Praise for the Fallen Blade novels

BLADE REFORGED

"Once again Aral and his Shade, Triss, find themselves in the middle of a royal mess—literally. Yet this time it is assassin versus assassin versus assassin. That alone promises readers some high-quality entertainment. But Kelly McCullough adds several twists, backbends, and handsprings that only a mind as devious (or demented) as his could possibly conceive."
—*Huntress Book Reviews*

CROSSED BLADES

"Kelly McCullough has once again written a magnificent story which deals with love, betrayal, and redemption."
—*Fresh Fiction*

"If you are seeking a fantasy unlike most others, you will not go wrong by choosing any title by this author. Kelly McCullough's writing style is indefinable, his imagination is creative and unique, and his [plot] execution is simply exquisite!"
—*Huntress Book Reviews*

BARED BLADE

"The second Fallen Blade fantasy stars an interesting hero with an irreverent, self-deprecating attitude . . . Fans will appreciate the magnificent McCullough mythos."
—*Genre Go Round Reviews*

"Full of action, fun characters, and an interesting plot."
—*Whatchamacallit Reviews*

continued . . .

BROKEN BLADE

"Creative world-building really helps the reader to immerse themselves . . . A strong beginning to a new fantasy-mystery hybrid series." —*Fantasy Book Critic*

"*Broken Blade* explores a different side of dark fantasy than the typical European/medieval fare . . . I could definitely spend hundreds of pages wandering around in the wilds of McCullough's newest creation." —*Flames Rising*

"*Broken Blade* is a compelling read that was hard to put down . . . Mr. McCullough has the ability to make even his dastardly characters sympathetic." —*Fresh Fiction*

"Filled with multifaceted characters, layered plots, and the type of quixotic scenarios that only the imagination of Kelly McCullough could possibly create. The author, once again, crosses genres . . . Stories by Kelly McCullough are one of a kind—just like him. I found Aral's world to be compelling and highly addictive. Brilliant!" —*Huntress Book Reviews*

"McCullough's atmospheric little tale of betrayal and skullduggery is brisk, confident, intelligently conceived, and suspenseful . . . With as promising a start as this, McCullough's new series is looking like one sharp blade indeed." —*SF Reviews.net*

"*Broken Blade* is perfect for a fan of political/hierarchal conspiracy in a fantasy series . . . It's also filled with some heart-pounding action . . . The story is positively bursting with excitement." —*Whatchamacallit Reviews*

More praise for the novels of Kelly McCullough

"Entertaining and rapid-fire." —*San Francisco Book Review*

"One long adrenaline rush." —*SFRevu*

"Original and outstanding . . . McCullough handles his plot with unfailing invention, orchestrating a mixture of humor, philosophy, and programming insights." —*Publishers Weekly* (starred review)

Ace Books by Kelly McCullough

The WebMage Series

WEBMAGE
CYBERMANCY
CODESPELL
MYTHOS
SPELLCRASH

The Fallen Blade Series

BROKEN BLADE
BARED BLADE
CROSSED BLADES
BLADE REFORGED
DRAWN BLADES
DARKENED BLADE

DARKENED BLADE

Kelly McCullough

ACE BOOKS, NEW YORK

THE BERKLEY PUBLISHING GROUP
Published by the Penguin Group
Penguin Group (USA) LLC
375 Hudson Street, New York, New York 10014

USA • Canada • UK • Ireland • Australia • New Zealand • India • South Africa • China

penguin.com

A Penguin Random House Company

DARKENED BLADE

An Ace Book / published by arrangement with the author

Ace Books are published by The Berkley Publishing Group.
ACE and the "A" design are trademarks of Penguin Group (USA) LLC.

For information, address: The Berkley Publishing Group,
a division of Penguin Group (USA) LLC,
375 Hudson Street, New York, New York 10014.

ISBN: 978-0-425-27001-1

PUBLISHING HISTORY
Ace mass-market edition / May 2015

PRINTED IN THE UNITED STATES OF AMERICA

10 9 8 7 6 5 4 3 2 1

Cover illustration © John Jude Palencar; dragon © Shutterstock.
Cover design by Judith Lagerman.
Interior text design by Laura K. Corless.
Maps by Matthew A. Kuchta.

For Laura, my bright shining star

Acknowledgments

———◦•◦———

Extra-special thanks are owed to Laura McCullough; Jack Byrne; Anne Sowards; Neil Gaiman; my mapmaker, Matt Kuchta; and cover artist John Jude Palencar and cover designer Judith Lagerman, who have produced wonders for me.

Many thanks also to the Wyrdsmiths: Lyda, Doug, Naomi, Bill, Eleanor, Sean, and Adam. My Web guru, Ben. Beta readers: Steph, Dave, Sari, Karl, Angie, Sean, Matt, Mandy, April, Becky, Mike, Jason, Jonna, and Benjamin. My family: Carol, Paul and Jane, Lockwood and Darlene, Judy, Lee, Kat, Jean, and all the rest. My extended support structure: Michael, Lynne, Bill, Nancy, Sara, James, Tom, Ann, Mike, Sandy, and so many more.

Penguin folks: Rebecca Brewer, Anne Sowards's wonderful assistant; managing editor Michelle Kasper; assistant production editor Julia Quinlan; interior text designer Laura Corless; publicist Nita Basu; and my copy editor, Mary Pell.

Thanks also to the readers who've been so helpful in answering my crowdsourced questions about things that happened in earlier books: Allen Monette, Benjamin Billman, Chad Elstad, Dextre Tripp, Keith Williams, Taylor McCoy, Vicki Brown, Yann Le Scouarnec, and Zedd Epstein. With six Fallen Blade books in print now, it's gotten much harder to hold it all in my head.

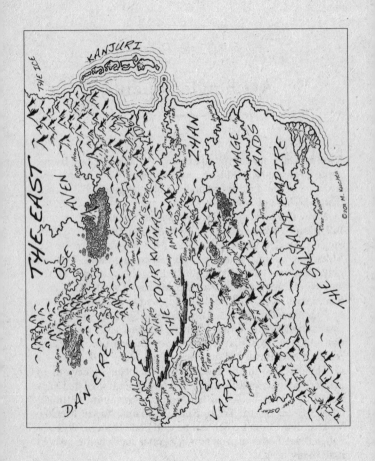

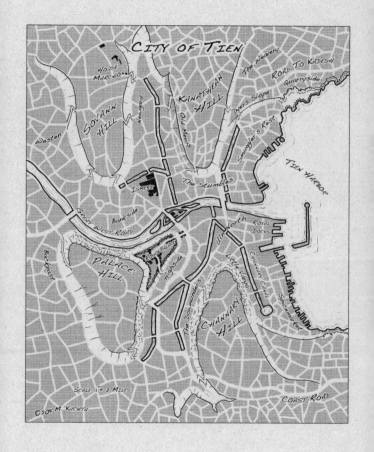

1

I speak to the dead. Usually they don't answer me back. Usually . . .

This time was different.

It's been nine years since the death of Namara and the destruction of her temple. Nine years that saw my few remaining fellow Blades driven and harried before the forces of the archpriest called the Son of Heaven. Nine years of death and darkness and retreat. But only recently have I learned the real reasons for the fall of my goddess and her temple. . . .

My goddess was murdered by her peers for the crime of caring more about justice than the safety and comfort of those who inhabit the Empire of Heaven.

We were assassins once, killers in the service of Justice who used magic and the sword to bring death to those high lords of the eleven kingdoms who considered themselves above the law. Where courts and trials could not reach the great, we could. And they hated us for it. Us and our companion shadows, the elemental creatures of darkness known as Shades who conceal and complete us.

We knew of the hate of the mighty, and their fear, and we welcomed it. It was a sign that no one was beyond the reach of justice. What we *didn't* know was that the gods themselves were also frightened, for Namara had made the swords that she gave us into a tool that might slay even a lord of Heaven, and that was the true reason for our fall. I know it now, but what to do with the knowledge? That is the question that had me calling out to the dead. That is the question that had brought me an answer.

Perhaps.

The bar was the Gryphon's Head, a place I knew as well as I knew the dark parts of my own soul. It was the place where I had plumbed the depths of despair back in the days when I was trying to drink myself into the grave so many of my fellows had already entered. But this time it was different. None of the regulars were in evidence, not even Jerik, the bartender, who was one of my few true friends in the world.

No, tonight, the Gryphon was peopled with the dead. When I walked through the door, the first person I saw was Alinthide Poisonhand, whom I had loved from afar as a boy and who had died trying to kill a king. She nodded to me, but she said no words, merely pointing to an empty table by the back wall. It was my usual place, and the only table without a full complement of the fallen. Most of the closer dead were Blades and priests—those I had known at the temple in my youth.

But not all. At another table sat two kings that had fallen to my swords, forever changing my name from Aral Brandarzon to Aral Kingslayer, as the world knew me now. They glared hate at me, Ashvik and his bastard half brother Thauvik. Nor were they alone. Nea Sjensdor sat with them, Lady Signet, and preceptor of the Hand of Heaven—the order of sorcerers that had destroyed my temple—and another I had slain. There were more, for somehow the taproom of the Gryphon's Head now looked both exactly as it ought and seemed to stretch out to encompass hundreds of tables.

Here were all my dead. Those I had loved. Those I had

hated. And those who had meant nothing to me at all. These last were perhaps hardest to face, for I had killed many over the years, most for no more reason than that they had stood in the way when there were those I needed to slay. I will not attempt to excuse their deaths. Not here, and not when I, in my turn, stand before the lords of judgment. I did what I felt was right at the time, and I will pay the price when it comes due.

Slowly, I walked through the ranks of the silent dead, approaching the place that waited for me. There were only two chairs there, though five could have sat at the table comfortably. That, too, was in keeping with my past experiences, for once I had called the Gryphon's Head my office and used that table to conduct my business. One chair was mine, and one belonged to my client, whoever that might be at the time.

I paused then, looking for my shadow and, with it, my familiar Triss. For Blades are sorcerers as well, dependent on our darkling companions to focus the gift of our magic. My Shade assumes the shape of a dragon made of shadow when he is not concealing himself within my own. But, there and then, though I could feel that he lived through the link that bound our souls, I had no shadow. I missed him dearly, for I love Triss more than I love myself, and I rely on his advice in all things.

Still, I drew back my chair and sat down, as I knew that I must. When I looked up, I was no longer alone. The greatest of my dead had come. Namara. My goddess.

"Hello, Aral, I've been waiting a long time to speak with you."

When I had met with her in life, she usually wore the shape of a great stone statue with six arms and skin like granite. Today, she had assumed the size and shape of a beautiful woman in a scarlet dress. The only obvious evidence of her divinity were her six arms, but even without that, I would have known her, for her image was forever burned into my soul.

"You're dead," I said, wishing once more for Triss to come and stand beside me.

Namara inclined her head ever so slightly. "I am."

"The dead do not return to us." The words came out flat and hard.

"No, we do not."

"Then, how . . ."

"I was a goddess, Aral. I am allowed certain dispensations."

"I don't understand."

"You carry me in your heart. As long as it beats, there will a tiny part of me remain. When I knew that I was to die, I took steps to see that what I cared most about might live on beyond my own ending."

"I . . . what do you want of me?"

"Only what I have ever wanted of you. Justice."

"Is that why you're here? To tell me you want me to . . . what? Do justice?"

"Yes."

I was suddenly achingly furious. "Why now? Why not when I was in the fucking depths of despair and half dead from drinking myself unconscious every night?"

"Because I am dead. I'm not really here, Aral. I exist now only in your heart, and the hearts of those who once served me and may yet again. I do not speak from beyond the grave, I speak from within it. I could not come to you before you yourself summoned me up. Only in following the path I would have wished of you have you become again the man who can hear this message."

"And your message is to seek justice?"

"That, and nothing more."

"How?" I yelled. "I don't know what I'm doing. I want justice, but I don't even know where to look to find it."

"Here," she said, and reached a hand across, placing her palm on my chest above the heart. Her touch burned.

"That's no answer."

"It's all the answer there is or ever was. You have found the path. Follow it."

"But I can't see it."

"Neither could I. To seek to follow justice is to walk in shadows. Some days they part and you can see clearly where to put your feet. Some days they thicken and you may stray far from the road, at great cost in blood and souls. Know that now, for a little while, your feet are exactly where they need to be. That is all there is." She began to fade.

"Wait, will I see you again?"

"I have delivered my message."

"That's no answer."

"It's the only one I have. Now let me leave you with a gift."

One of her hands turned over and a cascade of efik beans spilled out of it. I looked at them with a sort of horror, expecting the drug craving again, the hunger that had been slowly devouring my soul. But I felt nothing.

"I . . . I don't want them."

"When you passed through smoke you left the flesh behind for a time and, with it, the needs of the flesh. That broke the physical desire in a way that only the power of a god could. What the Smoldering Flame began, I can finish here in this place and time, sealing the wound that was opened by the Kitsune." She seemed little more than a ghost now.

"Will it last?" I asked, needing desperately to believe that it would.

She shrugged. "My power is broken. So that is up to you. It always was."

"And the alcohol . . ." I couldn't even ask the question.

"Was never sacred to me. That demon you must fight alone."

Alone.

I sat bolt upright in my bed at the Roc and Diamond gasping for air.

What just happened? Triss spoke into my mind, his mental voice sounding muzzy and confused as though he were rising up from a deep and enchanted sleep. *I had the strangest dream. . . .*

"Aral?" It was Siri, waking beside me. "What . . ." Her voice trailed off as she touched the skin over my heart.

I looked down. Clearly visible in the late-morning light was a mark on my chest—like an old burn scar. It took the shape of a six-fingered hand.

I speak to the dead. My fallen brethren. The people I have killed unjustly whose forgiveness I beg in the small hours of the night. Most of all, my goddess. Usually, they don't answer me back.

I think it's better that way.

The Roc and Diamond was a typical example of architecture in the city of Wall. The ground floor was sixteen feet wide and sixty feet long, its shape determined by the nature of the gigantic magical ward that separated the lands of the Sylvani Empire from the human kingdoms to the north. The ward took the shape of a wall eight feet tall and eight feet wide, enclosing and confining the magics of the First within a perfect half circle that started and ended on the shore of the great eastern ocean. It was thousands of miles long and served as the only street of the strangest city in the world—a city a thousand miles long and forty feet wide.

The gods had created the wall as a sort of prison for the First, and they had endowed it with certain magical properties. Nothing could be built upon or remain atop the wall for any length of time. Stand still on the wall and you would find yourself slowly and inexorably sliding toward the nearest edge. Nothing could breach or harm the wall. For exactly sixteen feet on either side, the ground was as hard as granite, perfect footing for buildings, and the foundation of the city. For another hundred yards beyond that the ground looked normal but acted more like slow quicksand. Holes filled themselves in. Trees of any size couldn't root properly and quickly fell over. And any attempt at erecting a building met with a similar fate. They called it the Fallows.

The wall was a bizarre place to build a city, but that interface between the human lands and the older Sylvani

Empire provided opportunities that could be found nowhere else in the world.

My childhood mentor, Kelos Deathwalker, had once quoted a scrap of an ancient lay describing the place, and now that I was temporarily living on the wall, it came back to me often: "A stone snake five thousand miles long coils its way around the empire, a city riding on its back. Within is the oldest and mightiest civilization in the world, a dreaming land of decadence and corruption ruled over by ancient immortals fallen from grace. Beautiful and terrible they were in the power of their youth, and beautiful and terrible they remain, though they are ruined now and their strength broken—a decayed remnant of the world that was, bound forever within a wall built by the gods."

The requirements of magic kept the city from growing out into the Fallows or over the wall, and the crowding of centuries prevented much expansion side to side. That meant that the more successful buildings went up. The Roc was no exception, with a number of towers reaching as high as six or seven stories—more than that made the edifice vulnerable to tipping in the wind, for there was no way to fasten the building to its footing.

The eight of us had taken rooms in the tallest of the towers while we sorted out what happened next. Four of us were human and Blades once; me, Siri, Faran, and Kelos the Traitor. Four were Shades. Triss, Kyrissa, Ssithra, and Malthiss. The first and most pressing question we had to deal with was the matter of Kelos.

What to do with the traitor who had betrayed the Temple of Namara to the Son of Heaven? It seemed a simple enough question to answer. The man certainly deserved to die, and there wasn't one of us who didn't want to kill him. But he was stuffed full of secrets, secrets that we might desperately need in the days to come. Especially if we decided to move against Heaven's Son.

That didn't even take into account that Kelos had all but raised Siri and me. A Blade enters the temple somewhere around the age of four or five. I have vague shadowy memories of the man who had begot me, but when I thought of a father, I pictured Kelos Deathwalker. Him I loved as much as I hated, and Siri felt likewise.

There was Malthiss to consider as well. Killing Kelos would kill his familiar, since the death of either half of a familiar-bonded pair always killed the other. How complicit was Malthiss in the crimes of his partner? Had Kelos compelled his familiar to join his treason? Persuaded him? Moved in harmony with him?

It was a tangle, and not the worst we faced. That was Heaven's Son.

"Namara wants you to go after the Son of Heaven." Kelos rose from his perch in the bay window to pace our small parlor. He was a big man with one eye covered by an old leather patch, and heavy with muscle, his skin a maze of scars and tattooed snakes' coils. His familiar took the shape of a shadow basilisk, lying mostly invisible amongst the tattoos at the moment. "That was the message of Namara's visit. Isn't it obvious?"

I was beginning to wish that I'd had the sense to keep my dream a secret. But Siri had demanded an explanation for the fresh burn over my heart. And, whatever had happened to the temple, Siri was the last of us to wear the title of Namara's First Blade—my superior in the order still. When she asked a question, old loyalties read an order.

"No," I replied. "It's not obvious. Not to me anyway, and I was told to follow *my* own heart in this and all things. She cautioned me, too, about how easy it is to stray from the path of justice and spoke of the great costs that follow. For that matter, I'm not sure the dream was anything more than wish fulfillment."

"Which left you with a burn scar on your chest?" Siri asked mildly from her place beside the fire.

Wisps of smoke wafted off the fire to coil and curl around her before sliding back to roll up the chimney. More smoke ran through the long thick braids that hung down her back and across the coal black skin of shoulders exposed by the tight vest she wore instead of a shirt. Likewise exposed was the fresh stump of her left arm, which ended just below the elbow. Her familiar, Kyrissa, took the form of a winged serpent. Alone among the Shades she was no longer a thing purely of shadow, but wore feathers of smoke on her wings and the coils of her body.

"Briefly . . . and maybe." I opened my shirt to expose the smooth skin over my heart—the print had faded away. "Do you see a scar there now?"

"No, but it was there in the morning. Both Triss and Kyrissa witnessed it."

Triss nodded, and whispered into my mind, *Sorry, but I have to agree with Siri here.*

"There," said Kelos. "The word of a First Blade is good enough for me."

I shook my head. "Even if the dream was real, and Namara was somehow speaking to me from beyond death, that doesn't mean I'm supposed to hare off after the Son of Heaven at this late date. She said I was already on the right path, and that I should follow justice. I had no plans to face the Son of Heaven when she said that. It could as easily have been a warning not to move against him."

"What could be more just than killing the man who destroyed the temple?" demanded Kelos.

"You know"—Faran spoke up for the first time in several hours—"he's got a point there."

I started at that—Faran agreeing with Kelos? That would be a first. I turned to look at my apprentice. She was taller now than when I'd first met her, a young woman rather than a girl, and lovely in a hard and cold sort of way. Her hair was long and brown, her skin a bit paler than my own deep brown. A vicious scar carved its way down her forehead and across her cheek where she had nearly lost an eye—a scar that burned red now with barely suppressed anger.

"Those who destroyed the temple *do* deserve to die." Faran drew her swords as she rose—swords of the goddess that had once belonged to a traitor Blade by the name of

Parsi. "I think we should start with this one." She lifted the point of one of her swords to prick the skin at the base of Kelos's throat.

Kelos shrugged, but didn't otherwise move. "I've certainly earned it. I won't stop you."

Faran's arm remained perfectly still, but a drop of blood welled up on Kelos's skin and began to roll its way down the length of the sword toward her hand. Tension hovered in the air like the bright moment before lightning rips open a stormy sky. She was a child of nine at the fall of the temple, thrown out into the world to make her own way. None of us had suffered more than she had.

"Well," she demanded after a few long beats, "isn't one of you going to order me to back off again?"

"No," I said, my voice flat.

"No?" She turned her head to look at me, but kept her sword up.

"No. You know all the arguments against killing him as well as the arguments for it. If you aren't yet convinced, demanding that you change your mind isn't going to change anything. The goddess told me to seek justice. I say the same to you."

I waited for the lightning to strike, vaguely relieved that I wouldn't be the one who had to make that decision. The red drop rolled on down the sword until it finally touched the lapis oval of the guard—Namara's all seeing eye. It clung there for a long moment, then dripped to the floor like a bloody tear.

Faran muttered a curse and flicked the blade back and up, away from Kelos's throat. Slamming it home in the sheath on her back, she turned and stalked silently out of the room.

"Interesting play there, Aral." Kelos raised an eyebrow. "I didn't know whether she'd go for it or not."

"And I didn't care," I replied. "You're on your own with her from now on." I followed Faran out.

2

The dead should stay dead.

For six years after the fall of the temple I believed that Kelos had died defending our goddess and our people. Then I discovered what really happened and that he was still alive. I wish that he'd stayed dead.

I had climbed to the top of our little tower, an octagonal deck surrounded by a low wooden wall. The sun had long since set, but the moon was more than bright enough for eyes trained to the darkness, and I could see as well as I needed to. The wall stretched away east and west, its shape picked out by the magelights and oil lanterns glowing along its length, like some phosphorescent eel from the deep ocean.

"I liked him better when he was a corpse," I said.

"It's never too late. . . ." Faran's voice spoke from behind me.

I turned, looking for the deeper bit of shadow I must have missed when I first came out on the rooftop. I found it in an angle of the wall not far from the stairhead. Or, at least, thought that I did—a shrouded Blade is all but invisible, especially at night. I crossed my arms and waited silently. A moment later the shadow thinned and resumed Ssithra's phoenix shape, revealing Faran, who sat cross-legged with her back against the boards.

She lifted her chin. "It's really not too late, you know. I could go back downstairs and kill him right now. Or . . . you could."

"That wouldn't solve the problem."

"It would put an end to it."

"No, it would only put an end to Kelos. It wouldn't undo the fall of the temple or the death of Namara or any of the other horrors he helped perpetrate."

And it wouldn't salvage your memories of the man he was before he did those things, Triss said quietly into my mind. *That man is already dead, and with him a part of you.*

That, too.

Faran rose to face me, and her eyes were on a level with mine. "Then what is the lesson?"

"Huh?" I asked.

"You took me on as your apprentice, right?"

I nodded.

"So, teach me. How can you stand to let him live after all that he's done? How can that be right? Namara's Blades exist to bring justice to those who would not otherwise receive it, those who are protected by power from the results of their actions. Doesn't Kelos fit the bill?"

"Namara's Blades are gone."

"That's a dodge, Aral, and a pretty bad one at that. You're still here and the ghost of the goddess told you herself that you should seek justice, that you should continue down the path she set you on."

"I don't know." I turned my back on Faran and looked out into the darkness again. "I don't want to kill him."

"Not two minutes ago you said that you 'liked him better as a corpse.'"

I nodded. "I did that. But the corpse I liked him as was a martyr to our goddess, not a traitor to her. That ship sank. Now, he *wants* me to kill him, or if I won't do it, Siri or you. He believes that he deserves to die for his treachery."

Faran put a hand on my shoulder and turned me to face her. "He's not wrong."

"No, he's not. But what will it accomplish? He wants to die for his crimes, but he doesn't repent them. He would do the same thing tomorrow in the same circumstances. He believed then and still does that by giving people hope for justice, Namara was relieving pressure that otherwise would have destroyed a corrupt system of governance. Is he wrong about that?"

"I don't know." Faran sighed. "In the lost years I made my way in the world by spying and commissioned theft. I saw a lot of corruption in the ruling classes, and I didn't do anything about it because: hey, my goddess is dead and it's not my fucking job. Then, I found you, and you showed me that there may be something to this whole justice business even without Namara to show us the way. But I don't see it as clearly as you do. *Is* the system so corrupt that the only thing to do is burn it down and start over? Or is it more important that we keep righting the individual wrongs?"

"That's really the question, isn't it?" asked Triss. "The big one that we're all fighting over without actually talking about it. Do we kill Kelos because of what he did to Namara, or do we back his play and move against the Son of Heaven?"

"Even that oversimplifies things," I growled. "Is killing Heaven's Son justice of the kind we were raised to deliver, or is it revenge? He is practically the personification of injustice rendered untouchable by power. If ever there was a man who deserved to die on the sword of a Blade, it's the Son of Heaven. Killing him alone would certainly serve the old ideal."

"But then there's the problem of the risen," said Faran.

I nodded and began to pace. The Son was more than just a priest, he was a rapportomancer—a very specialized sort of magic user, one with the familiar gift but no talent for actual magery, and his familiar . . . that was the rub. His familiar was a sort of death elemental, a strand of the curse of the restless dead—the one that gave birth to the risen.

Once the curse had advanced far enough, the risen were easy to spot, with their rotting hides, and mindless hunger for the flesh of the living. But there were ways to prevent or hold off that deterioration for months, or even years if you were willing to spill enough fresh blood.

In the shape of the hidden risen, the Son's strain of the curse wore the bodies of thousands of nobles and priests all through the eleven kingdoms, maybe even tens of thousands. They bathed in the blood of the living to disguise their undead condition and they gave the Son of Heaven de facto control over much of the East. Individually, killing them was as just as killing the Son himself. But, all at once . . . that was another thing entirely. What happens to a civilization when you remove the structures that rule it? The people with the experience of governing? In destroying the risen we might destroy kingdoms entire. Would it be just to ignore that cost?

Kelos believed that a new, more just, system would arise from the ashes of the old, that the inevitable civil wars and banditry and bloodshed would all ultimately prove to be worth it. But his vision of justice had led to the death of Namara and nearly all of my brethren, and that was a cost I could never accept.

Nuriko Shadowfox, his sometime lover, sometime foe who had started him down the path he now walked, had been even more radical in her plans. She didn't believe in government at all, that somehow eliminating it entirely would lead to a new and better world. Her plan had been to destroy the system and then to spend the rest of her life preventing a new one from growing in its place at a blood cost I couldn't even begin to imagine.

I didn't know what I believed, but I knew damned well that killing the Son of Heaven would result in a bloodbath of epic proportion. For every one of the risen that died with him, tens or even hundreds of innocents would fall in the chaos left behind. If the weight of my dead was already crushing me when they numbered in the hundreds . . .

"I don't know what to do, Faran. It was so much easier

when the goddess told me where to go and who to kill. The responsibility was hers. I *hate* being the one who has to make the decisions."

"Would you go back to living that way . . . ? If you could?" Faran's tone was gentle, her expression sympathetic, but the question was as sharp as any knife, and it cut straight through to the pain that knotted my gut.

I desperately wanted to say yes. But . . . "No. I have seen too much of life's grays to ever go back to that kind of certainty. Even knowing, as I now do, that Namara herself was uncertain . . . No. I lie to myself when I say the responsibility was hers. My actions were and always have been my own, and somewhere down deep I've always known that. If the responsibility for what I do belongs to me, so do the choices. I couldn't go back to being a tool in another's hand if my soul depended on it."

"Then, stop letting Kelos manipulate you."

Her mind is as sharp as her blades, sent Triss. *She's grown so much since we first found her.*

I laughed a grim little laugh. "That would be much easier to do if I knew what he was trying to bend me into doing, and whether or not what he wants of me is the wrong thing to do. Because the flip side of the risen problem is that allowing the Son of Heaven to live is a decision with heavy consequences of its own. How much of the evil done by and for him am I responsible for if I refuse to end his life?"

That was the question that made me feel as though I was carrying shards of broken glass around in my chest.

Triss rose up and wrapped his wings around my shoulders. "Sometimes you come to a place where there are no right decisions and all paths lead to fell ends."

"And then?" I whispered.

"You still must choose your way," said Triss.

"But I don't know how. . . ."

Faran stepped closer then, taking my hands in her own. "You do, you know."

"If so, I can't see it."

"That's because you're looking at it the wrong way. The

question is not, what should you do? It's: who do you want to be?"

"I don't understand."

"You can't control everything that will result from your actions, you can only control the actions themselves. If you died tomorrow, how would you want to be remembered?" She put one palm on my chest where the goddess had touched me. "Who are you, in here?"

I thought back to the decisions I had made over the last few years as I crawled my way back out of the gutter, what I had done that had made me proud, where I had failed. . . .

I took a deep breath. "I fear that I must face the Son of Heaven."

Faran nodded, but she also asked, "Why?"

"I am a hunter of monsters in human guise. It's what I was born to do. It's what I trained to do. It's who I am. Who knows? That might even make me into something of a monster myself. But, if so, I am a monster whose job is taking greater monsters out of the world. I may not be able to stop new ones from rising up where I have brought down the old, but I can't let that stop me from doing the job I was made for, and the Son is a very great monster indeed."

Going after the Son of Heaven was a scary decision, but it felt like the right one in that moment and in my heart, where it beat under Faran's hand. I covered it with my own. "How did you get to be so wise, my young monst— apprentice?" I clumsily switched words there as I realized that my usual nickname for her carried a different weight in this discussion.

She grinned. "This is the part where I'm supposed to say that I have a good teacher, right?" She pulled her hand free of mine and very gently leaned forward to kiss me on the cheek. "Which, I do, and he is also a good man, and no monster." She turned and walked back to the head of the stairs.

"Thank you," I said as she started to descend.

She nodded, but didn't answer me back.

"What about Kelos?" asked Triss.

"I don't know. But it matters less now."

"How so?" asked Triss.

"If I seek to confront the Son of Heaven, Kelos can help me—none better. But even with all the help in the world, this will be a very difficult play. The chances that either of us will survive the attempt are not great, much less both of us."

Triss snorted. "What you mean is that you're hoping to push off the decision long enough for it to become somebody else's problem."

"Or no problem at all, yes. Is that so wrong?"

"No. If we're going to go against the Son of Heaven we will need all the help we can get, and, sometimes, the enemy of my enemy is enough to get you through to the end."

I had made my choice, or thought I had, and I desperately hoped it was the right decision. But somewhere, down deep in the back of my mind, a voice kept saying: *But what is the cost if you're wrong?*

I appreciate irony as much as the next man. I just wish it didn't have to be quite so biting when you were on the receiving end.

"Absolutely not." I slammed my palm down on the table-top. "I will not have anything to do with that woman." Faran had already stormed out, while Siri sat quietly behind me radiating a sort of cold rage.

Kelos looked stubborn. "Don't go all squishy on me now, Aral. We need allies and I can't think of a better one. At least talk to her. We share a common enemy."

"Yes, and she's part of it."

Kelos crossed his arms and waited. Siri leaned forward and put her hand on my shoulder. It reminded me of the one she'd lost—a price willingly paid for ending a greater evil.

I sighed. "All right, I'll talk to her, but I won't promise not to kill her when we're done."

Kelos grinned. "That works for me. If you come to an agreement, we advance things in one manner. If you kill her, we do it in another. Chaos to our enemy either way. I'll tell her you'll be along momentarily."

He went to the stairs and headed down into the pub below.

"Siri, am I doing the right thing here? I mean, this is the fucking Signet of Heaven we're talking about."

She shrugged. "Probably, but I wouldn't let Jax in on this part of the deal when we bring her into the matter."

I shuddered at the very thought. The Signet was the head of Heaven's Hand, the Son's own personal sorcerous storm troopers—the people who had tortured Jax more than half to death when she was taken prisoner in the fall of the temple. Actually, there were any number of things I didn't want to mention to Jax. Like the way Siri had lost her hand, for one. Jax was my ex-fiancée as well as one of the handful of remaining Blades, and I didn't fancy explaining the weird magical mess that was my brief and unexpected marriage to Siri, or the bloody but amicable divorce that had ended it. . . .

Triss had followed Kelos to the head of the stairs. Now he looked back at me, his posture questioning.

"All right, I'm coming." As I reached the head of the stairs he let his dragon shape go and faded back into my shadow.

The taproom below was all but empty, a very unusual circumstance here in the early hours of the night. The only members of the local crowd who remained belonged to the staff of the inn, and *they* didn't look any too happy about being there. I couldn't fault them for wanting to leave given the newcomers—a half-dozen members of Heaven's Hand. Priests and sorcerers of the most deadly and fanatical sort. I wanted to leave, too.

They had shed their uniforms for loose dark pants and shirts cut in the style of the steppe riders of the Kvanas. They weren't fooling anyone. Everything about them spoke to their true origins, from the hard, cold expressions on their faces, to their military bearing and the many weapons that hung in use-worn sheathes at hips and shoulders or tucked into boot tops. Long ponytails bound with the ritual knots of their order identified them more exactly for any who knew what to look for. And then there were the Storms.

Each of the six companioned a cloud-winged familiar. The Storms were elemental creatures of air that assumed a myriad of forms, everything from the lucent shapes of huge gemstones, to wheels of golden flame, or abstract swirls of color. Their only commonality, one to another, was that they flew on wings of cloud.

The obvious leader of the troop was partnered by a tight bundle of colors and tentacle-like streamers that reminded me of nothing so much as an octopus trying to conceal itself on a bright coral reef. She had taken a seat at a small table not far from the base of the stairs, where she sat as ramrod straight as if she were occupying a bench in the front row of the master temple at Heaven's Reach. Her followers had ranged themselves around the room in a loose cordon that allowed them to see every entrance and exit and to cover each other as needed in case of attack. I had to give them points for execution at the same time I deplored their very existence.

Kelos, being Kelos, had taken a stool at the bar with his back to almost everyone, as though he was daring someone to stick a knife in it. Tempting as that idea sounded from time to time, I ignored him in favor of approaching the woman at the table. A second glance refined my first impression. For one, she was absolutely ancient, her hair bone-white rather than the blond I had first thought, and the lines in her face many and deep.

If she were not a sorcerer I might have guessed her age at eighty, but her life was tied to her familiar's, and the Storms, like the Shades, may live for hundreds of years. For her to have aged so much, she must be at least three hundred, and maybe as old as six.

"I am five hundred and thirty eight," she said, her voice crisp and more than half-amused. "Also, I don't read minds, just faces, and I've had lots of practice. My name is Toragana, and this is my second time wearing the ring."

She waved her right hand, where the Signet's insignia of office circled her thumb. "After a hundred and ninety years of retirement in a peaceful hermitage I have been drafted back into the role of head of my order and I am not at all pleased about it. Now, sit. We have much to talk about and our time is short. The Son would kill us all if he knew I were here talking to you. Besides, I'm ancient and angry. Apoplexy could carry me off at any moment."

I suppressed a grin and sat. Despite all of the weight of history and blood that lay between our two orders, I found myself instinctively liking this woman. "Angry?" I prompted.

"Extraordinarily so. Mostly at Corik Nofather. First, for failing to succumb decently to the risen curse fifty years ago, thereby sparing me the trouble of doing something about his continued reign as the Son of Heaven. Second, for doing such a horrible job on the throne, *necessitating* my doing something about it. Third, for being an inhuman monster that makes doing something about it a task that requires me to seek help. And, before you put on that curious tone and say 'Mostly?' I'm also mad at myself for hiding away in my hermitage and missing out on the chance to simply kill the little bastard off before he got too powerful for one old woman to handle."

I like her, Triss sent rather bemusedly.

So do I. This time I couldn't stop a grin. "So, you know what he is, then—" She cut me off with a chop of her hand.

"Yes, and all of his history, though I haven't been able to do anything with the information, since he's converted the bulk of the curia into undead slaves." She sighed. "I admit it's an improvement in some cases, but still, it complicates things. The only ones I've been able to bring in on this are certain members of my own order and that idiot Devin Nightblade."

I started at the name of my onetime best friend, now head of the Blades who had gone over to the Son of Heaven after the fall of the temple. He had been Kelos's chief pawn in the matter, and he hated me with a rare vigor.

She nodded at my reaction. "A piece of work that one.

Venal, dumb in a clever sort of way, and more than half a coward. He speaks very highly of you, which would have been enough for me to look elsewhere for help if it weren't for the fact that it's obvious he despises you and that it pains him to feel the way he does about your abilities."

"So, he sent you here?"

"No, I sent me here. Devin—gods help us—heads one of the five branches of Heaven's forces on earth. I head another. Together we *ought* to be able to push the Son of Heaven off his throne without any help. But in addition to Devin's cowardice, his traitor Blades are bound by terrible oaths that prevent them from acting directly against this Son of Heaven, and my own order is a hollow shell of what it once was. For which, curse Corik's name for five thousand generations." She spat on the floor.

"As much as I agree with you about the Son of Heaven, I'm finding it hard to feel a lot of sympathy for you after what your order did to mine."

Her mouth tightened at that, but she nodded. "I can understand your position on that conflict. What would you say if I told you that I mostly shared it?"

"I . . . what?" That was not what I had expected.

"That attack killed over half of the active members of my order, and it utterly destroyed our command structure. Nor was that result unintentional. The Son of Heaven cannot convert mages without revealing himself, and that means that his control over the Hand has always been the weakest element of his command of the forces of the church. Since he took office, he has been systematically throwing our most powerful and independent members into the riskiest of situations, and the pace has accelerated dramatically of late.

"Seven Signets have died in the last ten years. Two at the fall of your temple, counting Taral's single hour in that role. One in an ill-planned mission to Aven. Another, you killed two years ago at the abbey outside Tavan along with more than thirty of the Hand. One vanished shortly afterward, no one knows where. One fell in the battle understairs during the conflict over the Key of Sylvaras. His replacement was executed for treason three weeks later. For comparison, we lost three in the hundred years before that. Discounting half-trained novices and dotards like myself, the order has one fifth the number of members it did before your temple fell."

She slammed a fist down on the table. "The Son has killed far more of us than your Blades ever did. Following the death of the last Signet there were only three active officers left who had held significant command roles in the organization, and not one of them felt up to the task of assuming the office—which is why they came to me. Privately, and *before* I took the ring, the three of them told me that they thought it would be a death sentence for any of them to do so. All of them were willing to offer up their lives if they thought it would save the order, but not one of them believed they could make a difference."

"And you think you can?" I asked.

"I honestly don't know. But I had to try. That's why I'm here. The Son of Heaven has made *this* into little more than a shiny bauble." She took off the ring and tossed it to me.

Reflexively, I caught it out of the air. When I opened my hand to look at it I realized for the first time what was missing. "What happened to the magic . . . ?"

I held it up to my eye and looked through the circle at Toragana. I had held the ring of a Signet before. Two of them, actually, and each had glowed brightly in magesight, infused as they were with many spells. Among other enchantments, they were, or had been, keys that opened every one of the many wards that guarded the great temple at Heaven's Reach.

"Two years ago *someone* slipped into the Son of Heaven's bedroom." Toragana gave me a pointed look.

"Really?" I asked, my face as blank as I could make it.

"Really. Though the story has not been widely shared beyond the upper echelons of the temple, the intruder stabbed two swords of your goddess into the headboard of the Son of Heaven's bed, bare fractions of an inch above his face. When the Son of Heaven woke up, he ran into them, putting twin slices into the flesh over his cheekbones. Those wounds have never healed."

"That's fascinating," I said.

"Oh, do stop. Kelos was the one outlawed for the thing— losing his place as head of Heaven's Shadow to Devin and garnering a death sentence in absentia—which is part of why I sought him out. But he's already told me who actually marked the Son of Heaven's face, and how, and why. That's also when he told me that you're the one I have to deal with if I want your people to help us with the Son of Heaven."

"Me, not Siri?" Toragana nodded, and I glanced over her shoulder to where Kelos continued to pointedly ignore us all, wondering what he was up to. "Interesting."

"Look, I don't care about your internal politics. What I care about is rescuing my order and my religion from the half-risen monster who currently heads it, at any cost. If bringing him down means I have to work with the sworn enemies of the Hand and start the biggest war in a thousand years, well, that's what I intend to do. My duty to Shan demands nothing less."

"Do you believe that killing the Son will mean war?" I feared that it would, but I wanted to hear the Signet's feelings on the matter.

Toragana nodded, her expression grim. "Half a dozen civil wars at the very least. How could it not? Corik Nofather controls most of the ruling houses of the East. When the old rulers fall, there will be a rush to fill that opening, the likes of which the eleven kingdoms have never seen. There will be pretenders, and wars of distraction, and bloody crusades to root out more of the hidden undead. I don't like it, but I don't see any way around it. We cannot allow a half-risen monster to sit the throne of Heaven's Reach."

Triss hissed silently in my mind. *Do you think she's right?*

I don't know, I sent, though I very much feared that she was. "How did you discover the Son's true nature?"

"After you left him with those slices on his cheeks, the

Son of Heaven went a little mad—paranoid and vindictive. He executed every guard who had been within a hundred yards of his rooms that night. Then he cut off all access to the innermost temple for the Hand, the Shadow, and those members of the Sword who are also mages.

"He restricted entry to a very few at first, his risen slaves within the priestly hierarchy and the military orders. But that also restricted his ability to get things done, so he started converting more and more risen. Concealing their true nature takes enormous amounts of blood. Too much to hide from someone with my connections and history in the church. Combine that with things that I scared out of Devin, and I knew what the truth had to be."

"That's when you decided to come to me."

"Well, Kelos initially, but yes. Will you help me make war upon Heaven's Son?"

I took a deep breath, as I tried to decide how to answer her. That's when a large boulder smashed right through the Fallow-side wall of the Roc and Diamond at shoulder height. It passed directly over the table where Toragana and I faced each other before punching out the wall on the other side. A few inches left or right and it would have killed one or the other of us.

Triss wrapped me in a shroud of darkness as I rolled backward out of my chair. In a hand-off we had practiced thousands of times, he released control over his senses and substance to me as I bounced to my feet. My view of the world changed as my own vision became irrelevant and I shifted to seeing through Triss's borrowed darksight. Color went away as textures and how they reflected or absorbed light became central to my awareness, and shadows took on a depth of meaning beyond anything I can ever hope to describe. . . .

As I drew my swords, a tattered horde of risen came pouring up the main stairway from the lower level.

The Son of Heaven had moved first.

3

---·◆·---

Death or Justice?

Sometimes, when I'm being especially honest with myself, I wonder what impulse I truly serve. The memory of my goddess? Or the darkness of the grave? I have always tried to kill only those whom Justice demanded I slay, but how far does Justice's writ go?

Ashvik was my first, King of Zhan, and as clear a case for the justice of the sword as you could ask for. But he was not the last. Many have died at my hand since that day. Some deserved their deaths as clearly as Ashvik deserved his. Some put themselves between me and my rightful prey. Others . . . others merely stood too close.

I might say that I took no pleasure in their deaths, that I would have spared them the edge if I could have, but I would not be telling the whole truth. For I love my work. There are few pleasures that can compare with being one of the best in the world at what you do. I do not like being responsible for the deaths of those who do not deserve it, but the cut and the parry, the interplay of steel and spell and knowing that the ultimate price will be paid by the less skilled

player . . . that is another thing entirely. To deny the shock
of joy that went through me as I unsheathed my swords and
prepared to wade into the ranks of the risen would be to
deny who I am.

I would like to believe that I wouldn't have felt the same
way if my opponents were living breathing humans with
wills of their own. I would like to believe that very much.

I do not.

The Hand met the risen at the stairhead with spells and
steel and the miniature lightnings of their familiars. Heads
fell, rotting skin crisped and burned, a score of the restless
dead fell in a matter of seconds. But more came bounding
up the stair. Indifferent to their fallen comrades as anything
more than an impediment to decent footing, they came on
in their hundreds. By sheer weight of undead flesh they
forced the Hand back and back again, establishing a bridge-
head.

Kelos had shrouded himself at the same time that I did,
but I could trace his path across the room toward me by the
line of fallen bodies he left in his wake. The swords of
Namara are one of the most effective tools against the
undead. Even now, after the death of the goddess, that part
of their enchantment will work for the proper wielder. But,
the next wave of the risen rushed toward the Signet and me
then, and I lost track of Kelos and his swords. Before the
dead reached us, another great rock smashed through the inn.

It killed one of the Hand and tore a dozen of the risen
into rotting shreds—not that they seemed to care. The death
of the sorcerer-priest engulfed his familiar Storm, causing
a great roar of thunder to shake the inn as the heavens
mourned one of their own. Though I couldn't see it, I knew
that the clouds would already be forming overhead—a har-
binger of the wind and rain to come.

The Signet drew a pair of short, leather-bound rods from
her belt, like a pair of truncated axe handles. Crossing them
in front of her face, she snapped them down and out in the
manner of twinned whips. Bright coils of lightning lashed
outward, crisping the entire front row of the oncoming

horde, but more of the dead quickly flowed in behind. She struck again and again, but the risen kept coming. I moved to one side to intercept a couple that had slipped around the edge of the zone of death described by her lightning whips.

She was one of the most accomplished magical warriors I'd ever seen, but even with me guarding her blinds, the dead forced us back, and back again, until we were wedged into one corner of the long common room. That uncovered the base of the spiral stairs that led to the apartments above, and more of the risen swarmed upward. I hadn't the time or breathing space for more than a passing worry about what that might mean for Faran and Siri.

Periodically, the engine hurling stones from outside would fling another through the inn. Mostly they killed the restless dead, but I had just beheaded another—the surest way to make this their last rising—when a lucky shot turned the Signet's legs into a mass of pulped flesh and shattered bone. She fell at my feet and faceup, her eyes somehow seeming to pierce the shadow that hid me from my foes.

"You must end Corik. He profanes the world by his very existence." She coughed then, and red bloomed on her lips. "Do what I could not," she whispered, and was gone. Thunder boomed again and again and again, as a mighty wind hammered the inn.

Though I had only just met Toragana, I felt her passing with a sharp pain—mourning the friendship that might have come with time. I wanted to stay and make those who had killed her pay, but she was right. The risen might fall here like autumn leaves before a northern wind, but there was no end to them, and they seemed to care nothing for the final death. If I remained longer I would die as surely as the Signet had.

A glance around the room reinforced the futility of our situation. All but one of the Hand were dead or taken, as were the inn's staff. I couldn't speak to Kelos, nor Siri and Faran for that matter—if they'd even come down to join the fight here instead of meeting the dead above. I couldn't see any of them—though that would be as true if they were simply shrouded as it would if they'd fallen under the seething horde of the dead. The building itself stood on the brink of collapse after all the rocks that had ripped their way through its walls. The growing storm was already causing it to creak and sway. When it fell it would bring ruin to any who remained within.

By dint of a very controlled sort of manic flailing I cleared a brief hole in the fighting and sent up a shock of magic. Pink and orange—invisible to the mortal eye, but a bright burst for those with magesight—the colors my order traditionally used to signal one another. The flare formed itself into a blazing arrow pointing toward the side of the inn that faced the wall and the Sylvain, slipped through a hole, and then shot away, paralleling the magical wall's top in the direction of the sea. I hoped that my companions would see it, but I couldn't wait around to find out. I cut my way to the nearest window and vaulted through, dropping toward the wall below.

The risen were thinner here, but still present in great numbers, so it was more luck than skill that allowed me to land in a clear space. Even through the pounding rain I could see that many of the nearer buildings had their doors and windows broken in. Here and there knots of fighting had sprung up where the restless dead had met with some resistance, particularly on the empire side of the wall.

As I watched a swarm of them bring down a tall Sylvani lord in his shining crystalline armor, I revised my estimate of the scope of the battle radically upward. It wasn't just the inn under attack, but this entire section of the city of Wall. The living were losing badly, and too many of those who weren't torn apart or devoured would join the ranks of the enemy over the next few days as they rose from their graves in turn.

The thought of it made me sick at heart. Again, I found myself wanting desperately to stay and fight. Again, I forced myself to move on. My goddess-forged swords and their enchantments might give me an advantage against the restless dead, but even if I slew scores before I fell, hundreds

would remain. There was no winning this battle. The dead
were simply too many. It was hard to believe the scale of the
thing. Nothing like it had happened in more than a thousand
years, not since Master Corvin and Resshath Ssura ended
the Necrotariat that had risen in Dan Eyre of old before the
merging of my order and the worshippers of Namara.

Over the next quarter of an hour I fought and shadow-
slipped my way through the horde of dead mobbing the wall.
The warm rain was my ally in the latter, making my
shrouded presence even more invisible than usual. I finally
broke free of them a half mile or so east of the inn.

There, a small group of heavily armed and armored Sylvani nobles had taken a position on the wall with a more
slapdash force of human irregulars backing them up. Facing
a sharp and organized defense heavy with magic and
enchanted weapons, this ragged edge of the army of the
dead was faring badly. I pressed myself into the shadow of
a broken door and took a momentary rest while the dead
focused on the Sylvani and their human allies.

The Sylvani all stood at least a head taller than their
human auxiliaries, with one or two taller yet—close to the
seven feet and change of my friend Ash. The Sylvani had
donned full armor and close-faced helms against the threat
of the risen, all in varying hues and shades of crystal. As I
watched, one of the risen struck their leader in the center of
her breast plate with the terrible strength of the dead. The
point of impact flared and sparked, sending light crazing
away from the spot like cracks running through a dropped
mug, refracting the force of the blow by a sort of elemental
light magic.

The Sylvani struck back, whipping a slender dueling
blade up and around with inhuman speed to stab the risen
in the eye. A bright spark of light flashed down the length
of the crystalline blade from the hand that wielded it toward
the point of the sword. It vanished for a moment when it
passed the point where sword met rotting flesh, but the
risen's head started to glow from within a moment later, like
a bright lamp glimpsed through paper walls. The glow

spread down and out, filling the risen with light. Then, there was a bright flare—viciously so to my borrowed darksight—and the risen collapsed in on itself.

The sudden brightness had come as a painful surprise, leaving me blind for several long beats of my heart. I hadn't realized that the Sylvani could perform magic atop the warding wall as well as within its boundaries. The gods had created the thing to bind the power of the older race among other things—preventing them from using their magic in the lands beyond its bounds.

As the battle intensified, I saw my chance. Sheathing my swords, I climbed up the nearest building to the rooftop, and slipped past the barricade along the chimney road. I finally released my hold over Triss once we were well and truly beyond the fighting, though I kept moving. He rose at once from the dreams where he'd retreated to allow me finer control over both shroud and magic.

Faran? he sent anxiously as soon as he was fully himself again.

I don't know. I shrugged, and then winced as the motion sent threads of rainwater crawling down my back—I was going to regret not having had time to grab my poncho, or any of my gear beyond the bare minimum—I always kept my sword rig on. *I didn't see her join the battle before the risen stormed the upper stairs, and I've no idea what happened above.*

I hope she's all right. . . . Triss rather dotes on Faran, but then, so do I.

Me, too. And then, because I could feel a weight of worry behind his thoughts, *She's tough and smart and her new swords should serve her well against the dead.*

I know, but— He stopped speaking when another shroud brushed across us—a familiar and welcome presence.

"Siri!" I said.

We were far enough away from the fighting now that I halted, signaling Triss to drop his shrouding effect so that we could see and be seen. The shroud collapsed into a dragon-shaped shadow at my feet as Triss shifted forms to show his public face. Kyrissa did the same, becoming a smoke-feathered serpent who hung in the air behind Siri as we faced each other.

"Aral." She nodded hello and I nodded back.

"Do you know where Faran is?" asked Triss.

"No, we were separated when the risen swarmed the sitting room. She went up and I went out a window."

"Dammit!" I growled.

Siri put her hand on my shoulder. "I'm sure she's fine. She's very good with her swords, and an excellent mage."

I nodded. "And smart and tough, and all of that. I know, but . . ."

"Dead sexy, too," said a familiar voice.

I spun around in time to see Faran drag herself up over the fallow-side edge of the roof. Her tone was light, but her right sleeve was drenched in blood and she had no shadow because Ssithra had wrapped herself tightly around Faran's arm above the biceps reinforcing a rough bandage. Faran staggered as she got closer and I leaped to catch her. She was soggy and cold, though the rain was warm.

I ran a finger along the lower edge of her shadow bandage. "Is that . . ." I trailed off, too horrified to say more. When you fight the restless dead . . .

Faran grimaced. "One of the risen nicked me with a claw, barely more than a scratch really."

"The curse?" demanded Siri, her voice sharp and tight.

"That's what all the blood's about. I shaved off a rather large chunk of meat, making sure it didn't go any farther."

A shadowy phoenix head lifted free of the darkened bandage. "She acted quickly enough," said Ssithra. "The curse will not take her, but she has lost a great deal of blood and if I let go she will lose more."

Faran looked embarrassed. "Yeah, I had to cut and run after this." She touched her arm and winced. "Sorry I couldn't stay to guard your back. I wanted to, but my swords weren't affecting the risen the way yours do—I had to cut them apart or behead them—and Ssithra kept yelling at me to get out."

Not good, but also not wholly unexpected. I had hoped that the enchantments on Parsi's swords would perform properly for Faran as Devin's had for me the two times I had been forced to borrow them before recovering my own. But Faran had never been confirmed as a full Blade and the circumstances under which she'd taken possession of them were unprecedented in the history of our order.

Faran pulled a bundle free of her sword rig then and handed it to me. "I did manage to grab your poncho on the way out. You don't know how relieved I was when your signal arrow passed me back that way." She nodded over her shoulder.

"It came so far?" I was surprised because I hadn't specified a duration for the spell, just let it fly, but I'm no great shakes with magic.

"No idea. It passed me a quarter mile or so from the inn and kept right on going. A little gaudy maybe, but good for me, and . . ." She wobbled and suddenly sat down on the roof, putting her head between her knees. "Oh my."

"Can you do anything for her?" asked Ssithra. "Between the blood she's lost and my needing to play tourniquet, we haven't had the resources for any sort of healing magic."

"Lie down," Siri told Faran. "Aral, cut that bandage away."

"Shouldn't we get in out of the rain first?" I asked.

"After. The longer we wait, the worse it will get."

I did as ordered, hissing sharply when I got a look at the tight seam of shadow sealing the wound beneath. Faran had carved a strip at least three inches wide and half an inch deep out of her upper arm.

"Nasty," I said.

"Less wouldn't have been enough," replied Ssithra. "I could see the curse moving through her flesh and showed her where to strike."

Meanwhile, Siri had knelt beside Faran. Now she reached out to touch the injury with both hands and . . . wait a second. I did a double take as I looked for Siri's missing hand. The limb was still gone from about halfway down her forearm, but, where the flesh used to continue on, a sort of ghost wrist and hand had formed out of whirling smoke.

"Is that . . ." I didn't even know what I wanted to ask and trailed off.

"I've been experimenting with the connection between me and the buried god," said Siri. "With my sword in old Smokey's black heart, the link's even stronger than it was when I put him in his grave the first time. But I have more freedom now. The sword is binding him much tighter than the eye dagger ever did. Now, shut up, I've a tricky task to perform."

I shut up, because that's how orders work.

"Faran, this is going to hurt, probably a lot. Are you—"

"Do it!" snapped Faran.

"All right." The smoke defining Siri's left hand grew darker and thicker, especially around the base of her fingers, like it was coming straight off a flame. The palm there took on a faint orange cast. "Ssithra, I will need you to move in three, two, one. Now."

The shadow slid away from Faran's arm and blood welled up behind it. Before it could go farther than that, Siri placed her smoking palm against the wound. There came a sizzle like a freshly forged sword going into the quenching trough. Faran whimpered and then fainted. A moment later, Siri pulled her hand away and promptly tumbled over onto her back with a splash. Where she had touched Faran's arm, the flesh looked hot and pink and shiny, like a new burn scar, and the bleeding had stopped, though a clear fluid was oozing out here and there.

Before I could examine it any closer, Ssithra hissed angrily and wrapped herself around her injured companion's arm again. The Shade's tone didn't invite any further prodding. So, I checked Faran's pulse quickly—thready but distinct—then turned my attention to Siri, who looked very nearly as wrung out as Faran. Her eyes were closed and she had her stump pressed tight against her forehead. The hand of smoke was gone.

"Siri, are you all right?"

"Not really, no, but I think I might be later . . . after I've had a bath or six. I had to touch *him* pretty deeply to do that, and it's left me feeling unclean inside and out. That and like a troll just used me as a chew toy. Now, be quiet and let me meditate here in the rain for a little while. I need to put this aside, and the storm will help me wash my soul clean."

I stood and walked to the nearer edge of the roof, leaving Siri in peace as I began a slow circuit of the building. I didn't have to ask her who "him" was or why she felt unclean. She meant the buried god known as the Smoldering Flame. As I had once been bound to him, too, however briefly, I knew something of the sense of violation his presence brought with it. One of the two swords our goddess had forged for Siri was buried in his heart now and would remain there unless the god's own magic burned it away over the next thousand years or so—it was the only way that we knew of to keep him safely in his grave.

The buried gods had once been almost inconceivably mighty sorcerers of the Others, or First as they called themselves. The Sylvani, Durkoth, Vesh'An, Asavi, and all their lesser known brethren. In the days before the birth of humanity they had grown in power to rival the gods themselves, and that had resulted in their downfall. The gods are jealous of their place, and they had gone to war to break the strength of the First.

It was a close-run thing, and ultimately, while the gods defeated those who had risen against them, they could not destroy them. So, the gods had entombed their enemies and created the Wall to bind the power of the First. Mostly, the buried ones remained in something like sleep, deep in their tombs, but now and then one would rise for a time and trouble the living.

The buried gods were enormously powerful still, and couldn't be slain, though they were something less than alive. They were also incredibly alien in their thinking and desires, and being bound to one, as Siri was, meant sharing the dreams of a sleeping abomination. Much of the time she could push that awareness back and down, keep it in a sort of box of the mind, as we had been taught to deal with the guilts and horrors that our profession sometimes brought.

But here, for Faran's sake, she had chosen to actively broaden and deepen her connection with the Smoldering Flame if only briefly. I shuddered at the thought. I had seen into his mind, and I do not think that I would have had the strength to do what Siri had just done. Once again, she had demonstrated the will and skill that had led her to supplant me as First Blade back in the days before the temple fell.

I was just passing the women for a second time, when I heard a faint splashing sound from the far edge of the roof. Even as I drew my swords, Kelos stepped out of shadow and waved to me. There was something hunched about his outline and it took me a moment to realize that he had a body slung over one shoulder. I raised an eyebrow as he came closer.

"Hand. We were close together when you gave the signal to make a break for it, so I brought him along. I'd have been here sooner, but I was on the Fallows side of things and had to get out that way when the building got blown over by the storm. We rode the wreckage down, which event turned out to be a good thing, as that was where the risen were thickest and the fall of the building squashed or buried a fair few of them. Then I had to run most of a mile out of my way before I could cut back to the wall."

"Why are you carrying him? Did the risen get to him?"

"He's missing an ear and a healthy strip of scalp, but I'm pretty sure I saved him from the curse with that cut. Even so, he wanted to stay behind." Kelos shook his head. "I presume he intended to die there, taking as many of them with him as he could to avenge his Signet—damned Hand fanatic!"

Kelos had left out an important detail. "But then you talked him into it somehow?"

Right . . . sent Triss.

"Don't be ridiculous. I knocked him on the other side of his head with the flat of my blade, threw him over my shoulder, and started running."

"So, he might wake up angry," I said dryly.

"Good chance, if he wakes up at all. I hit him pretty hard, and head injuries are funny things. I didn't have time to sort it out gently, and he was the last of the Signet's personal guard. Have to admit he's a hell of a fighter. . . . But the important thing is that he might know something we need."

"I'm so glad that you continue to place such a high value on other people's decisions," I said.

"I value other people's decisions exactly to the degree that they make good sense."

"To you!" I snapped.

"Is there any other measure a man can make beside what's reasonable to him? If I think a person's making a bad mistake, should I pretend it's not so? Because that sure as hell won't help things."

Aral, let it go. You won't change him.

I know, it's just that he makes me crazy! I took a deep breath and tried to push my anger away.

It wasn't productive right now, and it was clouding my thinking. It's funny how the people who raised you can knock your best efforts at reacting like a reasonable person on the head. There's something about having been a child to someone's adult that leaves marks on you that can never be wholly erased. Somewhere in every exchange you have, there is the ghost of that old relationship trying to make itself felt.

"Speaking of which," continued Kelos, "what are you doing up on a rooftop in rain like this with wounded? I thought I taught you both better than this." He included Siri in his gesture.

She had abandoned her meditation and come up beside me while we were speaking. Now she used her remaining hand to flip Kelos a rude gesture.

That's when I started to laugh. It was that or kill Kelos, and, as tempting as I found the idea, all the old arguments still held. I still needed what was in his head.

"Fine, we'll get in out of the damned rain, Grandpa."

And then what? That was the real question.

4

———◆———

"**Y**ou may rob a grave, but you cannot steal from the dead." This was not the first variation we'd had on this particular conversation, but it didn't hurt to say it again.

"If that's not it, then why won't these work for me, Aral?" Faran whipped her swords angrily through the air, then winced and rolled her injured shoulder.

It had been nearly a week, but even with much better magical care than we could provide, that arm was going to trouble her for a very long time . . . if not the rest of her life. We had camped for the night in the loft of an abandoned barn somewhere east of Tavan in the Magelands.

We should have made it to the city by now, but the risen continued to hunt us, and avoiding both them and the locals working to exterminate them was slowing us down—the last thing any of us wanted to do was to try to explain the whole thing to anyone official. Nursing the priest of the Hand we'd dragged along was another factor in our travel time. Kelos's blow had left him with both a concussion and a pretty scrambled view of what had happened at the inn—a fact that became incredibly apparent during those few brief moments when he came awake enough to attempt conversation.

It would have been simplest to abandon him at another inn, or, better yet, a church facility, but there was still the chance that we might get important information out of him. Also, he might draw the risen down on whomever we left him with, and I didn't need that on my already stained conscience if it could be avoided. At the moment, our unwelcome guest was sleeping in a corner.

"Namara's swords will slay the risen for you." Faran jabbed one of her swords in my direction. "And for Siri." Another jab. "Hell, they even work for old one eye!" She jerked her chin at Kelos. "And he *betrayed* the temple!"

I shrugged. "I don't know what's wrong, but the fact that you took them from Parsi's corpse isn't the problem. What made her Parsi was gone by then, moved on to face the lords of judgment and the wheel of rebirth. There was no one there to steal *from*, and we know there are other reasons that may cause the enchantment of the swords to fail. Devin's wouldn't work against the risen either, not for him anyway."

"Are you saying I'm like Devin?" Faran's voice went up a half octave as she stabbed the blades deep into the floorboards of the old barn loft.

Way to put your foot in it, my friend, sent Triss.

I took a deep breath. "No, Faran, that's not what I'm saying at all. I'm just noting that it's possible to have been handed your swords by Namara herself and for them still not to do everything they're supposed to. And no I don't know why that is."

A shadowy cobralike head lifted over Kelos's shoulder. "I have been pondering it for some time, and I begin to think that I might know the answer. In this case, at least. Devin is another thing entirely."

Triss flicked his wings sharply. *Interesting . . .*

He wasn't the only one who started at Malthiss intruding himself into the conversation. The old Shade had always leaned toward the quiet side, a trait that seemed only to have deepened in the years since Kelos had betrayed the temple.

Faran's reaction was sharpest. When she wasn't advocating for chopping Kelos's head off, she tended to pretend that neither he nor his familiar existed. The fact that the two of them might know something she desperately wanted to obviously caused her considerable distress. I refrained from welcoming her to my world, but only by chewing on my tongue.

After several strained seconds, Faran turned to Malthiss, and nodded a jerky sort of nod that didn't quite cross the line into a formal bow. "You have something to add, Resshath Malthiss?"

"Kelos won't remember the conversation, but when I was much younger than I am now, I once spent a long evening discussing the swords with Falissil."

"Falissil?" I didn't recognize the name, and I found it difficult to imagine why Kelos wouldn't have remembered the conversation.

Kelos actually blushed. "He was companion to Master Voros, who was First Blade a hundred years before I was born. Voros taught me to fence, and later, in my fifties, we had something of an . . . understanding." He snorted. "It's hard to believe I was ever that young."

I nodded. That would explain Kelos missing that conversation *and* his blush. The Shades always tried to give their human partners at least the illusion of privacy when sex was involved. Kelos's preference for bedding women was a fair bit stronger than my own, though he had been known to make exceptions over the years as well. But he wouldn't have wanted to discuss the thing if it were a woman, either—he is too private a person.

Malthiss continued as though the interjection had never happened. "Falissil and Voros had moved on to teaching the younglings about the history of the order and the way of Justice. Part of that was sword lore, and Falissil knew much that I did not. It was a passion of both his and Voros's and they had learned many things that lay outside the scope of the teaching of basics to children."

I thought back to my own time in those classes. More than anything, what they had been about was channeling youthful

energy and habits of thought into the pursuit of the right. A
Blade has to walk a narrow path between loving death and
being crushed by it.

From the day we entered the order at the age of four or
five we were trained to kill the unjust, and to do so without
regret or hesitation. That requires a ruthlessness that can all
too easily slip over into a sort of blood hunger where killing
becomes a goal in itself. More than one Blade or Blade in
training has become the very sort of monster that the order
existed to destroy.

But it is all too easy to tip the other way instead, to feel
the deaths of those we must kill too keenly. If you are raised
to see injustice and to look at its costs with unflinching eyes,
you will see much of the aftermath of death. You will see
the harm it does reflected in the eyes of the survivors, those
who have lost friends, parents, lovers. . . . If you have any
compassion at all, you cannot help but see that the Ashviks
and other monsters also have friends, parents, lovers. . . .
Most Blades die by violence, but it is not always an enemy
that spills their blood. Too many die by their own hand.

I had come closer to that edge than I would ever admit to
anyone, even Triss. . . . No, *especially* Triss. I shook off the
thought, and forced myself to listen as Malthiss continued.

He was speaking directly to Faran. ". . . and so, the goddess
only ever made around six hundred swords. Even with all of
her strength, it took her centuries to manage that many. The
swords that Kelos carries, or Aral or Siri, once belonged to
another Blade, just as yours did. But where their swords were
rededicated by the goddess herself and consecrated to their
new wielders, yours are still attuned to she who used them last."

"Hang on." I held up a hand. "I knew that the swords
returned to the goddess, but I don't think I knew that." It wasn't
a complete surprise—some things I had been told over the
years implied it in retrospect—but I hadn't ever really thought
about it. I drew one of my swords and looked down its length
at Malthiss. "I wonder who this belonged to before me."

Malthiss leaned forward and touched the tip of his forked
tongue to the steel. "Alinthide Poisonhand."

I very nearly dropped the sword. Alinthide had been one of my favorite teachers, a smart, strong, wonderful woman. She was one of the Blades who had died trying to kill Ashvik, and I had held a mad secret crush for her in my heart from the age of fifteen to seventeen. Her death was the thing that had driven me to ask Namara to make me a Blade before my time and to give me Ashvik as my first assignment.

"Are you sure?" I asked him. "There were several killed in the time between when I was made a Blade and the investiture of the journeyman who came before me."

Malthiss nodded. "There were also a hundred or more sets of inactive swords at that time without counting the two that were reforged into one for the Kitsune. It had been more than three hundred years since the goddess had last had a full complement of Blades." He twisted his head in a gesture that took in the four of us. "Making *you* was a much harder task than making the swords."

"Then how do you know that these were Alinthide's?" I found that I desperately wanted it to be true, to know that something of that old love lived on.

"I can taste Serass in the swords," said Malthiss, naming Alinthide's companion. "Part of the darkness of the steel comes from the way it is bound to the Shade who partners its master. That leaves a record that only a great length of time, or the conscious effort of the goddess can erase. Falissil showed me how to touch the echo of that in the rededicated blade, though it only works if you knew the Shade personally. It's something like recognizing a shadow trail, though fainter and more complex."

Let me try. Triss rose up and touched his tongue to the sword. "I don't . . . I'm not . . ."

Malthiss said something long and complicated in the hissing tongue of the Shades, and Triss responded in kind. Kyrissa came forward then to touch the sword as well, though Ssithra held back.

"Ssithra?" I asked.

The phoenix shrugged her wings. "Alinthide died before we came to the temple. I wouldn't recognize her taste."

"Perhaps not," said Triss. "But you know mine. This is important knowledge and Malthiss may be the last of the old Shades who knows it. You should learn, too, so that it doesn't die out."

Ssithra nodded and moved forward. "Oh. I hadn't thought of it that way. Thank you, Resshath Triss."

Well? I sent. I didn't trust Malthiss and I wanted this to be true, but I was unwilling to ask my question aloud, for fear of the answer.

Serass, he sent, very firmly. *Now that I know what to*—he sent something incomprehensible in Shade—*for, there is no doubt.*

Why do you think Namara gave me Alinthide's swords? Do you really have to ask?

No, I guess I don't. I closed my eyes and sent a silent thanks to a fallen goddess for a grace that I only now recognized— both for the connection to one I had loved and for the rightness of the thing. Ashvik might have killed Alinthide, but in the end it was Alinthide's sword that killed Ashvik.

"All right," asked Faran, "but what does that mean for me with Parsi's swords?"

"I think that we might be able to attune them to you," said Malthiss. "The six of us working together."

"Even with the goddess gone?" Faran's voice dropped to a whisper.

"Even so."

Is that possible? I sent to Triss.

You'll have to ask Malthiss. I don't know enough about it yet. There was a long pause, then he added, rather reluctantly, *But I can't imagine that it will be easy, especially given Faran's . . . loyalties.*

What does that mean?

Justice matters here. It has to for anything that addresses the power of the goddess. And justice is not Faran's first loyalty, nor has it been since at least the fall of the temple.

I couldn't argue with that. *She had to make hard choices. Without that self-reliance and self-centeredness she wouldn't have survived.*

No, she would not. But that, too, has passed.

What do you mean?

*These days, her loyalty belongs to you. She is a warrior
and you are her captain.*

I didn't know how to answer that, and the conversation
was moving on without us, so I remained quiet.

"How soon can we try it?" asked Faran.

"That depends on our route," replied Malthiss.

Faran frowned. "I think I missed a step in there somewhere."

"The ritual I envision will have to be performed at a place
holy to Namara, probably the grotto on her island in Lake
Evinduin. It still may not work, but, from what I know of
the swords, that is the only way it could."

Faran turned to look at me now. "Aral?"

It was almost a thousand miles out of the way if our plan
was to go after the Son of Heaven straightaway, which
brought up another thing that needed addressing.

"Siri is senior to me." Both Faran and Kelos had taken
to treating our course as though the final authority for choosing it lay with me. "The decision belongs to her."

Siri shook her head. "I don't think so. Faran is your
apprentice, and dealing with her needs is a choice you have
to make." I opened my mouth to demure, but Siri held up a
hand. "But that's not all. I know that you still think of me
as First Blade, Aral, but that's over. Namara is dead and the
temple has fallen."

I shook my head. "You are still my better in the skills of
the Blade *and* Namara's final choice to lead the order."

"That was before this." She raised her stump and formed
a hand of smoke. "The injury isn't a problem, but the Smoldering Flame is. I owe my allegiance to Namara's ghost, but
my soul is bound to another god now, one who seeks to
subvert my will even in his dreams. To be tied to one of the
buried gods is to be forever compromised. Without Namara
to protect me from his influence I can never fully trust my
judgment again, and you shouldn't either."

"Siri . . ." I didn't know what to say. I had felt the hand

of the Smoldering Flame close around my heart, and I knew that she was right, but still . . .

"No. I've thought about this a lot over the last few weeks, and I have made my choice." She swallowed hard and raised her chin. "You are all witness to my words, and I call on you to pass them along to any other members of the order as and when you see them. This is my final command, for I am rendered unfit by circumstance and hereby resign my place as First Blade."

"I . . ." Well, fuck. Now what?

"Further," Siri continued as though I hadn't said anything, "I wish to point out that with Namara dead and the temple fallen, there is no structure to replace me in that role and no higher authority in what remains of the order. That being the case, I think it is only right and proper that it fall to the Blade who preceded me in that role, and I, for one, intend to act accordingly."

Before I had time to really make sense of what she had just said, Siri knelt before me. With a lightning-quick movement, she whipped the single sword that she still carried from its place on her back and laid it on the ground at my feet.

"First Blade Aral, I am yours to command."

Kyrissa moved up alongside Siri and bowed her head. "As am I."

Oh. Shit.

Faran was only a half second behind, wrenching her swords from the wooden floor and laying them at my feet. "I am no Blade, and, with Namara gone, may never be such. But you have my allegiance, First Blade . . . for what it is worth." Ssithra joined her.

I didn't want this, not any of it—I wasn't strong enough for the role. I had proved that in my collapse after the fall of the temple, in my surrender to drink and darkness.

I felt utterly paralyzed, until Triss spoke into my mind. *Say something, idiot! She just handed you her soul with both hands. Be worthy of it.*

I nodded jerkily and reached out to put my hand on Faran's

forehead. "Your loyalty is worth the world, my apprentice, and I accept it. Likewise, yours, Siri." I placed my other hand on her forehead. Whatever I might think about the way she'd trapped me as neat as neat could be, I owed her the same sort of consideration I owed Faran. "And you," I nodded to their Shades, "I accept and honor this trust you give me."

Triss moved around in front of me then and bowed his head. "First Blade Aral."

Stinker, I'll get you for this. I bowed back and gave him the almost-never-used honorific of a chief Shade, "Resshath-ra Triss." If I was stuck, so was he.

Kelos leaned forward then. "First Blade Aral, I know how you feel about my past, and I would not expect you to accept my service or my oath. I am no longer worthy to give you either, and I won't put you in the awkward position of formally denying me by laying my swords at your feet. Nonetheless, they and my life are yours to spend as you see fit from this day forward."

Malthiss bowed to me and then to Triss. "And mine as well. First Blade, Resshath-ra."

I wasn't sure whether I wanted to punch Kelos in the face, or weep, or what. I hadn't seen any of this coming and it was going to take me a while to deal with all the implications.

"The goddess is dead, and I think that you're all crazy to offer yourselves up to a dried out wreck like me, but I thank you for your confidence and I will attempt to live up to the honor." I lifted my hands away from the women's heads. "Now, both of you, take your swords back and let's figure out what happens next."

"That's entirely up to you," replied Siri, and I saw a hint of her wickedest grin as she spoke, "oh, First Blade. I merely serve and obey."

"As I recall," I growled, "the First Blade has a council to rely on for good advice, Siri. And if you think you're getting out of that particularly joyous duty, you are so very wrong. One of the traditional seats on that council belonged to the order's most skilled mage. I believe that chair now belongs to you, Magus Siri."

"A hit." Siri mimed taking a blow to the heart and winked at me. "Well struck, sir, well struck."

I turned an eye on Faran. "As for you—" But she shook her head.

"No. I am no Blade, Aral, nor likely to be named one with the goddess dead . . . however much I may wish it. Your council has no place for me." There was a deadness there in her tone that worried me.

It also decided me. "I don't think that I agree with you there, and I believe I know a way to prove you wrong."

"What do you mean?" asked Faran.

In the same moment, Triss sent, *What are you up to? You'll find out soon enough.*

I put my hands behind my back and stood up very straight. "We've been heading for the mountains above Tavan and the Goat's Pass at Uln, so that we could cross into Dalridia and go on from there to the refuge that Jax and Loris built to gather in our surviving apprentices and journeymen on our way to Heaven's Reach. I know we didn't have anything as formal as a plan, but we all felt that with Jax being the only other surviving master who refused to go over to the Son of Heaven, it was necessary to bring her into the discussion of what happens next and to let her know what we have learned about the Son and his relationship to the risen."

Siri raised an eyebrow. "I take it that's not what we're doing?"

I grinned as I started to find my footing. I might not believe I was up to the task, but that didn't get me off the hook. Even if I failed, I would try to do what was right, both by the remnants of our order and the broader world.

"Oh no, that's exactly what we're doing, but now it's official. It's still on the way, and I want Jax on any future council I'm stuck leading. But more than that, we have a good dozen journeymen who ought to have been confirmed as Blades long ago. If we four are going to attempt to bring justice to the Son of Heaven, the chances are good that some or all of us will not come back. As First Blade it has become my responsibility to see that those who we leave behind are in the best possible position to carry on."

"And?" asked Kelos.

"And, I had originally hoped to move on directly from Dalridia to Heaven's Reach and the Son."

"But not anymore," he said.

"No. We're going to the temple. We have to, if I am going to revive the order. When we get there, we are going to attempt to attune Parsi's old swords to Faran and Ssithra. If we succeed, I will, under my authority as First Blade, invest her with all the duties and rights of a full member of our fallen order."

Faran's eyes had gone very wide, but she didn't speak.

You realize that if this doesn't work it will break her, sent Triss.

Yes, but it's the only thing I can think of that has any chance of making her into what she was meant to be, and the order needs her.

What do you mean?

You were right about her loyalty being to me first. If she is going to become a true Blade, it has to be to justice. That means I have to give her something to live up to. And, if you can think of something greater to live up to than swords consecrated to her on the goddess's own island, we should just make you First Blade and have done.

Point. We do it your way. Aloud, Triss added, "What about the other journeymen? You seem to have some ideas there as well."

I turned. "I do. Malthiss, you said that there were over a hundred pairs of Namara's swords that were inactive at the time of my investiture. The number would have been much the same at the fall of the temple only a few years later."

Malthiss nodded. "Yes . . ."

"Where are they?"

"I don't know."

"Well, neither do I, but I intend to find out. If the order is going to live on, it needs those swords and the masters we will make with them."

5

———◆———

Making a corpse of an enemy is infinitely simpler than trying to make a friend of one.

The Hand of Heaven had killed almost everyone I had ever cared about. They had done so without pity or remorse, and they had gone on to torture many of the survivors. Hell, Jax, whom I had loved and nearly married once upon a time, bore a network of fine scars that threaded her skin from head to toe from her time with them.

Later, these same sorcerer-priests had tried to blackmail her into setting me up for their nets. In the process of that confrontation they had been responsible for the death of one the four remaining free masters of my order, as well as the death or maiming of several of our onetime apprentices. During the fight I had been forced to take actions that led to the deaths of hundreds of souls who were innocent of anything but proximity. The guilt of that had nearly broken me, and I was a harder and colder man for the experience, one long step closer to the monsters. The deaths were accidental and I had done what I felt I had to do, but I could never erase the stain taking those innocent lives had left on my soul.

All of that went through my mind as I stared at the sleeping priest and his watchful Storm familiar. I *wanted* to kill him, to visit on him some of the horror his order had visited on mine. It would have been the easiest thing in the world to cut his throat there by the little stream where we had camped. To simply be done with the problem that he presented. Easier in many ways than abandoning him, and *much* easier than doing what I intended. For that matter, I would have enjoyed it, but that wouldn't have served the mission.

I glanced at the Storm. "Do you understand Varyan?" I asked in the language of my birth. Then switched to the one I'd spoken most over the last decade. "Or Zhani?" I was moderately fluent in a half dozen more, including the formal church dialect of Heaven's Reach, but I was best with those two.

The Storm, which took the shape of a hoop of braided silver centered by a catlike green eye the size of my head, flicked gray wings and rose into the air. It hovered there for a long beat before bobbing twice in an unmistakable nod.

"Both?"

Again, the Storm bobbed in place.

"But you don't speak?"

It twisted back and forth in the air, and small lightnings danced in its wings.

"I'll take that as a no."

The Storm bobbed again.

Up to this point, Kelos and Siri had been the ones having the most to do with our addled priest. I hadn't the magic for it, and Faran had neither the patience nor the mercy. She hated the Hand much more viscerally than any of the rest of us, for they had stolen more than friends and home from her—they had taken her childhood.

If we'd left him to her care he probably would have *died of his wounds, unexpectedly in the night . . . see.* After which, Faran would have pointed to the brand new slice in his throat and smiled sweetly. Which, admittedly, would have made my life simpler.

I sighed and looked at the Storm. "Do you know why he's not recovering better?"

The Storm twisted in the air, its wings darkening noticeably.

"Neither do we, which means we need to take him to a real expert. The university at Tavan has one of the best healers' halls in the eleven kingdoms, and we'll arrive in that city tonight."

The storm rocked in the air but the agitation of its wings faded.

I don't think it understood all that, sent Triss. *It's not much brighter than Scheroc . . . or a big dog for that matter. Air elementals just don't seem to have any real intellectual depth to them.*

It really doesn't matter as long as it calms down and lets us hide them both in a rug so that we can carry them up to the university without drawing too much attention.

Like all the cities of the Magelands, Tavan was centered around a great magical university whose governing council also ruled the city. The council was an elected body made up of senior members of the faculty, all of whom were mages. Likewise, most of the larger towns had magic colleges or individual mage orders making the important decisions. It was a land of refugees formed in the aftermath of the wars that had turned the West that was into an uninhabitable wasteland, and any mage from anywhere in the eleven kingdoms could ask for Magelands citizenship and expect to receive it.

That had the unintended but fortunate effect of rendering the country all but immune to the risen takeover the Son of Heaven had arranged throughout much of the rest of the eleven kingdoms. It did not, however, free the city from the usual pestilence of temples. There were many gods, and the Son was titular head of their various earthly hierarchies in his role as chief priest of the highest church of the East.

Most of the Son's predecessors hadn't managed to exert much control beyond the priesthood of Shan, current Emperor of Heaven, whose archpriest he was. But, there, too, the curse of the risen had allowed the current Son to change the balance of power by the simple expedient of converting the majority of his fellow hierarchs into his undead servants. Now, the combined churches danced to his whim, and that made carrying an obviously injured Hand through the streets of any city in the East a dangerous prospect.

I wonder where Siri found this rug, I sent. *It smells like the wrong end of a manticore.* It was my turn to carry our guests.

Do manticores even have right ends?

They certainly have better *ends,* I grumped as I rolled my shoulders.

We had covered about two-thirds of the distance from the outer edge of the city to the university. Normally, we'd have rented or bought some horses somewhere along the way, but the sudden and unexpected manner of our departure from the Roc and Diamond had cost us badly in both coin and gear.

There had been a time when I might have addressed our lack through a bit of minor burglary, but I was trying to put Aral the jack and all of his bad habits behind me. I was, once again, First Blade, and however much I might wish the job belonged to someone else, I would do my best to do it right while it was mine.

We all preferred to travel in the dark, so we had passed the walls of the city just shy of sundown—as late as we could push it before gate close. The night hunters were out and active by the time we arrived on their turf. Not that we worried about them attacking us. The local shadowside toughs had come sniffing around at first, but they'd veered away quick enough once they got a better look. Which is what you would expect given that Kelos all by himself is scary enough to make battle-hardened soldiers cross to the other side of the street when he gives them that one-eyed basilisk glare of his.

That's why I was so surprised when Siri cried out, "Ware the roof, Aral!" from her place behind me.

I had let my guard relax, and it cost me then as something

dropped onto the rug across my shoulders with force enough to slam me to the ground. Even as my forehead bounced off the cobbles, I heard the heavy sounds of more attackers landing around me. I'd have been in real trouble then if I were alone, maybe even dead, but I had the best in the world covering my back, and *my* shadow bites.

I'm sorry, Aral! Triss shouted into my mind. *I didn't see—*

I lost whatever he said then when the whole street lit up with a tremendous booming crash. Two bursts of magelightning and a lance of black ectoplasmic energy all intersected at a point about three inches above the back of my head. Whoever or whatever had landed on me came apart rather spectacularly at that point. There was a noise like someone had caught a burst of thunder in a bucket and mixed it with a cartful of crockery going over a cliff, followed by a spray of red mist, and a sudden lessening of the weight on my shoulders.

I slithered backward out from under the rug, and vaulted to my feet. My first instinct was to shroud up, but we were trying to keep our profile as low as possible, and vanishing like that would practically scream Blade for any who knew what to look for. Besides, there only seemed to have been about a dozen of them to start with, judging from what I could see—a mixed and very lightly armed group—and that number had already been halved by the time my swords cleared their sheaths.

It wasn't until the nearest lunged for my throat, hands hooking like claws, that I got a good whiff of rotting breath and realized that they were risen—either recently converted or mostly preserved by frequent immersion in fresh blood. I changed the target and manner of my thrust then, jamming my sword through the creature's left eye socket instead of skewering its throat, while I hopped back and away. My point lodged in the back of its skull, as intended, halting its rush and keeping it well beyond arm's reach.

Torquing my whole body leftward, I twisted it off its feet and threw it to the ground. It landed hard on its back, and the true death took it as I slid my blade free. By that time, the rest were also dead. Kelos had cut down two, Faran had beheaded another, and Siri's black ectoplasm had devoured the remainder.

"You're really going to have to show me how to do that someday," I said as she approached. "It looks like it hits harder than magelightning."

Less painful for a light-sensitive familiar, too, sent Triss.

Siri shook her head. "I don't think that would be a good idea. It's lightning's smoky mirror, and much much riskier than it looks—Kayla Darkvelyn taught me the trick I built it on top of, but without the Smoldering Flame to buffer . . ." Then she trailed off, looking abashed. "But, all that's beside the point. I'm sorry. I should have called out sooner. I didn't see that risen until it was actually dropping toward you."

"Don't fault yourself too much," said Kelos. "None of us saw it . . . saw any of them. They were in place long before we got here and they didn't move at all until they attacked. It's amazing how still something can hold when it doesn't have to breathe. What makes me truly curious is that none of the street players seemed to know they were there either, and I'm not sure how they managed—"

A muffled yammering from the dropped carpet interrupted him then, and we all turned to look at it.

"Better check on him," said Siri. "The rug caught it pretty nasty when Kelos and Faran's lightning met my darkburst and vaporized the risen that was on your back. That's a weird combination of elements, and no telling what it might have done to our guest."

But, when we unrolled the carpet, we found the Hand not only unharmed but actually looking out at the world with real awareness for the first time since we'd started dragging him around. His Storm rose into the air above him and began flitting about like a kitten after its first mouse, which seemed another good sign.

He sat up and looked me in the eyes. "You're the Blade, aren't you? Aral? The one the Signet was talking to before . . ." He shook his head. "We were attacked, weren't we? All of us."

I nodded. "Yes, by the risen."

He paled visibly. "The Signet?"

"Is dead." Kelos spoke then, his voice flat, but almost gentle.

"Then, I've failed. We all did. Utterly." He hid his face in his hands for a moment. But then, with a visible effort he lifted his eyes to mine. "The Son of Heaven sent them?"

"He did."

"I will kill him myself."

"Excellent sentiment that." Kelos bent to offer the man his hand. "But we probably ought to hold off on the rest of this conversation until we get somewhere a bit less public. We should also see about making that whole less public thing happen sooner rather than later."

I looked around as Kelos helped the man to his feet. The street had emptied as soon as the trouble started—it was that kind of neighborhood, where concerned citizens ran *from* rather than *to*—but there would be watchers at the windows and probably listeners in the alleys. And, even here, the guard would be along soon, given the circumstances. The risen were the sort of problem that drew official attention in force and with speed.

"You're probably right." The Hand smiled a crooked sort of smile. "It's odd, really, to *be* the disruption of proper order rather than responding to it." As we started moving, he shook his head. "I'm sorry, I should have said before, but my brain seems scrambled, my name is Chomarr."

Aveni, then, though of the older, darker, families, since his skin was nearly as brown as mine. "I'm Aral."

"The Kingslayer, yes." He nodded. "No introductions needed, though it feels very strange to be talking to you instead of trying to kill you." Before I could answer that, he continued. "I recognize the Deathwalker from his time at Heaven's Reach." He jerked his chin toward Siri. "And she can only be the Mythkiller."

"Faran," said Faran, before he could do much more than turn his eyes her way. "No other name."

His expression went distant for a long beat. "Faran, the spy?"

She blinked surprisedly. "I've played the eavesman a time or three, yes, though I didn't think that was widely known."

"Not widely, certainly, but I worked security for the office of the Signet. We kept files on every top player on the shadowside. A child spy who can breeze her way in and out of the most secure buildings in the eleven kingdoms draws our attention."

"No one ever saw me." Faran sounded defensive when she said it, but her face suggested that she felt some pride at having the sort of reputation that drew the attention of the Hand.

"No, they never did." He shook his head. "We didn't have a picture or even a description beyond young and female, and the name Faran was more than half a guess, but we had good reason to suspect the Ghostwind was one of . . . Namara's missing apprentices. There, we had resources that other intelligence services did not."

Faran's expression hardened at the Hand's brief hesitation, just as I felt my own doing. It was clear Chomarr wasn't used to giving the goddess her proper name, or any respect. I briefly regretted not killing him earlier when it would have made the most sense, but then I put it aside. We had a common enemy, and whatever Chomarr might have been thinking, he'd had the sense or grace to make what finally came out of his mouth sound both proper and respectful.

Chomarr went on, apparently oblivious to the anger his pause had generated. "Your identity was one of the great mysteries, and we weren't the only ones who wanted to know it. The Son of Heaven had . . . has unusual access to a lot of state secrets. Every government that we had contact with wanted to know who the Ghostwind was. You're a legend."

"Ghostwind." Faran rolled the word out slowly, like she was testing its flavor. "I think I like that."

"It suits you," said Siri.

I agreed. "Doubly so. Back in Tien, ghosting is shadowside argot for making someone into a corpse."

"The killing wind," whispered Faran. "Yes, I do like it."

Kelos ducked into a narrow gap between two buildings.

"Down this way. I know a place we can lie up till tomorrow night, if it's currently accessible. An alley-knocker of sorts."

A half hour later we were climbing down a rough-built ladder into a deep cistern. Wide cracks in the walls of the tank showed why it had been abandoned. Someone had knocked a hole in one wall, and a narrow tunnel descended farther from there. Thirty feet and two light-blocking turns led us into what looked like a natural cave with several tables in it and a low archway leading onward. A crudely lettered sign hung over the arch, marking the entrance of the illegal tavern: The Honest Man.

I had to laugh. Tradition named alley-knockers after the false or mythic, and that one cut deep.

"Where are we?" said Chomarr.

"There's a layer of limestone underlying the whole city," said Kelos. "It's rotten with caves and sinkholes, and it houses much of shadowside Tavan, though it rarely breaks through the harder capstone layer to the surface. There's been an alley-knocker in this location under one name or another for most of the last hundred years. Every so often the city guard rousts out the current version and plugs up the main entrance, but it's such a handy spot that it always gets re-excavated after a while."

The main room of the tavern was surprisingly well lit, and more than half-full, but we didn't stay there long. An unpleasantly large chunk of our remaining cash bought us private use of a side cave for a night and a day. We could have gotten a cheaper room if we hadn't wanted one of the three that had its own rabbit run to the outside world—a kick panel that opened a slide into the sewers, and the cheapest of the trio because of it.

The mole-faced fellow who showed it to us had said, "It'll get you out, but it won't be a bit of fun, and no doubts. There's a drop at the end, but you land in a deep pool, so that's less a problem than the smell you'll be trailing when you eventually crawl out at t' far end."

Kelos dropped into a chair across the table from Chomarr.

"So, what can you tell us about current security arrangements at Heaven's Reach?"

"I don't think . . ." Chomarr began heatedly, but then trailed off while his Storm's wings darkened with agitation. He took a deep breath. "Sorry. It's going to take me a while to get used to the idea of working *with* you people, instead of against you."

Chomarr tried again. "Even then, I'm not sure how much help I *can* be. After you marked him, the Son started changing everything around in the heart of the temple precinct, and he mostly kept the Hand out of the loop. That's only gotten more true with the passing days. I haven't been past the outermost ring of the precinct in almost a year, and neither has any other member of the Hand save only the Signet and her predecessors."

"None of whom are available for discussion," said Kelos sourly.

I saw a flash of grief and anger pass across Chomarr's features, but if he wanted to make a sharp reply, he fought the impulse down.

Kelos either didn't notice or didn't care. "All right then, tell us what you *do* know. Start with the border patrols and work in toward the city and the temple precinct."

Heaven's Reach the domain was a small temple state in a long valley in the rough hills that separated the Kvanas from Aven. Heaven's Reach the city was its only significant urban area and that more as a support structure for the temple precinct than anything. The business of city and realm was religion, and the Son of Heaven was its absolute ruler.

Kelos had spent the better part of five years living there in his role as chief of the traitor Blades of Heaven's Shadow. He was perhaps the greatest assassin who had ever lived and he had gone in with the intent of betraying his new master as thoroughly as he had his old. He knew the city and the temple precinct and how they were defended as well as anyone, and now he grilled Chomarr on every changed detail.

It took long exhausting hours and I listened to every minute. My one trip to the city had been almost two years before, and brief, but I'd gone there to kill, which meant I had paid very close attention to everything. At the time, Kelos had supplied me with a magical skeleton key in the shape of a Signet's living finger and ring minus the original owner. That had allowed me to bypass a lot of the work I'd normally have done, but the habits of a lifetime meant I'd done extensive reconnaissance anyway.

Without that knowledge I'd have been lost now. With it, I managed to keep up, but only at the cost of a nasty headache. Triss didn't say anything—all the Shades were lying low with only the thin door between us and the common room, and servers coming and going—but I could tell by the way he kept squeezing my shoulders that he knew I was having a hard time of it.

Five hours on, Kelos finally let up. "I think I've about wrung you dry."

"It certainly feels that way," croaked Chomarr—his voice had gone from hoarse to worse some time ago. He threw himself down in a corner, going to sleep within moments.

"What do you think?" I asked Kelos.

"It's going to be really nasty. He didn't know what goes on in the deeps of the precinct these days, of course, but it sounds like every aspect of the outer cordon has tightened and hardened. Beyond the brute physical layout inside the precinct, it's safe to say that very little of what I know from the old days is likely to hold true anymore. I suspect it wouldn't help, but I wish you hadn't left Signet Eilif's finger on the Son of Heaven's chest when you marked him. It'll be like cracking a fresh nut."

I nodded. "That's what I thought, too, though I've only been there the once." I had noticed that in all his questioning Kelos had very carefully avoided saying anything that might even imply the existence of a second ward key in the shape of Signet Nea's finger, so I wasn't surprised that he didn't mention it now. It was a secret that only the two of us and our Shades knew, and I didn't see any reason to expand that circle just yet. "Siri, do you have any thoughts?"

"I never had call to enter the Reach before this, so that was about one third gibberish to me. I've got nothing." The smoke wreathing through her hair and shadow might supply us with some possibilities on that front, but again, not something I wanted to share with an officer of the Hand of Heaven in the room—not even an ostensibly sleeping one on our side.

I looked at Faran, but she shook her head. "I was offered one or two jobs there when I was spying, but I turned them down. I never went within a hundred miles of the place, not even in transit. I didn't want anything to do with the Son, or the Hand, ever again." She looked pointedly at our guest, and made a subtle throat-cutting gesture. I flicked my hand in a sharp "no," and she shrugged. "Worth asking. Maybe later."

Just then there came a sharp rap on the door. A moment later, Mole-Face poked his nose through the gap. "It's an hour past dawn and word just came down from one of our ears—there's a couple of priests asking around up top for a group of four malcontents and a renegade Hand. Boss thought the description sounded like your lot, and that you might take kindly to a nod before they got much closer, as they're trailing a good score of badly disguised temple soldiers in their wake. . . ."

"Your boss is a smart woman." Kelos tossed the fellow a silver coin. "How close are they?"

"Not so close that you need to take shit's highway." He nodded toward the rabbit run. "But close enough you might want to go out the long way behind the bar . . . for a small fee, of course."

"Of course."

6

———•◆•———

There is nothing, absolutely nothing, half so tedious as
messing about on barges.

As a mode of travel barges drive me to distraction.
They're slow. They're cramped. They're damp. It would have
been a good deal faster to walk from Tavan to Uln on the
tow path that followed the river, and much cheaper, and
that's almost certainly what we would have done, too, if it
weren't for the risen. Running water impedes the passage
of the restless dead and the Tamar River was deep and wild.

The barge master had cleverly used the load of planks
she was carrying upriver to Uln to create a sort of second
deck atop the barrels and crates of her other goods. Add in
the padding of heavy tarps, and it made a perfect fencing
ring—irresistible to a bunch of bored Blades. . . .

I stopped my swords halfway to their sheathes when Siri
indicated she wanted to go a round—I'd just finished a pass
with Faran. "I'm up for it if you think you're ready." I flicked
a look at the all too fresh scar where her left forearm ended.
"But one hand against two hardly seems fair."

It was only a few weeks on from the self-amputation of

her left hand, and the first time she'd indicated any desire to spar with anyone.

Siri's smile was confident. "It's all right, Aral. I'll go easy on you."

Don't underestimate her just because she's lost a hand, sent Triss—the barge master couldn't miss that we were something well outside her normal run of passengers, but there was no reason to *give* her the answer, which meant the Shades had to stay hidden. *Siri's handled the risen all right.*

The risen aren't exactly a challenge on the individual level. It's numbers that make them dangerous. Five or ten on open ground is a serious problem. In ones and twos with walls to guard your flanks, not so much.

I seem to remember them very nearly having you for dinner a couple of times back when we were helping Maylien recover her baronial seat. And that was only ever one or two at a time.

That's different. I was a drunken wreck then, and *I hadn't recovered these yet.* I squeezed my hilts.

We'll see.

As Faran waved for us to begin, Siri and I circled each other slowly. It had been nine years since the last time we'd had a bout, and both of us had changed a lot in that time. Siri's missing arm was merely the most visible sign of that.

Despite what Triss might have implied, I had no intention of treating Siri lightly. She was one of the deadliest swordswomen that my order had ever produced. In the last year before the fall of the temple we'd fenced regularly, and if I scored one point for every three she did, well, that was a good day on my part. For that matter, I was only two years on from my drunk days. While I had been rotting away in a dive bar in Tien, Siri had been training daily with Ashkent and Kayla. My extra hand would probably reverse the old advantage in my favor. But I didn't expect to get off without losing points and, probably, a little blood into the bargain— given that we were sparring with live steel.

I sensed more than saw Kelos when he arrived and took up a position opposite Faran to watch us, so focused was I on Siri. We circled and counter-circled and circled again, all without engaging. Finally, impatient to get things moving, I offered her a very slight opening. Low, and left, ideal for a right-handed sword and her current edge position. She ignored it, and ignored the next one as well.

Fine, if she insisted that I move first, I would. I'd been very careful to keep my edges at angles to each other and the blades well apart to maximize the advantage that extra sword gave me. Now I attacked in the same way, driving in a low line thrust on the left, while simultaneously whip-snapping my right sword at Siri's face in a cross chop. I could have gone for a more cautious approach, using one sword to attack and keeping the other ready to defend, but while playing it conservatively *might* keep Siri from scoring on me, it would *never* land a point on her.

She caught my left-hand sword with a parry and as neat a bind as I'd ever seen her manage, jerking it and me forward and out of line, while simultaneously ducking under the edge of my right. *Damn, but I'd forgotten how very fast she was.* Still, I'd hedged my attack by snapping my upper blade rather than committing to a full cut. Now, I was able to twist my wrist and bring it down toward the top of her head in a drawing slice as she dragged me to her left.

But she wasn't there. In the instant after she'd pulled my left sword down and out of line, she disengaged, moving forward and left. Spinning past me, she flicked a backhanded cut at my right shoulder blade. But I turned with her, parrying her easily enough, then riposting with my free sword. She blocked it with the end of her hilt, catching my edge an inch below her pinky.

And so it went, for a good dozen passes. She had gotten *much* better, while I was only just recovering to what I had once been, and I couldn't touch her. But my extra sword meant that she wasn't having any more luck at scoring on me.

I was growing increasingly frustrated at my continued failure to even come close to a point against a one-handed opponent. I decided to force the issue, going in hard with a doubled thrust and a long lunge at maximum speed and power. That was mistake one. Mistake two was getting into the habit of ignoring her missing hand.

She parried my left-hand sword with her right, and blocked my left with a beautiful back fan kick that caught the side of my blade and knocked it out of line. At that point my arms were spread wide, with my points forward and on either side of Siri. That's when she snapped her stump arm across my throat as if she were making a neat, short, cut.

Wait, what? I thought.

My confusion turned to grudging admiration when a smoky hand holding an equally smoky sword suddenly formed on the end of her stump, hiding the raw scars underneath. A moment later, a faint slithering burn kissed the front of my throat. What should have felt like a brief puff of warmth somehow grew an edge, tracing a bloody line across my skin.

I put up my swords and stepped back. "Killing point, since I assume that if you'd wanted to do more than edge kiss me there, you could have."

Siri grinned and nodded, panting when she spoke. "I've been working at it for weeks now, and I can make the smoke as hard as steel for a few tenths of a second."

"Which is all it takes," I replied, somewhat acidly.

"Yep. Of course, it makes me feel like I've got maggots crawling through my brain every time, and I'm going to need to sit down now and catch my breath. It burns nima like a runaway soul tap."

"Is it worth it?" I asked. That kind of magic drain could kill you—and very nearly had done for me once.

Siri laughed. "Oh yes! The look on your face alone justified the cost. When you realized that you'd been suckered . . . a thing of beauty." But then she swayed on her feet, and went to one knee. "Still worth it, but ugh. The brain maggots are soooo much worse than the exhaustion. Stop giving me that look, Aral."

"What look?" She raised her eyebrows, and I blushed and bowed my head. "And another point for Siri."

She always finds a way to win, sent Triss, *no matter what it costs. That's what makes her great.*

"I *have* to do this," said Siri. "To get a handle on what I've become. If I don't learn to master the buried god within, he will master me. Maybe not so directly as the way he tried back at the Brimstone Vale, but fear and revulsion are also types of control, and I will not give in to them." She grinned abruptly. "Actually, this is your fault."

I startled. "What do you mean by that?"

"Not fault really, since I appreciate you allowing me the opportunity to do this more than I can say."

I was still baffled, and shook my head.

"When you took over as First Blade, it freed me from responsibility for anyone but myself. I can afford to risk things that I couldn't before. Where I had to fight against the smoke within every single minute, now I can strive to make it mine, to own it instead of the other way round. You might even say that it's become my duty. If I can master this, it will allow me to do things for the order that maybe no one else can."

"And if it devours you?" Though I didn't entirely believe there *was* an order anymore, I let that part of her remark pass unanswered.

Siri shrugged. "You'll kill me. Before, you would have hesitated, bound by your sense of duty to my authority as well as our friendship. Now, that same sense of duty will force you to do the right thing. I find that enormously reassuring."

I didn't know what to say to that, so I turned away. Only to find myself facing Kelos, his eyes unspeakably sad. If I had believed for an instant that he was capable of betraying his own inner emotions, and not just aping sentiment to manipulate those around him, I might have taken some comfort there. As it was, I had to restrain myself from spitting at his feet.

"What do you want?" I growled.

"Are you exhausted yet, or would you care to go another couple of rounds?" He looked hopeful, almost wistful—more manipulation, certainly.

"With you?" I couldn't keep the incredulity out of my voice.

He nodded, but his expression closed, and sarcasm laced his response, "Believe it or not, I need to practice as much as the rest of you."

"Why not with Faran?"

Are you mad? Triss asked me silently.

"I would prefer not to bleed out if I miss a parry," replied Kelos. "I trust you not to kill me out of pique. Your apprentice . . ."

"It wouldn't be pique," said Faran. "It would be cold-blooded justice, and I'd be smiling all the while. Sunny, even."

"So," said Kelos. "Are you too tired to spar with me or not?"

"I'm good to go," I said, surprised to find that it was true. Even six months ago, one serious round with Faran had been enough to wind me—maybe I really was the Kingslayer again.

"Will you?" Again he gave me that faux-wistful look.

I rolled my eyes, but nodded. "Fine, let's do it."

Are you sure about this? asked Triss.

Not even a little bit.

Kelos stripped off his shirt as he crossed to the far side of our tiny arena. When he drew his swords and turned to face me, I couldn't help but remember the last time I'd crossed blades with him. That had been in the Magelands, too, atop the roof of the proctor house at the University of Ar. . . . I say crossed blades where I should probably not. I'd drawn steel right enough, but Kelos hadn't bothered. He hadn't needed to. He'd taken me down using little more than his bare hands.

It was embarrassing in the extreme and I couldn't help but relive that humiliation now. Would he defeat me as easily again? I was in much better shape than I'd been then, but he hadn't even needed to draw on me. I felt a bead of sweat form at my hairline and roll down the side of my face.

No.

I would not let him outface me this way. I refused. He

might beat me anyway, but he would have to do it with steel. I wouldn't let him win the fight inside my head. Not ever again. I forced myself to be calm. Forced myself to *be* the Kingslayer, and not just Aral. Kelos might be a legend, but so by the goddess was I.

I drew my swords and advanced on my old master, every sense at maximum alert, every nerve alight. There was none of the cautious circling that Siri and I had indulged in this time. Kelos came in hard and fast. He outweighed me by a good fifty pounds, all of it muscle. He used that advantage ruthlessly, hammering away at me with blows that would have shattered lesser swords, driving me back and back again with sheer raw power.

It was daunting. Doubly so since I knew that he could shift styles in a heartbeat, moving from force to finesse with ease. He had done so all the time back in the days when he taught me to use my swords—mirroring the styles of a dozen of the order's most dangerous foes in aid of teaching us to defeat them. Through him, my childhood self had lost fights with the Elite, the Dyads, the Hairi . . . And, dammit, there he was again, beating me in my head instead of on the field.

He had backed me to the very edge of our impromptu ring, though I'd kept him from pinning me in the corner. I was in danger of letting him push me right into the river if I didn't do something quickly. By sliding sharply to my left and at the cost of two points—one to my wrist, another on my shoulder—I managed to get around Kelos and shift back toward the center of the ring. It might not be in my head, but he was still beating me, and maybe he always would.

Kelos scored a third point then, knocking my right-hand sword aside with another smashing cut followed by a reversal of his blade to slap my hip with the flat, and that was the match.

"Again?" asked Kelos.

I wanted so very much to say no, to plead exhaustion and slither away to lick my wounds, though I was far more injured in spirit than flesh. It would have been the easy thing to do, the smart thing, even. But I refused to give up. I won't say that I couldn't have walked away, because I could have. I just wouldn't.

"Again," I said.

He switched styles now, shifting from hack and slash, to flit and flick, dancing his edges around me in swift and shimmering network that let him prick two points off me in less than a minute. He was so very good. But, dammit, so was I. I would not let him do this to me.

Kelos came in for the third point, but I deflected him. Barely. And again. And yet again. I was fighting him off, but only by pushing myself to the very top of my form, and only for a time. He really was better than me, and not just in my head. For some reason it was far harder to admit that than it had ever been to admit that Siri was.

So, I couldn't win. Accept that, move on. Maybe I could still at least score a point if I waited for the right opportunity. My tactics stayed much the same—Kelos had kept me on the defensive from our first moment of engagement—but my attitude shifted. Instead of fighting a sense of defeat as well as Kelos, I embraced it. I was going to lose. The best I could do was lose with style.

I saw an opening that I wouldn't have tried for before—too risky, too little chance of scoring a point. This time, I went for it hard. I missed, but Kelos had to actually hop back to keep my edge away from his skin. I had surprised him, and he grinned. He likes surprises. Another minute went by with me somehow managing to keep him from scoring that final point. I saw a second opening—low, and riskier even than the last. If I missed, Kelos couldn't help but finish me off.

Why not?

I started a lunge at Kelos's chest, but at the last moment I let my forward leg collapse, dropping my whole body toward the floor. I released my left-hand sword and caught myself on the palm of that hand. My thrusting hand shifted with me as I fell, angling up now at the meaty part of Kelos's thigh rather than straight into his chest, just as I had planned.

My point went home, sinking a good inch into his leg before I had the presence of mind to stop my thrust, so

unexpected was my success. We both froze then, him standing, me balanced precariously on knee and toes and palm.
A trickle of blood ran down half the length of my blade
before meeting the edge and dripping to the deck in a series
of bright drops.

I didn't know what to do or say. In all the years I'd known
Kelos, and all the times I'd sparred with him, I had never
once needed to pull a blow before. Even in those moments
where I'd scored a point as a boy I had never been in any
danger of actually hurting him, so thoroughly had he controlled our exchanges.

"I . . . I'm sorry. . . ." I stammered as I reverted briefly to
nine. "I didn't . . . I . . ."

Kelos stepped back, pulling himself free of my sword.
"Good point, boy. Excellent!" He had a huge smile on his face.
"Totally unexpected and you'd have hit bone if you hadn't
pulled it. No one's pricked me that solidly since Nuriko."

"I didn't think I would actually hit you," I said. "You're
so much better than I am . . . I just . . ."

"Stop apologizing, Aral. That thrust was a thing of
beauty. Riskier than anything you'd want to try if you didn't
have to, but I *am* better than you are, and if you can't out-
fence an opponent you have to outrisk them. You're a thinker
and a planner, always have been, and damned good at it.
But that's made you overly cautious. Sometimes you simply
have to take a leap in the dark and hope."

I realized then that I was grinning like a madman, and
mentally kicked myself. I hated that praise from this man
could still light me up like a fucking schoolboy. But somewhere, deep down inside, no matter how much I hated what
he had done to the goddess and my order, no matter how
much I might hate *him*, he was still *my* master, still the man
whose approval mattered most to me.

Would I ever be able to let that go?

Whether it was the two weeks on untamed water, or simply
that the last of the risen who had attacked us in Wall had

fallen to the forces of the Magelanders, I couldn't say, but we didn't encounter any more of them in Uln or on our way into the mountains above. The series of high passes that led from there into Dalridia were little more than goat tracks, totally unsuitable for trade or anything other than the fittest of foot traffic.

We climbed higher and higher, now edging our way along the narrowest of tracks, now skirting huge drops, now scrabbling up one of the many short vertical climbs that punctuated the trail. Often, as we negotiated a particularly difficult stretch, I thought back to my last passage this way hauling three badly injured comrades and wondered how we had made it at all.

It snowed twice. Both falls were light enough, but a reminder that we needed to hurry if we wanted to get through the mountains to the temple before winter closed the passes on the west. We were midway through the month of Harvestide, which meant summer was winding down, and the western road that led down into the Kvanas lay at the far end of Dalridia. Though travel usually continued well into Talewynd, early blizzards had been known to shut the passes down before Harvestide's end.

By the time we descended into the mountain valley that held the kingdom of Dalridia we were all pretty ragged and grimy. Fortunately, the royal castle Jax's brother had set aside for her and Loris and their students was on the south end of the kingdom, and we didn't have to pass through any heavily populated areas to get there.

When we reached a point on the road where the castle was visible high on the slopes of the mountains ahead, I waved our little group to a stop. "I think it might be best if Kelos and Chomarr waited here in the wood below the village, while Siri and Faran and I go on ahead."

It was a cold afternoon with a fine rain falling, and waiting in the evergreen forest wasn't going to be much fun, but Kelos nodded. "That's probably the wisest course, given the time Jax spent with the inquisitors of the Hand, and Loris's death. I don't think she'll be at all happy to see either of us."

"Neither will her students," said Faran. "Most of them would kill you both given the chance."

Chomarr pointed back up the road. "Perhaps we should meet you above the western pass? We could wait for you at Riada on the lake."

It was tempting for a number of reasons, not least that it would give the rest of us the option of simply skipping over the part where we picked them up, but I shook my head. "No. We have plans to make with Jax and her students and we'll need you both close for that. I just want to warn them that I'm bringing you in so that no one does anything hasty."

"Premeditated, on the other hand . . ." said Faran.

I shot her a look, but she ignored me. And that kind of closed the conversation down. With a sigh, I turned toward the castle and started walking. Siri and Faran fell in behind me.

An hour later, as we finished climbing the steep series of switchbacks that led up to the castle's main entrance, the drawbridge came down to let us pass. It was a rough-looking old fort built heavy both for defense and to withstand the terrible mountain storms. Like the mountains behind, it was carved of some rough gray stone, but I knew the inside was comfortable enough, having been retrofitted as a luxurious royal retreat and then later converted for Jax's use. Though she had surrendered the title when she was inducted into Namara's service, Jax had been born a princess of Dalridia, and her brother now sat the throne.

A trio of figures was waiting for us at the far end of the plank bridge. Jax stood in the middle, looking ridiculously tiny between Maryam, a tall slender woman with black hair and beautiful eyes, and Roric, who was shaped like a bog troll—deep chested, long armed, and preposterously broad of shoulder.

As I got closer I couldn't help but focus on what the Hand had done to them, and what I was about to ask. Jax's entire skin was threaded with fine scars, like intricate lace, and she was missing about half her left hand, including her pinky and ring fingers. She hadn't brought her cane, but I expected that she could tell the weather from the aftereffects of a leg broken in four places. Maryam had a huge burn scar across her right cheek and neck from the fall of the temple, and she'd lost the ear above it to the events that had brought Jax and I back into contact two years before.

Roric had fared the best, with only his missing right ear to mark his time in the dungeons of the Hand. Well, that and the fine scars across his cheekbones, but then Maryam and Faran and I all shared those, as did Javan, who was elsewhere at the moment. Roric was Avarsi. As was the custom of his people, he'd sliced those lines into his cheeks himself, both as a way of mourning for Loris and in promise of avenging him. The moment had been full of blood and rage and madness, and the rest of us had joined him in marking our pain on our flesh.

When we got close enough to speak without shouting, Siri extended her right hand and forearm to Jax. "Sister, it's been too long."

"SIRI!" replied Jax, leaping past the hand to wrap her arms around Siri's neck and, literally, hang there—Siri being more than a foot taller than her old friend. "What on earth have you done with your hair?" Jax ran a finger through Siri's smoking braids.

"That's a very long story," replied Siri. "I promise you all of it, but not till later."

"Master Aral," said Roric.

"Journeyman Roric." I grinned and clasped forearms with him while Maryam did the same with Faran. Then we switched, while shadows mixed and mingled around our feet with a susuration of Shade voices. Next, I turned to Jax, who had finally let go of Siri, and bent to hug her. "Hey there."

"You're late," she said into my ear while poking me in the ribs. "Clever, but still late."

I let her go. "I . . . wait, what?"

"It's been nearly two years since you said you'd come back to help me with the school once you killed the Son of Heaven. Don't think I didn't notice when you sent a letter to Faran asking her to meet you in Tien instead of coming to collect her yourself. You *knew* I wouldn't let you leave so easy. Coward."

I grinned at her. "First, I didn't say I would come back, I said that I *might*. Second, the Son of Heaven isn't dead yet, so even if I had said what you're claiming I did, I'm still not in violation of my word."

"Technicalities," humphed Jax.

"Well, you did say I was clever, though I still haven't figured out why."

"Because of this." She grabbed hold of Siri, who had just finished greeting the other two and pulled her up between us. "You brought me a Siri! Which means I'm not allowed to be mad at you for at least a day and a night."

"Is that binding?" I asked.

"Of course, why do you even mention it?"

"Because of what else I brought you."

"You can't mean Faran. She's a delight." She put out her other hand and dragged Faran in for a hug as well. "And don't think I didn't notice the swords on your back, girl. I'm going to want the whole story on that. So . . ." She turned back to me. "What else did you bring me?"

I decided there was no way to sweeten it.

"Kelos."

7

─────◆─────

Hate looked at me out of eyes that once held love. All that I had said was a name, but it was enough to transform the smile on an old lover's face into the merciless stare of an angry killer. The warm raucous sounds of reunion went utterly cold and silent.

"The whole, living, breathing Kelos, you mean? Not just his head or his heart?" Jax's tone was quiet, almost joking, but I didn't for an instant make the mistake of thinking she was anything but furious. "I presume that's what you mean from the way you said it, but it seems so unlikely that you'd let him live. . . ."

"It's not really Aral's fault," said Siri.

"Yours?" Jax turned hard eyes on Siri.

Siri held up her one hand. "No. Nor Faran's either. You should know that Kelos is always and only ever Kelos's own damn fault."

"That, yes." Jax nodded. "It's the allowing him to live thing I'm having trouble with. . . ."

"Well, *I* wanted to kill him," mumbled Faran. "But nobody would let me."

"That's not strictly true either," said the shadowy phoenix who now formed herself from the shadows at Faran's feet. "Aral said very clearly that he wasn't going to stop you ever again."

Jax reached up and pinched the bridge of her nose. "I can see this ugly little story is going to require time for the telling. We'd better take this inside, where the Shades can talk out of the light and I can get a nice cup of efik."

For the first time in ages, I heard the name of the drug without twitching. That felt almost unspeakably good.

I nodded to Jax. "You might want to brew up a whole pot. It gets worse."

"Worse than Kelos? I don't even . . ."

"Well, more *in addition to* than *worse* exactly," I said, "but yeah. Inside is good."

Jax took a deep breath. "Come on then, Javan's waiting in the council room with Inaya and Xin, and they'll want to hear this as well."

Along with Maryam and Roric, Javan, Inaya, and Xin were the seniormost of the surviving journeymen from the temple. The first three I knew well from the abbey raid where Jax, Faran, and I freed them from the Hand. The latter two had been left in charge of the castle while all that was going on, and I had only had minor dealings with them in the time I had been here between the abbey and my previous visit to the Son of Heaven. Together, the five made up the council Jax and Loris had formed to help them run their school and refuge. With Loris dead, their influence had only increased.

"How's Javan's leg?" Faran asked Jax as we headed across the stone mosaic floor that centered the castle's entrance—a hunting scene with turbaned lancers surrounding a wounded chimera. Javan had lost the leg from the knee down during that same abbey raid.

Jax sighed. "The flesh has healed well enough, but he's still trying to come up with a peg that doesn't thump when he walks or a magical construct that won't shine through his shroud. I don't think he'll ever be able to do proper fieldwork again."

"Has he tried the Durkoth?" asked Faran.

Jax raised an eyebrow. "There's a thought. They don't come cheap, but the Durkoth can do some very fancy things with locks and toys. They might be able to do a working foot as well. So"—she turned back to me as we passed down a short hall lined with tapestries depicting a variety of scenes from the history of Dalridia—"did you bring me any *good* news?"

"Besides Siri and Faran? Isn't that a little greedy?" Before she could answer, I held up my hands. "Sorry, couldn't resist. But, actually, I have. Maybe. It depends on how things work out with Faran's swords and . . . dammit, there's so much to tell you and I've no idea where to start."

Siri interjected, "I do. We made Aral First Blade."

Jax turned. "You what?"

"Made Aral First Blade."

"On whose authority?" she asked. "The goddess is dead, or hadn't you noticed?"

Siri's face went as cold as Jax's. "On *my* authority, as the last First Blade personally named by Namara. Aral was First Blade before I was, and the only other living person to hold that title besides me and Kelos. I thought it only fit and proper that he reassume the role, and that's why I asked him to do it when I stepped down. Do you have a problem with that?"

And now it was Jax's turn to put up her hands. "No. Sorry. It was just startling is all. Do you mind if I ask why?"

"I was no longer able to do the job, and with only we three left of the true Blades, it was him or you."

A flash of pain burned its way across Jax's eyes. "That does narrow it down a bit, doesn't it?" She opened the door to the council chamber. "Given that I missed the meeting, I guess I got off light. I'm just as glad that you didn't pick me."

"I'm not." Maryam's voice came out flat and hard.

"Not what?" Javan asked from within.

The young man was sitting at a long wooden table with his amputated leg up on a small stool beside him. The flesh ended just below the knee, giving way to a glossy black calf and a foot of glazed ceramic—golemite clay if I was any judge. Whatever it was, it registered as an intense shining green in my magesight. His familiar, Thiess, who generally took the form of an enormous horned owl, perched on the back of his chair. Like Maryam and Roric, Javan was missing an ear, and for the same reason. A previous Signet had delivered them all to Jax in a sack once upon a time.

Inaya and Xin were sitting across the table from Javan. The former was a short, muscular young woman with long dark hair that was nearly as curly as Siri's and skin the color of strong tea. Her Shade, Ssayath, took the form of a tuft-eared lynx. Xin was a typical northern Zhani, with fine black hair, a round face, and a slender build. Alone of all the people in the room he carried a pair of short axes instead of any kind of sword. His Shade, Gulthiss assumed the shape of a hump-backed camelopard.

Maryam jerked a thumb at Siri and me as she crossed the threshold and went to stand beside Javan's chair. "I'm not happy that these two decided to make Aral First Blade over Jax. She's the one who gathered us all up from the various corners of the eleven kingdoms and brought us here. Her and Loris. She's the one who has trained us and sheltered us and done what she could to re-create the order while Aral was playing the shadow jack in Tien. I think that if there's going to be a new First Blade it ought to be Jax."

Maryam turned back to me. "I owe you my life after what you did for us at the abbey, but while you were tucked away in Tien, Jax was rebuilding the order." She bowed formally now. "No offense meant, Master Aral, but that's how I see it."

I returned her bow. "None taken, Journeyman Maryam. You make a good case for Jax's dedication to the order, and for her dedication to its lost children, though I have never doubted either. That's why, if the order continues and if I continue as First Blade, I intend to make Jax chancellor of our school and chief of my council. Rebuilding will start with you and your generation. Jax is the bridge between us."

Siri spoke now, quietly, but with a cold and deadly precision. "I can't speak to the matter of the order, but while I live and unless he voluntarily relinquishes the title, Aral *is* First Blade."

Faran didn't say a word, but she stepped up to stand with Siri and nodded.

Javan rose then to stand beside Maryam, and Roric joined him there. Across the table, Xin and Inaya backed them.

That's when Jax moved between the two factions. "I. Don't. Want. The. Job."

"What?" Maryam looked shocked. "But . . ."

"But me no buts, Maryam. I have no interest. Even if I did, I would accept Siri's word in this. She was the goddess's final choice, and, as far as I am concerned, in this matter Siri speaks for Namara."

Maryam continued to bristle, but Roric and the others visibly relaxed. Jax turned and knelt before me then, placing her swords at my feet. "First Blade Aral, I am yours to command." She had rehilted her swords as a way of concealing them, and she wore them on her hip in the Dalridian style, but once they were unsheathed, the black steel of the goddess was unmistakable.

When Jax spoke, Triss emerged from my shadow and took his place beside me, as was right and proper. *I am having real trouble getting used to hearing that oath again.*

Tough. If I have to live with being First Blade, you can suck it up, too.

Sshayar formed himself out of Jax's shadow, taking the shape of a great tiger and kneeling before us as well. "I am likewise at your command, First Blade. Yours and Resshath-ra Triss's."

Jax didn't look over her shoulder at the journeymen, but neither did she make any move to get up or retrieve her swords. She just waited.

Roric joined her a moment later. "I have no swords to lay

at your feet, but if I may serve the order through you, First Blade Aral, I will."

His Shade, an enormous six-legged badger named Ssolvey, emerged then and silently touched his forehead to the ground in front of my feet. Javan and Thiess followed next, and I marveled at how well his golemite leg worked. Xin, Gulthiss, Inaya, and Ssayath quickly joined him there, crowding the space in front of me.

Finally, after several long beats, Maryam knelt as well. "If it is Jax's will that we accept you as First Blade, Master Aral, I will follow you into hell itself." Not quite the traditional phrasing, but it was hard to fault the sentiment.

The many-headed hydra that formed Maryam's shadow slid forward. "First Blade Aral, I am yours to command."

"Thank you, Vrass. I hope to be worthy of all of you. Now, will you please get up and take your places around the table? We have many things to discuss before I drag Master Kelos in here—"

"Kelos! That—" Javan snapped, then cut himself off and took a deep breath. "Sorry, I can see there's much to hear." Rising, he returned to his chair.

Once everyone had taken a seat I nodded to Javan. "There is, and much of it you're all going to hate. Kelos is probably the worst of it, but he's not alone in the woods. There's a Hand named Chomarr with him."

A low murmur arose at that, but only Jax spoke. "Kelos and a Hand. Why does that not surprise me?"

"For what it's worth, we picked them up in two different places," said Triss—as was traditional in a meeting of the order he had taken a place on the wall behind me where he could easily see and be seen. "Kelos has been with us since the rising of the Smoldering Flame some months ago. The Hand only for a few weeks. He is the last member of a delegation led by the now deceased Signet Toragana."

Jax nodded approvingly. "You've killed another Signet then, Aral?"

"No. Sorry to disappoint, but I rather liked this one." More quiet murmurs. "I know, I'm not making anyone happy with that, but there it is. Toragana came to ask me to help her kill the Son of Heaven."

"Finally, something we can approve of," Maryam growled. Then she flushed. "I'm sorry, First Blade, it's just . . ."

I smiled rather grimly. "That I am not your choice for this role and I keep giving you bad news."

Gently, sent Triss.

I nodded to his unspoken prompt and continued. "I understand that, and I pardon the interruption. Also, the next one, but do try to save it for something big. This is going to be a very hard story to tell, and I can't fault anyone for not liking it much. I know that I hate having to tell it, but we'll get through it much faster if we save our outbursts for my most truly egregious faults."

Maryam chuckled. "Thank you for that, First Blade, and again my apologies."

I wanted to tell her to drop the First Blade nonsense, but I knew that if I really wished to have my authority respected here, I was going to need to get used to hearing it—at least in formal settings like this council.

"That being the case," I continued, "why don't I give you the better news first as something of a cushion. I know that none of you will have failed to notice these." I reached over and touched the sword hilt that jutted over Faran's right shoulder. "They belonged to Master Parsi—given to her by the goddess—and Faran claimed them from her corpse. One of the better reasons Kelos is still alive is that Malthiss thinks he can help us to properly seal them to Faran so that we can make her the first new Blade the order has seen since the temple fell."

"Is that possible?" asked Xin. "I mean, without Namara's personal blessing?"

"Malthiss thinks so. My own swords belonged to Alinthide Poisonhand before they came to me, just as Jax's and Siri's swords came to them after other masters. Malthiss says that we must go to the ruins of the temple to attempt it. If we *can* do this thing, I intend to proceed directly from Faran's investiture to a search for the place where Namara kept those swords that were not currently sealed to a living master. If I can find them, I will induct all of you who are of the proper age."

There were tears on Roric's scarred cheeks as he choked out, "I . . . that would be . . . I mean: Thank you!"

"I hope that I will be your First Blade for some years to come, but I believe the next thing I must attempt after the visit to the temple, is to address the problem of the Son of Heaven." I still had very serious misgivings about whether that was the right path, especially given the cautions of the goddess and Toragana's visions of war, but the idea of it would help to unite the order I hoped to build. "Without the aid of Kelos, I can't see any way to succeed there—another reason he lives yet. There is no guarantee that I will survive the experience. If I die in Heaven's Reach, I want those of you who are left behind in the best shape to continue the order that I can manage."

There. At least for the moment, that should reduce any impulses to advance Jax's case for First Blade via a dagger in my back. In the days of the goddess, such an idea would never even have occurred to me. But now, with all the betrayals I'd faced over the last few years, and the simple fact that I was leading a society of *assassins*, it was a possibility I couldn't afford to ignore.

"Does anyone else have any questions before I tell you where we are with respect to the forces of Heaven's Reach and how we got here? It will take me some time to get through it all, but hopefully by the end you'll see why Kelos yet lives, why I have a Hand in my train, and understand the full story of the fall of the temple."

Jax raised a hand. "I want to know what is going on with Devin and the other traitors, and what you intend to do about them."

"To the extent that I know anything about the first part, I'll get there. As to the second, that will be a matter for the new shadow council. It's not a decision I feel that I should make alone." As much as *kill them, kill them all* appealed to me at the moment, I suspected it wasn't the best choice.

Jax nodded and looked thoughtful.

Inaya's familiar Ssayath, spoke from the wall behind her next. "Master Aral, in that same line, I would like to know what you intend to do about Master Kelos and Resshath Malthiss."

"Assuming that they and I both survive our visit with the Son of Heaven, I think that we will have to bring him before the shadow council as well. His crimes were against all of us, and all of us who remain should have a part in deciding his fate."

"Thank you," said Ssayath.

Once, you would have said that his crimes were against the goddess. . . . Triss sounded sad and wistful in my mind. *You have changed so very much these last few years.*

For the better, I hope. I am no longer as certain of things as I once was, but I feel wiser.

Even as Triss and I continued our silent conversation, I began to speak aloud, relating all that I knew and had guessed about the Son of Heaven, the fall of the temple, Kelos, and, well . . . everything I had been doing since Maylien had come to me for aid in regaining her legacy. Well, nearly everything. There were a number of secrets I wasn't yet ready to share.

You are wiser, I think, sent Tris, *and you have stopped drinking. But you are a harder man now and a colder one. You have always been capable of great good. Now I think you are also capable of great harm, and that concerns me.*

I wouldn't worry too much. I have you to advise me.

That is part of what concerns me. I think that I understand your people better than most of my kind, but I am not of you. I attempt to live mercy because it is—or was— important to you and to Namara, but it is a learned thing. Darkness does not know restraint. It is all devouring and without pity, and, as much as I am bound to you and, through you, to humanity, I am still an elemental creature of darkness. In my mind, I may share your ideals, but in my soul . . . I look at what Thiussus was like and I wonder how easy it would be for me to become her.

I thought back to what I had seen of Nuriko's mad Shade familiar . . . *I can't see it.* I simply couldn't imagine Triss ever acting like she did. *You're better than that. Sane, for starters.*

I thank you for that, and I hope that you are right, but still, I worry.

But then I was coming to my first encounter with Devin after the fall of the temple—a particularly dense section of the story I was telling aloud—and I had to drop the conversation with Triss to give my full attention to the details.

Hours later, after I had passed through the revolution in Zhan, the events that had cost Jax half her hand, and the rising of the buried gods, I finally wound down to the last few weeks, the death of the most recent Signet, and what she had told me. I elided some of the details about the powers Siri had gained through her forced connection to the Smoldering Flame—that was her story to tell, if she chose, and not mine.

When I was done, there was a long silence, into which the growling of Faran's stomach made an especially loud interjection—it *had* been a long march on tight rations. Taking that as a sign, and because I wanted to give all the information time to sink in before we started arguing about Kelos and Chomarr, we adjourned for a late lunch.

In another place it would have been supper, but much of a Blade's training and life happened at night, and Jax ran the place on the same timeline as the temple, which meant four meals. First breakfast came shortly after dawn, for the convenience of those who had to operate on the sun's time for one reason or another. The shepherds who maintained the flocks that fed the castle for example. Blade's breakfast happened at midday and provided lunch to the grooms and other morning folk. Dinner, or Blade's lunch was served around sunset, and supper happened at midnight.

Dalridian cuisine was heavy on frying, sausage of the unidentifiable bits variety, and other foods that could be stored for a long time without spoiling. It reminded me strongly of the things my family had eaten back in Varya before the temple took me, and not in a good way. There was some nostalgia value to it, but after years of eating spicy Zhani noodle dishes and Sylvani curries, it sat very heavy on the stomach.

Not that I faulted Jax for that. The castle stood in a remote village in the mountains in a country that was cut off from the rest of the world for half the year, and the fancier sorts of culinary preservation magics were extraordinarily expensive. One of the things I was going to have to do sooner rather than later if I wanted to properly reestablish the order was figure out some way to get in better food and some really good cooks. If I didn't, the next generation of Blades was going to be terrible with poisons. You have to know how to cook and how to season if you want to successfully dose a meal or drink.

"So." Jax leaned in close as she finished her food. "Now that we're done stalling, can we talk about Kelos, and whether or not we should leave him out in the rain to rot with his Hand friend?"

I responded just as quietly. "You saw through that, huh?"

"Aral, we were engaged through several possible but never realized wedding dates. I can spot your stalling face from a mile away on a dark night with a patch over one eye."

Ouch.

Hush, Triss. Aloud, I said, "Point."

"Well?" asked Jax.

I looked around the large room. The group that had met in the council chamber was alone, the majority of the castle's inhabitants having eaten their lunches at a more reasonable hour. There was no reason not to continue the discussion here.

"I think it's time we brought them in," I said. "Siri, will you go collect Kelos and Chomarr for me?"

She rose instantly from her chair. "Of course. I presume you would like me to bring them in as quietly as possible."

I nodded. "Not that it's going to do any good. I know exactly what young Blades are like. There's not a chance in the world that the whole school isn't going to know they're here within five minutes of the drawbridge going down to let you all in. Still, I'd like to keep the fuss to a minimum for as long as possible. We'll meet you in the council chamber."

The school likely already knows, Triss sent as Siri faded out of sight.

Oh? I asked as we rose and headed out in the other direction.

Maryam is not happy with how things are going. She fell to the back of the group on our walk here, and Vrass fell back farther still. I expect that she passed word along to those she thought would support her.

Lovely. Do you think I will need to do something about Maryam?

Perhaps. It would certainly pay to be ready for that.

I don't want to fracture the remainder of the order any worse than it already is, I sent.

I hope that it doesn't come to that.

But you don't believe it.

No, not really.

8

———◆———

"**H**ello, Jax." That was all that Kelos said. A simple *hello* as he stepped through the door into the room. It was also, quite clearly, too much for Jax.

The council table was a long slab of some dark wood that could easily have seated twenty. I was at the end on the right as you entered the room with Faran and Siri flanking me on the sides. The journeymen were ranged around the far end, with Jax at the seat across from the door, bridging the divide between us.

When Kelos spoke, Jax made a little choking noise and then moved as I had not seen her move since our temple days. In one long fluid motion she launched herself up and out of her seat and landed in a crouch on the table, all in perfect silence. A flick of her wrist dropped a knife into her good hand as she made a backhanded cut at Kelos's throat. It was blindingly fast, and it would have killed most men. But Kelos was not most men.

He caught her hand almost casually, not even interrupting the flow of her spin, just a brief squeeze and twist as it approached his face. The knife fell to the stone floor with a

harsh ting while Jax continued her rotation, turning past
Kelos. But Jax was very good, too, and she brought her right
foot up as she pivoted on the ball of her left when her hands
touched the table, lashing a heel at Kelos's face.

It was a powerful kick, with the whole weight of her body
behind it. Kelos caught Jax's ankle with the same hand that
he'd used to disarm her, and she just . . . stopped—like she'd
hit a stone pillar. Before she could do anything else, Kelos
pushed, throwing his weight behind the move. Jax skidded
toward the far edge of the table.

She lifted her free foot and stomp-kicked at the hand
holding her ankle. Kelos caught that foot as well, and now
he pulled and twisted so that Jax ended up dangling upside
down by her ankles facing away from Kelos. She wasn't
completely helpless that way, but nothing she could do was
going to put someone like Kelos at serious risk.

That's when Maryam struck. Sometime during the
action, she had drawn her right-hand sword. Now she thrust
in sharply at Kelos's ribs from the side. Malthiss appeared
then, batting the sword away even as Kelos turned and inter-
posed the dangling Jax between himself and Maryam as a
shield. That put his right side toward the table and his back
to Siri.

"Child, I would prefer not to hurt you," Kelos said, quietly. "Please don't strike at me again."

Jax sighed. "Maryam, do as he says. Kelos, put me down."

"Are you going to attack me again?"

"No. Not while you're awake anyway."

Kelos chuckled. "Good enough. Smart, too. You might
even get me that way." He tossed Jax into a flip that allowed
her to land gracefully on her feet facing him.

She turned a hard look my way. "I thought you said he
had a death wish, Aral."

I shrugged. "I thought he did. Perhaps that was all reflex?"

"I choose not to die today," said Kelos. "But it won't be
much longer." He sounded old and tired and unspeakably
sad. "Once the Son of Heaven is gone, I will have no reason
to keep fighting. Until then . . ." He shrugged. "Until then,

well, it could go either way. Depends on mood more than anything."

He turned and stuck his head out into the hall. "I was right to have you wait back there, but you can come in now, Lieutenant Chomarr. I think that the bulk of the killing rage has been burned off for the moment, though I wouldn't turn my back on anyone but Aral and Siri, if I were you."

The Hand entered cautiously with a terse, "Noted."

Chomarr took a seat between Siri and Kelos as the latter closed the council room door and leaned back against it. His Storm flew down to perch on his thigh.

"Aren't you worried that one of my students might put a sword through your back from the hall?" Jax asked Kelos.

"Do you think Malthiss would let that happen?" he countered, and I noticed that his shadow vanished under the door rather than taking basilisk shape behind him.

"No, probably not. But a girl can dream, can't she?" Jax vaulted back over the table and reclaimed her seat. She assumed a calm tone, but I could read the fury in the lines of her neck and the set of her lips—I had seen it often enough when we were engaged.

"Lieutenant Chomarr?" she said. "I understand that you have information we need. In light of that, I'll refrain from letting my students kill you before we've extracted it, but, your people gave me these." Jax traced a finger lightly along the scars on her cheek. "And this." She lifted her half hand. "Give me the slightest excuse, and I will cut your living heart out of your chest."

The Hand nodded, his face almost serene. "I have served my god all the days of my life. My soul is always prepared for death. I do not fear to meet the lords of judgment. Nor the wheel of rebirth."

I recognized his expression by the way it felt from within. When my goddess yet lived I wore it often enough myself— utter religious certitude, perhaps the most fundamental problem of fanaticism.

Roric cleared his throat. "Just say the word, Lieutenant, and I can speed you on your way." He touched the scar where his ear used to be. "Like Master Jax, I have a few debts I owe where your kind is concerned."

I can't quit, can I, Triss? I sent. *Right now, what I want more than anything in the world is to get up and walk away. I want to go home to my horrible little room in the hayloft at the Gryphon's Head and go back to being a shadowside jack whose only problem is where to find enough money for my next drink.*

Is that really what you want? To become a drunk once more? Because, as I remember it, you were fucking miserable doing that.

I sighed and rubbed my forehead. *You're right, and it was killing me. But I don't want the weight of the order on my shoulders, much less what's going to happen if we kill the Son of Heaven. I really don't know if I can bear it all.*

If we kill the Son of Heaven? I thought it was when. *But we can discuss this later; if you don't want another fight breaking out in this room in the next few minutes, you need to get your hands back on the reins.*

Triss was right, as usual. "Roric, that's enough. Everyone, Lieutenant Chomarr is here under my protection, and I will not have him threatened any further." I turned to Chomarr next. "I've told my people the basics of my conversation with Toragana and what we believe is happening with the Son, and in Heaven's Reach, but I've left the details of current security arrangements till now. Why don't you and Kelos give Jax and her students a full rundown of the layout of the temple precinct and the situation within."

Chomarr nodded and began to speak.

There, sent Triss. *Very leaderly. Was that so hard?*

Yes. Leaderly? Are you sure you speak human?

It's a perfectly good word.

It's really not, I admonished.

Hush, you should be listening to this.

I heard it all before, back in Tavan.

Triss made the mental equivalent of a snort. *You weren't listening that time either. Not really. I can tell when you're not paying attention by the way your daydreams start to leak.*

Fine. I'll listen.

I believe you.

I tried to force myself to it, but I kept thinking back to that little room in Tien. It was a hellhole and I was drinking myself to death, but there was something terribly seductive about the idea of going back to not owing anything to anybody beyond Triss and my bar bill.

I may have agreed to try to deal with the Son of Heaven, and he certainly deserved it, but I couldn't stop worrying about what the aftermath was going to look like. The responsibility might ultimately belong to the Son of Heaven, but, if I succeeded, it was going to be *me* who killed off an entire ruling class. There was a potential there for death and destruction across the eleven kingdoms on a scale that hadn't been seen since the mage wars had devoured the western lands more than two thousand years ago. *Then*, the survivors had moved into what was now the eleven kingdoms, variously conquering, assimilating with, or being massacred by the people of the-East-that-was.

You're not listening.

And so it went.

It was sometime after noon when a gentle tap came at my door.

"Yes?" I mumbled from under my pillow.

The door creaked open, so I flipped the pillow aside. It was Altia, who had been Faran's closest friend back before the fall of the temple. She was compact and muscular with a round face and golden brown skin that marked her out as Kvani—Dvali if I was remembering right. Her familiar, Olthiss, took the shape of a Kvani-style manticore—a bat-winged horse with saberlike teeth and a scorpion's tail. But, for the moment, he remained hidden in her shadow.

"They're serving breakfast in the great hall, Master Aral,

if you would like to come down." She had a deep, rough voice and a warm smile. "Otherwise I can bring a tray up for you."

I blinked. "A tray would be lovely. Did Jax send you? Or Kelos?"

Altia laughed merrily. "No. I overheard the servants arguing about who they ought to send to"—and here her voice shifted higher and took on a sharp worried undertone as she quoted—"'wake up the First Blade.' I could tell that the thought of bothering the Kingslayer made them all very nervous, so I offered to come in their stead."

"That was kind," I replied. "Even among Blades in training there aren't many who would think of the servants' feelings and choose to take on a duty that they might feel was beneath them."

"Beneath me?" She shook her head. "Hardly that. I was raised to become a Blade, but I was born in Dval. You are First Blade, and that makes you my clan chief. I owe you my sword and my service. Bringing breakfast to the head of my new clan family and my khan is no burden. Now, let me get to it while the food is still fresh."

"All right. Thank you, Altia."

"Back as quickly as I can." She grinned and was gone a moment later.

I see why she is Jax's favorite, sent Triss. *She's very sweet.*

She is that, which explains some of why Faran and she no longer get along. Faran's life since the fall has left her hard where Altia had things gentler. She and Faran are of an age, but if I didn't know that I'd give them a ten year difference.

I flopped back down amongst the pillows and tried to convince myself that crawling out of the truly marvelous featherbed was a good idea. I had been assigned the best of the castle's guest rooms. Somehow, leaving it didn't seem like a step in the right direction. Probably because I knew what the rest of my day looked like. . . .

Triss, tell me I don't have another fucking meeting to go to this afternoon.

You want me to lie to you?

Yes, if you *want me to get out of bed.* I flipped the covers down to my waist.

But then I would have to go to the meeting, too. Triss pulled them back up.

I left them there. My original plan had called for a two or three day stop at the castle at most. Breeze in, give Jax a briefing, collect a few journeymen to make into masters, and head for the temple. . . . But no. We had been there for nearly two weeks already, dealing with a never-ending series of decisions and discussions, with no escape in sight. I was beginning to suspect that Jax was *trying* to trap us there until the snow fell. I knew she wanted both Siri and me to stay on and instruct the youngsters, and she had more than enough guile to trap where she couldn't convince.

I don't remember playing the First Blade involving quite so much in the way of politics back at the temple, I sent.

It didn't. Many of the duties they are trying to assign you used to belong to the high priestess or to Namara herself. Others were handled by the council on a much more routine basis.

Do you think Siri had any idea what she was getting me into when she vacated the role and insisted that I fill it?

Siri is very nearly as good a strategist as Kelos. . . .

I'm going to get her for this if it's the last thing I do. I flipped the covers back again.

This time Triss didn't pull them up. *I'll help.*

Habit carried me out of bed and into the routines of dressing and equipping myself. Since there was no one actively trying to kill me, I put my shirt on before my sword rig. Then pants, and boots with their built-in sheathes and knives. I'd worn my wrist sheathes to bed, mostly because a lifetime of practice meant I slept poorly without them. My hood came next, though I left it and the attached scarf down since I wasn't going a-hunting.

I was just bending over the ewer to wash my face and hands when I noticed smoke swirling wildly above the banked coals on my hearth. Siri, and unannounced. Never a good sign. Especially since she had stopped sleeping with me once we had decided to go after the Son of Heaven—she preferred not to indulge in such entanglements during a mission. I couldn't blame her, and ours had always been an off-again, on-again casual sort of affair. Friends first, and lovers only when it seemed convenient.

I moved away from the ewer as the smoke thickened, giving myself space to draw if she needed my swords. "What is it?"

Siri stepped out of smoke. "News from the north and none of it good. Journeyman Kumi has just arrived from Riada. She foundered two horses getting here and went straight to Jax. I thought it best to listen in. There's an army storming up the pass from the Kvanas."

"The fortress at the mouth of the pass?" I asked, skipping over the obvious question of how she'd managed to listen in— she was Siri. "What happened there?" The Dalridian people took pride in the fact that it had never fallen but through trea-son in all the years since the founding of the kingdom.

"It was taken. The details are hazy, but Kumi said that they believe the invaders used catapults to launch a force of the restless dead over the walls into the courtyard in the deep of the night."

"Risen," said Triss.

"Almost certainly, with their hidden brethren leading the army. The Kvanas are the lands closest to Heaven's Reach and among the most vulnerable to the Son of Heaven given the fragmentation of their governance and relative lack of mages among the clan leaders."

"It's a Caeni army?" I asked.

"Kumi didn't say before I left to tell you, but that's most likely. They're the most settled of the great clans and least aggressive, but the pass lies deep in southern Caen. If it were Avarsi, Amrli, or Dvali they would have to come through the Caeni and that would mean internal war."

The high arid plains of the Kvanas were terrible for farm-ing and sparsely populated. The clans that eked out a living there were nomadic, a horse-centered culture that followed the herds as they grazed their way back and forth across the landscape. They lived most of the year in round felt tents, coming together only at the height of the green season for the swapping of brides and grooms and the renewal of old grudges.

They were ruled locally by their clan chieftains for the most part, though the chiefs in turn answered to the four high khans, who were nominally obliged to the great khan. But it had been generations since a great khan held any true power. These days, the Khan of Khans, Ruler of the Kvanas, and Protector of the Clans mostly served as a game piece for the power struggles of the high khans, alternately being raided or traded from one to another along with his family and official court.

"I appreciate the warning, Siri, but why not just wait for Jax to tell me herself?"

"Because the job of First Blade has become political. I believe Jax when she says she doesn't want it, but there's Maryam to worry about at the very least. If it appears that you have unusual sources of information, it will help you build your authority in the long run, and that means less chance that someone will try to stick me with the job, or force it on Jax."

"Good thinking," said Triss.

"Politics!" hissed Kyrissa.

Siri continued, "Now, you don't have much time. If I've a portal of smoke to use as a shortcut, I can move faster than Jax or her messengers, but I expect the knock will come any—"

Someone hammered on my door.

"And that's my cue to slip out the same way I came in—which ability is a secret I've yet to share with anyone here." Siri vanished in a puff of smoke.

Somehow I didn't think it was Altia back with my breakfast. "Come."

Faran opened the door. "The Kvanas have united under the new great khan," she said without preamble. "They're burning Riada as we speak."

I blinked. "How did *you* know that?"

"I take it from your lack of surprise that I'm not bringing fresh news." She grinned. "Good on Siri."

"Not entirely fresh, no, though I didn't know that the clans had united."

"Siri didn't stay long enough to hear that, then. Sensible of her, since she didn't know how soon they'd head this way."

"But you do?" I asked.

"Not precisely, but Kelos said he'd delay them as long as he could without making it obvious what he was doing."

That set my head a-spin. "Since when do you and Kelos get along?"

"We don't. But the venues for listening in on Jax's receiving room are very limited if you can't slip in and out by way of the hearth smoke. Kelos and I bumped into each other in Javan's garderobe, and that didn't leave a lot of room for lies about what we both were doing there."

"And Javan?"

"Still asleep when I left. We're neither of us amateurs. Now, do you think it would be best if you waited here for Jax to come to you? Maybe sitting over at the desk and looking bored when she announces her news? Or would it be better to casually meet her on the way and ask, 'What news of the invasion?'"

I sighed. I really didn't want to have to play this game, but if I was going to do it, I might as well do it right. "Meet her on the way. Better to have it happen as publicly as possible, since this school's walls have a lot more ears than most. That means I need to get going."

"I'll close up behind you. Best if you aren't seen to have an obvious informant."

She was right, so I went. I hadn't gone fifty feet before I bumped into Altia. She had a tray with a wide variety of breakfast options on it. Apparently she had decided to bring me half the kitchen.

"Master Aral?" she said, obviously surprised to see me up and moving. "I thought you weren't planning on coming down. . . ."

"Things have changed, for the worse. The Kvani are

invading Dalridia, which means I'm going to have to eat on the move. If you're willing to follow along with that tray, I'd appreciate it."

"Of course, anything you need," she said, and the softness had left her voice while one hand dropped to check the hang of the long dagger at her hip. Here was a young Blade in training ready to do whatever was required of her, even if it meant killing her former countrymen. Maybe she wasn't as naïve as Faran had told me—though that conversation lay two years in the past now, and things change. "The sausages are cool enough for fingers and so are the rolls. Let me make you a quick sandwich."

She did so, and I chewed on that while we headed down the main stairs of the guest wing. Jax occupied the royal chambers, which lay in the opposite wing of the castle. The arrangement was specifically designed to make it difficult for guests to slip quietly across and murder the royal family, which probably says a good deal about Dalridian politics, and meant that I had to pass through the entrance to the great hall to get there. Whether it was by happy chance—possible—or the machinations of Kelos—far more likely—that most public of central foyers is where I met up with Jax. She was trailing Kumi, Maryam, Roric, Kelos, and a man I didn't know dressed in the royal livery of Dalridia.

Before she could speak, I asked, "How bad is the situation in Riada?" I kept my voice calm but pitched it to carry—again, if I must play the part I would do it up properly. "And with your brother?"

Maryam and Kumi both visibly started, though Roric hardly blinked. In general Roric retained the same stoically placid expression right up until the point where his temper cracked and he started twisting people's heads off. It was one of his stronger assets as a potential assassin. The great hall was open, and I could hear the sounds of eating from within begin to go quiet as a ripple of whispers led away from the door. Kelos showed no surprise, of course. To her credit, neither did Jax, only sadness.

"My brother is most likely dead," replied Jax, her voice

steady. "As king, he led the counter-attack that met the Kvani at the top of the pass. If Riada is burning, and Garis tells me it is"—she touched the shoulder of the messenger—"then he will have fallen in the battle. Dead, badly wounded, or taken. I see no other chance. Given that the risen lead the van, I can only hope that Eian has died the true death and that his corpse will not be used as some undead puppet to sit the throne for the Son of Heaven."

"He was a mage," I said. "There is no concealing the death of his familiar. Would not the people notice?"

Jax shrugged. "The ones who knew him, certainly, but if his tenure were brief enough, it might go unremarked. Were it me in charge of the thing, I would stage a formal surrender and abdication using his animate corpse to dress up the wounds of conquest a bit." Her voice had grown bitter and angry by then and I was reminded that she had taken over the direction of her brother's spy service when she returned home.

"Do we know the pretext of the invasion?" I asked. The real reason was obvious enough—the Son knew that Toragana had come to us, and he feared what we might now do.

Jax turned to Garis. "Give him the scroll."

Wordlessly, the messenger reached into his bag and handed over a slender roll of parchment. I unrolled it and . . . began to swear.

It read:

> Be it known that Hasar, Khan of Khans, has learned of the revival of the cult of Namara, so-called goddess of justice under the auspices of the throne of Dalridia. The society of assassins must never be allowed to flourish again, and so it is with the utmost sadness that Hasar has united the clans and leads them now in war against this harborer of heretics.
>
> The people of Dalridia will be harmed only inasmuch as they give succor to these cultists. Further, once the scourge of Namara's cultists has been stamped out, the great khan will withdraw his forces from the lands of

Dalridia. He will leave only those troops needed to properly restore order and see a new king set upon the Dalridian throne, one who shares none of the tainted blood of the so-called crown princess, Jax Elarson, known by some as Seldansbane, who is proscribed of Heaven.

"What does it say?" asked Faran, coming from the great hall.

I read it again, aloud this time.

"Crown princess?" asked Siri—she had just entered through the door that led to the drawbridge, as though she'd been out of the castle and only recently returned. Nice touch that, since no one knew to suspect that she had secret ways of coming and going.

Jax rolled her eyes. "I renounced all titles and inheritances when I went to the temple. Eian wanted me to reclaim the coronet when I came back to Dalridia, but I refused. I am no princess, nor ever shall be again." She turned now to Garis. "*Which* is why you must take the crown to someone else."

"The crown?" I asked.

Jax nodded. "Along with the scroll, my brother sent the crown to me."

"I left the king an hour before the battle," said Garis. "Since I bore the crown, he sent me by gryphon back and told me to wait on the heights above Riada city to see how things fared. When the city burned I came here, arriving on Journeyman Kumi's heels." He bowed to Jax. "I'm sorry, Your Highness, but your brother's orders were very specific. I was to bring the crown to you, and you alone." He lifted a slender circlet of gold studded with emeralds from the bag and held it out to her.

"I don't want the fucking thing!" Jax snarled, slapping it out of his hands so that it hit the floor and rolled away. "There is no one in all the world who would be a worse choice for the throne of Dalridia right now. Or, hadn't you noticed the army that is currently burning its way across the kingdom on its way to this spot? The army that is coming here to kill all of us?" She threw her hands wide to encompass the whole of the school.

"I am a poison to this realm as are all of my kind," she continued. "When we had nowhere else to go, my brother took us in and gave us sanctuary. For that kindness he has now paid with his life and the lives of who knows how many thousands of our people. And it is only just beginning. If you wish to see anything of Dalridia survive, you will take that crown as far away from me as you possibly can, because putting it on my head is no more nor less than shoveling our people into a fire, and I have killed enough of you already. Don't you think?"

Her back was straight, and her tone as hard as iron, but there were tears rolling down her cheeks. Suddenly, all of my worries about the politics of the order and playing things just right tasted like bitterest folly. What did any of that matter? We had not even moved directly against the Son yet, and already the dead numbered in the tens of thousands. A toll that included the much loved brother of a woman I had very nearly married. And this was only a foretaste of the wars that would follow if I killed Heaven's Son.

I moved to put a hand on her shoulder. "Oh, Jax, I am so, so sorry. This is on me, not you. If I had not come here—"

Jax wheeled on me. "Aral. Shut. The. Fuck. Up. You did not build a school here on ground given to me by my brother. You did not collect what was left of the order and bring them here to my brother's kingdom. You are not responsible for this."

"But—"

"Did I, or did I not, tell you to shut up?" Her eyes burned with a cold rage that I had never seen there before—Jax normally ran hot. "Your arrival may have been the trigger that set the bolt winging from the crossbow, but this is on my shoulders and I will *not* share my guilt with you.

"Now, you are First fucking Blade, and what is left of your charge has an army bearing down on it. You need to get over your whole tragic angst thing, and make some decisions about what happens next. I have contingency plans about getting out of the country, but which way we go and what happens after that is all on you."

She's right, sent Triss.

I know.

I took a deep breath before speaking. "Roric, you're with me. I need to know what the plans for evacuating the castle look like. Siri, Faran, go with Maryam and do whatever she tells you needs doing to get us out of here. Kelos . . . you'd better come with me, too. I need to think out what happens next, and you're the man who taught me strategy. Jax, I'm going to the council room. I want you to take at least a few minutes of time for yourself, but come as soon as you're ready. Doing something won't help with the grief, but it might distract. Move, people!"

As I walked away I found that Altia had fallen in behind me. "Shouldn't you be collecting your gear?" I asked.

"You haven't finished your breakfast, and you may need a runner on short notice. I keep a bag packed, as Master Jax has taught us. Maryam saw me with you, she will have Jaeris fetch mine. Anything else I can do without. Here is another sandwich, with a bit more in it than just sausage." She had not been idle while the rest of us talked.

I took the sandwich as we continued on. "Thank you, I do need this."

"Never ride out on an empty stomach," she said, in the manner of one quoting a proverb.

Behind me I heard Jax speaking quietly but firmly with Garis. "I will not take the damned crown, and it should not fall into the hands of the invaders. Take it over the mountains to Ar in the Magelands. I'm going to give you an address. My cousin Jafsica is there—she runs our intelligence service in country. She will make a better queen than I ever could have. Don't look at me like that. Get moving!"

9

———•———

The line between fault and responsibility is a razor that cuts deep. Jax might claim that the ruin of Dalridia was not my fault. She might even be right. But when I had become First Blade again, all that remained of the order and all that we did had become my responsibility. That now included the destruction of an entire kingdom to strike at us, and the weight of it lay heavy on my shoulders as I tried to sort out what happened next.

Not counting Kelos and Faran—each of whose status was ambiguous for different reasons—we had three master Blades, nine journeymen, and nine apprentices. That was all that was left of the legacy of Justice, barely a score of survivors where once there had been four hundred masters and trainees. My original plan had called for taking three or four journeymen on to the temple and leaving the rest in Jax's care until we sorted out the matter of the swords. Now?

Well, that *was* the question.

"How did the Son of Heaven know you were here?" asked Roric.

"What?" I looked up from the table.

"I mean, this attack had to have been at least a couple of weeks in the planning. I'm not foolish enough to believe it's a coincidence. The Son must have known you were coming here almost as soon as you did."

I sighed. That question had occurred to me as well, and there was only one answer that made any sense. "I imagine that Lieutenant Chomarr told him."

"What?" demanded Triss.

"I said that Chomarr probably told the Son of Heaven where we were going and what we were planning."

Triss began to swear venomously in the hissing tongue of the Shades, as he realized that I was almost certainly right.

"How long have you known?" asked Roric, and I could see that he stood on that line between placid and killing rage.

"Known?" I replied. "I don't *know* even now, though I can't imagine any other answer that's half so likely."

Roric leaped up from his chair. "I'll kill him!"

"I hope so," I said. "But do sit down. We have a castle to evacuate and Chomarr's been gone for what, two days now? Kelos?"

The big man shrugged. "Could be nearly three. I haven't seen him since we discussed the outer wall wards for the temple precinct the afternoon before yesterday."

I nodded. "The timing's about right. That night would have been when the Kvani attacked the fort at the base of the pass. That's the latest he could have stayed without at least tripling his risks. He's clearly a calculating man and a risk taker, but that's the point when hanging on would have shifted from acceptably dangerous to foolhardy."

It's a damn good thing we never told him about Signet Nea's finger and ring, sent Triss. *Or about Siri's powers over smoke.*

It is that. Siri had kept her own secret, and Kelos and I hadn't even discussed the finger between ourselves. I'd thought about it, but the castle was full of young Blades with eager ears, and there was no need to share that bit of intelligence before its proper time. *Not that I have much hope in it being useful anymore. If I were the Son of Heaven and*

I'd gone as paranoid about mages as he seems to have, I'd have had all those wards rekeyed first thing.

You're probably right. Triss sighed mentally.

Roric, who had been looking back and forth between Kelos and I for several seconds, finally asked, "How can you be so cold about it?" He still looked angry, but he had deflated somehow. "Aren't you even going to check?"

"Kelos, we both know he's gone, but why don't you go take a look. If he's still here, he's a colder man than I imagined and too dangerous for any of the apprentices. I want someone who can handle him to deal with the problem."

"He's not here," said Kelos, but then he nodded and ducked out through the door.

As he went, I saw Altia waiting patiently in the hall in case she was needed. When we had arrived at the council chamber she'd simply handed me the tray and taken up station with her back to the wall before it had even occurred to me to think about whether she ought to be in where the decisions were made. When I thanked her again for taking care of me, she'd looked a bit embarrassed and repeated her earlier comment about my being her khan. It wasn't exactly proper Blade doctrine, but then, the temple was gone and if we were going to survive as an order there would have to be many changes in doctrine.

I turned back to Roric once the door was closed. "You didn't get to finish your temple training and you were never sent into the field, so you didn't get to learn the most important lessons. The things that only experience can teach." I held up a finger. "One, the plan always goes wrong." Another finger. "Two, you never know how it will go wrong until it happens. Three, don't panic when it all goes in the shit, and don't get angry—you don't have time for any of that. Four, cut your losses and move on. Do it smart, do it now, and don't look back until it's all over. *That's* how I can be cold about it."

"But . . ."

"No buts. I fucked up. Badly. People died. I can wallow, or I can salvage what I can from the situation. Jax reminded me of that rather forcefully earlier. I have some idea what it cost her to do that and I am not going to throw that away. Later—if

I have a later after I do what I can to deal with all the problems in front of me right now—I'll take my pain out of its box and wallow in it. Until then, I can't afford the luxury."

Roric nodded and I could see him forcing a return of his usual calm. "Thank you for the lesson, First Blade. I think I have some idea of what it cost you."

He's about five times as sharp as he appears, isn't he? sent Triss.

He is that. Those who survived the fall of the temple and escaped the Hand did so because they were the best of their generation. You know, I think he even echoed me back just now for the right reasons.

The door opened and Jax came through. "Is Kelos off to check on Chomarr?"

"You think it was him as well."

She nodded. "If it's not Chomarr it's Kelos himself, and I think that you and Siri are right about him. We can trust Kelos as long as killing the Son of Heaven is your plan and until you've carried it out. His insane focus on bringing the whole system down is the only thing that makes any sense of his motivations so far."

"I'm glad that you believe me."

Jax laughed. "You're a sentimentalist, but you're also damned smart. Mind, I wouldn't buy it if Siri hadn't also been convinced. She doesn't have a sentimental bone in her body, and she will have gotten to her conclusions in a very different way. Of course, I think that young Faran is right as well and that Kelos really ought to be killed now. No matter how useful he is. He's too dangerous to leave alive."

"There's that," I said. "But I'll need his help if I'm going to face the Son of Heaven and have any chance of getting out alive afterward. Especially now. Chomarr knew that Devin had thrown in with Toragana's plot. Which means that Devin is either dead, imprisoned, or fled. We aren't going to have anybody on the inside to help us out. Kelos is the only one we have left who really knows the inside of the temple precinct in depth. We have to have him or this just won't work."

Jax nodded, her expression grim. "That's why I haven't

let anyone kill him in his sleep, though I've had several offers. You might piss me off, but Siri's right that you're our best bet for putting the order back together for the future. I want you back in one piece." She sighed. "You know, this all could have been avoided if you'd just killed the Son of Heaven when you went after him the first time."

"Don't think that hasn't occurred to me. Of course, if I'd done that, Kelos would have become the next Son of Heaven right in the middle of the greatest upheaval in the history of the eleven kingdoms. He'd have ended up ruling the world."

"And that's not an acceptable answer, either," said Jax. "I know. It's just so frustrating to be playing a game where no matter what you do, Kelos the Traitor wins."

"It's hard to beat a man at a game of strategy when he started planning his moves out five years before you were even born."

"Do you really think it reaches back so far?" she asked.

"Some of it probably goes back farther, but if Kelos is telling the truth, thirty-one eighty-five is when the Kitsune told him about the Son of Heaven's risen curse and how she wanted to use it to bring down the entire ruling structure of the eleven kingdoms." I closed my eyes. "So much blood, and it will all be on my hands."

"You take too much on yourself," snapped Triss. "What blood is spilled with the Son's fall will be on his own head. Well, his and the Kitsune's and Kelos's."

I didn't agree with Triss, but neither did I want to argue with him, so I turned to Jax. "Are *you* going to be all right?"

She shook her head. "No, I'm not. But that's not really what you're asking. You want to know if I'll hold it together and get through this." She smiled the bitterest smile I'd ever seen. "And the answer to that is yes. I have no other choice. Not if I want to keep my students alive. We had the same training, Aral. I can put my pain in a box as well as you."

"I hope you can do a better job than that," I replied. "Mine broke me, if you'll remember. If it hadn't been for Maylien Dan Marchon, my lady of the red dress, I'd very likely be dead by now."

Maylien had figured out who I was and more or less pressed me into helping her remove her sister, Sumey, from the baronial seat that rightly belonged to Maylien. In the process we had discovered that Sumey was a hidden risen, and I had used one of Devin's swords to end her. That had been the start of me recovering my soul and climbing out of the gutter.

I continued. "She showed me that I could still do some good in the world and helped me find a new purpose." It was a bittersweet memory, as our relationship had broken hard a few years later, after I helped her to the throne of Zhan. "I wish that we had parted friends."

"How will she fare when the Son dies?" asked Jax.

"Well enough, I think. Her magery has kept her safe from becoming one of his slaves. She's going to lose a lot of nobles when this goes down, but she's tough and she's smart. Once she rides out the chaos, she may well be able to build a better kingdom."

"That's something," said Jax. "I'd like to believe that there are those who will come through the next few months unscarred. That some kingdoms will remain standing . . ." She paused for a long moment, looked away—out the window. "I was four when the temple took me. Four. My brother was six. He barely knew me as a person, and yet he gave me sanctuary without even a moment's hesitation. I was a fugitive with half the world against me and he handed me the keys to his kingdom. Do you know why?"

I shook my head.

"I asked him, you know. More than once, because I couldn't believe his answer. Not the first time anyway."

"What did he say?" I asked.

"Simply that I was his sister . . . and that he loved me. No worries over all the years I had been gone, or the fact that I had trained to kill men like him. None of that mattered to him. What mattered was that a six-year-old boy had loved his sister, and that he had missed her, and that he was glad that she had finally returned to him. He was a fool. A glorious, glorious fool, and I will mourn him all the days of my life."

She took a deep breath, and I could see her locking her

pain away. "But not right now. Right now, we have plans to form. Which means that you have a decision to make. Do I take the bulk of the students east into the Magelands where the Son of Heaven cannot easily reach us? Or do we all go west to the temple in the hope of finding the lost swords?"

"How many of your students are ready to take their oaths?" I asked.

Jax paused for a long moment. "That depends. By the standards of Namara? I don't honestly know. There are deep flaws in some of them, scars left by the fall of the temple and the wandering time before Loris and I brought them here. They are, every one of them, wounded in ways that can never be cured. I do not know how many of them the goddess would have taken into her full service. Roric here, certainly. Inaya, Xin, Kumi. Probably Javan. Before her torture at the abbey I would have said Maryam was the readiest of them all. Now . . . my answer remains yes, though I worry about the rage that lives in her heart."

I held up a hand before she could continue. "Namara is dead, Jax. The only opinion that matters to me right now is yours. You are the chancellor of the order's school. How many of your students would you trust with one of these?" I drew my swords and set them on the table between us.

"Entirely?"

I snorted. "No splitting hairs. The question is practical and immediate."

She sighed. "All of them except Malok . . . and, maybe, Altia." I raised an eyebrow in question, since the girl had impressed me with her efficiency and no-nonsense attitude over the last hour, and Jax continued. "Malok is still too young at fifteen. He was only seven at the fall, barely bonded with Yinthiss—I honestly don't know how he managed to escape."

"And Altia?" asked Triss. "She was one of Faran's closest friends before the fall, and I remember her as being a very promising young mage. She has done very well this morning, or so it seems to me."

"Altia is . . . my fault. Entirely. She's smart, and she's

efficient, as you've seen today. But she lacks the proper ruthlessness a Blade needs. In that, she reminds me of you at twelve or thirteen, Aral. Ultimately, the temple trained the worst of that out of you, but I haven't done the same for her. She was the first of the children that I rescued—not even a year after the fall—and I have coddled her because of my own pain. If she'd had to live on her own for a time, she might be stronger now, but she was lucky there, too. A band of Rovers found her scant days after the temple's ruin. She has been too much sheltered, I think."

"But if you had to make the decision right now?" I asked. "If this was the one chance to give or deny her her swords for at least the next few years?"

"I would hand them over and I would pray that I had done the right thing."

"That leaves only Malok, then." I took a deep breath and nodded. "We go west. If we can find the swords I will see every one of them invested."

"I just told you Malok was too young," said Jax.

"I will not have one boy singled out, alone of all who survived the fall on their own, and refused his swords. I don't know if we will find the swords. Further, I don't know when or if we'll be able to go back to the temple after this trip. It might be years, it might be never. Much will depend on how things play out with any attempt to deal with the Son of Heaven. But if this *is* our young people's only chance, and if you have that much faith in them, I will not see any of them denied. If I'm wrong, so be it. I will accept the consequences, however it falls out."

The door to the council chamber opened again. It was Maryam, with Faran and Siri trailing along behind. Siri had collected the rest of my gear as well as her own, and she slid it across the table to me now. I was particularly happy to have a trick bag again after going so long without—I had lost mine in the Sylvani Empire some months before, and hadn't had the resources to replace it until we got to the school. I started hanging things off my sword rig as Maryam began to speak.

"We've got all the students collecting their bolt bags and

their other gear. I gave them a quarter hour to get ready and meet us in the great hall. Those servants who don't have immediate duties are either helping out with readying the horses and the agutes, parceling out food for the locals, or have already gone out the gates and scattered into the hills."

I was glad to hear that we had agutes. The large wooly pack goats would be enormously helpful for getting supplies over the narrow tracks of the southern passes.

"So, we're ready to move out?" asked Jax.

"Very nearly. The only major task that's left is to rouse the sleepers and throw open the undergates."

"Sleepers?" asked Triss.

Jax smiled—a thoroughly predatory expression. "The Kvani will get no joy of this castle. When we took the place over, we knew that the Son of Heaven might send his forces against us at any time, so we made preparations to see that anyone who came for us would have a great deal more to worry about than hunting us through the hills. Loris labored long hours in the deep catacombs that lie beneath the lowest cellars. He created a lure and a trap for the ghouls and night-gaunts that roam the high wastes. It draws them in and lays an enchantment of deepest sleep on them until we need them."

Faran whistled. "Nasty! I like it. How many are there?"

"No one knows," replied Maryam. "They've been collecting there for seven years. Hundreds at the least, and not one of them has fed since they arrived. They will be *very* hungry when they wake, and trapped within the walls of the castle by Loris's enchantments."

"Setting the dead against a lord of the dead," said Siri. "There's a poetry to that."

"There is," said Jax, "though we didn't know about the Son of Heaven when we set the trap. I wish Loris had lived long enough to know how appropriate his work truly was."

Kelos arrived then. "Chomarr's gone. Looks like he went out the garderobe to avoid the watch you had set on his room, Jax."

"It's barely eight inches across," she said. "That's one of the reasons I put him there."

Kelos shrugged. "He widened it a bit, and by hand if I'm any judge of such things. Wanted to avoid any light of magic as he worked, I imagine. At least we have the small pleasure of knowing he had to wallow in his own shit to get out."

"Five minutes," said Maryam.

Kelos raised a questioning eyebrow at me.

"That's when the students meet us in the great hall," I told him. "At which point, we ride for the temple. Jax, if you're planning on rousing your sleepers, you'd best get to it. Take Siri and Faran with you. I'd like them both to see Loris's setup. It sounds like it might come in handy for future arrangements."

"Sleepers?" asked Kelos.

I was already out of my chair. "I'll tell you about it as we go."

"**There's** a party of Avarsi raiders camped out in the valley ahead," said Xin, his voice quiet in the darkness. "They're well ahead of the main army of the Kvani—probably sent to cut off the high tracks that lead over the mountains and down through the Evindine watershed to Varya."

The valley in question lay two days ride west of Jax's castle. It was a narrow vale just below the only viable route that ran directly between Dalridia and Varya. As with the goat tracks that crossed over from Uln in the Magelands to the east, *viable* was a term more of art than commerce. It was possible for a hiker in good health to cross from Dalridia to the birth waters of the Evindine, but only during a few scant months in summer, and afoot. Agutes were the only pack animal that could make the crossing at all, and the goats were unsuitable for really big loads.

"Can we get around the raiders?" I asked.

Xin nodded. "Probably, but only if we go shrouded. They're camped right up into the throat of the pass. Even now, in the early hours before morning, with most of the camp asleep it would be difficult."

Jax broke in. "That would mean abandoning the agutes

and any supplies we can't carry on our backs. If it snows before we reach the headwaters of the Evindine that gear and food could mean the difference between riding it out and freezing to death or starving."

"That's no good," I said. We had always intended to release the horses once the going got too tough for them, but losing the wooly goats with their ability to carry loads over broken terrain would be a heavy blow. "How many of the Avarsi are there?"

"Looks like a hundred or so," replied Xin.

"Any mages?" I asked.

What are you thinking? sent Triss.

That we are at war, and that abandoning our supplies could mean the difference between life and death for the people that have entrusted me with their care.

So, you will kill them all in their sleep? Triss sounded more surprised than distressed by the idea.

I fear that we may have to. I didn't much like the idea, but we *were* at war. The Kvani had invaded Dalridia with the express intention of killing us all, and they had already slaughtered thousands of Jax's people.

While Triss and I held our exchange, Xin was shrugging. "I didn't see an obvious shaman's tent, but that doesn't mean they don't have mages with them."

"And the same is true of any hidden risen," added Siri. "I would be quite surprised if the khan leading this party is not of the restless dead."

"So would I." I turned to Jax. "I hate to have to ask this, but how many of your students are ready to take a human life?"

She sighed. "Expedience has hardened many of them earlier than it did our generation. Perhaps two-thirds of them have killed, either at the fall of the temple or in the years since. Of those, a bit over half might be ready for the kind of task I think you're contemplating."

Kelos pushed forward. "I'll lead your throat cutters if you want. I've no compunctions about the thing."

I shook my head. "No. If it has to be done, and I think it does, it's on me. I *will* assign you their khan. If he or she *is* risen, we will need to take care of that first and preferably by beheading. That strikes me as your sort of work." I hated to rely on him, but that is one of the problems of a Kelos: if you have one, it's mortally foolish not to use his talents.

Kelos grinned. "It is that."

Though the swords of the goddess would not slay the risen Sumey for Devin, Kelos had demonstrated more than once that particular magic worked just fine for him, and I had begun to formulate a theory about it. Unlike Devin, Kelos still believed in his heart that he served the ideals of justice if not the goddess of justice. He might feel that his betrayal of Namara had earned him death, but he had never once wavered in his dedication to the principles that she had espoused. At least, not as he saw them. In the depths of his own heart he was still a champion of justice.

Are you really going to do this? Triss asked into the silence of my mind.

I thought about it. *Yes, I am. I never liked the idea of killing guards just because they were in my way, and this has some of the same flavor. But these people came here to make war on us and they have already killed many of Jax's countrymen for no reason other than that her brother chose to give refuge to our children. They are soldiers of an army whose sole purpose is our destruction. Whether we want to be or not, we are at war, and this is the enemy.*

We could go around them, sent Triss, but it was clear from the emotion that came through with his words that he simply wanted to understand my reasoning, rather than seriously suggesting that we try to avoid the confrontation.

Yes, we could probably get around them, but only by assuming risks that might kill us all. If it were just you and me in danger, I might be willing to accept those odds. But it's not, it is all that is left of Namara's legacy and that includes those like Malok who is still little more than a boy. The Kvani are here to kill us. If that doesn't make them legitimate targets, I don't know what would.

I agree completely. But are you going to be able to live with this decision?

I really didn't know the answer to that, but I would not let it put my people in more danger. *I will have to.*

"Siri," I said aloud, "you're on mage duty. You go in first with Kelos and do what needs to be done on that front. If you don't find any mages, move on to chain of command. Kelos will do the same. As for the rest of us, it's a big camp and that means multiple parties. Four, I think—pairs, or trios if we have enough volunteers for it. I'll lead one, Jax another, with Maryam and Roric taking the other two. Faran, you're in charge of dealing with those sentries that Siri and Kelos don't clear out on their way in."

Faran nodded and loosened the swords in her sheath.

"What if the camp wakes?" asked Jax.

"Then somebody fucked up," I growled. "Don't let it happen. If any of the raiders get away, they're going to run straight back to the main army and report what happened here. Even if the enemy can't take horses over the high pass, they'll send hundreds of soldiers after us, to say nothing of whatever risen they have with them. I don't think that will end well for us."

"Point," said Jax. "Since it's come up, what do you think the odds are of us getting all the way to the temple without running into another major force after this one?"

"Zero," I replied, "though hopefully we won't have to take them so directly. We never mentioned our plans to go to the temple anywhere that Chomarr could hear, but I don't doubt that he figured it out from things said in passing. I'm confident that the Son of Heaven won't have sent another Kvani army into Varya, but there's no doubt that he already controls some portion of the local nobility.

"There will certainly be troops guarding the temple, and likely more between us and it, but one battle at a time. Right now, we need to fight this one. Kelos, Siri, Faran, give us five minutes to put together our teams and then go in. We'll be right behind you."

10

————— ◆ —————

No matter how necessary, there is no honor to be had from killing a man in his sleep. There is no challenge to it. No effort. No art. It lessens you.

I slipped over the crest of the hill above the camp with Kumi and Gryss following in my wake. Or, at least, I assumed that they did, for I could neither see nor hear them. Gryss was a relatively talkative Shade who took the form of an enormous, winged rat, but for now he and his mistress were absolutely silent, ghosts in the night behind me.

There was a slain sentry tucked in under the edge of a bush a few yards below the ridgetop. His throat looked as though someone had torn it out with claws—unmistakably Faran's work and a reminder that at least some of my companions were less reluctant to take a life than I. There was a savage joy expressed in Faran's kills for those with the skill to read it. I paused beside the body to look down over the camp and plan my descent.

While the commanding khan and some of his officers had retired to felt tents, most of the raiders slept on blankets in the open. The Kvani in war mode traveled exceedingly

light, carrying more gear for their horses than for themselves. The open nature of the camp would make the coming
slaughter both easier and harder. Easier, in that we would
have no need to slip in and out of tents. Harder, because
there would be no way to conceal the dead from the living
should they begin to wake.

We were approaching the camp from four points—a
quarter turn off the cardinal directions. Kumi and I had the
greatest distance to cover and the hardest approach. So the
signal was mine to give. As soon as we reached the darkness
at the edge of our hunting ground, I let out the low hoot of
a cloud owl and moved in.

There is no skill involved in this, I sent to Triss as I slid
the edge of my knife along the throat of my first sleeper.

*Not in killing one alone, perhaps. But a dozen, without
waking the others? Each death must come in total silence
yet quickly. Strike, move, strike again. It's a dance, cold
and cruel and hard, but as intricate a series of steps as any
duel.*

I shook my head as I killed a second of the raiders. I
understood that Triss was trying to make me feel better
about my choices and my task, but I couldn't agree with
him. I am very good at what I do, and what I do is kill people. There is no way around that, but usually I am facing an
enemy who is awake.

Taking out an alert guard with her back to the wall and
a weapon in her hands? That is a challenge. Slipping past
her to kill the duke she guards without her even knowing I
was there until they find the body the next morning—there's
art to that, even joy. Likewise killing armed foes in a battle.
But this slaughter?

No. I would do it because it was necessary, but I would
take no pride in it.

I would like to say that something went wrong, that someone woke, and that great deeds were done in the aftermath.
But that would be a lie. A hundred and twelve Avarsi warriors died that night, mostly in their sleep and mostly without
so much as a grunt. It was no battle, it was butchery.

When the killing was done, we used horses and ropes to drag the bodies into a great pile with all of their gear and we set a slow burning magical fire that would devour the evidence of what had happened without making too great a light. That they were gone and that there had been a fire could not be concealed, but who had done it and why and how would be muddied. That would keep the enemy from throwing all of their strength over the pass after us. As long as they couldn't know that it was us or that we had not gone another way or divided our forces before or after, they must cover all of our possible paths.

After the talk I'd had with Jax earlier, I couldn't help but pay close attention to the students as they went about the task of hauling and burning bodies. Those who had helped with the killing mostly wore the grim mask I remembered from my own experiences in dealing with corpses. Those who hadn't participated in the killing looked more disturbed by the exercise, though none of them balked or vomited.

I paid especially close attention to Malok and Altia since Jax had worried about their readiness to take the formal oath of a Blade. The former actually appeared calmer than many of his older peers. The latter, well . . . she didn't look happy, but she did the work, and she did it without complaint or dawdling. And these were her people—well, the Avarsi and the Dvali did as much cross-clan horse and cattle raiding against one another as they did cooperating, but there were blood ties aplenty connecting the two clan confederations. I don't know that I'd have done half as well at her age if the corpses had been Varyan.

"How are you doing?" I asked her when the thing was almost done.

"Better than I would have guessed if you'd asked me about it beforehand, Master Aral."

"Good lass." I punched her shoulder lightly.

As soon as the fire was burning well enough that nothing short of major magic would put it out, we turned loose all the horses and began the long climb to the high pass. Kelos had made the trek many times in the training of young

Blades, so he led us, with Siri following just behind to keep a close eye on him. I brought up the rear with Faran. Again, I regretted the way that Kelos kept making himself useful. It would be so easy and so foolish to come to rely on him. . . .

As soon as the others had moved far enough ahead that we could speak with relative privacy, Faran turned a hard look on me. "You're doing it again, old man."

"Doing what, my young monster?"

"Bleeding over the wrong things."

"How do you figure that?" I asked, even as Triss sent, *She's got you nailed.*

"There are people who need to die. Sometimes, they're like the Son of Heaven and they need to die because they are the horrors that have always haunted the darkness beyond the edge of civilization. Sometimes they need to die because they are doing things that need stopping—I'd put this entire invading army in that category. But, even if I didn't, sometimes someone needs to die for no other reasons than because they are in the way."

"It really doesn't bother you," I said rather wistfully, "does it? Any more than it bothers the Shades."

She canted her head to the side. "The killing or the reasons for it?"

"Either . . . both. I don't know."

"Not really, no." Then she put her hand on my shoulder. "Which is one of the reasons I'd be terrible at your job. Somebody has to sweat those details if justice is going to be served, and I'm glad it's somebody like you, even if you do overthink absolutely everything and cut yourself up about it afterward."

"Today it's me. If the order survives, it might be you someday. What then?"

"I will think very long and hard to figure out whatever necessary choice would have made you least happy if it were you stuck with the decision. Then I will go with that."

Triss chuckled, but I shook my head. "No, really. From where I'm sitting, you're the shining star of the younger generations. You could very easily end up as First Blade."

"All right. Then, without the sarcasm: I will think long and hard about what you would do in the same situation and I will try to do that. You may be softer than you ought, and dither more than I'm capable of, but I have yet to see you take a life lightly or for the wrong reason."

She gestured at the trail ahead and the rest of our little line of climbers. "We're all of us killers, selected expressly for that purpose by the hand of a goddess now dead. Whatever else we might do, or want, or aspire to, an aptitude for death was one of the things that we had to have to make us appropriate candidates for the purposes of the goddess."

"I have no idea where you're going with this," I said.

"I've seen you in a fight, Aral, watched you when you didn't have time to worry about the details or when you felt the cause was unambiguously just. There is no hesitation in you then, and the joy you take in the work is obvious. You're a killer born. But you're also a thinker, and the lessons of the goddess sank into your bones. What you *do* is my model of what a Blade ought to *be*. How you get there is sometimes a mystery to me, but if I can *choose* to do what you would do simply by dint of your natural inclination, I think that I'll be all right."

"That's a hell of a thing to try to live up to," I said.

"So, don't fuck up." She punched me in the arm.

"That simple?"

"That simple. Now that I've knocked you loose of the worst of your brooding, we should probably catch up." She broke into a slow lope, and I fell in behind her.

I don't deserve that kind of faith, I sent to Triss.

Nope. But you'd better damn well do your best to be worthy of it.

In other words: Don't fuck up?

Don't fuck up.

Because I'm so very *good at that. . . .*

Triss didn't answer.

The great Temple of Namara stood upon the south shore of Evinduin, the smaller of Varya's two sacred lakes. A half mile offshore lay the isle of the goddess, a low wooded outcrop with a deep pool that was connected to the main body of the lake by an underwater arch. A series of granite flags surrounded the pool in a neat ring, with a second ring of carefully trimmed grass between the stone and the woods.

When last I visited, there was moss growing between the flags and the grass had given way to rank weeds, but right here, right now it was as it had been when the priesthood maintained it—as clean and perfect as it was on the eve of my investiture. That made no sense to me. Neither did the fact that I had no memory of how I had gotten there. But I had more important things to worry about.

On that long ago night the goddess had risen out of the depths of the pool to present me with my swords. Now she rose again, her six arms held in the classic pose of her sculptures, her heavy stone breasts bared to the night.

The top of her head stood nine feet above the surface of the water that girdled her waist. The darkness and reflections hid her lower body, though a hint of fishy scales and fins could be seen beneath the surface, suggesting that she wore her aquatic form. At other times she might assume the shape of a serpent from the waist down, or, for certain formal ceremonies, legs. As always, and despite her stillness and the cold granite of her skin, she seemed utterly, wildly alive—more so than any merely mortal figure ever could.

Namara extended her middle hands, then, offering me a pair of black swords, though I knew somehow that this was not simply a revisiting of my investiture. I walked across the surface of the water as I had back then, reaching for these swords that both were and were not mine.

My hands touch the hilts and my experience of time shifts, as it usually does only in battle. I move wholly into the present moment with no real sense of past or future. I turn the blades as I pull them to me, drawing their sharp edges along the open palms of my goddess. They cut deep, leaving an impossible trail of bright red blood welling in their wake.

Namara yanks her hand back and away, and her expression shifts from welcoming benevolence to shock and horror.

I feel the same way, but cannot do anything to affect the actions of my body as I whip the swords around and thrust them both up under her left breast, driving the points deep into stone flesh. I want to vomit when my blades enter her great heart. I can feel the ponderous beat of it through my fingers and palms, feel my own heart somehow matching its rhythm, as first it beats faster, then slows, and finally stops.

For perhaps a minute my own heart feels dead in my chest. Then, suddenly, and with a tearing pain, it begins to beat again. Above me, the life has left my stone goddess, rendering her into little more than a statue. I wonder then how I will be able to draw the swords from the stone. But when I tug on the hilts, they come away easily enough.

Namara topples forward and I step aside, letting her crash to ruin on the shore. Her granite neck snaps and her head rolls to the edge of the flags. I want to run and hide, or slit my wrists, or do anything that will let me move away from the enormity of what I've just done. But I still have no control over my body. I am an observer, my mind trapped in amber as my hands move of their own accord, chopping the upper arms from that great fractured torso. . . .

Time blurs as I butcher Namara's stone corpse, hammering and hacking away and levering the broken pieces of my goddess into a rough heap. I create a nightmare throne where I may rest my arms on Namara's and prop my feet upon her fallen head. As I mount my new seat, I hear a scraping noise behind me and I turn. Devin is there. He draws his swords and sets them before my feet before performing the formal obeisance a Kadeshi peasant gives his lord, banging his forehead thrice on the hard ground. The traitor swearing fealty to me, his new master . . .

I lean over one hacked-off arm of my goddess and vomit onto the greensward.

"Aral, hsst, Aral, wake up."

I blink my eyes open, instantly awake, and find Siri kneeling beside me. The fingers of her hand rest lightly on the back of my right wrist. By the sun it is late afternoon.

"What is it?" I asked. "Have the risen come?"

She shook her head. "No. Nightmare. Yours. You were twitching and your breathing went off. I heard it from clear over there." She flicked her chin back toward the place where she'd set her bedroll.

"I . . . it was a dream. That's a relief." I had put my horrible vision aside on waking, but now that she mentioned it, my dreaming murder of my goddess rushed back in to fill my heart with a guilty dread. "Sorry I was so loud."

"It's not the first time you've woken me up with a nightmare. I swear you get more of them than any of my other bedmates ever did. Was this the one about the stone dog that nearly killed you when you went after Ashvik?"

"Nope, this was a bright shiny new horror. I was at the pool of the goddess when she rose from the depths and . . ." I shivered at the memory and shook my head. The symbolism was entirely too obvious. "It was awful. I don't want to speak of it."

"Heavy lies the heart that holds command?" she asked, sympathetically.

"Something like that, yes." I wanted a drink then as I had not for months—with my whole heart and more than half my soul.

Aral? Triss could sense my mood if not my exact thoughts.

It's nothing, Triss. We both knew I was lying, but he didn't press.

Siri spoke again. "Remind me sometime, under the morning sun when the world is bright and sleep is far away, to tell you about the nightmares I had in the early months of my run as First Blade. But not here, and not so close to night. Now, you should get some more sleep. It's an hour still till the time you set for us to move on."

"Not going to happen. I'll take a turn around the perimeter and see how things stand with Altia and Jaeris and the other sentries." I needed to get my mind off foul dreams.

Siri looked dubious for a moment, then shrugged and went back to her bedroll. She was asleep by the time I passed her on my way to the nearest of the guard posts less than a minute later. It was the one I'd given to Malok. I'd assigned the duty to some of the younger students who had not participated in the slaying of the Avarsi, both because they were more rested, and to make them feel as though there were other things that they could do for the order. Important things.

Tell me about the dream, sent Triss. *Bits of it bled over our link, but only bits. All I could tell was that it involved the goddess and that it frightened and revolted you. If Siri hadn't woken you when she did, I soon would have.*

It's really nothing, Triss. Guilt at trying to take the place of the goddess in our order mostly.

Tell me.

All right. So I did, spitting it out in bursts of mindspeech as I climbed up the steep rock wall to the spot where Malok and Yinthiss waited and watched.

The place where we had camped was little more than a flatter section of trail at the bottom of a long winding crevice carved into the mountainside by the spring floods. It was dry at the moment and very defensible, but also a potential death trap if a big rainstorm came through, and this was the season where storms could yet bring rain as easily as early snow here at the lower altitudes. I would have preferred not to risk sleeping there, but Kelos said this was the last good place we could stop short of the actual top of the pass, and that was at least another seven hours of hiking and climbing ahead of us. At that point, exhaustion had won over caution, and we had collapsed on the spot.

"Any sign of clouds?" I asked as I poked my head out of the narrow chimney I'd used to reach the ledge where the young man and his Shade perched.

Malok had assumed a cross-legged pose—it was that or let his legs dangle—with his back against a bend in the rock. He smiled at me, exposing white teeth in a face nearly as dark as Siri's. That plus his straight black hair suggested that his family came from the high mountains in the northernmost part of Kadesh.

"Not so much as a wisp, First Blade. This sun has driven Yinthiss deep into my shadow. It's really brutal—*much* worse than it would be at this height in the village where I was born."

"Janpor Province?" I asked, naming the region I had guessed.

He nodded. "The western edge, more than three thousand miles north and east of here—mostly north—beyond Hurn's Gate even."

"That explains the difference in the sun. We're close to the dividing line between north and south here, and the light is stronger at every height." He gave me that look that youth reserve for when their elders tell them things that they already know, and I had to suppress a laugh. "I'll leave you to your watching then, if you have nothing else to report."

"Nothing at all, First Blade. The only things I've seen are the sun, a few birds, and a lone gryphon flying high up and far away an hour ago. I would have called an alert if it came closer, but it stooped on something not long after I spotted it, and I haven't seen it since. So it must have downed its prey."

That or fallen for a bait of some sort, sent Triss, though he didn't contradict the lad. *There are things that hunt gryphons here in the high mountains, and not just the rocs and garudas. . . .*

He's young yet, it's better not to distract him with too many possibilities. I began climbing back down to the trail.

By the time I'd checked in with our other three sentries, the rest of the camp was awake and making a cold sunset breakfast before heading out.

Around midnight, Siri dropped back to find me at the trailing edge of our little column. As soon as Faran spotted her, she moved forward to put eyes on Kelos. If there was anyone who trusted him less than Jax, it was Faran. Siri nodded her thanks as they passed each other, then waved for me to stop.

Siri didn't speak until the last of the trailing students was out of earshot and, when she did, she pitched her voice barely above a whisper. "The Kvani have found the remnants of the fire we used to get rid of the bodies. It's nearly burned out except for a few hot spots and wisps of smoke here and there, so I can't see much but impressions from around the edges."

"Can you tell how big the Kvani force is?" asked Triss.

Siri shook her head. "Not in any depth, but there are several dozen of them poking around the edges of the burn, and more near enough to register as blurry shadows, so it must be at least as many as were guarding the pass."

"Risen?" I asked.

"None visible, but fire is one of the few things that will destroy them, so I can't imagine the more obvious sorts would . . . hang on, something's changing. They've lit a fire of their own. Let me just hop over and . . . there. Oh, dammit."

"What?" I asked.

"If that's not the main body of the Kvani it's a reconnaissance in force. There must be a thousand horses at least. Also, risen, and lots of them. The Kvani have four-horse chariots with wicker cages mounted to them to hold the dead. The risen are packed in so tight they can't even move their arms, maybe eight to a box, maybe ten."

"Wicker? That's ridiculous," said Triss. "It wouldn't hold the risen for two seconds if they really wanted out."

Siri shrugged. "There are visibly glowing glyphs at the joints of the cages, and not just to magesight. That latter means they're mostly for show, a way to make the troops feel safe around them. If this group of risen are all controlled by the Son of Heaven's strain of the curse and the Kvani are led by more of the same, they have no need of fancy controls."

"True enough," I said. "How many chariots are there?"

"Hard to say. At least a dozen, but there could be more out of my line of sight. I wish I could hear what the khans and their lieutenants are saying, but at this distance I'm lucky to be able to see out of the smoke."

I'd been meaning to ask about her limitations there, so: "Siri, how far away can you be from a smoke source and still touch it? We're barely a day's march beyond this one and you're having trouble, but you were able to contact me from nearly two thousand miles away."

"It depends," she replied. "Mostly, my range is right around a day's hard travel on the flat, maybe fifty miles. But that's only if I've got a solid connection of some kind to the fire, like the spell I set to burn the bodies, or the line of sight that allowed me to jump from that fire to the campfire. If I don't have a good sympathetic link, I can only manage a mile or three under most circumstances."

"And when you contacted me?"

"That took days of ritual preparations, a ton of help from Ashkent and Kayla, including their direct participation in the ritual, *and* a specially designed fire on my end that burned in the shape of a great glyph of communication. Oh, and the god wanted to possess you as well as me, so he boosted the power of my spell. Even with all of that, I don't think I'd have been able to reach anyone I loved less, old friend. Love is the ultimate sympathetic link."

She touched my cheek affectionately, and I covered her hand with my own. We might be divorced now, but that wasn't from any lack of mutual affection. The marriage had served its ritual purpose, and we were neither of us the marrying kind. A circumstance I wished I had figured out *before* it blew up my relationship with Jax back in the day. It might have saved a lot of pain, and many years of estrangement.

"And afterward?" I asked.

"Afterward, we were married, which made us one person for the purposes of that particular magic, and I *still* had to stretch myself to the limit to contact you while you were on one side of the Wall of the Sylvain and I was on the other. That boundary is so much more than a great ward to keep the buried gods inside. I think sometimes that it is a divider between different worlds entirely."

Kyrissa hissed then, startling all of us. She had always been a particularly quiet Shade, and her transformation into a mixed creature of smoke and shadow had only increased her reticence. Now that she could speak mind-to-mind with

Siri, as Triss and I did—another side effect of our brief marriage—she hardly ever made a sound.

Siri's eyes went briefly far away as she listened to her familiar, and farther away still when she focused her attention on the fires below and behind us a moment later. "They're opening up the cages."

"That's not good."

"Most of the Kvani have moved to the far side of our burn. Only a few khans and shamans remain near the chariots, and I don't think the shamans are much happier about it than the bulk of the raiders. But they have to stay close to maintain the show-magic on the cages." She whistled. "They must have loosed a hundred or more of their risen."

"What are the risen doing?"

"They're milling around like a pack of hunting dogs waiting for the—there! They're off and heading up the trail after us."

11

---·—·---

There is no good way to break the news that tireless legions of the undead are racing up your backtrail. There really isn't. Especially not to people you still think of as kids on some level, not even when those kids are themselves assassins in training.

Given that, I went for the bald truth, and got us back on our way with only the briefest of stops. No one panicked, which was good. Very few of them even looked nervous, which was less so. It suggested that they had way too much faith in me, and/or themselves.

We *did* pick up the pace, loping along under the stars now in a slow jog where we could manage it—the fastest we could get the agutes to move, though how long the goats would be willing or able to keep at it was an open question. This time, instead of dropping to the back of the pack, I moved to the front. I needed to think through our options and make plans, and I wanted to talk things over with Kelos—damn him for being so useful! And, damn me for being a weak enough leader to need the help.

Siri, Faran, and Jax all moved forward, too, while we

sent Roric and Maryam to play tail guard. They didn't have proper weapons for dealing with the risen, but we were a good ten hours ahead of our pursuers still. Even if the dead ran every minute of the night—they had no need of food or drink or rest—they wouldn't catch up until sometime tomorrow night at the earliest. With a very few exceptions—the hidden risen being a notable entry on the list—the restless dead cannot bear the direct sun. That meant that our pursuers would have to hole up someplace shaded during most of the daylight hours, just as we had originally planned to do.

"How many are there?" asked Kelos.

"A hundred at least," replied Siri. "Could be a hundred fifty. Maybe more. I only saw the chariots that came within about thirty feet of the fire."

"Ugly, but not impossible," said Faran. "We killed more than that back in Wall before we had to run."

I shook my head. "We did, but only with a great deal of help and at bitter cost. Your shoulder is still healing, and if the cut had been so much as a quarter of an inch deeper you'd have lost the arm, and we might have lost you. I have a hard time regretting the warriors of the Hand that fell there, but I'll note that they were on our side at the time. That means half of our force died in the fight, including a former Signet who was one of the most powerful mages I've ever seen."

Kelos nodded. "Aral's right. We probably killed a couple hundred of them at Wall, but the *we* that did that included some damn fine battle mages, and, once *they* fell, we had no choice but to run or be overwhelmed. If the risen hadn't gotten bogged down in fighting the entire population of that part of Wall they might well have caught up to us and finished the job. The risen are tough as hell—hard to kill, even with Namara's swords—and strong and fast to boot."

"We do have a few advantages," said Siri. "The dead are none too bright, and the nature of the trail means they can't come against us more than two or three at a time. That's a narrower fighting front than we had at the inn."

"I wouldn't bet money on that," I said. "The first time I

met one of the Son's breed of risen, it came up out of a five-story sewer shaft polished nice and slick. The second flung itself off a keep's battlements at me right after scaling them. They can climb like insects, and they don't mind falling substantial distances. If we stop to meet them in a canyon like this one, they'll be dropping down on us from above within a matter of minutes."

"A rain of the dead," Jax said quietly. "That's how the Kvani took the Dalridian fort at the base of the northern pass—flinging the risen over the walls with catapults. Aral's right. I'd rather not reenact that particular defeat if we can avoid it."

"Hadn't thought of that," said Siri. "*Is* there a place on the trail ahead where a few could defend the way against many, Kelos?"

"I don't think so. Not the way the risen climb. They'll flank us in minutes if we stand to fight, and there are only four of us with the weapons to kill them reliably. Magic will do the job, too, but even our best aren't one fifth the mage Signet Toragana was, and they tore her limb from limb."

"Well," said Faran, "we can't outrun them either. Even if we push all through the day tomorrow, we have to stop sometime. Exhaustion will finish us as surely as the restless dead. They can move faster than we can and do it far longer."

"So, what *can* we do?" Jax asked.

No one answered her.

That is the question, isn't it? Triss spoke into the silence of my mind. *You're in much better training and shape than you were when those two almost killed you back while you were helping Maylien, but without the kind of magical support we had from the Signet and the Storms at the inn, I don't think you and I could take even half a dozen coming at us together. With only four true Blades, we'd have trouble handling much more than two score, and that with a good strategic position and excellent battle mages of our own.*

I know, Triss. It's . . . ugly. We need some way of killing a bunch of them from a distance. And . . . A thought occurred to me.

"We'll have to use the mountains against them," I said aloud.

"You have an idea?" asked Siri.

"Maybe. I'm thinking avalanche. It's a classic, and human troops would know to be on the lookout for it, but it might take the dead by surprise where the living would see it coming." I looked at Kelos. "Is there a place on the downward slopes where the trail runs along a ledge with cliffs above and a long fall below?"

"There are several," he replied. "Let me think about whether any of them would be suitable. . . . It can't be in among any of the switchbacks. An avalanche there might carry our own away, or wipe out the trail ahead—trapping us. There's also the chance some of the risen will survive any fall and dig themselves out. We don't want them getting ahead of us and coming in from two sides. What we need is a mountain shoulder above a valley that leads away from our line of travel. . . ."

While Kelos was mulling, I turned my attention to Siri. "You're our resident magic expert. I want you to cook up some way to get a big chunk of mountainside moving all at once. Borrow Faran or anyone else if you think you can use them."

Siri tapped Faran's shoulder and the two of them fell back, muttering quietly between them.

"Jax, most of the students are just going to be in the way," I said. "Pick someone to lead them and get as many of them out ahead of us as you can. Make them stretch those young legs. I'd send you to watch over them, but . . ."

"But if the risen catch up to us, you'll need my swords if we're to have any hope of thinning their numbers enough for the students to get away. I know. Let me think. . . . Malok's a mountain boy originally and I know that Loris worked with him to keep those skills polished. I'll have him take the lead, with Roric and Maryam to enforce his orders." She paused. "I'm surprised you're not sending Faran away, too, considering her injury."

"You really think she'd leave me?" I asked. "You were

with me on the ship that time I tried to slip away from her in Tien."

Jax snorted. "Fair point. Let me think. . . . Javan will have to stay with us. He's already having trouble keeping up with that golemite leg of his, *and* he's been working much harder on his magic since he lost the one it replaced. Kumi as well, I think. She's smart and fast and the best of my mages despite her Kanjurese background." Her eyes went far away for a moment. "The goddess almost refused her, you know."

I didn't. "Why?"

"She's from a Hairi family, the same as Nuriko Shadow-fox. Kumi is the first such Namara has allowed to join the order since Nuriko became the Kitsune and betrayed the order."

The Hairi were the ruling class of Kanjuri, rapporto-mancers who bonded with the intelligent swords crafted by the mage smiths known as Gojuru. Sometimes a true mage was born on the islands—usually to a Hairi or Gojuru family—but they were never allowed to remain. There was some ancient prophecy about a mage sinking the island chain, and the Kanjurese took it *very* seriously. The only legal choices for a fullborn mage living in the islands were exile or death—though there were rumors of a secret cult-like order of mage criminals.

"Having gone up against the Kitsune and Thiussus, I can see why Namara might feel that the Hairi were a risk," said Triss.

Sshayar suddenly formed herself out of Jax's shadow—a shadow tiger pacing us along the wall—and shook her great head angrily. "The goddess made a mistake when she took on Nuriko. She would have made another if she refused Kumi. It was not where Nuriko came from that made her into the Kitsune. It was who she was. Just as what makes Kumi, Kumi, is about what she is, not who her parents were. Looking at bloodlines is a foolish way to judge people."

The goddess was never foolish, Triss harrumphed into my mind, though he didn't verbally contradict Sshayar, for which I was grateful.

No, I responded instead, *but she was sometimes wrong.* Aloud, I added to Jax, "So, Javan and Kumi. Anyone else?"

"It depends on what Siri and Faran come up with. Altia's naïve and her technique is weaker than I like, but for sheer raw magical power there's none of us can match her. I include Kelos and Siri in that. She really has the gift." I could hear the worry and conflict riding just under the edge of her words—she really didn't want to need Altia.

"I'm sure she'll do fine if she has to, and we'll keep her out of harm's way as much as possible. The people setting off the avalanche shouldn't be in much danger. It's whoever ends up playing bait below that's going to have to watch out."

Jax shrugged, obviously unconvinced. "Let me check with Siri and then I'll get the young ones moving—they'll have to take some of the load the agutes are carrying now since the goats will never keep up, and they might need those supplies on the downslope if we don't make it." She slipped back to chat with the other two, leaving me alone just behind Kelos.

I moved forward. "Well, have you got anything?"

"Yes," he said. "I think so. There are two places we could stage such an ambush, actually, but the better of them is too far away for my liking. We'd have to push damned hard to get there in time, and I don't think the improved ground is a good enough trade for arriving blown. The nearer spot we can reach not long after nightfall tomorrow, and still manage a good four hours' sleep during the highest sun."

"What's the rock like there?" Siri had moved up behind me silently.

"Some sort of reddish stone that spalls and cracks. There's always fresh rockfall on that section of the trail, and at least once a decade they have to carve the trail deeper when it loses a chunk of ledge. Beyond that? I don't know that much about rock in its natural state. I'm more a castles man."

"You and me both," said Siri. "There's not much call for assassinating mountain goats, so I never bothered to learn about the stuff of mountains. I suspect I'm going to wish at least one of us knew a lot more about it before this jaunt is over." She sighed. "That means I'm going to have to err on the side of power over finesse."

"Jax!" she called over her shoulder. "The answer is yes."

At the next wide spot in the little canyon, we paused briefly to sort out the packs. If things went badly and we didn't catch up with the youngsters, they were going to be on mighty thin rations by the time they got out of the mountains—eating the goats had always been the backup plan if things went pear shaped. But hungry was much better than undead. Once they were loaded up, the group of us who were going to attempt the ambush slid over to the side along with Maryam and let the rest pass on. As soon as the last of the line passed Maryam fell in at the back.

"Time to move!" she called, and the lot of them started into a steady lope that would see them over the top of the pass several hours ahead of the rest of us.

It was a good thing they had been training steadily in the mountains above Jax's castle for several years, and that they were all young and fit, because the next few days were going to be brutal for them if we didn't make it. The downward end of the trail extended much farther than the one running up had, since Dalridia was already so high to begin with.

Kelos led us off at a steady walk. The slower pace would open the distance with the students, and we needed the mages who were going to bring down the mountainside to arrive at the ambush site as rested as possible. Nima, the stuff of magic, comes from the well of the soul, and exhaustion will drain it as thoroughly as spellcasting.

I put Siri up with Kelos to sort out what they could of the plan short of actually looking over the site, while I started to drift back to the rear with Faran again. Jax took Altia tight under her wing, slotting in right behind Siri and leading half the string of agutes. Kumi and Javan fell in together next, talking quietly as they led another half-dozen goats. As I passed them on my way back, I couldn't help noticing how pale and sweaty Javan looked in the moonlight.

"How's the leg?" I asked.

He flexed golemite toes—there was little point in wearing a boot on that foot. "The magic side works well enough, First Blade, but my stump is aching something fierce. I train with it all the time, but I haven't had to travel distances like this on it before. I'm learning that I should have pushed myself to go farther and faster." He straightened his back. "But don't worry, I'll do this. I have to."

I could see what saying that cost him, and I squeezed his shoulder lightly. "I know you will. Good lad."

Once Faran and I had dropped back out of earshot, I said, "You spent a fair bit of time with Javan when you were both recovering from the fight at the abbey." He'd lost his leg in the same battle that had nearly cost her an eye and left her with years of debilitating headaches. "How bad is he, really?"

She shrugged. "I've seen him worse, if not by much. But he's tough and his endurance is amazing. He'll make it even if he has to walk the last ten miles on a bleeding stump or crawl on hands and knees."

"I wish we could put him on one of the agutes," I said.

But there was just no way. The goats couldn't carry much more than thirty pounds at the best of times, and they started to get balky at twenty. I kept one eye on Javan's back after that, and I didn't much like what I saw. Well before dawn he was swaying on his feet. As we went, I watched for any place we could conceivably leave him that he'd have a chance, but there was nothing.

The canyon itself offered no shelter beyond a few little half caves that would do no more than pin him in one spot for the dead. Above, the slopes were high and steep with hardly any cover between us and the snowline. The valley of Dalridia itself was barely low enough for trees. Within a few hours of starting up the path, we'd climbed past the place where even scrub brush could grow.

Oh, it was possible that he might find a narrow ledge well above the trail where he wouldn't be visible to the risen passing below, but they didn't hunt by sight alone. Hell, half of them didn't have much left in the way of eyes. I had never made a serious study of the restless dead, so I couldn't have told you how they did hunt. It was hard to believe scent was involved when you considered how terribly and strongly they smelled, themselves, but they were known to follow trails well enough, and there had to be something there. Perhaps they had some life-sense or could follow life-scents in some way analogous to magesight.

Whatever their method, leaving Javan to rest would be the same as leaving him to die. On the other hand, though he swayed and stumbled and sweated, he kept up hour after hour in a way that I don't know I'd have been able to manage if we swapped places.

Two hours past dawn and shortly after we crossed the highest point of the pass, we came on another little half cave. This one was scooped out of the wall on our left. On our right the mountain fell away steeply to the next loop of the switchback far below. It was early yet, but Kelos thought this was the best place we'd find to catch a little nap.

When Kelos waved us over for a break, Javan simply lay down on the bare rock and was snoring in seconds. The rest of us sorted out the pack animals and chewed a bit of jerky and some dusty trail cakes before finding places to curl up. I was just thinking about setting watches when Kelos caught my eye and shook his head.

"I've got it," he said. "You sleep." And damn if he didn't look as fresh as if he'd only climbed out of a featherbed ten minutes ago—I swear that the man is made of dragon hide and tempered steel. Also, I hate the way he seems to read my mind.

"All right," I said. "But wake someone if you feel tired."

As I settled into an angle of the rock, Faran sidled over. "Do you want me to keep an eye on him? I'm still pretty fresh."

"No. The last thing in the world that we need right now is for you to get one of your headaches. If Kelos wanted to kill us all in our sleep we'd be dead by now anyway."

"You're not saying that you trust him?!" she hissed angrily.

"Not as far as I could drive him back in a fencing match

with one hand tied behind my back. Not in the way that you're asking about anyway. As long as our goals and his remain the same, he's the best ally we could have."

"And if that changes?"

"I promise to let you know far enough in advance to put a knife in his back before he suspects. Can I go to bed now?"

"Humph." But she stopped arguing and her breathing eased into sleep shortly thereafter.

I had a bit more trouble, though I did fall eventually. When I blinked my eyes open next I had to assume that letting Kelos stand watch had worked out all right, since all of us woke with our throats yet uncut. He had stood guard over us for the whole five hours he thought we could afford to sleep without waking anyone. I'd have chewed on him a bit about not resting himself if he didn't still look fresher than I felt.

We marched from just after noon to an hour or so before sunset without a break, and we only stopped then long enough to grab a mouthful of food and some cold tea from our waterskins. The mountains towered all around us, their reddish heads capped by white helms shining like polished steel in the clear light of a cloudless day.

Twice we had to slowly pick our way through the aftermath of major rockfalls, and once an ominous crack from above announced the imminent arrival of a huge slab of granite. It bounced once on the trail, shattering the edge, before spinning off into the void, barely missing both Javan and one of the goats as it passed. Not a good omen that.

Maybe an hour after sunset we arrived at Kelos's ambush site. The trail ran ribbon thin around a thick curve of rock with a nearly sheer drop on the left. Perhaps four hundred feet below, a valley pointed down and away to the south, while the trail looped off to the west. I could see both why Kelos thought it would make a good spot to take on our foes and why he wished for a better one.

If we could get our undead in the right place and bring a chunk of the mountain down on top of them, it would certainly thin their ranks nicely. There wasn't so much as a jot of shelter to protect them. If the rocks didn't crush the risen, the fall was such that even the dead would likely arrive at the bottom more in the form of loose sacks full of smashed bones than anything that might walk away.

At the same time, it was a big stretch of very narrow trail, which would string them out into a long line. So, the chances of bringing down enough of the slope to get them all were awfully slim. Also, simply climbing up the wall to get in position to bring on the avalanche would make for a hell of a task.

"Which means we'd best get to it," Faran said with a sigh when I pointed that out. "How do you want to do this?"

I leaned back to get a better look at the slope above as we neared the sharpest part of the bend in the trail. "We can't afford to let them scent us—or whatever it is they do—before they reach the place where the ambush is going to happen. That means the climbers are going to have to go around this corner, head up, and then work their way back past this spot above. I want you at the point farthest back toward the way we came, so you're first up the wall."

"Not Siri?" Faran sounded surprised.

"Entirely sensible," said Siri with a laugh.

"What am I missing?" asked Faran.

Siri held up her stump. "This. The less of this sort of climbing I have to do, the smaller the chance I fall to my doom. I'm going to be holding down the back end of the line, with Javan just in front of me since we're far and away the weakest climbers here."

Javan nodded, and I couldn't help but notice how pale and shaky he looked. I wished I could have spared him the climb completely, but that would have left him down on the trail with the risen—an even riskier proposal. I didn't like putting Faran out front with her injury, but I trusted her more than anyone else there, Siri included, and that made her my point woman.

Faran actually struck her forehead with the heel of her palm. "Of course. I'm an idiot. So, who's between Javan and me?"

"In order," I said, "Kumi, Jax, Kelos, and Altia."

That got me a very hard look. "Where are *you* going to be?" she demanded.

"I'm the tethered goat or, the plug in the bottle, if you prefer. Someone has to stay on the path and force the risen to bunch up before you drop the mountain on them."

"That's not acceptable," Faran said in the same breath that Kelos insisted, "It ought to be me."

Siri and Jax didn't look happy about it either, but the former nodded and the latter looked away. Kumi, Javan, and Altia kept their heads down and played the part of the three monkeys of legend.

I addressed Kelos first. "You're ten times the mage I am, and everyone here knows it. In fact, there's not a one of you can't cast rings around me—bright blue ones with fairy wings, even—and you all know it. You'd do better as the plug in the bottle than I will, too, but only by a narrow margin."

I looked at Faran. "The same argument holds for you as far as to what happens above, and you're not even in the running for down here. Not until you get those swords properly attuned. Of those remaining who have the weapons to match the dead, upside is Siri's show for obvious reasons, and I'm a hell of a lot better brute-force swordsman than Jax, which is what matters most in going toe-to-toe with the dead."

Faran's face grew grimmer still and I put my hands on her shoulders. "The trail *has* to be held for this to work, and I'm the only logical choice. Tell me I'm wrong and why, if you can think of some other plan that works better. If not, you need to get climbing."

She shook her head. "Dammit, Aral, that's not fair." Then, she leaned in to give me a quick kiss on the cheek and a punch on the shoulder before she started climbing.

She will not take it at all well if you allow yourself to get killed in the next few hours, Triss said into my mind.

I'll see what I can do, I sent as dryly as I could manage. *I'm not all that thrilled about the prospect myself.*

I suppose that will have to do.

You're welcome.

Kumi was right behind Faran. Then Jax, who gave me a kiss as well before heading up, though hers was on the lips.

"What's that for?" I asked her.

"Luck."

I raised an eyebrow at Siri then, but she shook her head and winked as she stepped aside to let the others go first. "I'll kiss you after, and maybe even a bit more than kiss if we've the chance."

"You sound pretty certain there's going to be an after."

"I am. If you do die here, I'm going to catch your ghost before it makes it to the wheel of rebirth and wedge it back into your body somehow, because I am *not* going to let them make me First Blade again so soon, if ever."

"Thanks?"

"Any time."

Kelos paused for a long moment then, like he wanted to argue with me, but he, too, finally sighed and started up the mountainside.

Altia pressed her right fist into her left palm—a Kvani warrior's salute to her khan, and whispered to me as she passed on her way to follow Kelos, "Thank you for trusting me to do this."

Javan went next, moving more slowly and carefully than Altia, and Siri brought up the rear. Then Triss and I were alone on the trail with the other goats. I led the agutes far enough down the path to get them out of the avalanche zone, loosened their packs, and tied them lightly to various spurs of rock. None of them would get free easily, but all of them could manage it given sufficient time and motivation. There was no sense in them dying, too, if we didn't pull this off.

I loosened my swords in their sheaths and walked back up the trail to meet the army of the dead with only Triss at my back.

12

I have faced the imminent possibility of my own death many times. There is something freeing about the moment before the axe falls that I will always love, even though I no longer seek my ending as I did in the days right after the fall of the temple.

I do not wish to meet the lords of judgment before my time. Not anymore anyway, but with each passing year, the tower of weights on the balance against me climbs higher, and the stains on my soul grow darker. My passing will not be an easy one, but with every corpse I add to my tally I know that my final reckoning grows that much harder. Knowing that, I do not fear death when she comes the closest.

I will not embrace her, but I always blow her a kiss as she approaches.

When I saw the first of the risen come around a corner on the trail far above—their rotting flesh pale in the bright moon's light—I did not flinch or blanch. I simply drew my swords, stretched my shoulders, and smiled. Even moving fast it would take them another quarter of an hour to reach me, but the waiting was almost over. One way or the other.

The risen hunt in silence, so I had no more warning that they were upon me than the time it took the first of them to cross the distance from coming around the last curve to lunging at my face. I had chosen my place carefully, and now I braced my back foot against the edge of a crack in the surface of the trail, snapping my arms wide in a scissoring cut with both swords that beheaded the monster. It felt like chopping through an inch-thick wooden staff, and the impact shocked through me, driving me down and back into the stone.

My footing held. Both then, and again when momentum carried the now headless and inanimate corpse forward to slam into my chest in a gruesome parody of a tackle. The bones of its neck scraped unpleasantly across my ribs, as it slid aside and fell into the void. I barely noticed, as I was already facing the next of its fellows. This one I skewered through the eyes and under the breast bone, twisting sideways to lever it off the cliff.

Again, I was driven back on my heels. Again, I held my ground. The third went over without any help from me, as the pressure from behind squeezed him up against the back of the second so that he was dragged along when that one fell.

If they had simply kept piling into me and each other at a full run, they might have carried me over the side at the cost of a dozen or fewer of their number. But they were either too dumb to realize that, or they cared more for their survival than my death.

Whatever the reason, by the time I faced the fourth, the front of the line had slowed down and forced those behind to do the same. In the brief moment of respite between three and four I heard a sort of gnawing crackle from somewhere far above, like a squirrel with stone teeth chewing away at a marble walnut.

This one swung at me with finger bones sharpened into claws where they punched through the rotting flesh of its hands. I took my first step back then, as I needed to give up some ground before the avalanche came. I parried at the same time, neatly cutting away its right hand. Before it could take another swing, I bent my knees and hacked sharply at its left ankle. Bone splintered. Support faltered. Another risen fell into the abyss.

I backed up again, taking a moment to look both above and below my next opponent. Just as I had expected, the risen that couldn't come at me directly had begun to climb—some up, some down. The stone walls were steep and sheer, but the creatures were finding grips enough to begin their advance around the bottleneck I had created. Far above, the gnawing away of stone grew louder, punctuated now by occasional sharp cracks and pops.

I levered another of the risen off the path, and tried to back up faster as I realized the first major flaw in my plan. I had seriously underestimated the speed with which the risen could climb along the rock face. They were faster there than I could have imagined. A dead hand snatching at my ankle emphasized that point, and I had to take a reckless leap backward to get clear—hoping madly as I did so that I hadn't misjudged where the path behind me lay.

The next risen on the trail lunged forward into the gap my move created, clawing viciously at my face and chest. I felt my shirt tear as I backpedaled, and then my heel came down on air and I almost went over the edge. I probably would have, too, had not the one that leaped in then gotten a grip on my left wrist and yanked me forward, opening its rotted jaws wide to take a bite out of my face.

He'd have had me then, if not for Triss, who formed himself into a wire-like loop of darkness that neatly nipped off the hand that had hold of me. I staggered and flung my arms wide as I tried to recover my balance. Fortunately for my survival, the risen's situation was even worse. It suddenly found itself pulling at nothing, stumbled, put a foot down on nothing at all, and started to fall. As it went over, it made a desperate grab for the edge with its remaining hand, but caught the shoulder of the foremost of the climbers instead. They fell away together to bounce and shatter on the rocks far below.

That gave me a tiny instant of room to think and to act. I used it to turn and bolt down the trail. I hated having to turn my back on the dead, but it was that or be swarmed under. I knew I couldn't keep ahead of them for long, but I also knew that I didn't have to. I just had to stay ahead of them long enough to—

CRACKOOOM!

How do you describe it when the world comes apart around you? When a dozen things all happen at once? When you see some, and only hear about others later? This is the dilemma of the storyteller, whether they live the moment or only tell it later.

Let me begin with the sound of shattering stone, with a great wall of falling rock that rolled past behind me like a waterfall gone mad—noise and dust and the world's ending. My people had outdone themselves almost to all of our ruin. A curtain of stone three feet thick and thirty feet tall let go along a front a hundred feet long. It hit the trail right behind me and obliterated it along with the dead there as well as those both above and below. In that, my plan succeeded beyond my wildest dreams when nearly all the risen were ground into paste by the avalanche.

But it failed, too. None of us had anticipated the sheer amount of destruction it would bring, nor what that would mean to the line of my people clinging to the rock face above the fall. That whole section of mountain *flexed* with the sudden change in the weight of stone. Faran and Jax and Kumi managed to hold on, if only barely.

Javan and Siri could not. Kelos and Altia, well . . . Let me take the four of them one at a time.

Siri first, as she is dearest to me. Siri felt her one-handed grip slipping, and anticipated what was to come. She flung herself up and out, kicking off the wall and spinning wings of shadow. Making the choice to do it intentionally gave her the extra height and time she needed to turn and wheel neatly. Her sail-jump carried her around and down to land a few hundred yards farther along the trail as cleanly as if she'd planned it from the start. And that is Siri to a tee.

Javan's fall was less graceful. He tried to hang on, but could not. He would have died had not Thiess realized what was happening before his partner did and acted to save them both.

Thiess was one of the great gliders among the Shades; it was part of his reason for assuming the owl's form as his use-shape. Javan's sail-jump was nowhere near as neat as Siri's, but he managed to glide down and around to a small ledge a hundred or so feet below the trail where Siri had landed. From there it was only a matter of climbing up to rejoin us.

Kelos? Kelos had a good enough grip to hang on if he chose, but he realized what was happening as quickly as Siri did and he made a different choice. When he explained it to me later, he said it this way: "I saw that the whole section of the mountain was coming apart, and I realized what it meant for you with the dead only inches behind you. So, I decided to fall upon them like lightning from above. The only thing I regret is calling out your name when I leaped—I fear that's what made up Altia's mind."

Altia. Oh, my poor girl. I owe you my life and I will never have the opportunity to repay you. Altia's magical power was everything that Jax had claimed and more. She was also smart and quick on the uptake and she had nerves of steel under that naïve front—or so I must assume. Because she saw what Kelos was up to, and also that it wouldn't be enough. Not if the mountain fell on *me*, too. So, she let go of the wall, and she rode the avalanche down, using that enormous power of magic to steer the fall away from me and from Kelos, at the cost of her own life.

Jax watched the whole thing, watched as her favorite student chose to save my life at the cost of her own. There wasn't a thing she could do to stop it. When she told me about it later, her voice broke as she described the power and control it had taken for Altia to turn that gigantic mass of stone away from us . . . and Jax's voice never breaks. I do not think she will ever forgive me for what happened there, though she is proud in her grief.

Me? I ended up hanging over the edge of the trail, saved by Kelos, and Altia, and by the goat whose legs I clung to as he dangled from the rope I'd used to tie him to the rocks.

When the world stopped coming apart, Kelos pulled me and the goat back up—the fall and my weight had broken the poor thing's neck. Six of its fellows had simply vanished, though whether they were crushed or escaped is anyone's guess.

It wasn't until Jax and the others had climbed down and Siri and Javan up that I found out about Altia. Her name we carved deep in the stone where she had fallen, along with that of Olthiss, and the balance that holds all the grief and guilt I have generated in this world tipped a little bit farther against me.

I do not court death, but I do not turn away when she comes close, and when she finally takes me, I will not be sorry to leave the world behind.

"I hope they saw that." Faran let her arms fall back down to her sides once the last glimmers of the column of spell-light faded from the sky.

It was midnight, and she had just sent up the third round of signals to let those who had gone ahead know that we had stopped the oncoming dead. The spell-light was very bright and they were supposed to stop and look for that signal at the appointed hour, but there are many turns on the path that runs down from the mountains, and it was always possible that they might miss it.

We would know for sure in a matter of hours, when we caught up to them or failed to—ten at the most. They couldn't have gotten any farther ahead of us than that. If they *did* miss our signal we had a backup plan to meet at the mouth of the Evindine where it fed into the sacred lake.

Faran rubbed her hands together. "It's getting cold fast, and it'll be worse before we see the sunrise. We should catch up with the others." They had moved on ahead to get out of the wind—brutal there on the broad outside curve we had chosen for the signal.

Kelos was in the lead again, with Siri a half pace behind. Kumi had the much reduced string of agutes a bit farther back, while Javan staggered in their wake, looking more than half dead. Jax had taken on the task of shepherding him along and making sure he didn't fall off the trail—as much I think because it gave her something to think about besides Altia as because Javan really needed the help.

Altia.

"Why did she do it?" I asked aloud.

"She thought you were worth it," said Faran. "I'd have made the same choice in her place."

I didn't have any answer to that, so I looked away into the darkness below the edge of the path.

"She told you the answer to that herself," said Triss. "You were her khan."

"That, too," said Faran. "You are First Blade, a role that weighs all the heavier now that Namara is gone along with the priesthood. We have no other leader."

"I don't suppose I could resign my commission?" I kept my tone light, but I really did want to bolt.

Killing people who were just in the way of those who needed killing was bad enough. Being responsible for the deaths of those who followed me, of those I cared about . . . I shuddered in the cold wind. What if it *had* been Faran? Or Siri? The very thought of it made me want to slip quietly away in the night never to return. I found myself riding the ripping edge of panic in a way that I had not since before the temple fell. In all the time since, I had only ever been risking my own life, and that generally hadn't mattered to me all that much.

"No, you can't resign," said Faran, her tone deadly serious. "Not if you want the dream of the goddess to survive. Not yet anyway."

"What do you mean by not *yet*?" Had she thought of a way to get me out of this?

She laughed in a way that suggested she had read my tone if not my mind. "I mean not today, and not tomorrow, nor any time in the next year or two probably. You're stuck for a goodly while yet because there is no one else right now."

"Siri—"

"Siri can't be trusted. She told you so herself, and she wasn't wrong. Not until she gets her god problem under control. I saw what the Smoldering Flame did to her when he woke up. If she were First Blade, everything might be fine, or it might result in handing the entire order over to a half-mad, half-dead god."

"Faran's right," Triss agreed slipping out of my shadow. "We were only deeply bound to the buried god for a few seconds, and . . ." He shivered. "No. I love Siri and Kyrissa, but they cannot be trusted."

"Maryam suggested Jax," I said quickly. I felt like a caged beast.

"Jax is competent, caring and entirely inadequate to the demands of the job," said Faran. "She is an excellent school teacher and den mother, and, from what I've heard, a hell of an assassin in her own right. But she is not going to be capable of making the kinds of hard decisions that a First Blade is going to have to make in the coming years. Can you imagine her sending one of us out on a mission that might kill us? It would shred her."

"Point," I said, in the exact same tone I used when someone snuck in an unfair hit on me in a fencing match.

"And, that leaves you," said Faran. Before I could put up any other names, she held up a hand. "Who else is there? Really? Every other one of the Blades formally invested by Namara is a traitor to one degree or another. That lets them all out en masse."

She touched a finger to the swords on her back. "Concede for a moment that the job doesn't require a properly attuned pair of these, and move on to the younger generation. Kumi hasn't the weight of personality. Neither does Xin. Roric might grow into it someday, but he's not there yet. Maryam is too angry—she can be goaded like a bull. Javan is wonderful, but he doesn't have the field experience and he never will now. Hell, lack of field experience is true of all the others, too."

"And Faran Ghostwind?" I asked. "What about her?"

"Maybe, someday, if I ever manage to get enough of my humanity back."

"You look plenty human to me."

"Said the man who calls me young monster."

I felt like she'd kicked me in the chest. "I've never meant it that way."

She laughed. "No, you haven't. But just as Siri is not wrong about how dangerous it would be to trust her, your joking name isn't wrong about what I am. Oh, it's more wrong now than it was when you rescued me from the Durkoth, and it gets a little wronger every day that I spend learning from you and Triss and the others how to be human again. But it's not wrong. I am more of a killer than any of you except maybe Kelos. I'm good at, I like doing it, and I sleep like a baby afterward.

"I am learning in here"—she touched a finger to her forehead—"when it is and isn't the right choice. But that's all head and none of it heart. If I'm smart, and lucky, and I continue to spend time with people like you and Triss, I may feel it here someday, too." She put her palm on her chest. "But until that day, the last thing in the world that anyone should do is hand me the leadership of an order of mage assassins. I want to not be a monster, Aral. I want it very badly, but I'm not there yet."

Oh, Aral, I bleed for her.

Me, too, Triss. Me, too.

I reached out a hand and caught Faran's shoulder. "Pause a moment, I want to look you in the eyes."

We both stopped on the trail and Faran turned toward me. For the first time I understood in my heart that she really was a girl no longer. She was a smart, tough, badly damaged woman, and perhaps my closest friend in the world barring Triss.

"I know that you believe what you just said, Faran. And I know that there's a good deal of truth to what you say about the girl I rescued. But I think you're at least a little bit wrong about who you are now." I touched a fingertip to the spot between her breasts. "I believe that you do feel these things here. I think that at least some of the stuff that you say you've only learned with your head is in your heart, too."

"Aral—"

"Wait. I'm not finished. I know you don't believe in yourself, but I want you to know that *I* believe in you. I want you to know that no matter what you think or what anyone else says, there's at least one person in the world who believes that you are no monster. You are a good woman. When you can't believe that for yourself, please remember there's someone out there who is believing it for you."

Faran caught my hand and lifted it to her lips, kissing the palm of it as gently as a courtier. "Thank you, Aral. That was . . . just, thank you. It means the world to me. Now, come on, if we keep stopping like this, we'll never catch up." She let my hand go, turned away, and started into a slow jog.

I fell in behind her.

That was well done, Aral, sent Triss.

Hey, every once in a while I get something right.

And, now you're *doing it,* he sent—his mental tone chiding.

Doing what? I asked.

Selling yourself short. I have known you all the days of your life, and with a few notable exceptions, I think that you do get it right most of the time. Especially on the big stuff.

Thank you, Triss. I appreciate it.

Don't think it means I won't keep riding your ass and pushing you to do better, but you're very welcome.

"**Fuck!**" Faran snarled as she crawled back into the tent. "I nearly froze some very delicate bits of my plumbing pissing in that snowbank. I wish we had a pot around that we didn't have to cook in later."

Siri laughed. "I, for one, am glad that's a bridge too far for you. I've known a few who would have chosen the dinner pot over even a short walk in a mountain blizzard."

Faran rubbed her ass. "I can't say that I might not change my mind later if the storm doesn't ease up. It really is colder than a snow drake's balls out there. Hell, it's not all that warm in here."

She settled down cross-legged between me and Kumi, which involved a good bit of adjustment on everyone's part. The little silk tents were designed for four people to sleep in—if they didn't mind getting close, and they left their gear outside. We'd originally packed enough of the things so that each one would only have had to accommodate three sleepers. Unfortunately, most of them had gone wherever the missing agutes went. Which meant that now that we had caught up with students, the tents were splitting at the seams with seven occupants each, and all our gear.

Well, except ours. We only had five. The reason for that was that one of our five was Kelos. Jax didn't trust herself in that small a space with him after the losses she'd suffered in the last few days, and she'd insisted on taking Javan with her to keep an eye on him. Since Kelos terrified the rest of the youngsters so badly that no one who hadn't been part of the rear guard with us was willing to share a tent with him, it meant we had a tiny bit of extra space. It wasn't much, but going on three days trapped by the blizzard, we had all come to appreciate it.

"We need to get down off this mountainside," said Kelos. "We've been pinned up here too long already. And that's even if the food weren't running short. The agents of the Son of Heaven who are running the Kvani invasion will have sent messages on to whatever Varyan forces he controls at the base of the mountains, as well as the Caeni clans across the river. The longer we're stuck here, the worse our odds of getting past whatever is waiting for us down below."

I shrugged. "I can't say I disagree, but the track is iced over where it's exposed and buried where it's not. We've got no good way to move on from here short of a melt. You remember what it was like hiking through the first rough edges of this storm. We nearly lost Javan and Maryam both when we hit that ice patch. I'm not sure we'd still be alive if we hadn't come on this little hanging valley when we did. It's provided a much needed refuge."

"And a trap," said Kelos. "If we hadn't found such a good shelter, we might have pushed on and gotten down below the storm's snow line."

"Do you have a suggestion for how we get out of it?" asked Faran. "Or are you just complaining because you like the sound of your own voice?"

"The former," he replied, dryly. "But it's not going to be very popular."

This should be a doozy, sent Triss.

"Tell me," I said.

"If we're where I think we are," said Kelos, "there's a place about a mile down the trail where the path overlooks a deep ravine carved by the Evindine. The path itself curves on and goes around another small peak and down through a much gentler valley before it comes back to the river. The snow is going to be ten feet deep through that second valley if it's an inch—maybe deeper if there've been avalanches. It'll take us several days to get through if we go that way, and that's assuming we can do it at all."

"*If* we go that way?" I asked. "That's the way the path goes. If you haven't noticed, this isn't great terrain for breaking new trail."

Kelos shook his head. "No, it's not. Not on foot at any rate."

"I don't . . ." And then a mad thought occurred to me. "Wait, are you suggesting what I think you're suggesting? Because that's crazy."

"Probably. I told you that you wouldn't like it."

"Hey, old man." Faran poked me in the ribs. "I missed a step in that dance. Clue a girl in here, would you."

I sighed. "He's suggesting that we sail-jump down the ravine that holds the Evindine. He's also insane. I came through this part of the mountains a time or two when I was in training. If it's the place I remember . . ." I shook my head. "The clearance is what, fifteen feet side to side?"

"In the narrower spots." Kelos nodded. "But most of the way down it's a good twenty-five feet. It's steep, too, excellent drop to distance ratio for a sail-jump. I think we could make it all the way to the base where it opens out, especially with the wind that'll be blowing up from the bottom in this storm. It'll slow the glide down, but it'll provide a lot of lift."

"Not to mention turbulence," said Siri. "That'll make it harder to stay centered."

I looked at her. "You said that like it's a done deal. You're not seriously agreeing with him, are you? What if he's wrong and the valley isn't steep enough for a sail-jumper to make it all the way to the bottom?"

Siri opened her hand in a what-are-you-going-to-do gesture.

"We still might be all right," said Kelos. "It's been brutally cold for a good seventy-five hours. The Evindine is shallow here, and the flow this time of year is pretty light. There's a good chance it's solid ice from top to bottom. Given how rough and stepped the bed is, I wouldn't want to try to ride it if it's not frozen. But if it is, it's probably survivable."

"Maybe," I said. "If you're lucky, and you don't mind a few fractures."

"I didn't hear a *no* anywhere in there," said Faran. "Just a lot of *I don't like it*. Are you seriously considering this idea, Aral?"

You are, aren't you? sent Triss.

I nodded. "We've got two, maybe three days' food if we keep eating the way we have to in order to stay warm. Five if we eat the goats. If Kelos is right about how hard getting through the valley the trail follows is going to be, we're going to be mighty hungry by the time we get down to the flatlands. Even that presumes that the storm stops in the next day or two and we get a melt. It's an unseasonable blizzard, but not so much so that it couldn't simply be the start of winter."

"Even if it's not," said Siri, "we're going to have to do some hard digging to move on. That is, unless it warms up a lot and fast. . . ."

"In which case we'll have to worry about flooding," I added. "Yeah, I've been thinking about the downsides of a melt, too. As much as I hate to admit it, Kelos may be right."

The older man smiled his grim smile. "I'll volunteer to take the first jump. I can signal when I get to the bottom if it works. If I'm wrong, and it doesn't, then at least I'll be too dead to have to listen to all the I told you sos."

13

———•———

Snow devoured the world in dreamy silence, swallowing sounds and sights with a cold, merciless hunger.

I glanced over my shoulder. The trail ended fifty feet behind us, vanishing into a white void. The snow-covered slopes both above and below disappeared even faster since they lacked the string of gray-clad walkers to contrast against the gently falling flakes. Ahead? Ahead simply didn't exist. The trail bent steeply to the right for all of five feet before it opened out into the teeth of the north wind and whirled away into infinity.

The blizzard had slackened considerably in the two days since our discussion in the tent, shedding most of its power. But the snow continued to fall gently if heavily. Big fat flakes had taken the sky from us along with almost everything else. The only things that existed at the moment were my fellows and a yawning crack in the world ahead. The sides of the canyon were too steep for snow to cling. Though the snowfall hid the bottom of the ravine and the Evindine, we could see the stone along its upper edges for some distance, a dark and ominous slice cutting through the white void.

Kelos glanced over the edge again. "I wish I could see the far end. I remember it running more or less straight west from this point to where it opens out at the bottom, but even a slight bend could be a major problem with this visibility."

He looked up into the falling snow and shook his head. "But then, wishes are terrible currency. You can spend all you want but they never buy you anything. If I make it, I'll try to send my signal straight back up the canyon—you'll never see it if I aim anywhere but right at you, and even then . . ." He shrugged. "I guess we'll just have to find out."

Without another word, or even a glance in our direction, he leaped up and out. Malthiss spun him shadow wings that hid his arms before he reached the top of his jump. He jerked hard to the left when he hit the main current of the wind and had to bank to compensate, but then he dropped below the edge of the canyon—out of the brunt of the wind, sliding down and away—a dark arrow shot at an invisible target. Within seconds, the snow devoured him as thoroughly as it had everything else.

When I turned away I saw that Faran had a dreamy smile on her face—a look I had rarely seen there. I quirked a questioning eyebrow at her—more conscious than ever that I had adopted the gesture from the man who had just left us.

The smile hardened into something predatory and wild, much more Faran. "Sorry, simply thinking that we're ahead either way."

"I don't understand," I said.

Jax shook her head from beyond Faran. "That's because you can't bring yourself to hate him the way most of us do. What she means is that either he will have found a way out of this trap"—she spread her arms to take in the falling snow—"or he will die. Either way, the rest of us win."

I winced inwardly, though I think I hid it well enough. Not at Jax wishing Kelos dead, mind you. She had every right to that wish, and to the same for me frankly, after the ruin my return had brought to her life in the past week. No, I winced because she was right about my feelings. Even though Kelos had betrayed my goddess to her destruction and was responsible for the death of so many of my friends and loved ones, I couldn't hate him properly, couldn't wipe away the memories of the man who had taught and nurtured me from the age of seven.

He might be the Traitor Kelos, but he was also the man who had sat beside me for two weeks straight when I nearly died from fever when I was nine. The man who had set my broken arm at twelve. The man who handed me a purse and wished me good hunting when the goddess had sent me after Ashvik in defiance of tradition, and who had done so knowing that the rest of the shadow council would be angry about someone so young being given the job. I *wanted* to hate him as the others did and, even more, to stop loving him as my father in service of Namara, but I couldn't do it.

So, while the others were probably split about half and half between hoping he'd crash into a wall and fall to a very painful death, and wanting him to succeed and get us out of this mess, I found that I couldn't wish for anything but his safe landing at the far end.

That's why it hit all the harder when no signal came up the canyon. Not within what would have been a reasonable amount of time, nor even an unreasonable one. It slowly became clear that something had gone wrong.

"The question is: what now?" Siri asked after a half hour had passed with no sign from Kelos.

"That depends on whether he made it and simply landed someplace he can't signal us from, or if his story has finally ended," I replied. "One means flying forward into mystery, the other going back to our tents and hoping for a miracle."

"He's alive," said Jax. "I can feel it in my bones. He's too damned mean to die that quietly. Mind you, I have never liked this plan. But I think we have to go forward anyway. There's no sign of the storm truly breaking, and we've got to get off this mountain. I think we have to send another sail-jumper down the run and hope that they make it, *and* that they land someplace better suited for signaling."

Siri nodded. "I'm with Jax on that. I wouldn't have agreed

to this in the first place if I thought we had any real alternative."

Faran sighed. "So, who goes next?"

"I do," I said.

"Javan's a better sail-jumper," said Faran.

"For that matter, so am I," added Siri.

"I'm sorry," I said. "Did I give the impression that this was up for discussion? Because it's not."

I don't think—

I cut Triss off. *Nor with you either.*

"I'm going," I continued aloud. "I won't send anyone else into that ahead of me." I pointed into the crevasse below. "I *shouldn't* have let Kelos go—sail-jumping is one of the few places where I ever surpassed him. You, too, Siri. Though you're better at almost everything else a Blade does, I can outfly you." I turned to Faran. "And we're not even going to consider Javan for this."

"We've had this conversation," said Faran. "If we lose you, we lose our leader. We can't afford that."

"Too bad." So, because I knew that we could go around on this argument for hours if I let it continue, I simply turned and jumped.

Dammit, Aral! Triss snapped into my mind, but that was all he had time for as he got busy spinning shadow wings from the substance of his being. After that, he had to hand control over to me if he wanted to give us the best chance of surviving the glide.

Above and behind me I could hear all three women swearing angrily, but only briefly. Then distance and the muffling snow wrapped me in blessed silence. I loved sail-jumping as I loved few other things. There was a purity to it that I found in very few places. And this was an exceptional experience of its kind.

The snow hid the river below and blurred the passing walls of the canyon just enough so that it seemed as though I was hardly moving. The north wind barely touched the air down here. With no turbulence and no way to judge movement, it felt like I was floating gently within a sea of white light. I could have lived the experience forever if not for my responsibilities.

For starters, surviving the flight and getting a message back to the others. The safest way to do the former was to stay high up in the canyon, as close to the top as possible, where the gap between the sides was widest and the chances of hitting some outthrust bit of floor or wall the lowest. But that's certainly what Kelos had done, and, even so, something had gone wrong somewhere along the line. I needed to try a different tack.

I decided to get down low and see what the floor of the canyon looked like. Was the river frozen? Did Kelos hit a wall and go down somewhere along the line? I couldn't tell any of that from up here. So I tilted my arms, angling my wings to steepen the angle of my glide. Down, down, do-ooooh! I flipped my wings back hard, braking and clawing for height. The river was indeed frozen or, at least, iced over and covered with a deep layer of snow that both made it almost invisible amidst the fall around me and silenced its burbling voice.

If not for a waterfall that suddenly dropped away below me, I might well have hit bottom hard enough to discover exactly how solidly it was frozen. I hadn't even known I was close to crashing until that waterfall widened the distance between my feet and the surface of the ice-covered river, opening like a dark pit in one of the training mazes below Namara's temple. My heart hammered wildly as I yawed from side to side while getting myself back under proper control.

This time when I headed down again, I knew what to look for when I approached the floor of the canyon. I stayed about ten feet above the stream from there on out—high enough to keep my feet above the level of the occasional upthrust boulder or low stone spire—while I watched for any sign of a crashed Kelos. But neither my old mentor nor any major trouble spot appeared. Time lost much of its meaning as I continued forward—a tiny bead of awareness

sliding down a long dark cord surrounded by white nothing-
ness. It was mesmerizing, and I very nearly made the same
mistake Kelos must have—would have but for the advent of
a bright spear of orange pink spell-light ahead and to my
left that jarred me back into the moment.

It came from below and in front of me at an angle that
seemed ridiculously steep given the slant of the river thus
far, and it was way out of line with my glide. I backwinged
more out of startled reflex at the sight than from any conscious thought. That slowed me enough to spot a huge drop
coming up in front of me, making possible a risky split-
second decision on what to do about it.

First, I flipped my wings horizontal to the line of my
forward progress, yanking myself almost to a standstill in
the air. Then I released them back into shadow, and simply
dropped the eight or so feet to the frozen river below. I hit
hard—betting on the thickness of the ice among other
things—and slid forward, almost going over the edge of a
fifty-foot waterfall. But the snow was a good ten inches deep
and that slowed me enough that I was able to catch myself
with an outthrust foot, bracing myself against a ridge of
stone that must split up the flow of the falls when they were
running. A moment later, the bright spear of magelight
repeated itself. The unusual orange pink color that Blades
used for such things marked it unmistakably as a signal from
Kelos.

Cautiously, I leaned out over the edge of the fall, and
saw . . . well, a whole lot of nothing because of the snow. A
change in the light suggested that the canyon opened or
ended somewhere not too far ahead, but that was about it. I
released my hold on Triss's will after sending an answering
flash back in the direction of the two I had seen so far. It
was answered within seconds, and this time the light came
straight back at me instead of pointing off to my left.

*Remind me later to yell at you for not warning me in
advance before you jumped off the cliff at the top of the
canyon,* Triss sent grumpily. *I'd do it now, but we have more
important things to manage.*

Oh, absolutely. I will, without fail, remind you to make my life more difficult later.

Why do I think you're lying?

No idea. I would no more do that than I would forget to ask for a grumpy lecture at some future point uncertain.

So that's how it is, is it? He did the mental equivalent of a haughty sniff. *By the way, where are we?*

I don't honestly know. Not beyond the fact that we're sitting at the top of a big-ass waterfall somewhere close to the end of the canyon.

And Kelos?

I waved vaguely into the snow. *Down there somewhere, and apparently still in one piece.*

Triss assumed dragon shape and crept out to peer over the edge of the fall. *That would explain why we couldn't see his signal. Once he went over this edge his angle for sending signals would have gone all wrong. Any idea if he's on the trail or not?*

Nope. I wish we had some way to make conversation with these signals. I created a tiny flash of the orange pink spell-light over the palm of my hand—visible only to mages and their familiars.

Blades typically worked alone. Even when we didn't, there was normally a major premium on hiding in darkness. Flashy signals were generally a thing of last resort, so we'd never developed a system for using them to communicate, as we had with the squeeze code. I made a mental note to add that to my list of things to do if I ever got to really settle into the role of First Blade. Then I paused and reviewed the chain of thought that had gotten me there. . . . *Squeeze code, hmmm.*

There might be something there. It was a rudimentary form of communication used between Blades on those rare occasions where we might be working together and need to communicate wordlessly. There were no more than fifty words, all of them of the *yes, no, stop, go* variety, and they were transmitted by holding hands and squeezing. What if I pulsed the light I was sending down to Kelos . . . ? I tried the sequence for "alert," repeating it twice and then stopping.

Kelos flashed it back at me a moment later, followed by "safe," and "in place." He had caught on instantly, and the play was moving again. Fifty words isn't much, but it allowed me to figure out that Kelos had shot out the end of the canyon and passed right on over the trail and the edge of the deep valley it skirted here. He'd had little choice at that point except to keep going, until he landed on a slope on the far side. From there, he'd eventually slithered his way down to the trail again where it continued on that side. Or, at least, that's what I think he was telling me. In any case, he wanted the rest of us to come ahead and join him.

With that established, I signaled back up the valley, hoping that the many smaller waterfalls I'd passed over wouldn't block *my* signal. After a few minutes of flashing spell-light up the canyon, I was beginning to think that I couldn't reach them either. But then, finally, I got an answering flash. I tried my new idea for emulating squeeze code with spell-light, signaling "safe" and "come." It was a simple enough concept once it occurred to a person, and I wasn't surprised when someone up there signaled "yes" back at me. And "I come."

Since I wanted the sail-jumpers to pass over me and go on down to join Kelos, I stopped lighting things up once I got that and sent a message to Kelos instead, telling him I would signal him when I wanted him to provide a light for the sail-jumpers to steer toward. Not long after that, I saw the first of a series of barely visible blots of darkness pass high above me, up near the top of the canyon. Once I was sure whoever it was had passed beyond the falls, I signaled Kelos.

An hour later we were all assembled on the trail far below, with only one broken arm, two sprained wrists, and a dislocated shoulder spread across four of our youngsters by way of an injuries-incurred list. I got the rest of the story from Kelos then.

Overshooting the trail and the valley meant that he had landed more than a mile's hike below where he expected to come down, an all but impossible distance, given conditions and the waterfall he would have had to climb at the end of it.

Sensibly, he'd decided to wait there for a bit, sending signals back in the direction he thought the canyon must lie. He wanted to see if some better solution presented itself before he tried to make the long icy hike back up to the base of the canyon.

We had come down close to two thousand feet between the canyon run and the long steep glide from there to the segment of trail where Kelos finally ended up. There was snow down here, but significantly less of it than where we'd started from. It was warmer here, too, and not long after we started making our slow way along the trail, the snow shifted over into a frigid, brutal rain that slowly melted the way clear.

There were still icy patches here and there for the rest of that day and into the next, so we went slowly and roped together. The damp cold made a map of my body, pointing out every major scar and deep injury I'd ever suffered in fine detail. But after a long, slow, miserable twenty hours of hiking with only short breaks for snacks and shivering, the storm slacked off and we finally began to warm up a bit.

That process picked up considerably when we hit the place where the Demon's Brew fed into the Evindine. The Demon's Brew ran hot, coming as it did from steaming sulfurous springs in the Demon's Mouth, a long wide valley full of mud pots and fumaroles that ran north-south here, following the line of the mountains. There were a number of similar places on the western side of Hurn's Spine.

Some of the more accessible ones had become the sites of great baths, claiming all sorts of health benefits to be had from soaking in them, but not the Demon's Mouth. The valley was both hard to reach and carried an ill reputation thanks to the choking fumes that sometimes rolled out of the various smoking fissures and rifts that cleft the ground.

If that weren't enough to keep people away, there was also the fact that they had a much better location for a health bath some miles farther down the mountains at Yellow Springs. The Demon's Brew was too hot to bathe in of itself, but a deep pool not too far below the confluence of the two small rivers provided us with a chance to get really warm and clean for the first time since we had left Jax's castle in Dalridia.

I didn't even bother to strip off my clothes—it wasn't as though they could get any wetter—just dropped my pack and dove in once we'd established that the water there wouldn't boil the flesh off our bones. At first, the heat burned along my skin like dilute acid. After a few minutes, though, the worst of my cold faded and the waters began to soothe and relax.

Despite the sulfur stink and the metallic tang to the water, that deep pool felt like the best thing that had happened to me in ages. A pure animal pleasure that required neither thought nor effort. I didn't even mind when the cold rain picked up again. It was actually kind of pleasant to soak there with only my head above the surface, watching the icy drops strike the water and send up little fountains at the impact.

There is something about hot water when you are bone cold that beats even the finest of dry heat. My aches faded slowly from the outside inward: skin, muscle, and finally bone and joint. Below me I could feel Triss gliding around on the bottom of the pool with the other Shades, enjoying the water in his own utterly alien way. It was a brief interval of peace in a life that hadn't seen many. Which, of course, meant that it couldn't last.

Not long after I finally felt well and truly relaxed, Siri slid over from where she'd been lounging in the shallows and talking quietly with Jax. "Any thoughts on what comes next?"

"You mean besides soaking until I dissolve completely away? And then sleeping the sun from east to west? Nope. Not a one."

She canted her head to the side and gave me a very skeptical look.

"All right, all right. We're going to have to move on, and do it sooner than exhaustion would like. You obviously have some ideas on that front. So why don't we start there."

As if he had sensed the change in conversational mode, Kelos appeared then, surfacing silently, like one of the enormous marine crocodiles that hunted the salty marshes of the Ruvan Delta in the Sylvani Empire. I nodded at him and quietly spoke Faran's name. Siri hadn't been on Kelos watch, so I figured my apprentice must be. She slid out of shadows behind Kelos moments later, followed, somewhat to my surprise, by Kumi.

"Do you want Jax to join us?" I asked Siri.

She smiled and shook her head. "No, we've already had a little chat, and she likes my thinking well enough. It's the pool here that gave me the idea."

"Which is?" asked Kelos.

"Correct me if I'm wrong, but the trail shallows out a lot another day or so down that way." Siri pointed along the line of the river.

"It does," said Kelos. "There's one more really nasty bit right after the Evindine goes over a long falls, but once we're past that, it's easy going."

"Which means that we'll start running into whatever the Son of Heaven has cooked up for us somewhere in there," said Siri. Kelos nodded, and she continued. "We don't know how much sway he has in this part of Varya, but I'm guessing we're going to have most of an army to play tag with all the way from that falls down to the sacred lake. Two armies, if you count whatever the Caeni park on their side of the river. That could make for very slow going."

"And you think you have some way to speed things up?" asked Triss, who had surfaced to listen shortly after Kelos arrived.

"I do," said Siri. "Between the Demon's Brew and, lower down, the Yellowtide, the Evindine runs fast and fairly warm all the way from here to the sacred lake. Given that, why don't we play at being Vesh'An?"

"That's got a lot of potential," said Faran.

The Vesh'An were aquatic cousins of the Sylvani, Others who had forsaken magic after the godwar instead of returning from their ocean halls to the area warded in by the Wall of the Sylvain. We couldn't change our shapes the way the Vesh'An did—assuming the form of dolphins—but with the right spells we might well use the river as our road west. Breathing water and hugging the bottom could take us far and fast. It wasn't something I'd have tried on my own—the magic was far too intricate for me. But with Siri and Kelos sorting out the spell work, the chances of us all drowning went down dramatically. . . .

"**Fucking** dukes of Seldan!" Jax snarled as soon as she'd finished coughing the water out of her lungs. "Always neck deep in anything rotten in Varya. I still think you should have let me slip out of the river and add a third Seldan to my total back there." She jerked a thumb over her shoulder, pointing back up the Evindine. "The duke's tent was within spitting distance of the river. I could have done it with no one the wiser."

I shook my head, just as I had earlier when she tried to convince me of the idea via underwater charades. "However clean you got in and out, leaving a dead duke in the middle of an army encampment pretty much screams *Blade*."

Siri added, "And not just any Blade, Madam Seldansbane. The fact that you already racked up the father and uncle of the one currently warming the ducal seat is not something that would be missed by anyone thinking about who exactly might have made a corpse of this one."

"Hey," said Jax, "I'm not the only Blade ever to kill a Seldan. At least nine of that name have fallen to the order over the years. The Seldan family tree is a poison oak." She nodded toward Kelos. "Hell, I'm not the only Blade standing on this riverbank who has killed a Seldan."

"It's been nearly two centuries since I bagged mine," said Kelos. "With the seven who've fallen since, I doubt they even think of me that way anymore. Especially after the manner in which you left the last one you ended for Namara."

Jax grinned—a thoroughly bloodthirsty expression. "The goddess told me to: 'Make of this one an example they will not forget for a generation.' So, I did."

"You don't think that hanging him naked from the bell

tower of Shan was a touch beyond the scope of your assignment?" I asked mildly.

"Do they remember his death a generation later?" asked Jax. "Oh yes, I think that they do. Given how much of his history involved rape and murder, I think that stuffing his dick halfway down his throat was an inspired touch. Don't give me that look! I killed him clean and quick. The nastier bits all happened to the corpse. Now, if you're all sure you're not going to let me go back and make this one into my third-time good luck charm, we should probably get moving."

Jax pointed across the broad lake toward the far shore—invisible at this distance. There lay the ruins of the temple and our order's best chance of rising from its own ashes. We had a long hike ahead of us. While a straight shot across the bottom of the lake might have served us better in terms of concealment, we had actually crawled out of the river a few yards shy of its mouth. There were things that swam in the deep waters of Lake Evinduin that we had chosen not to disturb just yet. Historically, they had avoided taking Blades, but the goddess was dead, and we did not want to tempt them before we had to.

There would be plenty of risk on that front when we reached the sacred island.

14

———◆———

My shattered heart lay before me, a vision of the unreachable past written in broken stone.

Namara's temple had stood on a low hill above Lake Evinduin and the sacred island of the goddess for nearly eight hundred years, its great dome staring up into the vault of heaven with the Unblinking Eye of Justice. I had first seen the temple at the age of four when I entered the service of the goddess. From that day until its fall twenty years later, it had been my home, and my refuge, the center of my life, and the hallowed cradle of my religion.

Now . . . I took a deep breath and tried to release the lump of pain that filled my chest. Now, it was as dead as the goddess who had made it holy and the priests and laity who had been slain when she fell. Nothing grew on that hill, nor in the fields that surrounded it. The temple centered a dead zone that ran a long bow shot in every direction but lakeside, where the barren ground ran down only as far as the shore.

After the slaughter and the fire, the Sword of Heaven had brought in peasants from the surrounding farms and forced them to sow the fields and grounds with salt, turning the dirt over and over until the top foot was as barren as a sun-baked rock in the deepest desert. Spells they had laid, too, of desolation and blight and sterility. The Son of Heaven had pronounced the site cursed in the eyes of the gods and ordered that nothing be built there for a thousand years, nor any stone taken from the shattered buildings for use elsewhere.

Eight hundred years the temple had lasted, and now it might take another eight hundred years before nature even began to reclaim the ruins from the horrors wrought there by Heaven's Son in the name of his gods. I stared at the shattered remnants of my only true home from our place of concealment in a little copse of fruit trees, with tears on my cheeks. Nor was I alone in crying. I could hear more than one of my companions quietly sobbing.

Faran stood beside me, her eyes dry and utterly bleak. "I haven't been back but the once, since . . ." She shook her head.

Kelos had vanished into shadow before we got close enough to see the devastation—an entirely sensible move on his part, and one that he had warned me was coming. He would meet those of us who were performing the ritual of attunement later, on the sacred island—presuming the scaly monsters that haunted the deeps of the lake didn't devour him along the way.

At the moment, I rather hoped that they would, though I doubted it. Professional courtesy between ancient horrors and all that. It would make the ritual that much harder, but I thought we could manage it without him, and with the ruins there in front of me, it seemed a small price to pay for that particular piece of long delayed justice.

"We're here," said Jax from behind me, her voice rough and throaty. "Now what?"

I turned to face her. "We need to find someplace to lay up for the day. Then, once night falls, the four of us will cross over to the island and attempt the attunement."

"More than four, if you're willing," said Jax. "I'd like to bring Roric and Kumi with, if I might, as representatives for the younger generation."

"Not Maryam?" I asked.

Jax shook her head. "No, this is a task that wants devotion more than anything. Roric and Kumi have more faith in Namara than any of my other charges retain. If she had survived, I would have wanted to bring Altia as well, but . . ." She clenched her jaw so hard I half expected to hear teeth cracking, but then she forced herself to relax.

Faran spoke into the suddenly charged silence that lay between us. "Any thoughts on *where* we can hide out till sunset?"

Siri leaned forward. "There are deep places under the temple that the invaders never reached, prayer rooms, a section of training labyrinth, even a long forgotten shrine to the Eye of Justice. There are rooms down there that haven't been visited by any Blade but me in at least a century. The locals view the grounds as cursed and they will not enter them, so we'll be safer down there than anyplace this side of the salt line."

"Really?" I asked. "A hidden shrine? I've never heard a rumor of anything like that. Not even when I was First Blade the last go-round . . . How did you find out about that? About all of it?"

Siri flushed, and touched a finger to the smoke that threaded her hair. "My divine affliction. When I came back here after my final mission for Namara, the temple was still smoldering. The Sword and the Hand burned everything that they could, furnishings, panes, doors, bodies. . . ."

She took a deep breath and let it out slowly. "Much was brought out and torched under the sky, but those things that were nailed down or otherwise inconvenient to move, they burned in place. Smoke was everywhere in the deeps, and smoke passes where people cannot. There were secret ways under the temple, passages long forgotten or that only the priests knew. Smoke found a way in, and I followed it."

"But you didn't find the lost swords." It was a statement rather than a question—I was quite sure she'd have told us if she knew where they were.

Siri shook her head. "I suspect that if they reside

anywhere within this mortal plane, they're on or near Namara's island. The pool there was sacred to the goddess millennia before the advent of our order, if Kayla and Ashkent are right, and I've no reason to doubt it. They told me that Namara hallowed that island before the first humans ever walked under sun or stars."

I blinked at that; it was the first time Siri had mentioned her Other connections in weeks. "They spoke of Namara?"

"Only when I begged them to," said Siri. "The First do not like to talk about *your gods* as they call them, though Namara they hated least."

I would have loved to hear more about what they'd had to say, but Siri's expression didn't invite questions. Instead, I waved a hand toward the ruined temple. "I think we've given everyone enough time to get over the initial shock of seeing it again. It's probably best if we got under cover now."

I turned to Faran. "Once Siri's shown us to our temporary refuge, I think you and I should pay a visit to the village up the coast and collect a couple of those floating baskets that the fishermen use in shallow water—it'll make hauling our gear across to the island much simpler."

This is giving me a case of the horrors like you wouldn't believe. I sent the words silently to Triss because I couldn't very well admit it out loud.

The First Blade wasn't allowed to fear, not even when he stood on the edge of the desecrated grave of his entire religion. Not where his followers could see him, anyway. In the years since the fall I had returned to this place twice. I had not lingered either time, and this creeping horror was why.

The first time I returned was only a few weeks after the fall, and I had only briefly passed the outer gates of the temple and gone no deeper than that. After seeing the names of the dead and the banned on the stele out front, along with the ruined stone orb that once held the spirit knives of the Blades, I'd had no reason to believe that anyone yet lived within those walls. On my second visit, when I recovered my swords from the deeps of the lake, I hadn't so much as set foot on the salted ground, swimming out to the island at an angle from the still living part of the shore to avoid having to do so.

We came in to the temple from the lake side now, avoiding the stele and the desecrated orb—both to keep from passing too close to the still active road and out of mercy for the feelings of the students. In through the postern gate we went, a narrow slit in the white stone wall that had once allowed access to the docks and the lake without having to circle the whole of the temple complex. In the old days it had been concealed from casual observers by a thicket of gnarled thornbrindle, but that had burned away with all the other trees and shrubs.

The gate itself lay twisted and broken beneath a pile of stones torn from the roof of the arched passage that led into the inner gardens. There were holes aplenty in the wall around the gate, but I chose to climb over heaped rubble rather than to further violate the integrity of the old building, and the others had followed in my footsteps without complaint. The gardens within had suffered even more than the outer dead zone, having been planed flat and covered with a good inch of salt. Rain and sun had hammered that into a dusty white sheet almost too bright to look at, and I led us past it quickly.

I couldn't give the temple proper the same courtesy I had the postern gate. The forces of Heaven's Reach had been more thorough there, bringing down the entire section of wall that had once held the door to the kitchens. This whole part of the building was little more than an unevenly mounded pile of broken stone. The inner temple, though, was made of sterner stuff, its walls yards thick and reinforced with deep magic. Though they had torn the roof off, exposing the passages to the elements, much of the structure remained. Somehow, that made the hurt all the worse.

Once we passed the ruined arch that had led into the inner temple, we moved beyond any place I had visited since before the fall. We let our shrouds drop away then and Siri took the lead. When we passed through the door that opened into the Sanctuary of the Blades, I bit my lips hard. It was that or scream and bolt.

The Sanctuary was a great oval with ends that came to points. In the old days a high stone dome sheathed in white marble had covered it over except for a cutaway circle in the center that remained open to the sky. Under that circle had been a huge obsidian orb set in a wide ring of lapis tiling. From above, the orb had played the role of the iris in a huge unblinking eye fixed on the heavens—Justice fixing her gaze on her peers.

The orb had held our kila in those days—tri-bladed spirit knives given to each Blade by the goddess herself on their investiture. The first task of every Blade was to bring his or her knife from the sacred island here to the orb where they sank it deep into the stone in a ceremonial marriage with Justice. The orb was gone from the Sanctuary now, of course. Its broken remnants lay beside the stele that the Son of Heaven had caused to be erected in front of the temple to proclaim the ban of the gods on our order.

The kila had been chopped free of the stone, and it was rumored that those that were associated with living Blades now adorned the back wall of the Son of Heaven's privy so that he could piss on them every morning. I hadn't been able to bring myself to check the one time I had been in his quarters, so I couldn't say whether that was truth or a petty fiction.

The missing kila I had known about. What I had not was that the stones from the shattered dome had been neatly moved aside to leave the lapis ring free of any debris. Then, someone had gone through and very carefully pulled up and destroyed hundreds of individual pieces of lapis, leaving behind voids that converted the whole into a necromantic circle of binding.

I forced my voice to a calm I didn't feel. "Siri, was the spell circle here when you came through last time?" I pitched my voice low and soft, so that only those closest could hear it, and I waved for the students behind Jax to stop moving.

"It was." She pointed to a place where the circle had been broken, the tiles shattered and burned by extreme heat, her voice equally quiet. "I broke the ring with lightning."

"Do you know what it was binding?" Faran and Jax had moved forward, and Kumi followed Faran, but I didn't think any of the others were close enough to hear.

Siri nodded. "I believe so." A long silence followed, and I began to wonder if she wasn't going to say more. "I believe that it imprisoned the souls of many of our fallen—bound here in torment. Though I didn't know it then, I think that it held those whose bodies the Son's servants had converted to host his risen curse."

"So, some of the dead we have fought in the last few months . . ."

"Might have once been our own, yes," said Siri. "Though, I don't think it likely, given the long passage of time. Whatever the case, they would be very far gone from human at this point, and it would be impossible to tell who they once were without some extremely fancy divining magic."

"That's obscene," whispered Faran. "Why would someone do that?"

"I don't know," replied Siri. "Necromancy is something I've never *wanted* to know more about. Maybe it makes the associated risen stronger or more durable."

In my head, Triss was cursing viciously in the Shade tongue. The Resshath-ra wasn't allowed to show his horror visibly either. Not here. Not now.

"I should have searched the ruins when I came back," I said. "I should have known about this."

"There was no point in you doing that," said Siri. "You didn't get back till weeks later, and I had already taken care of this. There was nothing you could have done, and no reason to believe that the Son of Heaven could be responsible for something this horrible. None of us knew what he was then. I doubt most of his people had any clue about this—not the living ones anyway—though he needed at least one mage to manage it. There was no reason for you to know, which is why I never mentioned it till now."

Kelos knew, I sent to Triss. The idea made me sick.

But Triss's response surprised me. *He may have known about the Son, but he couldn't have known about this.* His mental voice was very firm. *He would never have countenanced it.* Malthiss *would never have countenanced it.*

I hope that you're right. If you're not, I may have to change my mind about accepting his help.

And letting him live?

That, too.

I can't believe that he knew. I refuse to believe it, even of Kelos the Traitor.

Siri lifted her eyebrows at me, obviously wondering if Triss and I were done with our silent little conference. Only she and Faran would have noticed. I nodded very slightly to let her know that we were.

"I wouldn't have chosen to expose them to this," she said very quietly, indicating the students with a jut of her chin, "but this is the only path that a human can manage into the hidden ways. Come on." She crossed the broken magical circle defiantly—the message that she would not let it affect her expressed clearly in the proud lines of her back and shoulders.

I followed, doing my best to emulate her quiet poise. Siri's refusal to let the Son's work make her treat the temple as less than it had once been was exactly the thing I needed to fortify my own flagging nerves. She led us all to a seemingly innocuous point about midway between the top of the eye as seen from above and the left corner. There, she slipped around some of the roughly stacked fallen blocks from the ceiling and drew her sword before kneeling and inserting the point into an open gap between two of the stones that made up the wall.

"There was a false piece of mortar here when I found it initially," she said. "I didn't see much point in replacing it, since this can't be opened without the right key." She pushed then, sliding the short curved blade of her sword all the way home. "Let's see. . . ."

Siri rocked the sword ever so slightly, and was rewarded

with a sharp metallic click. She pivoted, gently torquing the hilt of her sword to the right, and a slim section of wall opened inward to reveal a narrow set of stairs descending into the depths beneath the sanctuary.

"Why don't you go first, Aral?"

Her tone made me quite sure she was up to something. Nor was I wrong. The stairs led down thirty or so feet to a landing where they doubled back in the other direction. Faint light was visible through an arch at the bottom. I passed through and found myself in a mirror image of the sanctuary above. Here, the blue circle of Namara's unblinking eye was set in the ceiling, and the iris that centered it was a great orb of white marble spelled to give off a gentle light.

Where the eye above looked up into the sky, this one looked down into a seemingly bottomless reflecting pool. It was beautiful and peaceful. Holy. One, last, pure fane to a fallen goddess. Seeing it healed something in my heart. I understood then that Siri's choice to send me first was a gift, a chance to spend one perfect moment alone with the Eye before the others followed me in.

Once everyone else was settled, I sat down beside Siri. "Thank you. I needed that."

She smiled at me. "I thought you might."

"Faran and I will have to go steal some baskets soon, but I want to sit here for a few minutes first. You mentioned that there were other rooms down here. . . ."

Siri nodded. "There are, but the only way for a normal person to get to them now is to swim." She pointed at the reflecting pool. "It's not far, but I wouldn't advise trying it if we don't have to. That connects to the lake, and those who haunt the deeps come here as well. There was once another way down, which leads more directly to other areas, but it's buried under the ruins of the outer temple. It would take a good-sized crew a couple of days to excavate it."

"Have you explored the underwater ways?" I asked.

"Not thoroughly, no. I see where you're going, but I still think that the island is a much more likely place to find the

swords. It . . ." She paused for a long time, before shrugging
and saying, "It just feels right."

I had made the swim out to Namara's island and back three
times previously. Once, when I asked her to make me a
Blade before my time and send me after Ashvik. Once, when
I returned my swords to her. And again, when I reclaimed
them. It's nearly a mile of deep water, and you can feel the
great scaly horrors that live in the lake sliding by beneath
you, but I have never feared them. The first time, I knew
that my goddess would protect me, and the two times since,
I had been indifferent to my fate.

Tonight was different. I had things that I needed to do. I
still might not have a huge emotional investment in living,
but dying would be damned inconvenient. So, this time,
when I felt a fast moving current of cold drag across my legs
as though something big were swimming past not far
beneath, I couldn't help but stick my face underwater and
look to see if I might spot what had caused it.

It was dark, but the moon was high and full, and that
gave me barely enough light to see something long and narrow and scaly. I only saw the back end of the thing, but that
was enough for me to be sure that it was neither dragon nor
crocodile. If it was a fish, it was a damned skinny thing for
its size. It reminded me most of an enormous eel or marine
snake, and it had to be at least thirty feet long. Then it was
gone, and it didn't return before I had to resurface and take
a breath.

Siri was closest to me then. "You saw?" she asked as I
began to swim again—stroking as quietly as I could manage.

"Not well enough to identify it. I don't know that I've
ever seen anything quite like that before."

"No surprise there," she said. "To the best of my knowledge they live nowhere in the eleven kingdoms but here and
in Lake Leivas."

"You seem to know quite a bit about them. What are
they? And where did you learn it?"

"Master Illiana made a study of them. She was the Master who brought me to the island for my investiture, and she was feeling chatty that night. They're creatures of magic from the wastes in the west. Freshwater eels once, or possibly snakes. They were bent and twisted by the runaway magic that created the wasteland."

"Then why have I never heard of their like in the River Dan?" I asked. "It's supposed to meet the Leivas out west somewhere, beyond the edge of Varya."

"The Dan doesn't touch on a body of water big enough to support them—not within the eleven kingdoms anyway. I imagine that they know that. Illiana said that they're at least as smart as we are in their own way. She said that both Namara and the Lady of Leivas had made treaties with them."

"I didn't know that." The Lady was . . . a special case in every way, a mage that was only just this side of being a goddess, if the legends were to be believed. Though her power supposedly ended at the edge of that greatest of all freshwater lakes.

It's news to me, too, sent Triss.

"So," I said, "Master Illiana subscribed to the idea that the Lady is a real person?"

Siri nodded. "Absolutely. She told me that she had met her once, on a special commission from Namara—that the lake itself was somehow the Lady's familiar, and that was why she is so powerful within its bounds."

"I wish that I had gotten the chance to know Master Illiana," I said—suddenly wishing that I had not been so intimidated by her in life. But she was another of the grand old legends of the order, Illiana Spellslayer, and she had seemed all but unapproachable when I still had that opportunity. "The Son of Heaven robbed us of so much. . . ."

Whatever Siri might have said in answer to that was lost when a hiss sounded in the darkness ahead of us. We had reached the island, and Kelos was there, waiting.

"You and I need to talk," I said, ignoring the hand he offered to help me out of the water.

"All right. Alone? Or would you prefer an audience?"

"In this case, I think I'd like the audience." He nodded and stepped back, crossing his arms impassively while he waited for everyone to come ashore.

I do not believe that he did it, sent Triss.

I don't think I do either, but this has to be dealt with openly and immediately. I won't let it fester.

"In front of the goddess." I jerked my chin in the direction of the sacred pool.

Kelos raised an eyebrow, but didn't say anything before turning to follow me to the pool.

"Stand there." I pointed to the place where an initiate waited for the goddess to invest them as a Blade.

Once he was in place, with the rest of us facing him in a semi-circle, I told him what we had all seen in the Sanctuary at the temple and what Siri had to say about it. His face visibly paled, and he looked absolutely stricken by the time I finished. I hoped—almost prayed—that was an honest reaction. The alternative was simply too horrible.

After a moment, he shrugged out of his sword rig and extended it toward me hilts first. "There is no oath I can make that any of you would believe. I have earned that mistrust, and I won't insult you by pretending I haven't. I have earned even your suspicions about that abomination in the Sanctuary. I will swear no oath, nor protest my innocence with fair words."

He took a deep breath. "I will say only this: I did not know about the spell, and I would have died to prevent its setting. If I am lying to you, I pray that the ghost of the goddess will send one of the hunters in the deep into her pool and have it devour me right now. If you don't believe me, please take my own swords and put an end to me."

I nodded at him, but neither took his swords nor suggested that he put them back on. Instead, I said, "Malthiss?"

The shadow basilisk rose from the tattoos that wrapped Kelos from waist to neck and bowed before me. "He speaks the truth, First Blade. I would have taken him into the darkness before I would have let him participate in something like that. I know that we have done nothing to earn the faith of any here, and much to betray it, so I, too, will make no vows. I will tell you that we have not been back to the temple since the day of the fall, nor have we stepped beyond the ring of salt on this visit. Were it not for the ritual of attunement we would not tread the shores of this island tonight either. We have not the right."

"I have a question," said Kumi, startling me with the firmness of her interjection. "I know that Kelos betrayed the order, but how exactly? It doesn't seem to me that one man could convince the gods themselves to move against Namara."

I turned to Kelos. It wasn't something I'd thought about in quite that way before, and I wanted to hear his answer.

"Of course not," he said. "The gods had long since decided that Namara was a problem. She had created weapons that could kill a god and she didn't subscribe to the idea that the gods were themselves above justice. The question was always when. Never if. I only helped to decide the timing, and that because I thought I might make the inevitable serve the estimable, and bring an end to the rule of kings once and for all."

15

———◆———

Liars are exhausting.

Take your favorite goblet. Shatter it. Pick up the pieces. Use magic to fuse them back together. Even if the repair is seamless, you know that it was broken. It may hold water now, but can it ever be the same? I don't believe that it can, but others may reach different conclusions.

Trust is like that. Break it once, and no matter what you do to mend it, it will have become a different thing. The greater the degree of trust and the more badly it is broken, the harder it is to make whole.

With Kelos we haven't even reached the part where you put the pieces back together—might never—but much of what he said seemed to hold water. It *felt* true. But the nature of his betrayals meant that the simple fact that it was *Kelos* saying it made it feel false, too. Every single thing he said had to be weighed and judged on its own merits as much as possible and independently of the source. Dealing with that wears on the soul.

Take his statement about the intentions of the other gods about betraying Namara. It was a self-serving answer, but,

I thought, an honest one, too. It fit with what I had learned from other sources, and it made Kelos seem to be less powerful than he might otherwise, not an easy choice for a proud man—and he was that. All things that made it feel true. On the other hand, while the story made him seem less powerful it also made his betrayal less extreme, and that might serve his interests better than the other way around. Feeling false again . . .

And so it went, back and forth with every single thing he said or did. As long as he lived he would always cost me in time and energy I could ill afford. I didn't want to kill him myself, nor to have one of my fellows kill him for that matter, but my life would be much eased by his passing. . . .

I took a deep breath and nodded. "Put your swords back on, I believe you about the necromancy, and we have a thing that needs doing." I turned my attention to Roric and Kumi. "I want you two to sit over there." I pointed. "Don't move or say a word if you don't absolutely have to. This will be tricky enough without interruptions. Siri, I know that you and Kyrissa have been discussing how best to do this with Malthiss and Kelos for weeks now and have created a ritual structure for the thing. You're in charge. Tell us what needs doing."

"There are actually two main possibilities for how to go about the attunement," said Siri. "One involves a lot of ritual fancywork on the part of the petitioner and the assembled Blades. It has a decent chance of success. The other is harder, darker, faster, and a lot more painful. It also increases the chance of success enormously. I crafted a ritual for each, but I've had extensive talks with Faran about the two methods, and she's expressed a strong preference." She turned her eyes on the younger woman. "Last chance to change your mind."

Faran lifted her chin and spoke clearly. "I choose the way of pain."

Siri nodded, her expression grim. "It's what I would have done in her place, and it's much surer, but it's not a decision one person can make for another."

"Siri, what do you need from the rest of us?" I asked,

trying to conceal the concerns Siri's speech had raised for me. This was Faran's future at stake here, and the choices were hers to make.

"From most of you, I need little beyond following simple orders and a promise not to interfere when things get bloody. You're going to have a rougher task, Aral, but I'd rather you don't have too much time to dwell on it in advance."

I don't like the sound of that, sent Triss.

I don't either, but Siri's our magic expert and Faran knows her own mind. I won't interfere . . . however much I might like to.

I know, it's just . . . I worry.

I didn't have an answer for that.

Siri turned to Kelos. "Can you fetch me the head of the goddess up from the deeps? It's no more than stone now, but it will serve better than any other choice, and I think that Namara would have approved of what we are about to do."

Kelos nodded, whispered a few phrases, and touched fingers to his lips when spell-light answered his call. Without so much as another word to the rest of us, he turned and dove into the pool. I chewed on the inside of my cheek, and tried desperately not to think back to my nightmare about the throne.

Aral? Are you all right? sent Triss.

Not even a little bit, but I told Siri this was her show, and she asked me not to interfere. This is me not interfering, hopefully without drawing blood from my own cheek.

She doesn't make it easy.

That she does not.

Siri spoke again. "Jax, this is going to be a directional magic. The pool faces north and the deep lake. That's going to make you and Kelos the Wardens of East and West respectively. I will be the South Warden. Aral, as Faran's sponsor, you get to assume the role of the Warden of the North since that is the direction of Justice in this case. While we wait for Kelos we can set up the warding patterns—a diamond rather than a circle or something fancier, in this case—and fifteen feet on a side. You two cover your directions.

I'll do for me and Kelos both, as well as making the connections. Be about it."

Ritual wards come in a relatively small number of flavors, and they are drilled into every mage at a very young age. The simplest arrangement of all is the ward of the four directions, though a circle or octagon sealed to the eight elements is nearly as easy and buys you more flexibility. It scales up from there. Considering how nervous all the talk about blood and pain and fetching the head of the goddess had made me, it was a damned good thing that all I had to handle was the ward of the North.

I had to recenter myself and force my breathing back to calmer rhythms twice before I was able to assay it properly. By the time I was done, Siri had finished both the ward she would hold and the one for Kelos. Then she started in on laying the connections down, using the tip of her index finger to draw lines of light across the paving stones.

I turned to Faran while Siri was finishing up, and spoke quietly. "How upset am I going to be with you later that you didn't give me plenty of warning as to what's coming?"

She grinned at me, though it obviously took an effort. "In the short term? Extremely. Once you've had time to think about it? Less . . . I hope. Now, shut up and let me concentrate. This is going to take a lot out of me, and I need to prepare myself."

I wanted to pace and swear, but, again, the First Blade doesn't get to do that sort of thing. Not with Roric and Kumi there at any rate. Instead, I settled cross-legged on the pavers a few feet south of my ward, and pretended to meditate.

Good try, but you're not fooling anybody, sent Triss. *Well, maybe the youngsters, but Siri and Jax and Faran all know how you feel about meditation.*

Then I'm fooling the only ones I need to fool. Now, shut up and let me pretend to be peaceful in something resembling actual peace.

Too late, sent Triss. *Kelos is back. Which means you probably need to move.*

Kelos came up out of the water as I returned to my feet.

He was trailing a thick blue chain of spell-light from his left shoulder. Once he'd coughed the water out of his lungs, he unlooped the chain. One end of it vanished into the skin of his chest, just above his heart, as though it were anchored there.

Once he had the chain free, he started pulling it up out of the water hand over hand. From the way the thick muscles of his shoulders and back bunched and strained it must have taken enormous physical effort to supplement the magical working. With each pull, the slack he created vanished into his chest, like a capstan winding up one of the heavier ropes on a sailing ship.

As much as I didn't trust the man or want to be anywhere near him, I didn't like to think about what would happen with that chain if he slipped or stumbled. But he was Kelos, and he didn't. Not even at the end, when the great weed-encrusted head of the goddess rose out of the water, drawn by a golden loop of light set in the center of her forehead.

I couldn't help but draw a sharp breath when I saw her. While the goddess had lived, that stone face expressed a deeper sense of presence and vitality than any dozen human beings. Now, it was just another chunk of lifeless statue, albeit depicting someone I had once loved with all my soul. It burned my heart to see her ruined so.

Though he could never have done so physically, Kelos's magic allowed him to lift the enormous stone head completely free of the water, so that it hung a few inches above the pavers. Holding the head clear of the ground, he turned and slowly carried it into the diamond of the wards. Siri pointed at a spot maybe six feet south of the northern ward, and he set the head down there, facing away from the pool.

She had him hold it in place for a moment while she did a fancy little bit of magic that fused the broken neck to the stone pavers beneath, fixing it there as firmly as any statue on its plinth. That put the top of Namara's head about five feet above the ground. Together, they made a few more quick preparations that left the stone glowing faintly with a spell-light that fluctuated between a dark green and a deep red.

Siri turned to me as Kelos stepped away. "Come here for a second, Aral. I need you to look into the face of the goddess that was and not move until you're ready to let go of that knot of pain I saw you swallow a second ago. This will be hard enough without you trying to hold your breath. Trust me when I say that I believe with my whole heart that Namara would have approved of what we will do here tonight."

I didn't want to do it, but I *had* put Siri in charge, and she wasn't wrong about my feelings. So I went and I faced my goddess once again. Not there on the stones—Namara was dead, and the sculpted head was nothing more than an elaborate and broken tombstone at this point. No, I faced her in my heart, and I asked for her forgiveness for what we were about to do here.

She didn't answer. The dead rarely do, and then it's never good. But, after some minutes, I found a measure of peace. Enough, I thought, to face whatever I would have to do next. When I was done, I returned to the north ward and took up station there, with one foot on either side of the glyph I'd inscribed and my arms behind my back—left hand clasping right wrist as I had been taught.

Are you prepared for this? Triss asked into my mind.

Most definitely not, but that won't change, so I might as well deal.

Good luck. I'll see you on the other side. With that, Triss subsumed his will to my own, going into a sort of waking dream that would allow me to control our joint actions, a necessity for any elaborate ritual magic.

Thanks, old friend. I will meet you there. I whispered the words into the silence of my mind, knowing he couldn't register them now, but might remember them later.

Faran stepped up to the edge of the diamond then, between Siri and Jax. I was only slightly surprised to see that while I had been communing with my past she had stripped down to nothing more than a loincloth and her sword rig, exposing a lean muscular figure with high, small breasts. For one so young she had a lot of scars.

"Who comes before the ghost of the goddess?" Siri

stepped in front of Faran, and drew her sword as she asked the question. "I am Siri Mythkiller, Blade of Fallen Namara and the voice of the challenge." Her tones mimicked the ritual delivery of the priests who had once served Namara.

"I am Faran Ghostwind."

"And why do you come to this place of the dead, Faran Ghostwind?" Siri touched the tip of her sword to the base of Faran's throat. A moment later, it was matched by a sword of smoke held in a wisp of a hand.

"I come here to the tomb of my goddess, seeking a boon." Faran's voice was firm and clear. "Justice the goddess may have died, but justice the ideal lives forever."

"Then pass within." Siri dropped her swords away from Faran's throat and stepped aside. When she did so, the left one puffed away into nothing.

Faran moved to the middle of the diamond, facing the head of the goddess, while Siri sheathed her sword and returned to the southern ward. As she did so, Kyrissa flowed up from the ground to enclose her in a second skin of smoke and shadow, giving her will into Siri's keeping for the duration of the coming ritual.

"The Warden of the South is in place and ready to defend the rights of the petitioner." Siri bent and touched a hand to the glyph between her feet. As it flared to golden life, she looked at Kelos.

"The Warden of the West is in place and ready to defend the rights of the petitioner." He touched his glyph and it burst into light, igniting the line that lay between Kelos and Siri, who turned and nodded to Jax.

"The Warden of the East is in place and ready to defend the rights of the petitioner." Jax placed one finger on the glyph, waking it and sending another line of light to meet Siri's glyph.

Siri didn't bother to prompt me, and I had already pulled the stuff of shadow up and over my skin in anticipation of what came next. "The Warden of the North is in place and ready to defend the rights of the petitioner." My will and the touch of my flesh lit up my glyph and connected it to those belonging to Jax and Kelos. "With my seal, the warding is complete. None may force the ward while any Warden lives."

More light jumped up from the spell lines, enclosing us in a translucent pyramid of golden light. Below us, and invisible within the earth, another such extended downward. We stood within a fortress of magic until such time as one of us released their glyph or all of us died and the warding failed.

Siri stepped away from her glyph and walked up behind Faran. The warding was a part of her now, drawing nima directly from the well of her soul so that she no longer needed to maintain her position physically. "Faran Ghostwind, you have come here to the final resting place of Namara, Goddess of Justice, to ask a boon. State your desire."

"I bring the swords of one who once served justice." Faran drew Parsi's swords with a snap and held them high over her head. "She is as dead as Namara, but her weapons may serve on, if justice wills it. I would take these swords up in the place of she who once held them, and serve justice as a Blade full and true." She knelt before the stone head, her arms crossed with one sword held straight up on each side of her face.

Siri placed her hand atop Faran's head. "With the goddess departed, the duty of justice falls to the Blades she left behind. Who sponsors this woman to become one of us?"

I had been expecting something like that, so I was ready, stepping forward to stand beside the head of the goddess. "I am Aral Kingslayer, First Blade of Fallen Namara, and I stand sponsor for the petitioner." Like Siri, I mimicked the intonation of the priests who had served with us before the fall.

Siri nodded solemnly to me, though I thought I saw a twinkle somewhere in the deeps of her eyes, suggesting she approved of my language. "There is none better to speak for you, Faran Ghostwind. You may rise and approach the statue of the goddess."

Faran did so, stopping and bowing once again when she stood a few feet in front of the great stone face. For perhaps ten heartbeats she stared deep into Namara's cold, dead eyes.

Then she straightened her back and let her swords fall to her sides.

"I am ready," said Faran.

Siri nodded. "Will you petition the goddess by entreaty or by ordeal?"

"Ordeal." The word came out flat and cold—a strong woman making a hard choice. The spell-light that danced across the surface of Namara's head stopped shifting colors, settling on a deep crimson, like the sun shining through a curtain of blood.

"So be it." Siri crossed the short distance to stand behind Faran. "You know what comes next. Face me when you are ready."

Faran took a long step forward so that she was practically touching the head of the goddess before turning around. "I am ready."

Siri drew her sword again and placed it on the ground between Faran's feet and the head of the goddess, perpendicular to both. Then she looked at me. "Your first duty as sponsor is to close the doors of steel around the petitioner."

I drew my own swords and laid them so that a triangle of goddess-forged steel enclosed Faran hilt-to-point-to-hilt in a never-ending loop. When I stood up, Siri's eyes met my own, and I knew her well enough to read a clear and simple message there.

Don't fuck up.

I nodded even though it felt like my heart and stomach had decided to wage the most devastating sort of magical war on each other, laying waste to the whole of what lay around and between them in their battle. Siri turned her attention back to Faran, stepping to her left.

"I am Siri the Mythkiller. The Challenger's sword is mine to deliver." She extended her hand.

Faran nodded and flipped her left-hand sword around, extending the hilt to Siri, who took it and looked at me. "Sponsor, the other sword is yours."

I took a deep breath and forced a calm I didn't feel as I stepped to Faran's right—I had a horrible suspicion that I knew where this was going, and I didn't like it even a little bit. But the decision was Faran's. "I am Aral the Kingslayer. The Sponsor's sword is mine to deliver."

Faran offered me her other sword, and I took two steps to the north, following Siri as she made the same move on the other side. We now stood slightly behind Faran, with the head of the goddess between us.

Siri spoke again. "Faran Ghostwind, you have chosen the way of ordeal. Assume your place."

Faran nodded and leaned back against the head of the goddess, extending her arms behind her so that the backs of her wrists touched the goddess's temples. "I am ready."

Siri looked at me again as she raised the sword and turned it carefully, placing the point against the inside of Faran's right wrist, its back toward her palm. I mirrored her action, though what I really wanted to do was swear and shout and call the whole thing off.

"The ordeal begins now." Siri drove the sword through Faran's wrist, sinking it deep into the stone.

I did the same. There was a tiny bit of resistance as the point passed through Faran's flesh, but virtually none at all when it hit the stone. Pushing it forward until the hilt touched Faran's skin took virtually no physical effort, though the emotional cost made me want to vomit.

Faran's back arched and every muscle in her body went tight and hard. But she didn't cry out. It wasn't until the blood started dripping from the corner of her mouth that I realized she'd bitten her lip through in her efforts to remain silent. More blood rolled slowly down the stone from Faran's wrists, though nowhere near as much as I would have expected from such wounds.

Nor was Ssithra spared the ordeal. Faran had drawn her familiar around her, forming a second, shadowy skin as part of the ritual, just as the rest of us had. Now Ssithra's substance roiled and twisted around the place where the steel pierced her partner's flesh, and I knew that Ssithra had submerged neither will nor sensation for the ordeal.

I couldn't resist the urge to tug ever so lightly on the

sword as I stepped back and slid my grip free of the hilt to mirror Siri's actions. It felt as tightly fixed in the stone as if it had been pounded into place with a sledgehammer. When Siri moved back around in front of Faran and lowered herself to sit cross-legged there, I quickly joined her. It reduced the temptation to try to wrench the sword from the stone—an act I knew to be both against the spirit of the ritual and quite futile. That sword wasn't going anywhere before the proper ritual conditions had been fulfilled.

Siri didn't look any happier about the thing than I felt, and I could hear her slow-counting the seconds away under her breath. By the time the tally reached ten minutes, I thought that I would burst. More than ever I wanted to scream this horror to a halt. But if Faran could bear the pain in silence, I knew that I couldn't fail her by doing less.

When half an hour had passed, Siri touched my shoulder and we rose together.

"Faran Ghostwind, you have stood the test of pain," said Siri. "You may now release yourself or ask for aid. In either case, the time has come to see if you have proven worthy of the swords of justice."

Faran nodded grimly. She was covered in sweat, and the blood from her lip had run down her chin and neck all the way to the tip of her right breast. Without speaking, she tightened the muscles in her shoulders and chest, pulling. . . .

For nearly a minute nothing seemed to happen. Then, with a low grating sound, her wrists moved an inch or so out from the stone, dragging the swords with them. Faran paused for a moment, visibly relaxing her arms. Blood flowed more freely now, though still only a fraction of what I might have expected. Ten seconds she waited, breathing slowly. Then she strained again. This time the response from the swords was faster. The hilts moved a good ten inches, pivoting forward as well as sliding outward, without leaving any obvious marks in the stone head.

Another brief pause. Faran's breath came quicker and more erratic now, and the blood from her bitten lip dripped faster. Her eyes found mine then, and held as she pulled again. I willed her success as I matched her gaze and refused to look away.

With the faintest of pops the swords came free of the stone—later, I would look and find that they had left no marks there. I bit my own lip nearly bloody as Faran brought her arms around in front of her and took the hilt of the sword that pierced her right wrist in her left hand.

"I am Faran Ghostwind and I claim this sword in the name of justice." She pulled it free of her flesh in a long smooth motion that must have cost her dearly in pain.

The blood that should have burst from such a suddenly opened wound didn't come as she turned her right hand and caught the hilt standing out from her left wrist before pulling it loose as well. "This sword, too, I claim as mine by right of ordeal. What say you, Challenger?"

Siri stepped forward and rubbed the blood away from Faran's wrist. There was no wound, only a narrow scar that looked as if it had been there for years. Healing without spell-light and beyond anything a mortal healer could manage. It smacked of god-magic.

"I am Siri Mythkiller and I speak for the challenge. The sword has accepted its master. I say that the petitioner has earned the right to call herself Blade. Sponsor?"

I repeated Siri's performance with Faran's other wrist, exposing a second scar. "I am Aral Kingslayer, First Blade of Namara, and I speak for the order. Welcome, Faran Ghostwind, Blade of Justice."

Faran sheathed her swords. "Blade of Justice . . . I like the sound of that." She smiled at me, then swayed alarmingly. "Can I pass out now?"

"Only if you really want to."

"Will you catch me?"

"Of course."

She fell into my arms and darkness together.

16

---·---

A scar is a history of pain written on skin. Mine are palely drawn, cream on sepia—the book of my past reversing the typical colors of ink and paper. But then, my whole life reverses the order of day and night and so many other conventions.

Such were my thoughts while I waited for Faran to wake. Scars and what they say about us seemed terribly important as I contemplated the fresh marks on Faran's wrists. Once Siri and the others released the wards, I had carried Faran to the grass beyond the stone circle and gently lowered her to the ground, placing her head in my lap.

Kumi brought over a couple of ponchos to make a blanket for the unconscious girl, covering her from toes to chin. For reasons she didn't choose to share, she had very carefully crossed Faran's arms on her chest above the fabric, exposing her new scars to the moonlight and my contemplation. I don't know how long I sat there ruminating on the way the past writes itself into our flesh, but after a time Siri came and stood above me. I didn't really notice her until Triss gave me a mental nudge.

I looked up. "Yes, Siri?"

"We've cleaned up from the ritual and figured out how we can improve it next time. Now we need to start looking for those lost swords. Do you want to leave Faran here, or should we start without you?"

Before I could answer, Faran stirred, roused perhaps by the speaking of her name. She looked up into my face and smiled. "Hey there, old man, you look worried. I hope it's not about me, because I'm fine." She blinked and her expression clouded. "Unless that whole thing was a nightmare . . ."

"Nope. You, my young monster, are now the first fully initiated Blade since the fall of the temple. Welcome to the club. It's small enough that we can hold meetings in a rowboat these days."

"Well, we'd better do something about that, then, hadn't we?" She looked up at Siri. "Did I hear you say it was time to look for the swords? Because I want a piece of that."

"You heard right, *Master* Faran." Siri grinned down at the younger woman. "And, may I say that it feels just this side of miraculous to welcome a new sister to the order at this late date." She squatted and extended her arm in formal greeting.

"Master Faran, and for real, finally and truly . . . that sounds fucking fantastic." Faran laughed and sat up, clasping forearms with Siri. "Thank you, Master Siri. I am delighted to . . ." She glanced down then, and I could see a blush darken the back of her neck, as she snatched up the fallen poncho and covered her breasts. "You know, maybe I ought to shut up and put some clothes on before I contemplate doing anything else."

I blinked at that. Faran had never exhibited much in the way of modesty before this moment—take for example the cheerful way she'd stripped down and tossed her clothes into one of the floating baskets before swimming across to the island earlier—and I wasn't sure what had triggered an attack of it now.

"It's up to you," I said, "but I suspect that we're going to be doing a good bit of our searching underwater along the edge of the island."

"Maybe just a bandeau then. Siri, would you be so kind as to . . ." She trailed off when Kumi appeared to offer her a scarf of mottled gray silk—repurposed from someone's cowl.

"Thank you." Faran nabbed the scarf and slid it under the poncho, deftly tying it in place. "Good to go now. Let's find those swords."

Siri took Faran's arm again, pulling the younger woman to her feet as she stood.

I think I missed something there, I sent to Triss. *Any idea what it was?*

None at all . . . Well, that's not entirely true. It is often the case that when your people do things that confuse mine it has to do with the way your species absolutely obsesses about sex. Given that, and your occasionally bizarre fixation on nudity, the odds are decent that it was a sex thing of some sort, though I couldn't say what.

Not sure why it would matter now when it didn't two hours ago, but you might be right. I shrugged. *I guess it's not my worry, whatever it is. Let's hit the water.*

Aral, *I don't want you to make any sudden moves, but you should probably turn around.*

Triss's mental voice sounded more cautious than alarmed, so I didn't immediately spin away from the underwater crevice I'd been prodding with the tip of one of my swords. Instead, I very carefully pulled my sword free and, as casually as I could manage it, rotated in the water. That allowed me to bring my sword around to a place where I could easily use it without making an overtly threatening gesture. I didn't know what Triss had spotted, but his tone suggested that it was potentially dangerous, if not immediately so.

And . . . I blinked several times.

. . . So *that* was what the front end of the hunters in the deep looked like. The enormous face reminded me of nothing so much as what you would get if you crossbred one of the ancient bewhiskered bureaucrats that ran Tien's government offices with a catfish.

A wide lipless mouth big enough to swallow me whole. Scales the color of new copper coins danced across black in jagged lightning-like bands. One long whisker at each corner of the mouth, with a half-dozen shorter ones along the jaw. Barbels, really, or maybe tentacles, since they looked more flexible than the ones you normally found on carp or catfish. High bulging forehead, like no fish you ever saw, and wise eyes, green and luminous—totally unlike anything else in the piscine world.

Well, hello there! I sent silently to Triss.

The fish flicked the longer tentacle-whiskers at the side of its mouth back and forth in a distinctly apologetic gesture. *I'm sorry, could you repeat that? You spoke quickly, and your mind flavor is . . . odd to these ancient tasters.*

That was a surprise and a half, but I nodded. What? I was going to say no to the enormous but thus far polite fish who could as easily have devoured me?

I'm sorry, I sent, aiming my thoughts forward now instead of inward, and trying to enunciate as slowly and clearly as I might when trying to make myself understood in a language I had not yet mastered. *I was speaking to my companion, and I didn't realize you could hear me. What I said was: "Well, hello there."*

Ahh, sent the fish. *Much better. May I make an enquiry?*

You may, I replied, unsure of how literal minded it might be.

Companion?

Yes. Triss? I carefully directed the second word down the link between me and my familiar. *Make yourself known, please.*

Of course, he replied and my shadow shifted, assuming the form of a small dragon that flicked its wings to rise and hover beside me in the water.

The shadow of a dragon without the dragon, sent the fish. *Excellent. I was sent to find the one called Kingslayer, and now I see that I have.*

Sent? I enquired, wondering without asking, by whom? And, for what? *Also, may I ask whom I am addressing? It's customary among my kind to introduce oneself.*

Oh. How odd. I am: image of scales flashing bright in a cloud of churned-up bottom mud. *In your tongue . . . Mudlight? Yes, I think Mudlight is closest. The chief of my clan/school/pod, Slitherstrong, asked that I find and lead you to the gullet of Namara.*

I felt a surge of excitement, and wished that I could mindspeak to Triss without any danger of sharing my message with other ears. I responded to Mudlight instead. *If that is what I hope it is, I should collect some of the others first. . . .*

Mudlight flicked his barbels again. *Slitherstrong has already anticipated you. Others were sent to find Mythkiller, Ghostwind, Deathwalker, and . . . Is it Dukesbane? The translation didn't make much sense. Oh, and the two who do not yet own proper callings . . . Kumi and Roric, I think they are . . . named.* The huge fish sounded out the syllables as though the idea of names that didn't describe were utterly alien to it.

I thank you, Mudlight. Though I must admit surprise that you know all of our callings.

We watched you cross from the . . . groundsea? Would that be the word in your tongue? Doesn't matter. That is how it ought *to translate, that is how I will call it. We watched your passage through our realm to the dirtplace of the goddess, guarding your flanks and unders as we promised your Namara that we would when we made our bargain with her.*

Thank you, sent Triss, his mental voice possessing a sort of weird echoey quality as he projected it outward. *We did not know that you were there to protect us.*

The fish bobbed its head in a sort of bow. *Namara is gone, but as long as her children, both of flesh and shadow, remain and return, we will watch and ward you, just as we watched and warded when you raised the head of the goddess. Or when our shamans listened from the pool while you made the Ghostwind one of you. There is very little that passes through our realm that escapes our attention.*

I guess I'm ready then, I sent. *Lead on.*

We will go faster if I tow you. May I hold your hand? It will not harm you.

All right, I sent, though the idea made me nervous.

Mudlight turned his head and reached out with his long right barbel. It wasn't until he actually caught my hand that I realized the last ten inches of it could split apart, giving the fish a pair of large and very flexible tentacle-fingers. Before I had time to do much more than register surprise, Mudlight rolled sideways, pulling me away from the rocks. Then, with a sort of sinewy twist, he began to slither through the water at a speed that would have torn me free of his grip were it even a tithe less firm. As a mode of travel it lacked something, and we left my stomach far behind in the first few seconds.

If you don't mind my asking, I sent once I had recovered some measure of my calm, *what do your people call yourselves?*

We are: sweeping tails, flashing scales, churning fins, songs and sins . . . The images and sounds went on for some time in a sort of kaleidoscopic poetry of the senses that I found as deeply beautiful as it was incomprehensible.

But that is not, I think, what you really want to know, Mudlight sent when he had finished. *The Lady of Leivas named us Storm Eels, and that suits us well enough for dealing with your kind.*

Speaking of which, I sent, *all these years and you never contacted us before this—at least not that I ever heard about. Why now?*

When your goddess lay dying, we comforted her as best we could, buoying her soul up with our songs. She made of us certain requests then. Till now, the conditions to fulfill any of them had never been met. . . . He sent the mental equivalent of a shrug, or, at least, that's what I took away from the image of gills flicking, and the emotional undertone that went with it.

I— Mudlight's mental voice went suddenly silent. He stopped swimming a moment later. *Bide. One calls.*

I caught only the faintest hint of whatever was occupying him . . . the spillover from an absolute torrent of images and sensations shooting back and forth from one alien mind to another. It felt a bit like overhearing a fast discussion conducted in a foreign language by people who are experts in a very complex field of endeavor—tons of information being conveyed quickly with little in the way of the sort of side talk that happens in normal conversation at the market or tavern. Finally, it stopped.

I'm sorry, sent Mudlight. *There has been an unpleasantness at your temple. The*: images of rotting corpses that moved where no life should exist, anger at a violation of nature, decaying smells as conveyed through water, *have come. They tried to get in through the water ways, but we stopped them there.*

The risen?!? I sent, urgently. *Were any of the students harmed?*

Your younglings are fine, but we will have to get them out. There is a chance that the . . . risen, you call them?

Yes, sent Triss. *They wear the bodies of fallen humans, but really they are a sort of elemental of death, just as I am a spirit of shadow.*

Thank you for the word and the explanation, sent Mudlight. *The risen, then. There is a chance that they will be able to get at your young from above somehow. They are much stronger on land than they are when they enter our element, so we will bring your young out here to the dirt-place of Namara, where we can better protect them. Your Dukesbane has gone with Finflyer to explain it to them so that our presence will not bring them fear.*

That's a great relief, I sent. *Thank you.* I thought for a moment. *I don't know how far beyond the edges of your realm you can see. Do you know if there are other forces besides the risen around the temple?*

No, nor how many of the risen there are above the waves. We cannot see more than a few body lengths beyond the edges of our realm, though we can tell you that the undersanctuary where your young lie hidden remains yet inviolate. We see and hear much through the wellhead there.

I'm not sure what brought you to our aid at this time, Mudlight, I sent, *but it is very good to find that we have allies still in this world, however unexpected.*

I wish we knew more about what might be happening with the temple, Triss sent to me.

Mudlight answered him with the shrug image. *The risen entered our domain, and so we found them. Some few very strong ones came on toward the dirtplace, burrowing through the muck on the bottom, but most moved into the temple tunnels once they entered the water. If they are truly death elementals as you say, they probably sensed the life there, and hoped to pry it out like a clam from its shell. I imagine that once we move your young they will turn their attention this way again.*

Are there very many of them, do you think? I asked.

We have already devoured more than your numbers, and at least that many remain in sight of our shores. We will feed well tonight. They are very easy prey once you break their connection with the floor of the lake, but you must eat them quickly or lose the best meat—the currents scrub the flesh from their bones if they're exposed to it for long.

You eat them? I was appalled. *Doesn't that make you ill?*

Our kind began as bottom-feeders. We have grown much since those days, and we have learned to hunt for fresher prey, but the old ways are good, too. Horrible your risen are and steeped in evil, but delicious as well. The magic in them makes a fine sauce to go with well-aged flesh for such as we. But, come, we have stopped here too long already. I was supposed to see to it that you arrive at the gullet first. I must make haste if I am not to fail in my charge.

I thought that we had been traveling fast before, but now . . . The enormous eel-like fish tucked me in tight against its side and flew through water like a stooping gryphon. In a matter of minutes he had brought me around to the far side of the island and down almost to the bottom of the lake.

There, he aimed directly for a jagged rock ledge without slowing.

For a brief moment I thought we would collide with it to our ruin. But then, what had looked like a band of dark rock turned out to be a deeply shaded and overhung rift in the stone. Before I had time for more than the briefest flash of panic, we were through and into a column of incredibly clear water with bright stars shining down from somewhere above.

Where are we? I asked.

My initial thought was that it reminded me of the sacred pool, but we were about halfway around the island from where it ought to be, if I'd kept anything of my bearings. More importantly, there was something decidedly wrong with the sky, though at first I couldn't think of what. It was only as we climbed higher in the water column that I realized the moon had vanished and taken all the familiar constellations with it. I repeated my question about our whereabouts, as Mudlight hadn't yet answered.

This is Namara's hallow, her abode in the mortal world.

What's wrong with the sky? asked Triss, his mental voice querulous. *Those aren't the stars as I know them. They are too dim, and some of them move. . . .*

They what? As we got closer, I could see that he was right. Some of what I had taken to be stars were moving slowly and seemingly randomly across the dome of the . . . heavens? Sky? The color of the "stars" was wrong, too, a green-tinged blue that exhibited none of the variation I was used to seeing above me. *I don't understand.*

They are no stars, sent Mudlight. *Nor is that the sky. The goddess did not wish to be observed here. Neither by mortal eyes or divine, or so our ancient legends tell us. She made this cave under the heart of her island and she hallowed it and sealed it against all scrying and prying. But she missed the stars, for she was a goddess who loved the night.*

So, he continued, *she made her own stars from what she had to hand—tiny worms that hunt in the dark. She gave them light to comfort her, but she was a wise goddess and*

*made sure that it would serve them as well, by drawing the
gnats and flies that are their prey.*

I felt a stirring then in the waters beneath us. But when
I looked down, I could see nothing but blackness. Even my
night-trained vision couldn't penetrate the darkness below
without more light than worms could provide.

Tailnipper has joined us, sent Mudlight. *He brings Mythkiller, and Deepdiver comes behind bearing Ghostwind. I
will take you to the surface and then get out of the way. This
well can only hold a few of our kind, and there will be much
coming and going as we deliver your young. Call for me if
you need me anywhere within the bounds of our realm. I
will come as quick as I can.*

Mudlight's head broke the surface as he finished sending
that last, and he deftly swung me over to the shore. I have
made the transition from water-breathing to air-breathing a
dozen or more times, and it is never a graceful one. I spent
the next several seconds coughing water out of my lungs.
By the time I was in any shape to speak again Mudlight had
vanished.

"Not much on good-byes, are they?" Siri said a moment
later, though not in a way that invited a response.

Honestly, that was all to the good, because I had found
the lost swords. . . .

The goddess had forged her weapons out of black steel
taken from the hearts of fallen stars, and then she imbued
them with the stuff of the everdark. Namara's swords are
assassin's blades and all but invisible in the night. But where
the swords themselves could not be seen, the glowworms
that hung from them made each one into a sort of constel-
lation of its own.

If the glowworms made a shimmering heaven of the cav-
ern's ceiling, the swords were a swarm of slashing comets
cutting their way through the false night. They were scattered
in pairs throughout the cave, seemingly at random both in
terms of height and placement.

"What's holding them up?" Faran asked after some minutes of silence had passed. "I'd expect more of those glowing

worms to be attached to whatever it is, but I'm not seeing anything like that."

"I have no idea." I'd been wondering that myself. "Let's go look."

The six of us—Kumi, Roric, and Kelos had arrived shortly after Faran—crossed the short distance to the nearest low-hanging set. There were two pairs we could have gotten to quicker, but both were well out of easy reach. These weren't much above eye level. But on closer examination we were none the wiser.

"They look like they're just hanging in space without so much as a wire for support." Triss formed himself into a ring and passed completely around the swords as a test. "I can't find anything, physical, magical, or other dimensional. For all that I can tell, Namara simply put them there and told them to stay."

I looked over at Siri. "You're the order's magus, our highest officer for things of spell craft. Any thoughts on what we should do next?"

"God-magic makes me nervous," she replied, "even Namara's god-magic. It doesn't project spell-light, or follow any of the rules the rest of us have to play by." The worms cast enough light that I could easily see the pensive look on her face. "I really don't know."

Faran snorted. "Too much thinking, not enough doing." She reached up and grabbed the paired hilts.

I found myself drawing in a sharp anticipatory breath, but nothing blew up or started on fire. In fact, nothing happened at all.

I let myself breathe again. "Faran, don't ever do that again, all right?"

She turned and grinned at me without letting go of the swords. "Done. I will never ever be the first person to touch one of these beauties again."

"Thank you for drawing the narrowest possible lesson," I grumbled.

"Any time. It's one of my best skills, you know."

Siri glared at both of us. "If you two are done with the

witty banter, I'd like to hear more about why Faran hasn't done anything more than touch the swords yet."

"Can't," replied Faran. "Watch." She lifted herself off the ground, using the hilts like parallel chinning bars. "They're as firmly fixed as if they'd been sunk in stone."

"That could pose a problem for initiating more Blades," I said.

"May I try?" asked Kelos.

Faran shrugged and dropped free of the swords. "Be my guest, though I don't think adding an extra helping of manly to the table is the answer."

"It almost never is," agreed Siri. "But they just keep trying."

"It's sad, really," replied Faran.

Kelos ignored them as he reached up and yanked on first one hilt and then the other. Nothing. Next, he shifted his grip, so that both hands were on one sword, and swung up to brace his feet against the other. His shoulders creaked and popped as he pushed on it with everything he had.

More nothing.

After a few minutes of various brute force efforts, Kelos dropped free. "They're not moving for anything."

I was still wondering what to try next, when Kumi stepped past me and bowed deeply to the hanging swords. "I honor the goddess who placed you here. Please honor my desire to follow in her path." Then she reached up, took one sword in each hand and, as easily and gently as you could imagine, she pulled them free of whatever held them.

Kelos turned sharply to look down at the young woman. "How did you do that, girl?"

She smiled and bowed to Kelos. "I realized that the problem might not be one of how, Master Kelos, but rather, one of who. You have no need of more swords, and they have no need of you."

17

<hr />

I despise the ease with which the horrific can transform itself into the routine. Extraordinary ordeal becomes expected ritual. Ritual becomes practice. Practice becomes convention. And, all too soon, something that should never have happened in the first place becomes *the way it has always been done*.

Kumi claimed that having the swords come loose at her touch put her next in line to attempt the rite of attunement. A fair argument. Like Faran—and despite having witnessed exactly what she was getting into—Kumi chose the way of ordeal. She asked Faran to be her Sponsor and Kelos her Challenger. Roric came next and chose ordeal as well—I suspect because he didn't want to be seen to have less courage than the pair that had gone before. Jax was his Sponsor with Faran as Challenger, and Siri and Kumi playing the roles of the Wardens of the East and West. Maryam chose Jax as well, with Roric applying the challenge.

And so it went, ordeal after ordeal after ordeal, with Jax playing the role of Sponsor most often. Challenger shifted quite a bit, as did the Wardens, but Kelos played no role after Kumi, while Faran, Siri, and I were only rarely called on. Not one of the students failed, though several passed out while hanging from the swords. Many screamed and swore or cried, and only a few had the same degree of miraculous healing that Faran had. But even in those cases, the Shades could taste the difference in the steel and verify that the rite had taken.

Would the gentler petition by entreaty have worked as well? I don't know, and I doubt that I ever shall.

Every Blade that comes after this class will choose ordeal. Of that I have little doubt. Assuming that we are able to continue forward, those who take up their swords after the death of the goddess will see those wrist scars as much as a mark of passage as bonding with a Shade or being made a journeyman. An extreme event, designed in haste, and chosen out of expedience to suit the exceptional, will have become the customary because it will ever and always be *the way these things are done.*

If I survive as First Blade, I will certainly endeavor to find a means to gentle the thing, but my experience with my fellows does not leave me much room for hope on that front. We are, as a group, dedicated to the darkness of our calling as much as the light. The horrible romance of making a personal blood sacrifice to demonstrate devotion to the ideal of justice will have a powerful allure.

It took two nights of blood and magic and pain, but at the end of that time, the number of full Blades stood at twenty-one—excluding Kelos and the others who had betrayed the goddess. Nearly a tenfold increase from a week ago, but still only a tithe of our strength before the fall. I hoped that what we had begun here was a new era for justice, but feared it might amount to little more than putting a boot to the headsman on the way to the block.

Not that I intended to stop kicking one instant before the axe fell.

"I hate this!" snapped Jax.

"I know," I answered her. "That doesn't change my decision."

The rituals were all done. We'd slept the sun from east to west. And we'd eaten as much of a celebratory banquet as we could manage. Now that I had done all that I could to ensure there would be an order to come back to, and despite the gravest sorts of misgivings, it was time for me to head for my long delayed appointment with the Son of Heaven.

But I had dealt Jax out of that play, and she didn't like it one bit. Exhibiting wisdom earned the hard way in the years when Jax and I had been a couple, Triss and Sshayar had decided to let us work it out on our own, and simply vanished into the surrounding shadows.

I put my hands on Jax's shoulders and spoke quietly. "You know as well as I do that there's only one logical choice to leave in charge of this crew." I inclined my head toward the place where most of the others were picking over the remains of our meager feast. "Siri is compromised by her divine infection. Kelos is Kelos. Faran simultaneously scares those who know her well and irritates most of the rest by being younger and obviously better than they are. I *have* to go. That leaves you."

Jax took a deep breath. "I know all that, and I didn't say I wouldn't do it. I just hate it." Now she fixed me with her hardest stare. "Oh, and if you don't come back from this, I swear that I will track your ghost down and pickle it in a bottle of vinegar."

"Harsh." I grinned. "But probably fair, though I do have to protest the vinegar. You could at least make it good Aveni whiskey. Kyle's eighteen, maybe?"

"Don't you think you've spent enough time marinating in a whiskey bottle?" she asked.

She said it gently enough, but it burned, and I actually welcomed the pain. That I had even mentioned the Kyle's said things about what was going on in the back of my head that I didn't like. I had conquered my drinking for the moment, but I was under no illusions that I couldn't lose myself in the bottle again if I let my guard relax.

There were too many times when I really, really wanted to just let everything go for a while, as I used to be able to when I had a bottle to hand. Like, say, every single time I remembered what it felt like to put a sword through Faran's wrist, a memory that wasn't going to fade any time soon. Or when I thought about actually killing the Son of Heaven and what that would mean for the world as opposed to the more straightforward task of reaching him.

"Aral?" Jax spoke with a note of real concern. "Are you all right? I'm sorry. I didn't mean to—"

I put a finger to her lips. "I know you didn't, and you've no reason to apologize for anything. But that was point and bout together, and . . . well, let's leave it at that."

"All right." She nodded. "So, next thing on my list."

"Wait, there's a list?"

"Of course there's a list." She glanced skyward as if asking for patience. "It's like you don't know me at all . . . which might explain why our engagement foundered on the rocks, actually."

This time I smiled at her tease. It was delivered in a manner more barbed and arch, but simultaneously much less painful than the whiskey comment. The book on that relationship had closed long ago, and I couldn't imagine it ever opening again.

"It might explain it at that," I said. "So, your list . . ."

"First, I don't want you to go alone."

"We won't," said Triss, obviously deciding that we had moved away from the dangerous personal topics. "Siri will be with us, and Faran."

"Yes, and Kelos." Jax lifted an eyebrow. "The very three people you said couldn't be trusted to run things here in your absence."

"Not fair," said Sshayar. "The reasoning and structure of a mission to kill the Son of Heaven is completely different from that of maintaining the beginnings of a new order of Blades."

Jax snorted and put the back of a hand to her forehead. "Betrayed by mine own shadow. Oh, the indignity. La."

"Not that she's wrong about any of that," I said.

"Not that she's wrong," agreed Jax. She held up a finger.

"I suspect that Faran would eat her own heart raw if she thought it would protect you at this point—foolish girl." Another finger. "I trust Siri completely where neither you nor she does. Even if you have killed another king since the last time I saw you, she's still better than you are. And that's without whatever new secret talents she's added along with the smoke in her hair." She added a thumb. "Kelos is Kelos. I don't trust him, but if your interests and his coincide, as I think they do here, there is quite literally no one in the world better to guard your back."

I suppose that I should have been surprised that she'd figured out Siri had a new set of hole cards, but I wasn't—Jax is very smart. "So, what's your point?" I asked. "Or list? Or whatever it is you were about to get at?"

"I want you to take Maryam with you, and Roric."

"Absolutely not. This mission is already too big for my comfort. Trying to sneak four assassins in close to the Son of Heaven is probably three too many. An army isn't what I need here."

"And I'm not suggesting you bring one." Before I could respond, Jax held up a hand. "I'm not finished. I don't want them to go all the way in with you. I want them to ride along as observers and to be there to provide an outside distraction if you need one unexpectedly—not to help directly. I damned well want to know *exactly* what happened if you don't come back, and they're my way of keeping an eye on you. Besides, they'll keep Kumi company."

"Who said Kumi was coming?" asked Triss.

Jax rolled her eyes. "Have you not noticed that Faran has a second shadow now? Or a third, if you count Ssithra. Faran will go because Aral is going, and no one is going to be able to change that. The same I think is true of Kumi and Faran."

Now that she had pointed it out, I realized she might have a point. Kumi had stayed very close to Faran ever since the fight on the trail. "Huh, I wonder why that is."

Jax shrugged. "If I understood how the young think, I might have done a better job at that age myself. All I know is what I have observed while trying to play den mother to this pack of wild young killers. One such pithy observation is that they form all sorts of deep attachments for no apparent rhyme or reason and without any recourse for talking sense into them. She might look up to Faran as an idol despite being the older of the pair. She might see her as the sister of her heart. Or she could be head over heels in love. Sometimes it's very hard to sort out the one from the other even for them, I think."

I thought back to my own mad crushes and inseparable friendships from those days and laughed. "Those were interesting years. I wonder if what has happened between Devin and me since then would have turned out differently if we'd been lovers instead of just friends?"

Now it was Jax's turn to laugh. "It might have done his obsession with you a world of good. Sharing your bed for a couple of years certainly disabused me of any notion that you were perfect. Too bad he's never gone for guys."

I nodded. "I did offer once, but he's much firmer in his preferences than most of the rest of us. Or, most mages in general, for that matter."

"The familiar gift does seem to walk hand in hand with a more omnivorous sort of desire," said Jax. "I wonder why that is?"

"Does this mean we've finished with your list?" I asked.

"Not even close. Besides, you haven't yet said whether you'll take Roric and Maryam."

"I will. I think you're right about Kumi, whatever her reasons, and having her added officially with the other pair will make that all less awkward. So, what's up next?"

"Mostly sorting out the shadow council and the succession in case you and Siri are both killed. There were ten members in the old days. I think we'll want to halve that unless and until there are a lot more of us than the current total."

I sighed. Jax was right that all of this really needed dealing with before we left, but it wasn't going to be much fun. "All right, you're obviously stuck with First Blade if I end

up as a stuffed trophy in the Son of Heaven's hunting lodge.
That probably makes Javan magus, and . . ."

"**Kill** them?" asked Kelos.

I looked down on the campsite below us and pondered
the question. The risen that had attempted the goddess's
island had come from here. That was clear enough, given
the evidence of the wicker cage chariots and the fact that
we were barely more than a couple of bowshots from the
shores of the sacred lake. The Caeni troops would certainly
kill us if they got the chance. So would the dozen or so
heavily armored types wearing the insignia of the Sword of
Heaven. The lone member of the Hand that they were escort-
ing might or might not depending on who was watching and
whether she was aligned with Toragana's faction or more of
a mind with Chomarr.

Finally, I shook my head and gestured for us to move
back over the crest before speaking. "It's tempting," I said
once we were far enough away to talk quietly without worrying about being overheard, "but no. I don't think killing
them would serve justice. They're not directly in our way
and, once the Son of Heaven is removed, none of them may
even be enemies of ours anymore."

I paused for a moment then as I found myself suddenly
in want of more air. While we had been sorting out the matter of the students and the swords, I was able to put aside
most of my worries about the Son of Heaven and what killing him might mean for the broader world. I had even been
able to convince myself that I was comfortable with the
decision to go after him.

But that was all a lie. Actually talking about it brought
every one of the doubts and fears that had been lurking in
the back of my mind roaring in again as if they'd only been
waiting for the right moment to pounce.

There had been significant costs to this mission already,
both on the personal front and the broader scale of nations.
The battle at Wall. Dalridia engulfed in war. Jax's brother

falling to the invaders. The Avarsi we had slaughtered on our way out of Dalridia. Altia's death in the mountains . . . Enormous amounts of blood had been spilled, and we hadn't yet come within a thousand miles of Heaven's Reach. I had no doubts that there would be more blood spilled before we reached our destination. By us if we were smart and lucky. Our own if we weren't.

Even with Siri's new powers, and if I recovered Signet Nea's finger and it worked to our maximum advantage, I had my doubts about managing it. But if we somehow managed to succeed and make an end of the Son of Heaven and his risen puppets?

At the very least there would be wars and upheaval on a scale that hadn't been seen in a thousand years. The lakes of blood we had created so far would become a vast sea of crimson. And however much it might ultimately be the fault of the Son of Heaven, *proximally* it would be *my* decision that triggered the coming days of long knives. . . .

Aral? Triss sent, his tone rife with concern. *They're waiting for you to finish your thought. Are you all right?*

Not really, no, I replied. *But that doesn't change what I have to do.* I gave myself a little mental shake. *Thanks for the prompt, old friend.*

"We'll let them go," I said, as though I'd never gotten lost in my own head. "Both because we don't need to kill them, and because the death of that Hand down there would bring on a storm. That would seriously interfere with our progress if we take the lake path at the same time it alerted others to her fall."

"It's your call." Kelos sounded disappointed.

I looked at him. "It is that, but I'm willing to entertain arguments that go the other way. Did you have something you wanted to add there?"

Kelos sighed, and for the first time in all the years I had known him, he looked embarrassed. "One thing only. I was hoping for a chance to test a bit of magic I spent most of last year working on."

Siri cleared her throat before stepping in. "This is the

first you've mentioned anything like that. Care to elaborate?"

Kelos looked from her to me, and then over her shoulder to where the others knelt in the darkness farther down the hill. "Not really, but I'd better. You know that when I took service with the Son of Heaven, my initial plan involved getting Aral to kill the man and becoming the new Son of Heaven myself. Not for the power, of course, but for the chance to smash the very idea of a noble class."

"Of course." Faran's tone was deliberately colorless, but still managed to leave no doubt as to her true feelings about Kelos and his *noble* aims.

Kelos continued as if she hadn't spoken. "I presume Aral's also mentioned why I couldn't kill the Son myself?"

"You're talking about the geas all you Shadow of Heaven types had to bind yourself with before he would let you into his presence?" said Siri. "Yes, it's come up."

Kelos nodded. "I thought it might have. However, I don't know if Aral also told you that the geas bound me to do no harm to anyone who serves the Son either."

Siri and Faran both nodded, while the other three young Blades simply remained quiet, so Kelos continued. "Obviously it doesn't extend to the risen of his curse—the Son would have had to admit to what he is in order to set that condition. But, with that one exception, it was a very tight leash indeed that he bound us with. After Aral put me on the wrong side of my first plan, I suddenly found myself in need of a way to slip it."

"And . . ." said Siri.

"And I still don't know. I think I've found my loophole, but magical loopholes are inherently chancy things. Especially where god-magic is involved. I can't even *see* the portion of the spell that the Son arranged through his god, and that means I can't know if I've done the trick entire, short of a working test."

"Hence the interest in yonder batch of Heaven's Sword," said Ssithra.

Kelos nodded. "Exactly. I was rather hoping to take a

shot at these charming villains here while I have you all as backup, in case I couldn't touch them, and when there were miles yet to go to Heaven's Reach. Or, failing this particular bunch, others in the same sort of case. But if Aral's going to go all *no just cause* on us, that will make the testing of things a bit more challenging."

"I know you," I said, flatly. "You wouldn't have stopped experimenting with your spells unless you'd successfully managed some sort of test already. I would bet a pint of my own blood that you killed at least a couple of people wearing the Son's livery before ever you came looking for the Key of Sylvaras back in the Sylvain."

"Two Hands, four Swords, and three priests of the Voice." Kelos nodded.

"Not to mention all those Kvani who invaded Dalridia on hidden orders from the Son," added Faran.

Kelos shrugged. "Right enough, but every minion of his that I've killed has been far from home and short on any direct link to their master's orders. That tells me that I've loosened the leash considerably, but I won't know if I'm entirely free of it without facing off against someone operating directly under the Son's orders while wearing his colors openly."

"That does change the weight of things," I said. "We need to know what your limitations are *before* we get someplace where they might cost us the mission."

I thought the whole thing through again, and again decided against killing the group on the other side of the hill—in part because turning Kelos down would serve as something of a test of how he might react if our purposes eventually crossed for real.

"No," I said. "This isn't the time or the place. I still maintain that attacking this group wouldn't advance justice and, whatever else we are, we are servants of justice first."

Kelos sighed and nodded. "You always were the most stubborn of my students."

I let out a little mental sigh of my own at his surrender of the point. That was a good sign, if a small one.

Now to throw him a bone to gnaw on. "Mind you, if it were Lieutenant Chomarr down there instead of some random Hand and her Sword backers, I would happily grant the exception. He seems the *perfect* test case for you."

"True that." Then Kelos grinned. "It's not like we won't have plenty more opportunities to eliminate opposition on our way to Heaven's Reach. I imagine we'll be tripping over enemies the whole way."

"*Which* is exactly why I think we'll do better taking the water route and the long way around," I said. "If we go straight across the Kvanas we're looking at weeks of flatland and little cover beyond the grass sea itself. That would be more than bad enough, given that the whole country is roused against us, and even if you didn't add in the restless dead. With them? Getting caught out on the flats by the risen will get us all killed, goddess-forged swords or no. Anyone think otherwise?"

Nobody wanted to argue the point, so I continued. "That leaves three options. Skirting the mountains would be fastest, but it's also what they'll be expecting since it'd save us at least a month of travel time over the next shortest route."

"I don't much like the idea of following the Kvani scarp, either," said Siri. "Yes, it offers cover on one flank, but it's flat above and a hard scramble over broken rock below. Add in the Avarsi patrols and fortifications and it's one of the least hospitable places I can think of."

Three of the four Kvanas shared a high flat plateau. The scarp ran along its western edge, loosely defining the border between Avars and Radewald on the southwest and Dan Eyre on the northwest. It was a huge natural fortification, and the Avarsi had been using it to drop boulders on the neighbors for centuries. They had a thick network of forts strung along its whole length and they patrolled the area constantly.

"Which leads us back to the water route," I said. "We'll need to acquire a good boat or two, but once we've done that we can cross Leivas, exit by the river, pass Hove and most of Radewald on the west, and then take the river Dan much of the way back east to the foothills of the Almarn Mountains."

"That or take the fork that leads past Luvarn Keep in Avars," said Kelos. "I think you're right either way, but it's going to double the distance we have to cover and add nearly that much in terms of time."

"But most of it spent on wild water," said Faran. "That's the thing that really sells me. The dead *hate* rivers and they're none too fond of lakes, especially ones as big as Leivas. That's without adding in the power of the Lady or a bunch of hungry Storm Eels. The risen will have a very hard job coming at us while we're on a boat, and an even harder one following us."

I looked at our other youngsters. "Do any of you have anything you want to add? You're all full Blades now. That means pointing it out when the old guard fucks up. Maryam? You're not one to shy away from speaking your mind. . . ."

"I'm fine."

I raised an eyebrow at her.

"Really. Jax was very clear that we three are here to observe and to learn. So that's what I'm doing. Observing."

"Roric?" I said. "You're Avarsi by birth. Anything to add?"

"No, sir."

"Kumi?"

"I like boats and know them pretty well, so I can help with the sailing . . . or paddling . . . or whatever it is the particular boat we end up with requires. Beyond that, think of me as invisible."

18

———◆———

A knife slices through a sea of stars leaving the shattered universe rippling in its wake.

That image alone is enough to make me take back every bad thing I have ever said about boat travel, though really, it's barges I hate. The sky was cloudless and moonless, the black waters deep and still. Where a barge is a battering ram forcing its heavy way through the water endlessly and tediously, the pair of slender hulled, sampan-like night runners we had purchased from a Varyan smuggler slashed through the water as effortlessly as a razor slitting an unsuspecting throat.

The boats were designed to move drugs and other small expensive packages back and forth across the lake between the Kvanas and Varya without submitting to silly things like taxes and customs inspections. Each one was long enough to hold six people, but had been rigged up for four paddlers with a couple of small watertight cargo cases in the middle. They had been stained a rough gray with the juice of the oris plant, and couldn't have been much more than two feet wide at the beam. Both ends came to knifelike points.

Despite a shallow hull, they felt remarkably stable. Possibly because of the solid metal lance that hung about a foot underneath the boat. The lance provided both an easily removable second keel and a ramming beak designed to punch an ugly little hole below the waterline of any craft with a deeper draft than our own.

"Best way to deal with customs boats," the smuggler who sold them to us had said. "Get up a fast run and give 'em a nice distracting fountain to think about." He tapped a device on the floor of the boat. "Once the lance is sunk in good and hard you pull the pins here and upfront and leave it behind. If you place it right, it'll foul either their oars or their rudder. Then you back-paddle, pivot hard, and run for the deep dark. Replacing the lance is an expensive bit of work, but it costs ever so much less than the headsman's cut if they catch you with the wrong cargo."

"Anything else we ought to know?" Kelos asked—I'd had him take point on haggling since he scared the resistance out of people even when they didn't know who he was.

The smuggler nodded. "Don't get caught out in the deep if a storm blows in. You probably won't capsize, and you'll stay afloat even if you do, but you'll be miserable. And if you do fall in and can't get back aboard on the quick, the hunters in the deep will take you. They love to come up to the surface when it gets nasty. Oh, and I wouldn't run by daylight if I was you. These little beauties draw the wrong kinds of attention."

"Not a problem we'll have," said Kelos.

"Somehow I didn't think it would be. And now, if'n you don't mind, I'm off to see a lady about replacing a couple of boats."

"You won't mention where these two went," said Kelos, and it wasn't anything even close to a question.

"She won't ask and I won't say. Building, buying, or using—these are the sort of fancies nobody talks about or admits to seeing. You've paid me more than fair instead of slitting my throat, which is what I feared you might do when first you showed up all dark and scary like there at the end of my little dock. As far as I'm concerned, you was never born and these here boats weren't ever made. Good enough?"

"Good enough," said Kelos, but as soon as the man was out of sight, he shook his head. "It would have been safer if you'd let me kill him."

"I have no doubt of it," I agreed. "That doesn't change my mind. Let's go."

Our meager gear went into the cargo bins in practically no time at all with room to spare, and we'd launched within minutes of the smuggler's departure. That first night we'd left Lake Evinduin behind quickly enough, but made slower work of moving downstream toward Leivas.

The boats took some getting used to, and we nearly capsized both of them more than once despite their relative stability. We'd also decided to put in well before dawn because we weren't sure about how tough it would be to hide the boats. But they were easy to pull out of the water and stow under the whorled dark green tarps provided for the purpose.

The second night we'd gone farther and faster. By the time we reached Leivas and that sea full of stars late on the third night, we'd had plenty of practice at managing the runners, both in the water and ashore. Slipping quietly past the watch at Emain Tarn on the river's mouth had been almost childishly easy—the Shades working together gave our little boats nearly as thorough a cover as they could give us individually.

Our plan for the lake was to hug the southern shore and put in each day a bit before dawn, but we wanted to start out by swinging wide to the north to avoid the most heavily populated section of the Varyan bank of the lake. That meant driving straight out from the river's mouth initially.

Aral, Triss sent about a quarter of an hour after we left the river, *I think you might want to look over at the other boat.*

Why? I glanced to my right but didn't see anything special.

It has two wakes.

What? I looked again, and this time I saw what Triss meant. In addition to the faint white line the keel of the little boat was drawing through the water, there was a thick silvery thread following along behind and beneath.

I noticed it because it changes the way the light comes off the water, and . . . Triss trailed off as the silver line suddenly vanished. *I suspect that we are about to find out what is going on.*

You are indeed, Dragonshadow. The mental voice was strong and sharp, like an axe blade, yet distinctly feminine. Kumi startled in the other boat when it began to speak, which made it clear that whoever was talking, she wanted all of us to hear her.

A moment later, an enormous whiskered head broke the surface silently between the two boats. *I am Shallowshunter. Mudlight asked me to look after you while you travel across our waters.*

I blinked a couple of times. *Thank you, Shallowshunter. I had no idea that your people could speak lake to lake, or that Mudlight even knew we were coming this way.*

Shallowshunter flicked the short barbels on her upper lip and sent a little mental chuckle our way. *Lake to lake would be a long reach indeed, but an unnecessary one. Mudlight swam beneath you on the water-road as you traveled from his lake to ours. He sent for me as you neared our waters, and only turned back for home once I had arrived to keep an eye on you.*

Mudlight followed us all the way out here? asked Triss. *And we didn't notice him?*

No, and yes. Or, the other way round, really. He followed you only as far as the end of the water-road, but he did not cross into the broader realm because that would have forced him to make a formal visit of it. And, obviously, he kept out of your sight if you had to ask about it.

Obviously, Triss sent my way dryly.

If Shallowshunter heard, she ignored him. *Mudlight told me little of your purpose beyond who and what you are and that you travel by night to avoid unfriendly observers. Given*

*whom you once served, I can do a bit more than keep an
eye out for you. If you like, I can arrange to bring you across
to the dirtplace of the Lady. None will bother you in the
waters there.*

That would be appreciated, I sent. *Perhaps a few nights
from now? Even the nearer shore of the island would make
an impossibly long paddle for us in one go.* It was well over
a hundred miles from the river's mouth to the nearest point
of the Lady's island and out here in the lake we wouldn't
have the current to help us.

Tonight, sent Shallowshunter. Then, without another
word, she sank beneath the waters.

"I wish they wouldn't just vanish like that without saying
good-bye," said Faran. "It's disconcerting."

Several minutes passed and Shallowshunter didn't return,
so we began to travel again. After perhaps a half hour, I felt
the boat suddenly surge forward beneath me. *What the fuck
is that . . . ?*

Tonight I said, and tonight I meant, the reply came from
below, alerting me to the fact that I had done the mental
equivalent of speaking my question aloud. *I have acquired
some help,* continued Shallowshunter. *We take you to the
island now.*

We were soon moving at such a clip that water foamed
along our bows, and putting a paddle in was nothing more
than an invitation to have it yanked from your hands—at
least as fast as a cantering horse, if not faster. The eels went
on and on at that pace without flagging. I don't know how
many of her fellows Shallowshunter had summoned to help
out, but our speed dropped only briefly and occasionally
when one of the Storm Eels passed off the job of towing to
another.

The sun was just beginning to spill blood into the sky
when we finally spied the nearer shore of the vast island that
belonged to the Lady of Leivas.

Do you wish to rest here on the shore, now? sent Shallowshunter. *The sun is not yet up, though it soon will be.
The slopes are very steep here and we have only another*

few hours' travel if you wish to reach better accommodation for your kind.

We should probably put in, I sent. *It's far more important that no one see us than that we have a comfortable place to bed down.*

The decision is yours, of course, but there are no hostile eyes here to see you. Boats do not approach within five hundred lengths of the Lady's isle uninvited, and she is not currently receiving. If we stay close to shore we can take you many thousands of lengths yet without any danger of detection.

Lengths? asked Triss. *Lengths of what?*

Of an adult of my kind, replied Shallowshunter.

So, a three- or four-mile exclusion zone, I sent once I'd done the rough math to sort out five hundred eel lengths in my head. *There's not many who could see us at that distance, especially against the dark backdrop of the island. All right. Take us where you will.*

Done.

The eels towed us north and east, hugging the coastline all the way. The island was tall and steep sided—a pair of low mountains really, rising sharply from the lake bottom a couple of hundred feet below. The underlying stone was a color near black, showing through the lush green forest in ragged stripes and scars where rockfalls had ripped away the growth. Perhaps three hours after dawn we arrived at a point due east of the larger peak and the boats suddenly slowed, turning sharply to the left.

For a moment it seemed as if the eels were about to drag us into the rocky cliffs, but then we turned left again and I realized there was a hidden opening there. A narrow channel of water ran north to south between two vast curtains of stone—all but invisible from the broader lake. After perhaps seventy feet we turned right into a tiny bay cradled between the arms of the mountain. The eels left us then with their usual lack of ceremony and we paddled in to a narrow, black sand beach that provided us a place to pull the boats up out of the water.

"Now what?" asked Maryam. "Set up tents and collapse?"

"I think not," replied Faran from farther up the beach. "Shallowshunter said we would have better accommodation, and there it is."

She pointed toward what looked at first glance like a darker patch of rock. It was actually a rounded stone arch, likely the top of an old lava tube. Sand filled the lower half and had been neatly raked flat. A cursory examination suggested that someone or something had brought the sand in intentionally.

Perhaps thirty feet back from the cave mouth we found a neat stone hearth beneath a chimney in the rock. Cord hammocks hung from pitons driven deep into the stone of the arched ceiling, and sealed amphorae sunk, point down, in the sand held water and a selection of preserved foods.

Roric held up a strip of salted pork. "Do we make ourselves at home?"

I nodded. "I don't think the eels would have brought us here to go hungry in sight of a good meal."

Once we had finished with our early morning dinner, we climbed into the hammocks. Even with light coming in from the entrance and down the smoke hole, it was dark enough in the cave to leave watch duty to the Shades, which we gratefully did.

I woke from a deep sleep suddenly and gently, as though a beloved voice had called my name. When I sat up, I saw that no one else was awake yet. The light from the entrance told me it was late afternoon.

Triss?

Here, nothing to report.

You didn't hear anything?

Nothing but insects and sleeping Blades.

Thanks. I rolled out of my hammock and grabbed my sword rig from where I'd hung it in easy reach.

Something wrong?

No. I could still hear the dream echo of the voice that

had called me, but I didn't want to try to explain. *I'm slept out and I want a walk. I thought I'd check out the deeps of the cave.* The direction of that echo.

Fair enough. I'll let Kyrissa know we're going.

The lava tube ran up and back at a gentle angle, curving this way and that as it went. It was lit by round shafts that had been bored through to the surface above every fifty feet or so. Maybe a hundred yards up from the place where I left the others, the sand ended, and I continued from there along a floor that looked as though someone had carefully smoothed it. I walked for perhaps an hour before I saw a much brighter light ahead.

The lava tube ended partway up the wall of a high-walled circular crater—one of the secondary peaks of the larger mountain perhaps. A steep trail led down to a deep pool that filled the floor of the crater. The water was an intense impossible blue with no visible bottom. A floating wooden pier continued on from the trail out to something that looked like a miniature version of one of those round, open-roofed theaters that were so popular in Dan Eyre. Only, where the groundlings would normally have stood, the floor was open to the deep water below.

I climbed down the path to the pier, feeling all the while as though I were following directions I had heard in a dream I couldn't otherwise remember. The theater-like structure was a sort of cross between a raft and a reception hall, with tables and chairs placed on the broad plank circle around the pool at its heart. One table, just to the right of the entrance, held a pitcher of clear water, a rock-crystal goblet, a plate of finely sliced raw fish and freshwater seaweed, and a pair of Zhani-style chopsticks. A lone chair sat at the table facing the pool.

I take it we're expected, sent Triss.

I believe that we are, though I couldn't begin to tell you how I know that. I followed a forgotten dream to get here.

My, but doesn't that just fill me with confidence and hope.

Have I ever mentioned that you have a sarcastic streak? I asked.

Not that I can remember.

Remind me to correct that later. For now, I think it best if I do the expected.

I sat and filled the goblet, taking a sip. The water felt cold and light on my tongue, and . . . like so much more than water. Drinking it reminded me of listening to someone reading a fine poem. It was as exhilarating as an exceptional vintage of the sweetest white wine, without any of the blurring of intoxication. I knew that I could drink down the whole pitcher without worrying about any loss of control.

For someone like me, who has to fight each day not to go back to the bottle again, it was a remarkable gift. After a few minutes slid past with no change in my surroundings, I picked up the chopsticks and took some of the fish and a bit of seaweed. It was fresh and quite as good as anything I could have found at one of the fancier dockside restaurants in Tien, but almost a disappointment after the revelation of the water.

When I had finished with the meal, I pushed my plate aside and poured the last of the water into my goblet. At that precise instant, a ripple began at the center of the enclosed pool, and something like an enormous pearl rose up from the deeps below. I nodded as though I had been expecting it all along. Somewhere, down deep, where dreams live, I knew that I had.

The pearl, if that was what it was, must have been a good ten feet through the center, and as perfect in color and luster as anything I'd ever seen gracing a great lady's jewelry chest. It rose up until only the bottom third of it remained in the water, and then it opened like the oyster that might have birthed it. Inside sat an absolutely ancient woman on a nacreous throne that faced me. The Lady of Leivas, whom some called more than half a goddess.

Her hair was long and silver, brighter than the finest chain made by any Durkoth smith and dense with curls. It rolled down over her right shoulder and across the arm of her throne, spilling to almost touch the floor. She wore a deep green gown that covered her from throat to wrists and hid her feet completely. The fabric looked like living seaweed. Her skin was dark as old mahogany, and the intricate wrinkles on her face could have mapped a hundred labyrinths. Her eyes were black from lid to lid like a bird's—a sharp contrast to the blinding whiteness of her teeth when she smiled at me.

"I see that you received my invitation," she said.

"I did, though I've no idea how you delivered it," I responded.

"And, somehow, I missed it completely." Triss reshaped my shadow into his own dragon form as he spoke.

"That's because you have no water in you, shadowkin. The lake can no more speak in your heart than a stone could. Whereas Aral here is more than half water, red though it runs."

"You know my name, then," I said. "I take it Shallows-hunter announced us?"

She laughed lightly. "You were born in Emain Tarn on the shores of my domain. I have known your name longer than you have, child. When your mother first whispered it to herself in the quiet darkness one morning in the sixth month of her pregnancy, I heard. I knew you before you were you, and in ways that no one other than your goddess ever did. The tides that turn in your blood were born of the rhythms of my lake of Leivas."

"Uh . . ." I had no idea how to answer that. "The stories paint you aloof to the concerns of mortals. I had no idea that you paid that much attention to the comings and goings of those who live beside the lake."

"How could I not?" she asked. "I am no immortal, and the water of your life is the water of mine. Leivas is the living heart of everything that lies between the mountains and the deep wastes. The lake is the center of her soul, but her awareness extends throughout the whole of the watershed. Her power is greatest in deep water and still, and weakest at the little springs high in the mountains or the dying, magic-slicked pools of the great western reach. You were born here, and became the Kingslayer on shores hardly a day away. Though I had nothing to do with the shaping of you, you are a child of my soul's sister."

"What is Leivas?" Triss asked suddenly. "As we crossed the water on our way here, I sensed nothing like what I would expect from one of the greater elementals. But you speak of the lake as a sorcerer speaks of her familiar, and you feel . . . both human and . . . not. I don't understand."

"That is because I *am* human and not. Once, long ago, in the years when our kind first walked under the blue sky, I was not so very different from your Aral. More naturally gifted than most sorcerers perhaps, but fundamentally a creature not unlike what you call human, though I am of the founding generation and I had no parents other than the will of the gods. Then I met Leivas and she made me her own, and we became one."

"I have never heard any of that before," I said. "The people of Varya speak of the Lady of Leivas and think of you as something more akin to the divine than one of us."

"The story was once widely known," said the Lady. "But it is not, I think, sufficiently grand to suit the standards of the tellers of tales. And so, they embroider here and there, each adding their own bits, ultimately making of me more than I am."

"I've some familiarity with that particular effect," I said, wryly.

Again, the Lady laughed. "I imagine that you do, Slayer of Kings." Then she turned her gaze back to Triss. "But I still haven't answered your original question, little shadow. Leivas IS."

"Uh . . ." Triss made a throat clearing noise, though he no more had a throat to clear than he had bone or blood or water in his substance—a bit of non-verbal communication learned from the humans who surrounded him.

"That is the fundamental truth," said the Lady. "Leivas IS. But she is also a lake, and a mighty queen, and the mother of all freshwater dragons, though she has not taken that latter shape in half a millennia. This pearl that houses my throne is a cast-off jewel from her forehead, a token of her third eye."

"Oh." Triss's voice sounded very small. "I . . . oh."

I had to agree. I felt utterly overwhelmed at the thought of that, of the Lady and her companion, and well, everything about the experience.

"Why did you call us here?" I finally asked, though I managed not to add, "What could we possibly have or do that you would care about?"

"Your goddess was dear to me. You were dear to her. I see her through you, and that pleases me."

"Nothing more than that?" I asked, confused.

"Oh, child." She shook her head. "You say that like the sight of a departed friend is a slight thing. I hope that you live long enough to understand that it is one of the true graces, even if, as in my case with you, you only have the chance to see your departed in reflection. There are few indeed who remember me in my youth—the Master of White Fang, some small number among the Sylvani and other First kindreds, the distant and detached gods. . . . None of them were friends to me in the same way that your Namara was. To see her as she is in your heart . . . it eases my old soul."

"And?" I said.

"And what?" she asked.

"Exactly. We both know there's more to it than that. Do you intend to tell me about it, or do I have to guess?"

Triss sat back on his haunches. *Aral, tread lightly. Her power here in the heart of the lake is as great as one of the buried gods.*

I won't be lied to.

Sigh. He flicked his wings in a so-be-it sort of gesture.

"You doubt," said the Lady.

"What?" I blinked. "I'm not sure I follow you."

"You doubt your course and yourself," she said. "I do not know what it is that you have set out to do, but I know that you do not know whether you can achieve it, or even if you should."

"You read minds," I said.

"No. I read hearts in the rhythms of the blood they pump. Yours is as troubled as any I've ever touched. You anticipate something that you cannot see your way through or around."

Is that true? asked Triss. *I thought that you had decided you must slay the Son of Heaven.*

"It's true," I said, answering both the Lady and Triss. "There is a thing I believe that I must attempt, and yet, I believe the doing of it will destroy me."

Oh, my friend . . .

"If you will unburden your soul to me, perhaps I can help you," said the Lady. "I am as old as humanity itself and have learned at least a little of wisdom in those years."

"All right." I didn't think there was anything she could do, but perhaps simply talking about it might help. "Where should I start . . . ?" I took a deep breath. "Perhaps with the man who should have died. In those days he was known as Corik Nofather and he was a priest of Shan. . . ."

I slowly spun out the tale of the way that Corik had first been infected with and then bonded to the risen curse. I talked about how he had used his knowledge of the curse to hide its effects on those he infected and made his own, by having them bathe in the blood of the living. I spoke of how he had taken over the High Church of the East by filling the hierarchy with hidden undead who owed him their abject allegiance, and the way that he had then used his undead priests to infect and master most of the rulers and high nobles of the eleven kingdoms, including the new great khan.

I paused then when she held up a hand and said, "Bide."

The Lady's eyes went far away, and I sensed that she was communing with the soul of Leivas.

After a time she returned. "The curse has spread far indeed. It is a subtle thing when leavened with fresh blood, very hard to sense. But now that I know to look for it . . ." Her expression was grave. "Leivas cannot reach those who stand too far from the edges of open water here in the western basin, but even that reveals many thousands who harbor the hidden version of the curse. So many rulers and priests and leaders of men . . . The world will shake to its very foundations when the Son of Heaven falls. Thrones will tumble and armies shatter. Blood will run in rivers as those who remain fight for mastery."

"And *that* is the core of my problem," I said. "Namara is dead, and my fellows have placed what is left of her authority in my hands. Justice cries out for me to face the Son of Heaven and make him pay for his crimes, but justice also cries for all the many innocent lives that will be lost in the ruin of empires."

"I think I begin to understand your dilemma," said the Lady. "It has fallen on you to decide the fate of the East."

"And no matter what I choose, the decision will unmake me," I said, finally speaking aloud the realization that had been growing in my heart. "If I choose to kill the Son of Heaven, all the ruin that follows will be mine. I will have become the Kingdomslayer, and that is too much weight for my shoulders. But, if I choose *not* to kill the Son of Heaven, all the evil that he does from that day forward will belong to me, and my heart will wither and blacken in my chest. So, each day, I move closer to facing the Son of Heaven, hoping against hope that something will relieve me of the choice before I must make it."

"The forces you face are terrible in their strength," said the Lady. "You may well fall before you reach that point of decision."

"Lady, were it not for my shadow, I would pray for that." I had not admitted the thing even to myself until now, but I could no longer deny it. Death in the course of duty attempted would buy me free of the burden of choice, and if it wouldn't end Triss as well, I would gratefully seek it.

"Aral, you can't mean that!" Triss spoke aloud, his voice thick with anguish as he climbed up onto the table and looked into my eyes.

I didn't answer him, because I couldn't bring myself to speak the words, but through our link I could feel how much my silence told him.

"I didn't know," said Triss. "I didn't understand it was hurting you so. Oh, Aral."

"It's all right, Triss. You couldn't have seen it. However well you know and love me, I had hidden the worst of it even from myself till this very moment."

"No, it's more than that," said Triss, sounding very worried indeed. "I am not human. I love you, and I think I understand your kind better than almost any of my fellows, but in the deeps of my soul I am not one of you. Regret I grasp, and remorse to a lesser degree, but I do not know guilt as your people describe it. For my kind, once a thing is done, it is done. If it was done badly, we might work to correct it, but that is the next thing, not a part of the thing passed. We do not carry the weight of our mistakes in the same way that you do."

"I don't blame you for not understanding, Triss. I have done everything I can to avoid understanding it myself. I have a choice that I cannot avoid short of death, and whichever way I choose it will shatter me."

"I could decide for you," the Lady said, very quietly.

"What?" I whipped my head up to look at her.

"You say that the decision will unmake you no matter which way you choose. Namara was my friend. I supported her goals if not always her methods. I have lived as long as our race, and there are many weights on my soul. One more will not break me, even one so great as this. You were dear to Namara and she would not have seen you destroy yourself if it were possible to avoid it. In service to our old friendship, I offer myself as a proxy for your fallen goddess. If you ask it of me, I will decide the thing for you. You have but to say the word and I will bear the weight in your stead. . . ."

19

———◆———

"**No**."

One word, and a tiny one at that, but when I spoke it then, it carried the weight of ten thousand dead souls.

"No," I repeated myself. "I cannot accept your offer, however much I am tempted by it."

"Why not?" The Lady of Leivas leaned forward a few barely perceptible fractions of an inch.

"Because the responsibility is mine. It has *always* been mine. Though I didn't understand it when I killed Ashvik all those years ago, you cannot transfer the responsibility for your actions to another, no matter how much you might wish to. The goddess sent us here and there, telling us to kill this one and spare that one, but she never refused a Blade who asked to retire, and she never used her power to bend us to her will."

The Lady nodded. "Go on."

"I could have refused to kill Ashvik. I could have walked away from the order at any time. Every life that I have ended, *I* have ended. It doesn't matter that I was raised for the purpose, the core of the credo of the goddess was ever and always that the great and the powerful must be held to account for their actions. Though I am not great, I am among the powerful, and no one else can answer for what I have done."

"You have said that the choice will unmake you. . . ." said the Lady.

"It will, but I have been unmade before, when the temple fell. I am a weaker man now than I was before my ruin, but also, I think, a better one. I don't know what will emerge on the other side of this decision, but it will be *mine*."

"And if the goddess were resurrected tomorrow and gave you an order one way or the other?"

"I have longed for that with my whole heart, but it's not possible. Even if it were . . ." I shrugged. "It would change nothing. I would still have to make the choice and own the responsibility. The choice to accept another's command, even the command of a goddess, does not come with an exemption from my conscience."

She nodded now. "Very good, child. Very good indeed. You, too, have learned some little of wisdom in the time you have walked under the sun. I think your goddess would have been very proud of that."

"I . . . thank you." It hurt my heart to hear that—in a good way, a healing way. "Was this a test?"

"Every choice is a test, child. But you know that. You said it yourself when you said, 'you cannot transfer the responsibility for your actions to another, no matter how much you might wish to.' Yes, this was a test. But I am not the judge, you are and always have been."

I took a deep breath and felt the weight of her words settle around my shoulders. "I needed to hear that."

"Then I am glad to have said it. Now that you have forced yourself to see that no one else can make the choice for you, do you know what your decision will be?"

I thought about it and, finally, shook my head. "No more than I did when I came here, but at least I finally know what it really means to make it." I took a last sip of my water. "Is that why you called me here?"

"Perhaps it is, though I didn't know it beforehand. You are the soul-child of Namara, one of my oldest friends, and you were heartsore. I did not lie when I told you that seeing those we love reflected in those they leave behind is grace enough for me to want to see you. That I could do some small thing that eased your turmoil as she would have wished . . . well, that is a rarer gift. The dead leave the world, but they never leave our hearts. You have given me a chance to do a service to the Namara who lives in mine, and for that I owe you thanks."

"I . . . there's really nothing more to say between us, is there? Nothing but good-bye."

"Only this: go with my blessing." The dome of the huge pearl lifted behind her and began to close.

"Thank you, Lady. I hope I see you again someday."

She smiled, but didn't speak as the pearl finished closing and sank into the depths.

Oh, my Aral, I'm so sorry.

You have nothing to apologize for, my oldest and dearest friend. The situation is none of your making. A long mental silence followed as I rose and headed back for the cave.

Just as I stepped off the floating pier, Triss spoke again. *What will we do?*

I don't know, Triss. I really don't. I paused then as the beginnings of an idea occurred to me. *There is no decision that will not unmake me, but perhaps, knowing that, I can at least choose which is the best way to be unmade.*

Triss didn't answer.

"**Where** have you been?" Faran asked quietly. Alone of those I had left behind she was awake when I returned.

"A visit with the Lady of Leivas."

"She's real?"

I nodded.

"What was she like?" asked Faran. "What did she tell you?"

"Nothing that I want to share right now." Faran looked stung, and I held up a hand. "I'm sorry, it was very personal.

But if I ever do share it with anyone, you will be the first to hear it. Now, I need more rest." I hung up my swords, pulled myself back into the hammock, and was asleep in moments.

Heaven's Reach.

It took us weeks to get there, but they were largely uneventful. Whether that was because the Lady asserted her will over the waters and broke our trail for the risen, or simply the natural effect of wild water on the undead, I couldn't say. Whatever the reason, we encountered no problems while we traveled by boat down from Leivas to the edge of the waste and thence back up the River Dan to the Almarn Mountains.

The Almarn range is much lower and gentler than the Spine of Hurn and we were able to cross over into Öse without too many problems even so late in the season. From there, we worked our way down through the foothills and entered the valley that held the temple kingdom from the northwest. Patrols were light on that side and we encountered none of the undead, suggesting that the Son of Heaven had concentrated his forces to the south and east as we had hoped that he would.

Right after we crossed the border we waylaid a half-dozen soldiers wearing the livery of Heaven's Sword so that Kelos could test the efficacy of the measures he had taken to free himself of the chains of geas. He killed two and pronounced himself satisfied, though I thought I detected the faintest hint of worry in his voice when he spoke. Or I may just be fooling myself when I think that I have finally begun to learn to read him.

The bodies we consigned to the everdark, though we salvaged their gear and uniforms. This close to the temple city, I felt little enough in the way of pity for them. Still, we didn't *have* to kill them, and I know they will ultimately weigh against me when I face the lords of judgment. But then, I have known for a very long time that my next life will be one of suffering. Perhaps my next several lives—I have much to answer for.

Kelos led us onward to the city then, taking hidden paths that he had scouted out long ago, and bringing us unde-tected to his carefully concealed fallback. He was Kelos, and his plans had revolved around the Son of Heaven for more years than I had lived, so the location and preparation were perfect.

Rather than co-opt a space in some structure made by man, and have to deal with the potential hazards of unex-pected renovation or other chance exposing a hidey-hole he intended to use for decades, he had bored a deep cave in the bluffs above the city. There he had hidden the entrance beneath an overhanging shelf of rock and built a counter-weighted stone door. The mechanism allowed it to pivot outward only when two of Namara's swords were shoved full length into crevices in the stone and levered just so in the same moment that a Shade slipped into the depths and tripped a complex catch.

"I hadn't planned on having to house so many for any length of time," he whispered, as he strained to move the block—it was designed so that even with the counterweights, it would take someone as strong as Kelos to move it from the outside. "We'll run short of supplies if we stay more than a few weeks, though we should have room enough and more." He sheathed his swords. "Now, move smartly, the door closes by itself after a few seconds."

Suiting action to words, he extended his arms in front of him and slid face-first into the black gullet of the cave. At my wave, Roric went next, followed by Maryam, and the others, with me playing the part of the last duckling. The door was already slowly closing when I launched myself into the opening. The space beyond was narrow, and low, barely larger than a crawlway. The floor had been polished to a fine degree and it angled steeply downward to make something that was much more of a chute than a tunnel. I quickly found myself picking up speed as I slid along.

It reminded me unpleasantly of a trip the Durkoth had sent me on just a few short months before, during the matter of the Smoldering Flame. Then, too, I had been sliding through stone and darkness on a trip to someplace unknown, though this one turned out much shorter—perhaps seventy feet in all—and the darkness didn't last. Right before its end, the angle of the chute shallowed and then reversed itself, so that I came to a stop a few feet short of the opening. From there it was a short scramble up into the main cave.

Someone had opened a bright magelantern by that time, and I used the light to examine the structure of the chute. Hand and footholds were carved into deep channels along the sides, making a ladder to climb back up without ruining the slide effect coming in. I hadn't noticed them on my way down because of a raised lip similar to what you would find on a children's slide between the sliding surface and the handholds.

The hideaway was enormous, a barrel-vaulted space perhaps fifteen feet across by fifty long, with the floor entrance near the middle of one side. With only the one magelight to provide illumination at the moment, the ends of the vault were in deep shadow. It reminded me of the sort of cellar you might find under the palace at Dan Eyre, or one of the main channels in the sewers of Tien, not a one-man fallback. Even stranger, I couldn't see the mark of a single tool. Every surface looked as smooth and polished as the flat of a finely wrought sword. Where there *were* edges, like around the lip of the slide by which we had entered, they were carefully rounded and almost organic looking.

"This is Durkoth work," I said. "The stone was persuaded rather than mined." I ran a hand along the wall and couldn't feel the slightest irregularity. "It wasn't done by one of their lesser craftspeople, either. I've never seen stone shaped so neatly. And this place is huge!"

Kelos nodded. "I once salvaged the honor of an Uthudor. The details aren't important, but the result is that he owed me a very serious debt. This was how he repaid me."

Note that he speaks of the Durkoth in the past tense, sent

Triss. *Somehow I don't think that Uthudor lived on to betray the secret of this place to anyone after he finished making it.*

I wish that I could disagree. I didn't particularly like any of the Durkoth I'd ever met, but the idea reminded me too much of all those rulers who'd built themselves vast tombs and then killed the workers they'd employed to prevent them from revealing the location to potential grave robbers.

Kelos pointed to our right. "There's a privy through a thick stone door down at that end of the vault. Opening it creates a pretty stiff breeze, since it has its own airshaft to draw out the stink. Another shaft voids the contents into a fast moving underground river." Next, he pointed left. "There's a small sleeping cubicle up at that end. Also, a bathing chamber that draws its water from the same river, though well upstream, of course. It takes a while to fill, and longer to heat, but we'll have baths as we need them. That's where the rabbit run is, under a stone grate."

"Where does it go?" asked Triss.

"Into the river," replied Kelos. "It's a rough, cold ride, but about a mile after you hit the water there's a ledge on the left bank and a shaft that leads up to a one-way hatch onto the surface."

"Nice setup," said Siri. "Though it seems a bit sparsely furnished for the size." There were a couple of chairs, a small table, and what looked like it might be another mage-light lamp by the door to the sleeping cubicle, but not much else.

"I knew I'd be spending weeks at a time here over the course of years, and I wanted plenty of space to train and stay in shape. Speaking of which, all you need do is say the word . . ." He pointed upward and spoke a simple spell of opening, sending a rope of silver light to touch the center of the ceiling where it split in two and slithered away along the stone surface in the manner of bubbles flowing through a poisoner's still. In the wake of the twinned lines, a row of tiny bronze shutters that ran the entire length of the vault overhead opened, revealing strong magelights and flooding the room with a pure golden light. ". . . and instant dojo."

"It'll be good to have a chance to train properly again," said Faran, "though I imagine the stone floor is going to produce some spectacular bruises. Where are all your supplies?"

"There's a trapdoor in the floor near the latrine with various tools of the trade stored below—targets, pells, magical gear, etc. It's designed to double as a bottle dungeon, should we need one. There's another just like it up by the sleeping cubicle. There's food in that one in big earthen jars, and plenty of blankets and the like. Speaking of which, there's only the one actual bed, but we can rig up a couple of hammocks easily enough for those who prefer not to sleep on rugs or mats. That's what I intend to do, since the sleeping cubicle goes to our First Blade."

I nodded because it was the obvious choice. "I'd say getting sleeping arrangements set up is our first order of business. We've been traveling hard, and I for one am ready for a long rest. Then come tomorrow night, we can start nosing around the temple precinct to see what it will take to crack the place under the new security regime."

Siri grimaced. "We're going to have to approach that with even more care than we normally would, given the betrayal of Lieutenant Chomarr." She ticked points off with her fingers. "They know we're coming, we can't trust a thing he said, and every question we asked will have given him insights into how we think about these things."

"In short," said Faran, "we're fucked."

"Not entirely," I replied. "But we *are* starting in a very big hole."

"One thing Chomarr *didn't* know about is the Signet's finger with its ring," said Kelos. "I presume you stashed it somewhere near the city, Aral. How fast can you get your hands on it?"

I blinked at the question and shrugged. "More than a day, less than a week." I was surprised that now that Kelos had finally chosen to bring it up he did so in front of everyone, if not by the fact that he knew me well enough to know that I must have stashed it near the city.

"Do you really think we'll have any use for the thing?"

I asked. "You saw Signet Toragana's ring, and heard what she had to say about the changes in the system—how paranoid the Son of Heaven has become." I didn't pretend for a second that I believed he hadn't been listening in on that conversation. "I can't imagine that he wouldn't have had all the wards rekeyed at the same time."

That was a big part of why *I* hadn't chosen to mention Nea's finger to anyone else yet—I knew we'd have to try it, but I didn't want to make anyone think we had an easy in and then disappoint them. Judging by the look on Faran's face just then, I suspected that I might have made a mistake there, though she didn't yet say anything about it.

"I can imagine it very easily," said Kelos. "Think on what Toragana said about the *way* things have changed. The Son of Heaven banished all of his mages from the heart of the temple complex, replacing the sorcerer priests of the Hand who guarded him with hidden risen. I think the reason Toragana's ring of office wasn't a spell key, is exactly *because* the Son can't control all of his wards now."

Kelos began to pace. "He's no mage, and he's alienated himself from the vast majority of his followers who are. There are about a million and one warding structures inside the temple precinct. He simply won't have had the resources to change them all after tossing out the bulk of his mages. I'm sure he'll have ordered them to change the wards in the areas where he allows them entry, and he's probably had some of the inner wards redone as well, especially around his quarters. It won't help us at all with the outer defenses, but I think a lot of the inner temple may well remain vulnerable to the key provided by a Signet's ring and finger."

I found myself nodding. "I guess I hadn't thought about it that way. All right, tomorrow night Triss and I will head off to fetch that finger—assuming it hasn't rotted away. I'll take Faran and Ssithra, and Kumi and Gryss to watch my back when I go."

You didn't even think to leave Faran behind, and *you remembered that for now at least, that means Kumi as well. You're learning.*

I suppressed a snort. *Hey, if you hit me in the head with a blunt object often enough, it eventually makes an impression. For that matter, since we're going to be heading toward the area where we think the Son has concentrated his risen, I'll need someone to cover my back. I can't think of anyone I'd rather have between me and a knife.*

Maryam held up a hand, and I couldn't help noticing that the look on her face pretty well matched the growing storm on Faran's.

"Yes?"

"I only understood about half of that," she said. "I know that Jax went to you to get help to break us free of the Hand of Heaven back at the abbey, and that Kelos gave you Signet Eilif's ring with his magically preserved living finger still in it as a key to the temple precinct at that time."

She knew all that because Jax knew it. We'd used the finger when we busted her and Roric and Javan out of the abbey prison that had cost them each an ear.

"But I *thought* that you'd left the finger behind when you marked up the Son's face," she said, and I heard a distinct note of angry suspicion. "That's what the letter you sent Jax said, anyway."

"That's all true, as far as it goes." I nodded. "But after the fight at the abbey when I killed Signet Nea, I took her finger and ring and half-assed myself a second key. It's not nearly as well crafted as Kelos's version, but I believe it will still have some life left in it yet."

"You never told me you still had a key to the temple quarter!" Faran said coldly, finally breaking her angry silence. "Don't you think that's something somebody besides you ought to have known about?"

"I never told *anyone* about the key, though there's a letter Captain Fei is supposed to give you in the event of my death, and another to be sent to Jax."

Part of my reason for keeping the secret from everyone was that I didn't want anybody else getting ideas about taking a crack at the Son of Heaven—especially Faran, who had a rash streak—and possibly getting killed in the attempt.

I wouldn't have been able to keep it at all if Faran hadn't been so badly hurt during the fight where I'd harvested that finger. But she'd very nearly lost an eye a few minutes before and had incurred a nasty head wound in the process. That, plus the fact that I'd had to work the spell very quickly or lose my chance, had made it just barely possible.

"I'm sorry, Faran," I said, "but it's a secret I've kept very close." And one that wouldn't have mattered anymore if those letters ever got sent—since the life of the finger was dependent on my own continued health—but I rather hoped Faran wouldn't think it through that far.

Faran's eyes narrowed sharply, but then her tone lightened. "You are so going to pay for that the next time we spar. Speaking of which, remind me to take some time to beat the rest of your secrets out of you later."

"So, how long *will* it take you to retrieve this finger?" asked Siri. "It's obvious you're not going all the way to Tien to get it."

"Three days round-trip, if I'm quick. Maybe four or five if the patrols are heavy. I decided it was best to cache it close to where I'd need it if the time came, but I had to make damned certain no one had tailed me before I placed it."

I shot a look at Kelos. At the time, he was the person I was most concerned about finding the finger. He smiled serenely back at me, and I suddenly suspected that he had known at the time exactly what I was going to do with the thing and simply hadn't bothered to follow me for reasons of his own.

"If there's nothing else," I said, "we should try to get that sleep now."

Nobody said anything, despite Faran's hard looks my way, so I headed for the cubicle to fall down for a while. Behind me, the others split up to sort out the sleeping arrangements. I heard Faran ask where the hammocks were, and Kelos tell her they were in with the other mission gear, which made sense. Assassins spent a lot of time waiting for the opportune moment, and a small hammock or sling hung high in a tree or under the battlements of a castle made a good place to lie hidden. I'd used one such when I killed Ashvik. Roric called out a moment later, asking how many people would prefer a rug, but I didn't hear the answer because I had just opened the door to the sleeping cubicle and a sudden ringing in my ears blocked out everything else.

The square little room looked exactly like the ones we'd had back at the temple, right down to the furnishings. One small, spare wooden desk with a built-in set of shelves on one end for books or scrolls. One wardrobe/weapons cabinet combination with a set of hooks on the bed side for a sword rig. One thick rug suitable for extended bouts of prayer. And, one moderately sized rope-frame bed with a feather mattress—people who sleep in the day can use all the help they can get. The bed was designed for one, but could accommodate two readily enough if they were friendly—the goddess had never expected celibacy of her followers.

Aral?

What? I realized then that I hadn't moved since I'd pulled the door open. *Oh, sorry. It's just* . . . My heart felt like someone had closed it in a mailed fist. *I'd better go in, hadn't I?*

The last time I'd seen a room that looked like this one was before the temple fell. The crushing homesickness the sight brought on now made me want to bolt from the underground vault never to return. Somehow, I forced myself across the threshold and quietly closed the door behind me. That plunged the room into utter darkness, and I felt a faint easing of the pain in my chest as I lost my ability to see anything.

What's wrong? sent Triss. *I can feel how much pain you're in, but I don't understand!*

I wondered then if homesickness, like guilt, was a thing that didn't affect Shades. I knew that Triss hated what had been done to the order and, even more, what had been done to me in the process, and that he had wished often enough that it could all be undone, but I don't know that I had ever heard him express anything quite like what I was feeling then. No surprise either way, given that I had spent the first few years after the fall refusing to talk about the temple and trying to drown my memories in Aveni whiskey.

For the first time in over a year, I didn't think I'd have been able to put the bottle aside if I had one available . . . and I had to sleep here. Of course, I couldn't tell Triss that. He was so damned proud of me for staying dry this long.

Just homesickness, my friend, I sent. *I haven't been in a room like this since the temple days.*

Oh, I hadn't thought about that. He sounded genuinely puzzled. *It hardly seems like the temple at all to me. The polish of the walls makes them shine much brighter to my senses, and the furniture is more highly finished, too. All that reflection makes it feel very close and tight in here to me, hardly like the temple at all.*

Somehow, I found that enormously reassuring. It freed me enough to step away from the door and pull off my sword rig. I wasn't ready to hang it up yet, but I found that I could almost breathe again. That's when Triss punched me in the gut.

Do you think Zass is still alive . . . ? And Devin? Or do you think that Chomarr's betrayal means they've been killed?

He didn't intend it as a gut punch, but there it was. If Devin was dead, it was due to my first major failure as the head of my order. Mind you, I had no love left for Devin. But I no longer hated him so much as I had when I'd first learned of his betrayal either. How could I?

Devin's fundamental flaw was that he had no spine, no center. If *I* couldn't bring myself to pass final justice on Kelos, how much harder would it have been for Devin to resist him when he was first approached about betraying the goddess?

Nor was Devin a long thinker. Kelos's arguments about the underlying flaws in the way we went about producing justice, and about the inherent unfairness of government by a noble few, were quite compelling. Enough so that I had yet to find it in me to say that he was simply wrong. The system was unfair, and nearly a millennia of action by my order under the direction of Namara hadn't fundamentally changed that.

How easy would it be to succumb to the idea that you had the opportunity to do what even justice's goddess couldn't achieve? Hell, it was only by repeatedly reminding myself of the human costs of such a massive revolution that I could keep my perspective on the thing. Devin might well have seen this as his chance, *finally*, to become one of the great names among the champions of justice. I believed that history would judge him very harshly. But might he not have believed just the opposite?

Faran would say that I was being soft and a fool to excuse him like that, and she might well be right. But Devin had been like my brother once, and if my recent failure had caused his death it would be another heavy burden placed on my heart, however much he might have earned such a fate.

Aral, have I upset you further?

No, Triss. It's not you. It's this place and what we've come to do, and Devin and, well, everything. I should never have agreed to become First Blade. I have enough trouble living with the weight of my own actions.

Should you . . . resign?

I don't know, maybe, but all of Siri's arguments still hold true. I didn't see how I could refuse the office then, and I don't see how I can step away from it now. There isn't anyone else.

But you're in so much pain. What if it's killing you?

I didn't answer him. *I'm sure it will all look better tomorrow, and we can talk about it then.* I began to take off the rest of my gear. *For now, what I really need is sleep.*

But I lay awake a long time in the darkness after that.

20

———◆———

"**C**an't we cut the tip off or something?" asked Faran.
"That thing is really gross."

I looked at the finger in its box on the floor, and shook
my head. "I don't think we should, though Kelos might know
better. I was really just copying his spell, and I don't understand all the finer points of it."

We spoke quietly as we squatted there, using the sounds
of the nearby waterwheel to cover our words. I'd hidden the
box inside a watertight jar wedged into a gap I'd made in
the foundations of one of the stone piers supporting the
stream side of the mill. Given the newness of the construction, I'd figured it would be at least a decade before anyone
even thought about messing around with those piers, barring
a truly extraordinary flood.

After I retrieved the jar, we'd slipped into the mill—
empty at this hour of the night—to open it up and visually
inspect the finger. It didn't look good, which was no surprise
to me. Though I hadn't mentioned it to the others, I'd been
able to sense that something had gone a bit off about the

spell as soon as I'd gotten within a few miles of the finger. It was tied directly to my life force, after all.

I could feel the link as a sort of feathery itch that ran from inside the back of my skull and down my spine to whatever point of me was closest to the finger. When I had first made the thing, the sensation had been more like a tickle, but now it prickled and itched.

"That's *so* disturbing." Faran prodded the middle knuckle of the finger, and I felt the motion as a sort of tug on the invisible line between me and it. "It's not quite blood warm down toward the stub, which is disturbing enough after two years, but up top where it's gone all black and puffy. That's just, eww."

Kelos's original spell had involved taking a finger from the living hand of Signet Eilif, affixing it to a carefully prepared disk of unicorn horn with a custom-made silver nail, and using that to bind it to Kelos's own soul, keeping it alive indefinitely. It was only after he'd finished making the thing that Kelos let the Signet die.

I hadn't had the luxury of planning my own version out in advance or preparing all the necessary materials ahead of time. Instead, I'd had to improvise on a short schedule, using a bent splinter of silver and a wedge of dracodon ivory, both hurriedly pried free of the abbey's altar furnishings for the purpose. Not to mention that the Signet I'd taken my finger from had already stopped breathing for several possibly critical seconds by the time I harvested it.

Kumi frowned and leaned forward, but didn't touch the box. "The finger is tied directly to your life force?"

I nodded, somewhat startled by her question. She'd been all but silent for most of the two days it had taken us to get to the ring, either by temperament or because she was following Jax's orders to play the observer.

"That seems kind of risky," she said.

I shrugged. "I didn't have much choice, but yes. It's not quite necromancy, but it comes from the same line of spell casting. An experienced mage could easily make that link into a weapon against me if they got hold of the finger and managed to get close enough to use it before I could stop them."

I nodded toward the place where I'd fetched it from the stream. "That's part of why I was so careful about where I hid the thing, and why Kelos was concerned about my leaving the one he'd made in the hands of the Son of Heaven."

"I wouldn't worry about Kelos," said Faran. "I've no doubt he figured out some way to cut the link before it caused him any problems. Maybe even before you left the temple that night. The man's a master at weaseling out of situations that ought to result in his death."

"I can't argue with that." I shrugged. "Honestly, given the way he thinks, he probably had the means to sever the connection before he even made the finger."

"Of course he did," agreed Triss. "He's not one to leave a loose end hanging like that. Not when it could get him killed."

"Actually"—Kumi shook her head—"that wasn't the danger I was thinking of at all."

"What do you mean?" Triss asked, his voice holding sudden concern.

She took a deep breath. "Well, I'm not as good at magical theory as someone like Faran or Master Siri, but I spent a bunch of time studying up on necromancy when I was seventeen—right after Loris and Jax found me."

"That's a bit . . . unusual," I said. "Did Master Loris suggest it?"

"No. I was pretty broken up by the fall of the temple. Do you remember Master Zara?"

I nodded. "I remember her investiture. It happened a few weeks before my final mission."

"We were . . . lovers, and more than that. She wanted me to marry her once I became a master. She was killed in the fighting at the fall. I never got the chance to say good-bye, and that gnawed at me. I wanted to fix it. Of course, I ultimately learned that necromancy can't really touch a soul that died unbound, only the body left behind. But in the process, I spent a lot of time reading the more disturbing sorts of grimoires."

"And somewhere in there you learned something that makes you worry about this?" I tapped the box with the finger in it.

"Yes." She nodded. "It's dying back from the tip."

"That's clear enough," I agreed. As Faran noted, it had gone black and puffy. Also, the fingernail was visibly loose. A line of greenish skin marked the divide between the semi-living and obviously rotting tissue. It looked grotesque. "What about it?"

"Well," said Kumi, "I'm wondering what happens when it dies all the way back to the ivory where the spell is anchored to your soul. Like you said, it's not necromancy, but it does share a lot of means and methods with the darker art. One of the big reasons necromancy is so very dangerous is the tendency for the spells to backlash through the caster. What I want to know is, what kind of echo will the death of that"—she pointed at the finger—"produce in your soul?"

"Right." Faran's voice was bleak and angry. "We're destroying this thing right now!" A ball of spell-light began to form around her clenched fist.

"Agreed," said Triss.

Kumi put her hand over the box. "I wouldn't do that. Without the proper precautions, *anything* you do to that finger could easily rebound back through Aral's soul."

"So what are the proper precautions, exactly?" asked Faran.

"I don't know," replied Kumi. "I was looking into a very different sort of necromantic spellwork. I didn't cover anything like this."

"That's not good," I said. "We'd better talk to Kelos and figure out how to sever the connection."

"**No** idea," said Kelos, from his place in one of the three chairs around the little table in the fallback. "Not with the finger half-dead already. If you look closely at the spell-light in the glyphs on the base here, you can see that the whole magical structure's gone corrupt. You say the rot has progressed another quarter of an inch since you picked this up?"

I nodded. The line of decay had advanced significantly during the two days it had taken us to return to Heaven's Reach.

"That seems like a mighty big coincidence." Roric was sitting on the floor opposite Kelos. "That it just *happens* to go bad right when we get here, and then starts getting worse that fast."

"It's no coincidence," said Siri, who had chosen to alternate standing with worried pacing. "I'd bet my eyeteeth the rot was triggered by Aral getting within some critical distance of the finger, and that the same effect is what's causing it to move so quickly now."

"So, what happens when it gets to the base of the finger?" asked Triss. He had taken on dragon form and settled on the floor in front of my chair, with his front legs up on the table.

"Nothing good," said Siri. "I can't say for sure, and necromancy's not my specialty, but after talking it over with Kumi, I don't like any of the answers. There's a slim possibility it won't have any effect at all, but I'd bet against that. Much more likely is that it will injure or kill Aral. It could even turn him into one of the restless dead, though that's almost as unlikely as it failing to hurt him at all."

"What!" Faran whipped around in her chair to glare at Kelos. "Did you know any of that when you made yours? Because that's crazy dangerous magic you were playing with."

Kelos shrugged. "I took precautions that Aral didn't. Also, I'm not as convinced as Siri that we can make any meaningful guesses about what will happen if worse comes to worst. Besides, none of that will matter if we get the enchantment sorted before it reaches that point. That means we need to seriously expedite our schedule for cracking the temple precinct."

"I think I must have missed a move somewhere in your play there." Faran's voice was low and dangerous. "Because if I *didn't* mishear anything, then Siri said that this spell going bad could turn Aral into something like the risen, and you responded with mouth noises that suggested fixing Aral's problem is in some way contingent on breaking into the temple, instead of taking a new place as our signal priority."

"It's not my call to make," said Kelos, "but if Aral really wants to solve the problem of the Son of Heaven, we need that finger in working condition. I don't know what we'll have to do to stop the spell from backlashing through Aral, but at the least it will involve severing the connection between the two of them and destroying the finger. But without that finger, *and* a major dose of luck, we're screwed."

Siri crossed her arms and nodded reluctant agreement.

Before Faran could argue further, I stepped in. "Let them explain."

Siri went first. "I tried, Aral, I really did. But I couldn't even *touch* the smoke inside the temple complex, much less use it as a way in. Part of that is simply distance. The farther I get from the Brimstone Vale and the tomb of the Smoldering Flame, the weaker the powers that come with being bound to the god. But there's more to it than that. This is the place where the powers and attention of Heaven lie heaviest in the mortal world.

"See?" Siri touched a finger to one of her long braids.

For the first time in weeks I really looked at her hair. What can I say? I'd been too focused on what was going on inside my head and heart to pay close attention to *anything* in the outside world. The smoke that habitually looped and slithered through her tightly bound black curls had faded almost to nothing.

"It's been like this since we scouted out the edge of the temple precinct three days ago," she said.

"Kyrissa?" I asked.

Siri's shadow reshaped itself into the form of a winged serpent, and I saw that the thick smoky feathers I had grown so used to were likewise faded and indistinct. Almost, she looked as she had in the days of our youth, before the fall of the temple and their entanglement with the buried god.

"I am much diminished," said the Shade. "If that loss of

power came with less of a sense of presence, I would happily make the trade, but alas, it does not. If anything, I have felt the attention of the Smoldering Flame growing as we traveled closer to this place of his enemies. His hate beats at my mind, and I fear how it will grow and burn if Siri and I actually enter the deeps of the temple."

I raised an eyebrow at Siri, and she nodded. "I don't know how far in we'll be able to go with you. Not all the way, certainly. There's god-magic at work here, both the Smoldering Flame's and Shan's. I started to feel physically ill the moment that Kelos and I entered the outermost loop of the temple precinct. Nausea and dizziness. Not debilitating, but whatever was going on also completely blocked my sense of smoke."

"And that's all the farther we've been able to get," said Kelos. "There are new installations atop most of the major gates. Ostensibly, they're shrines, designed to look like those little pagodas the Shanites are so fond of. But really, they're protective tombs—a safe place for the risen to lie up during the day. They come out at sunset. I spotted several of them slipping off to play gargoyle in the dark. Chomarr didn't mention them, either because they're new, or because he was playing us. Combine the dead with the way the wards on the wall tops will slow us down and we've got a major problem."

"Ugly," I said.

The temple precinct was a walled city within the greater city. It spiraled inward from the great gate through a series of inner baileys like the chambers of a nautilus. Each bailey had its own temples and shrines and its own gates, both inner and outer. As I had discovered on my previous sortie, all of the walls after you passed the outermost ring had wards built into the very stones, many of them created by or enhanced with god-magic—invisible to mage sight. The only thing that had allowed me to get past them the last time was the Signet-finger keys I had brought with me.

"Deeply ugly," agreed Kelos. "I'm beginning to think we'll have to do this in two stages. First, we go over the outer wall shortly before dawn and hole up in one of the lesser temples until morning drives the risen off the walls. Then, when they're clear, we do the rest of the job out in the sun."

"That's suicide," said Triss. "We can't hide you in the direct sun atop those walls."

"It's not suicide," said Kelos. "Not if we've got the Signet's ring and finger, *and* it still works for most of the wards. Not if we can move fast enough once the alarm sounds. There are places where we'll have to take to the rooftops and brave the direct light, but fewer than you might think. There are shortcuts between many of the loops, narrow gates and deep tunnels known only to a very few. The Signet's ring of office opens most of them. Or, at least, it used to."

Faran spoke. "You just said, 'once the alarm' sounds. Does that mean you've given up on our getting in and out without being caught and killed?"

"No," said Kelos. "I think our chances of making it all the way in without setting off the alarms is pretty close to zero given the things Siri and I have been able to learn in the past few days and the risks that a sunside approach are likely to add to the endeavor. That's why *we're* not going to be the ones triggering the alarm. But that's Siri's show, and I'll leave her to explain it after I'm done."

Kelos continued, "Once the alarm sounds, things will get hairy everywhere, but if we do this right the pressure will actually be lightest in the heart of the temple. If we strike fast and kill the Son of Heaven before what risen are there can swarm us, the resulting chaos when three-quarters of the curia and nearly all the inner temple guards die with him, should provide us more than enough cover to get back out."

I rolled the finger in its box. "And if this thing *doesn't* work anymore?"

Kelos smiled grimly. "Then we might as well go home, because we are well and truly fucked, and the Son of Heaven will soon become the uncrowned emperor of the eleven kingdoms. And since his life is tied to the life of the curse that is his familiar, he might reign for a thousand years. I think we have to try this, and I believe that we can succeed."

"Why am I not reassured?" said Faran.

"Because you're a hopeless cynic?" I asked.

"Yeah, that'd be it. Well, I know this isn't going to fly, but I'm going to vote we fix Aral's problem now, and leave the Son of Heaven for another day. Any takers?"

Silence.

"Yeah, that's what I thought." Faran sighed. "Moving along, when do we go after the Son of Heaven?"

"Given how fast the rot is traveling," said Kelos, "*and* that we have no idea what will happen when it gets to the base, or even what the mechanism of the spell is, I'm thinking that as soon as humanly possible is the only sane answer."

"Is that because you're worried about Aral?" Faran asked bitterly. "Or is it because you're afraid the key will stop working and ruin your chance at starting this glorious revolution of yours?"

Kelos frowned at Faran. "You're smarter than that, girl. It's not an either/or situation. I'm obviously concerned about both, if not in equal measure."

"Faran," I said quietly. "Let it go. Kelos, Siri, it sounds like you put together quite a detailed plan while you were poking around. Let's hear what you've got."

"Well," said Siri, "it starts off with us violating the hell out of Jax's desire that the youngsters remain in the background. They're full Blades now and I think we should treat them as such. I love Jax, but she's wrong to coddle them."

"Damned right she is," said Roric. "It's about time we got invited to sit at the adults' table."

"Not," said Ssolvey, from his shadow, "that we weren't going to just go ahead and move up on our own if we didn't get the nod."

"What's our role?" asked Maryam. It was the first time she'd spoken in nearly an hour, and I was surprised at the obvious eagerness in her voice. I'd expected her to back Jax, but maybe she was tired of being treated like a kid, too.

Siri continued. "While it's possible I would be able to function in the depths of the temple precinct, we've decided to assume that I can't. That means I'm stuck in the outermost loop, and it would be foolish not to do what we can to take advantage of that."

"Like what?" asked Faran.

"The temple of Zhen-Ki is in that outermost ring," said Siri.

"Now I'm confused," replied Faran. "What does the Binder of Demons have to do with anything?"

"In this case, everything," said Kelos. "Heaven's Reach is a church-state, and it has to fulfill all the functions of any government. That includes having someplace to put people who break church law. Mostly, they go to a stand-alone prison fortress operated by the Sword of Heaven at the far end of the great valley. But prisoners of the Hand stay here in the city, in a small dungeon below the temple of Zhen-Ki."

"So, right before dawn," Siri said, taking the lead back from Kelos, "I intend to lead our three observers here in to free as many of the prisoners as we can." She nodded to Maryam. "I don't know who's in the dungeons there at the moment, but I'm certain busting them out will provide Aral's crew with a hell of a distraction. If we're lucky, it will provide us with some allies, too. I don't know what their quality will be, but if the Son of Heaven has chosen to jail dissident members of the Hand and the Shadow instead of simply liquidating them, we might produce some major fireworks once we crack them loose."

Kelos spoke again. "Then, after Siri starts making noise and calling down hell on the prison right as the sun comes up, you and Faran and I will make our run at the inner temple."

"I really don't like the idea of working in daylight." Ssithra spoke from her perch on Faran's shoulder.

"No Shade does," Malthiss replied, without lifting himself free of Kelos's tattoos, "but I don't think we have any choice in the matter this time. There are simply too many of the risen in the temple precinct right now for us to do anything else."

"Is that it?" I asked.

Siri shrugged. "Pretty much. There are a lot of details

that we simply can't plan in advance on this one given the time constraints imposed by that"—she pointed at the finger—"and the way the risen are swarming all over everything. Kelos has some very detailed maps of the precinct in general and the targets in specific. Looking over those, I haven't seen any other good options."

"Sewers?" I said. "I'm asking because I want to be thorough, not because I think you haven't considered it."

Kelos shook his head. "They're kept brimful all the time, and even the best spells for breathing water won't work in sewage. There's just not enough of what we need to breathe in the stuff to start with. That's a problem the risen don't have, which makes it a perfect place for the Son of Heaven to hide an army. There are thousands of them down there."

"What about the clean water supply?" I asked without much hope.

A city this size needed a lot of water, and being in a valley meant it would come down from the hills. Usually, in situations like this, water was brought in through stone-walled tunnels that mirrored a sewer system. But anyone with any sense of security made sure that wards against water-breathing were built deep into the stones of the walls wherever the channels passed under protected areas. Such things could be broken, but it was long, slow, tedious work and it didn't buy you much even if it didn't trigger alarms. While the main arteries of an aqueduct might be big enough to pass a man, well shafts were always heavily guarded, or made too small for a human to move through.

"The supply channel wards are even nastier than usual," answered Kelos. "Some previous Son of Heaven convinced the Queen of the Waters to reinforce the wards with godmagic. They are completely unbreakable."

I nodded. "That's more or less what I figured. Let me think for a moment." I got up and walked away from the others. I was First Blade now, and the call was mine. I wouldn't make it lightly.

Well? sent Triss. *What do you think about all this?*

I think I want to go in and properly game the whole thing

out myself and make my own damn plan. I also think that would waste time we don't have given the way the spell on that finger is going bad. Besides, one of the key things I'm going to have to learn if I'm going to become a good First Blade is to trust other people to know their jobs. Siri and Kelos are both at least as good at this stuff as I am. Second guessing them is a waste of time we don't have.

Truth. He gave a little mental sigh, and I could feel him working himself up to tell me something he didn't think I'd want to hear. *You do realize that if we go all the way in and don't kill the Son of Heaven, getting out will be a major problem?*

It's occurred to me, yes. But . . . But what? Really? I know that he deserves death, Triss. I know it all the way down to my toes, but I still can't bear the idea of all the other deaths his will bring. That's part of why I have to go in regardless of my misgivings. If I don't actually face him, I will never be able to make the decision to kill him.

You're trying to force your own hand—give yourself no choice but to kill him.

Maybe I am.

What will that do to you? And what if it doesn't work? What if you get in there and you can't kill him?

I don't know, Triss, I really don't know. But this is the only way I can see forward. I just wish I could leave Faran with Siri.

Absolutely not!

What? Why?

Because I won't see you commit suicide. If you left Faran behind I would know that you had no intention of coming back, whatever lies you might tell yourself about the thing. I've seen you give up on yourself, but never on her. No. Faran comes, or we don't go in at all.

Maybe you're right. Will you back me?

You know I will. Always and to the end.

Then I guess it's time we put the play in motion.

I walked back to the others. "So, when do we hit them?"

"I vote for tomorrow night," said Siri. "I wish we could

go now, given the rapid decay on that thing, but it's late, you're visibly exhausted from your travels, and the rest of us need a good day's sleep before we're in top form, too."

"Siri's right all around," said Kelos. "We need a break, but we can't afford to wait even a minute longer than we have to after that."

I took a deep breath and let it out slowly. "All right, people, get some sleep. Tomorrow we face the Son of Heaven."

21

---•---

"**Y**ou played me?" I demanded. "Again?"

"You say that like you're surprised," said Kelos. "Now, are you going to take advantage of the opportunity I've opened up, or are you going to let hurt feelings make you throw away the one good chance we have at the Son of Heaven?" Then he ducked back through the hole in the wall.

Step back a moment in time to Kelos leading us to an air shaft on top of a poorly cared-for shrine built to propitiate the Spirit of Jealousy. . . .

Where the High Lords and Ladies of Heaven like Shan or Athera had mighty temples in the heart of the precinct, the more minor inhabitants of the Celestial Kingdom had to settle for lesser placement and inferior shrines. Some of them weren't even granted the courtesy title of "god" though they were said to come of the same stock as their more powerful peers. Jealousy, with his hideously painted face and furry back, was such a one.

"This will be the perfect place to hole up for a few hours." Kelos gestured for us to precede him down the air shaft. "It's exceedingly rare for any but the priests to make offerings to Jealousy. The shrine would have made a good secondary fallback but for one thing."

"What's that?" I asked a few moments later as he joined us in the circular room below.

An apelike stone idol hunched in the center of the floor, glaring enviously toward the door and the deeps of the precinct beyond. We had all lowered our shrouds far enough to expose our faces, but Triss remained in his dormant state for the moment. There was no point in waking him up until I was sure we had a secure place to settle in and wait out the hours till dawn.

"Let me show you." Kelos reached for the low pedestal beneath the crouching Spirit of Jealousy.

With a shove and a back-punishing twist, he forced the idol aside. Before I could say anything, he dropped through the hole he had exposed.

"There's something fishy going on here," said Faran. "I don't like the smell of it."

Neither did I, but I didn't want to risk the mission either, so I just sighed. "Not much to do about it now but follow him." Then I dropped into the hole myself.

Below, a second circular chamber echoed the room above. Only this one was half-full of the bones of sacrifices—mostly goats, but here and there I spied a human skull. They covered all of the floor except for the space directly under the trapdoor and a path that had been forced through the bones to a rough hole punched through the back wall.

"What is this place?" I whispered—I'd never heard of Jealousy having the kind of following that would have produced such offerings.

"Trappings of a secret cult a thousand years old," said Kelos. "A hidden priesthood concealed within the greater practice of the Spirit Fellows." The Fellows were the priestly hierarchy devoted to serving all of the lesser denizens of Heaven—a motley bunch looked down on by the rest of the church.

"I've never even heard of anything like a separate cult of Jealousy," Faran said as she joined us.

"No surprise," replied Kelos. "It died here about the time you were born. That's when I strangled the last of Jealousy's exclusive priests."

"Why do I think that I'm going to hate where this is going?" I said.

"Because you're a soft-hearted soul, and occasionally a fool." Kelos ducked through the low hole in the back wall. "You've never liked the expediencies of the job, and these people were an expediency, if a necessary one." He stuck his head back through the gap. "You're lagging, and you're sentimentalizing. Needlessly, I might add. The followers of Jealousy were as nasty a set of bloody-minded old murderers as you could ask for, and they needed killing for plenty of reasons beyond mine."

"How reassuring." I sighed. "Given all the preparations here, and the fact that you didn't mention any of them to anyone when we were gaming out our play yesterday, I have to assume there's more to this visit than holing up and waiting for sunrise and Siri's distraction?"

"Of course there is." Kelos barked a sharp word of command then and spell-light flared beyond the arch. "I've just started the aqueducts draining. It'll take some time and, flow rates being what they are, they'll likely start to fill again before they finish emptying. In the brief window before that happens we have a clear road to the Son of Heaven's palace and one chance to take it."

Which brought us full circle to my, "You played me?" and Kelos's response before he ducked back into the passage beyond the hidden chamber.

As soon as Kelos was out of sight, Faran whispered in my ear. "I'm going to kill him."

"Fair enough," I whispered back.

"But not till afterward, please," Kelos called back. "The waterways are a maze, and I'm the only one who knows the way. You'll need my help to get to the Son of Heaven."

"Fine," said Faran, no longer trying to avoid being overheard. "I'll wait."

"Deal," said Kelos.

Beyond the rough hole, a short passage led maybe ten feet forward and three down before ending at a circular opening in the floor like a well. Jealousy's shrine was built up against the outer wall of the temple precinct, which meant the well-like opening lay just inside the magical boundary of the precinct. Kelos was nowhere to be seen, but a rope ladder led downward. A glance over the edge showed a crudely dug shaft leading into the top of a vaulted channel nearly full of water. I started down the ladder.

"There's about three inches of air clearance at the top of the channel now," Kelos called up from below. "It'll get bigger as we go along, but that's enough to get started. We should be more than halfway to the Son of Heaven by the time Siri starts her diversion."

I wanted to scream and rant, or simply call off the mission. Instead, I eased myself down into the chilly water. I had no doubt that Kelos was telling the truth about this being a one-time opportunity, and I wondered idly how long ago he'd set it up. His mention of strangling the priest around the time that Faran was born, suggested that parts of it went back many years. But that wasn't all that important, so I pushed it aside. I might not *want* to deal with the Son of Heaven, but I knew that I had to face him, and this might be my only chance.

And, honestly, where we were when Siri started her diversion didn't really matter. It wouldn't affect her choices at all. I ducked my head under the surface and looked around. Kelos was perhaps ten feet ahead of me, unshrouded and pulling himself along the roof of the broad tunnel— easily visible because of the bright magelight dangling from his belt. The water was so clear that he seemed to be hanging in empty space, or clinging impossibly to the roof of the tunnel. The stone of the walls was the color of clover honey and rough cut. It also glowed very faintly golden with spell-light. I released Triss then, since we apparently weren't worrying about light or being seen.

What's going on? he asked.

Kelos is playing us again. I'll tell you about it as we go.

Of course he is. Triss continued to whisper into my mind for several long seconds after that, but he shifted to the language of the Shades, and all that I could tell was that he was swearing calmly and at length. I felt the same way.

"Do we even need Siri's diversion anymore?" I asked as I began to pull myself along behind Kelos—a faint but distinct current helped me along.

"Of course we do," said Kelos. "That's always been part of the plan if I could manage it. It's why I convinced Roric that he should talk Jax into sending along some of the youngsters as 'observers.' Though, honestly, I'm not sure whether the risen will be more or less susceptible to the call of distraction than the Hand and the Sword would have been."

"Always?" I said, rather shocked at the lack of any heat to my anger. I was more tired of Kelos's shit than anything.

"Well, since Chomarr told us about the new arrangements and I had to recalculate this version of the plan as a group effort, anyway. More recently, the water entrance was a third-order backup plan involving just you or Siri, with me trailing myself through town as bait to distract people from noticing the falling wells. But then you didn't kill the Son of Heaven, and I had to bump it up the list."

"I thought you said the wards down here were unbreakable," Faran called as she caught up to me.

"They are," replied Kelos. "That's why I had to get my Durkoth Uthudor to create a temporary way to rechannel the system inflow here. That's what I triggered with that spell, by the way. Without the air pockets created by diverting the water, this approach would be utterly impossible. That's why I'm so sure the Son of Heaven won't have bothered to rekey the wards on the gates down here. There is no good way for him to drain the aqueducts and access them without a massive investment of time and magic. He has plenty of the former, but has become ever weaker in the latter."

"Why are we using a light?" grumbled Ssithra. "Especially such a bright one?"

"Risen," replied Kelos. "The Son of Heaven has kept a few of his nasties down here since the beginning."

Faran made a face. "Ewww, what does that do to the water?"

"Nothing too horrible as long as he keeps the number small," said Kelos. "The only disease the restless dead carry is the curse itself, and they mostly stop losing bits after a while. Especially if they've been dry cured and then limed and pickled. It's not like wild water, so there's no conflicting elemental magic to wear them away."

"I know I'm going to hate myself for asking," said Faran, "but, dry cured? Limed and pickled? I've never heard of either of those things before, at least not with regards to the restless dead."

"I think the Son invented both techniques. For dry curing, he takes a risen and packs them in a barrel of salt for a few months. At the end of that time, their flesh is essentially the texture of jerky. Liming and pickling are a part of the tanning process, and comes after dry curing—he needs to get most of the moisture out of the flesh first. I believe that he has also tried smoking them, though that was less effective. And the natron method rendered them incredibly vulnerable to any kind of open flame."

"Is it my imagination," I asked then, "or is the current slowing?" I really didn't want to hear any more about the Son of Heaven's restless dead experiments and a change in current could be a serious issue if it wasn't in the plan.

"Not your imagination," replied Kelos. "The current should come to a stop in about a half hour, and then it will reverse for a while. At that point, the water will start to drop much faster. The mechanics aren't worth going into, but I needed a delay to allow whoever ended up making this approach to get clear before the big drain opened up. Without that, we'd be sucked right down into the deeps and drown there—because of the god-magic reinforcing them, the effects of the wards against water-breathing extend some hundreds of feet down and out from the temple precinct."

I don't like the sound of that, sent Triss.

Neither do I.

The water had come down another three or four inches

by now, making it much easier to carry on a conversation. The clarity of the water was kind of eerie. With Kelos's light carried below the surface you really couldn't see it at all, only feel it buoying you up. Any time I looked down, it felt like I ought to be falling.

"How far in do we have to get to prevent that from becoming an issue?" I asked.

"Beyond the first of the gates, at least," said Kelos. "It shouldn't be a problem."

"Why is it that I don't trust a word you say?" I grumbled.

"Because you're finally learning?" answered Faran.

Kelos laughed aloud—a growly sort of laugh. "Point. Though, to be fair, I am telling the truth this time."

"Of course you are," said Triss. "We have your word for it, right?"

"Of course." Kelos laughed again. "You should never trust me to tell you everything, but you can always trust me to tell you everything you need to know. How to avoid drowning while you're doing what I want you to do is definitely something you need to know."

"That's so very reassuring," said Faran.

"Don't let it get you down," said Kelos. "You're going to kill me when we're done here anyway, so what does it matter?"

"That's the plan, yes," she agreed. "But I'm pretty sure I'm not the first person who had that on their agenda, and you're still here. So you'll forgive me if I wait to put a mark on my hilt for you until after I see you bleed out."

"True, and fair enough, though you *will* have one decided advantage over every previous attempt." Kelos's tone became much more serious then, as he turned through an arch on the left—it was the third on that side and fifth overall, and I couldn't see anything to distinguish it from the others. "Once the Son of Heaven is dead, my job is done. I'm a tired old man, and at that point I shall be quite ready for my final rest."

Do you think that's another play? asked Triss.

I don't know anymore. I sent a mental shrug. *We were*

certain he wanted me to kill him back at Ashkent's castle, but he's still here. Is that because we outplayed him then? Or is it because we did exactly what he wanted us to do?

Or did he simply set it up so that he won either way? He can't be that good, can he really?

Maybe . . . or maybe he's got us so bamboozled he doesn't even have to play us anymore, we just do it to ourselves because we believe he's that good. We took a right turning then, following Kelos through another arch. *All I'm certain of is that he really and truly wants to bring down the current order. . . .*

And how do you feel about that, Aral? You sound wary. Have you made your decision yet?

It should be so simple. The Son of Heaven destroyed us. He's half-undead, a master of the risen, and a manipulator of kingdoms. But if I kill him, kingdoms will fall and tens of thousands will die. Maybe hundreds of thousands. If I leave him alive, he will do unmeasurable evil. . . .

But if you kill him, you will do unmeasurable evil. Or, at least, that's how you see it. You know I don't agree with you about that. From where I sit, the responsibility either way is his.

I know, Triss, and I know that taking it on myself isn't entirely sane. But I can't help it. I have always bled for the unintended victims of my actions. We took a left then, as I tried to think of how to express my feelings. *Here, try this: What would you have thought if I had suggested we poison everyone at a state banquet as a way to reach Ashvik? There are slow acting poisons that we could have used to do just that, things that would have gotten past his tasters because they wouldn't have taken effect for days or weeks.*

That's monstrous, Aral! You would never have done such a thing.

What if it was the only way to ghost him? He killed thousands of his own subjects including his own sons, and tens of thousands more in Kadesh. If we hadn't killed him, it would only have gotten worse. Isn't stopping that worth the price of a few dozen courtiers? People who supported

Ashvik in his madness and profited from it? Really, how many true innocents dined with the man on any regular basis?

I don't think the situation with the Son of Heaven is the same, though I can't quite explain why.

We turned left again.

But it is *the same,* I replied. *In fact, it's worse. The only way to kill the Son of Heaven is to do something that will kill an awful lot of other people as well. And, unlike that banquet scenario, a lot of the people who die will be genuine innocents, guilty of nothing more than being in the wrong place at the wrong time. That's what starting a war does, Triss. You can tell yourself that not starting it will result in worse evil, and maybe you're even right, but it won't bring a single one of those innocents back.*

But you can't know that this will start a war, can you?

Maybe not, but I believe that it will. So did Toragana, and the Lady of Leivas. For that matter, I think that was the true message of the goddess in my dream, that I must always be aware of the costs of my actions, that justice isn't just a matter of guilt and innocence, but also a question of weighing the benefits and the price. Independent of the innocent deaths I believe it will bring, slaying the Son of Heaven is clearly just. When you bring in the cost though . . . I don't know the answer, but I still have to make the choice and accept the consequences.

I . . . Oh, Aral.

The initial evil may be the Son of Heaven's fault, but I won't . . . can't use that to excuse my own actions. Not without losing my moral core. Not without becoming a monster myself. I may have *to kill him, but I won't look away from what that means.*

Before Triss could respond, Kelos called back, "The first gate is right around this next bend. Give me the key so I can open it."

At that point we had passed three openings on the right and one on the left in this section, and while I *thought* I could have found my way out on my own if I needed to, I wouldn't have bet my life on it. The place really was a maze—chock full of twisty passages with nothing to distinguish one from another.

"I think I'd rather open it myself." I slipped past Kelos to look through the arch.

"Fine by me," said Kelos, "though it'd be quicker for me to carry it if I'm going to lead."

"I'll suffer the inconvenience."

This passage was closed off by a large iron grate that sat about five feet back from the arch that led into it. The grate was perhaps eight feet tall, and ten across at the base where it was broadest, and it glowed a dim red in magesight because of the wardings woven into the iron. In the middle was a smaller, circular grate with a glyph-covered steel plate centering it. I pulled out the Signet's finger, briefly checking the progression of the rot before I dove to press the ring against a bright green spot that perfectly matched the size and shape of the seal on the ring's bezel.

The edges of the gate flared with spell-light and it pivoted aside, but I barely noticed. As I used the ring, I felt a sharp tugging sensation as if there were a thread running up from the spell lock, through the ring and finger to my own hand, and thence to my heart, where the sudden tug left a tiny hole—like a needle coming out of a finger. Nothing like that had happened when I had used the key on my last visit to the temple precinct, and I glanced quickly at the finger. I couldn't be sure, but I thought the line of rot might have advanced a hair's breadth from where it was only moments before.

What the hell was that? demanded Triss.

In a minute, I sent back.

I quickly tucked the finger away again—if there was something going badly wrong there I didn't want the others to know until I had a better grip on it myself. I swam through the little gate, closely followed by Kelos and then Faran. It had already begun to close itself as Kelos moved ahead of me in the passage again. We swam now rather than pulling ourselves along on the ceiling, as the water level had dropped too far to make the latter practical, and the current had completely stalled.

As we fell back into a line, Triss nudged me again mentally. *Well . . .*

I don't know, Triss. I think that using the ring on that gate did something to the finger. I couldn't say what.

Why do I think you're not telling me something?

Because you've been spending too much time around Kelos, and it's making you paranoid?

I fully intended to tell him more about the finger once I figured out what was going on. I just didn't want him panicking and trying to call the whole thing off prematurely if I was only imagining things. Well, and being honest with myself, even if I wasn't imagining it, I would be very reluctant to pull out now. We were so close, and this was the only chance we would have to make use of the water route.

Maybe you're right, sent Triss. *Maybe I am being paranoid, but if you're holding out on me . . .*

Would I do that?

You have. You do. You will again. Usually you believe you have a good reason. Usually, you're wrong. Next question?

Fine. Kelos led us into yet another branch of the tunnel. *When I used the ring, it felt like something tugged at my heart, and maybe, maybe, the rot line moved. But I might have just imagined that part.*

We should turn back, right now.

And give up what might be our best shot at the Son of Heaven?

Aral, you don't even want to do this!

But I can't not. You see that, don't you? One way or the other, I have to face him and decide the fate of the East.

I . . . Argh! You are the most frustrating creature I have ever met!

"Is the current moving the other way now?" asked Faran.

"Yes," replied Kelos. "I think you're right. Let's hurry, there's another gate just beyond the next arch. If we can get through it quick enough, that'd be a really good thing. I didn't expect to make it this far this fast, but we have, and that gives us a much better chance."

Perhaps two minutes later, we were at the gate. By then, the current going back the other way was strong enough that swimming against it had become damned hard. Having the grate to cling to was an enormous relief.

Watch the finger as I open this gate, I sent to Triss. *Tell me if the rot moves.*

Dammit, I don't think—

By then I was already pressing the seal against the spell lock. This time, I expected the tugging on my heart. That didn't make it feel any less awful, but at least it allowed me to brace for it.

The line moved, sent Triss. *It definitely moved.*

That's not good.

No! It's not. We have to turn back.

I don't think it's an option at the moment, Triss. Remember what Kelos said about getting sucked into the deeps and drowning?

I didn't wait for his response as I went for the gate. The current had increased enough that dragging myself through took real effort, and letting it press me against the grate on the far side was almost a pleasure. Faran came next, with Kelos last.

"Hang on tight," said Kelos while the flow increased and increased again till it felt like it was trying to press me right through the bars of the grate.

The water level dropped a good three feet over the next few minutes, leaving that much more flowing along the bottom of the tunnel, and the current made it foam and froth as it went through the grate. We were able to climb down and put our feet on the floor then, though there was no chance of moving against the weight of the water quite yet. I was about to ask Kelos how much longer we might have to wait before it slowed enough to move on, when I saw a pair of dark shapes eeling through the water at the edge of our light.

"Risen!" I shouted, drawing my swords and dropping

them into a low guard, though I couldn't do anything in terms of stance with my legs pressed back against the iron bars.

Kelos mirrored me on my right, bracing for the risen attack, but Faran was more clever than either of us. Pulling herself up out of the water, she kicked off the gate and launched herself forward, landing full on the back of the one coming in at me and punching her swords down and through its torso. A moment later, they both slammed into the grate a few inches to my left. Faran got up, the risen did not. The other one—coming in on Kelos's far side—suddenly kicked off the bottom then, bursting up and out of the water like a crocodile going after a pig that had gotten too close to the shore.

But Kelos was no pig. He scissored his swords up and out, meeting the thing's pounce. It still hit him square in the chest, but it did so minus its head and its arms below the elbows.

I had a sudden nasty thought. "How aware do you think those things are?"

"I don't know," said Kelos. "Why?"

"Because the risen curse is the Son of Heaven's familiar. If he can see through their eyes . . ."

"Then he might know we're here. Is that what you're suggesting?" asked Faran.

"Exactly."

"I don't think so," replied Kelos. "From what I've seen he *can* look out through their eyes, but mostly he doesn't. There are simply too many of them seeing too many different things all at once. You know how hard it is to look at the world with a Shade's vision. Admittedly, that's a much more alien view of the world than a dead man's, but it's only one set of 'eyes' as it were. My sense of the thing is that the Son mostly doesn't try to put himself into their heads, and when he does do it, he can't really focus on more than one or two at a time."

I let out a sigh. "There's a relief."

Kelos tilted one sword back and forth noncommittally. "Yes and no. While he probably didn't *see* any of that, he might have been able to *feel* the risen die. Hopefully Siri has started her attack above by now, and he's got lots of distraction on that front, but it probably wouldn't hurt to hurry things along from here on out."

He pushed forward, forcing his way through water that had dropped to about two feet, and against a much reduced flow. I fell in immediately behind Kelos, letting him take the brunt of the current.

You're not going to turn back, are you? asked Triss.

No. I'm not. I can't. I've come too far, and there's too much at stake. I've got to see this through, one way or the other.

Are you going to kill the Son of Heaven?

I wish I knew, Triss, I really wish I knew.

22

---·•·---

Walking into the darkness.

That's what life is really, one step after another toward the darkness that will inevitably claim us all. Some steps we take with eyes wide open and a firm sense that our feet will land on solid ground. Others are blind. Either way, we're moving forward with the knowledge that whatever happens in the next few seconds, the road ultimately ends in the abyss.

I was in the dark now, and any step might be my last, a fact that I was infinitely aware of as I lifted the Signet's finger to open the next gate. The grates had grown more frequent as we moved deeper under the temple precinct, and I was no longer under any doubts about whether the process of rot was being accelerated by my use of the key. The last gate, our sixth since the water fell to knee height, had pushed the line of rot beneath the thick band of the ring.

I couldn't see the point of failure in the spell anymore, and this gate might be the one that sent the rot to the root, the one that would show me once and for all what would happen if the spell backlashed through me. But there was no point in turning back, even if I'd been willing. The gates locked behind us, and we would need the key just as much going the other way. No matter what happened, I would come to the end of its magic soon. I could feel it in my heart where the finger's failing powers thrummed and fluttered continually now, like the beating of a trapped dragonfly's wings.

Here goes nothing, I sent to Triss as I pressed the bezel to the lock.

The fluttering in my heart briefly became a burning, gnawing pain, as though ants were biting it from the inside. Then a sharp click sounded and the gate pivoted aside. I held my breath, but no darkling band emerged from beneath the ring and the pain in my heart receded to the featherlight touch of phantom wings.

And we win another round. I breathed a gentle sigh. But as I went to tuck the ring away, the tip of the finger broke off and fell away. *Shit!*

I *really* didn't want Faran to see that.

I've got it, sent Triss. Shadow swirled in front of me and the bit of rotting flesh vanished into the darkness at the same time that I slipped through the gate. *Your secret is safe for a little bit longer.*

That's all I need, really. Kelos said this was the last gate. The finger just has to hold together for another half hour or so and then it won't matter.

What!? Triss's mental voice split the difference between furious and horrified.

Sorry, Triss. That didn't come out right. I mean that the secret won't matter. I do intend to live through this . . . well, I hope to anyway.

You'd damned well better!

The current had reversed once again, and the level was slowly rising, having come up maybe two inches in the last quarter of an hour. Faran followed me through the gate. Kelos was in the process of joining us when a pair of risen came a-slithering through the water. Faran and I were able to dispatch them easily enough in the shallows, bringing our total for the venture up to ten. Whether it was because the

Son of Heaven preferred not to taint the water he himself had to drink—Faran's theory—or simply because he wasn't worried about the aqueducts as a serious possibility for invasion, there just weren't that many risen down here.

"So, what now?" I asked.

Kelos had been very tight with information thus far, a fact that made me nervous. Without him to lead us we would have been utterly lost in the labyrinthine aqueduct. With the water rising again that was an ugly thought. We had passed a number of wells that we might be able to climb out of, but that would be the same as abandoning the mission.

He waved a hand ahead. "We walk up that way about seventy feet and duck around the corner. That will take us beneath the courtyard in front of the Son of Heaven's apartments."

I remembered it well, a huge area enclosed under a staggeringly expensive roof of the finest and clearest glass, which allowed for a very fair counterfeit of the Celestial City and the True Heaven itself. The paths—surfaced with chips of ivory and fragments of pearl—danced in and out through a garden filled with tropical rarities that had no business surviving in this part of the world. Jade tiles faced the walls of the buildings surrounding the courtyard as well as the gold-roofed pavilion that centered it. Even the fishpond was floored with fragments of precious stone.

"And then?" I asked.

"The pond," said Kelos. "There aren't any man-sized wells within the courtyard, but there is a ceramic pipe with a small bucket-chain pump in it for filling the pond. It's not big enough for a man either, but we can yank it out, and that'll give us a way up to the surface that doesn't require blasting a giant and noisy hole in anything. It'll be a damned tight fit for me, but a bit of grease and some luck should make it workable. I'll be going last, of course, in case I get wedged."

We were able to accomplish our demolition in relative silence by dint of getting Malthiss to send the pins that held the pump and most of the piping into the everdark. Soon we had a rough hole in the ceiling. Faran wanted to go first, claiming the right as the smallest, but I nixed that idea on the grounds that she didn't know the layout above and I did.

Are you ready for this, Triss? I asked as I looked up into the raw opening. *I don't know what we're going to encounter up there, but the chances are good that I won't be able to loose you until it's all over.*

He sent the Shade equivalent of a sigh. *I'll be fine. It's you I'm worried about. You might be able to hide your worries from Faran and Kelos, but I can sense exactly how conflicted you are about all of this. Don't let indecision get you killed, all right?*

I won't . . . I hope.

Not very reassuring. You know that, right?

I wish I had a better answer for you, Triss, but I don't. I could never go back to the way it was before, with Namara making all my decisions for me. I know that. I've grown beyond being that person, but sometimes I wish that I hadn't. I wish that someone else was making the hard choices. . . .

I don't. There's no one in the world I trust more to do what is right, Aral. No one. I may prod and push and tease, but I believe in you more than I ever believed in any goddess. You will *make the right choice when you have to. You always have. I just hope that it's a choice that's got a happy ending.*

That would *be nice,* I sent, though I had very serious doubts about it.

It would. But, if it isn't . . . well, I'll go with you to face the lords of judgment without any regrets. We've had an amazing run, my friend.

We have indeed.

Let's go get 'em.

My sense of Triss as an independent presence dropped away as he slid into the dream state that allowed me to use his skills and senses as my own. Kelos gave me a boost into the base of the shaft then, and I began to climb. I paused briefly when I reached the top to brace my feet solidly in the holes where the supports had once been. There, I pressed my ear to the thick jade plate that concealed the workings of the pump from defiling the garden view above.

Nothing.

But then, I hadn't expected to hear anything. Not unless Siri's distraction had grown into something earth-shattering. The garden was designed to emulate the peace and opulence of the Celestial City. Having guards, human or risen, visibly tramping around it would have interfered with the faux divinity of the setting, and that was true whether there was an emergency in the outer wards of the precinct or not.

Next, I extended the portion of me that was, at least temporarily, a thing of elemental shadow down the short ceramic pipe that led from the top of the pump to the concealed outlet in the pond. The pipe opened under the arched bridge that divided the pond into two unequal halves. But my borrowed darksight revealed nothing more than my ears had. The dawn light spilling across the courtyard garden was simply too bright for me to perceive anything much beyond the immediate area around the bridge with Triss's senses. Lacking any other choice, it was time to move.

I pulled my shadow back in tight around me and reshaped it into a shroud of darkness, rendering myself functionally invisible. Then I took a deep breath, put both hands under the center of the jade plate, and pushed straight up. It grated very faintly as it lifted free of the lip, and though I expected the noise, I winced. Straightening my back and shoulders, I rose up and tipped the plate to one side, lowering the edge silently to the rich soft earth of the garden.

The pump access was concealed within a small clump of shrubbery, allowing the gardeners to perform maintenance without visibly inflicting their peasant presence on those who believed themselves their betters. As had so often happened in the past, the triumph of aristocratic aesthetics over practical and security considerations created an opening I could exploit. Not to mention providing me with a protective patch of shade. It was a small justice of the poetic sort.

Once I had the plate stowed, I climbed out and pulled my sword rig up behind me, slipping it on over bare shoulders and reattaching my new trick bag. The shaft was too tight for me to fit with the rig or even a shirt on my back, though

I hadn't needed to strip completely. I chose not to waste the time and create the momentary vulnerability of putting my shirt back on now. With each minute that passed the sun would rise higher, weakening our shrouds and posing a greater danger to us and our mission. I sent a faint tickle of orange pink magelight down the hole as I moved aside.

Faran appeared a moment later—a blot of deeper darkness in the shadow under the brush, identifiable mainly by the sword rig she pulled behind her. Kelos took longer and had a hard time of it. Even after leaving shirt and pants at the bottom of the well and greasing his shoulders, he ended up with deep and bloody scrapes on his right arm and down his left shoulder blade—exposed to sight briefly when he lowered his shroud to check the injury.

"One of the many reasons I'd intended this route for you or Siri." He rubbed a bit of blue black ointment into his scratches—the bleeding slowed immediately, but his sharply indrawn breath suggested the effect came at some cost. "Damn, but that hurts. It's a Kadeshi recipe made from manticore chitin among other things. It stings like a whole swarm of wasps, but it'll keep me from leaving a blood trail." He hadn't bothered to reclothe himself, so he was wearing little more than boots and a loincloth as he slid to the edge of our little copse.

"The lights are burning bright in the Son's apartments despite the morning sun," he whispered after a long moment of looking and listening. "Judging by the shadows playing across the windows, there's a lot of activity within, too. I suspect that Siri's raid is having at least some of the desired effect. I hope she finds Chomarr out there and nails his hide to the wall." He started to edge forward. "We should move quickly."

"Wait," whispered Faran. "Do you smell that? There's rot under the blossoms."

"Risen?" I asked.

"That would be my guess," she replied.

"Good nose," whispered Kelos, "and better thinking. I'm impressed."

"Fresh turned earth, too," I added after taking a few deep

sniffs myself. "A lot of it. I wonder . . ." A thought occurred to me. "He's very image conscious, this Son of Heaven. Even if everyone this deep into the complex knows what he is now, I bet he doesn't want the risen making an eyesore of themselves."

"You think he's buried them all through the garden," whispered Faran.

"It'd be the best way to keep them close but out of sight," I replied.

"That changes things," whispered Kelos. "I'd intended for us to go straight for his apartments from here, but there's a lot of garden between us and it, and much of it shadowed enough for the risen to brave the dawn. Let me think. . . ." A brief silence followed. "Right, we'll go in via the gallery. It's much closer, and the Son had a door knocked through from there to his playrooms."

"Playrooms?" asked Faran.

"He's almost half-risen himself," said Kelos. "He shares their blood hunger, even if it's expressed somewhat differently. He ejected his chief aide and several other members of the curia from the suites below his own and had the whole place made over so that he could indulge himself."

"Torture chambers," said Faran.

"And more," he replied. "Come on, the wall of windows directly across the pond opens into the gallery. They're east facing and that whole section of garden catches the morning light, which will help keep the risen off us if they sense our passing. I presume I don't need to remind you to walk extra light and—"

"Watch for fresh turned earth," finished Faran. "No, you don't."

"I didn't think so." The dark blot that was Kelos slid back into the heart of the little copse and out the other side heading for the small bridge.

The sun started chewing painfully away at my shroud the instant I cleared the shadow of the shrubs, blinding my darksight and forcing me to peel back the shadows across my eyes. Operating in bright daylight came at a heavy cost in both efficiency and magic as I fed nima to a sleeping Triss to hold the shroud in place. But we didn't dare rush or cut corners.

Even on the shorter route we passed four or five carefully concealed disturbances in the earth, like shallow graves . . . rather exactly like. But nothing popped out at us. By the time we reached the windows, I was soaked in sweat. The fluttering of my heart in rhythm with the failing spells on the finger of the Signet in my pouch added another beat of urgency to the whole thing. I needed to get this thing settled one way or the other and quickly.

"These didn't used to be warded." Kelos's shroud blotted out the lower portion of a window. "Let's see . . ." The darkness briefly rose to hide the whole of the pane. "Yes." A low pop followed and, as the shadow retreated, the window pivoted inward. "They're often left open for days or weeks at a time to circulate fresh air through the wing."

Kelos vanished within. Faran went next, and I followed her, glancing back over my shoulder and sending up a silent prayer of thanks to my dead goddess that we hadn't wakened any of the sleepers under the earth. The paintings and screens we passed as we made our way through the nearer part of the gallery registered as weird, almost nightmarish mélanges of gloss and matte nothings in darksight, a marked contrast to the senses of my body. Shades simply didn't have the right vision for this kind of art.

The sculpture in the next section was a little better, though not much, as many of the figures were carved or shaped from a single type of material, and to Shade senses that made the representational pieces look disturbingly off. But none of the disconcerting effects caused by seeing the art through a Shade's "eyes" simultaneously with my own would have prepared me for the true nightmare of the next gallery. Nor Faran either, apparently, as I very nearly slammed into her when she stopped abruptly in the doorway. Our shrouds overlapped in an intimacy unique to our kind as I stopped inches behind her.

"That's human skin, isn't it?" she demanded, her quiet voice filled with anger. "What is this place?"

"Let me see." I put a hand on her shoulder as I slid through the narrow gap between her and the door frame.

I had suspicions cultivated from a long ago discussion with Devin, but I wanted to see for myself. As soon as I slipped past Faran, I took a look around. What I saw hit me like a punch to the heart, temporarily overwhelming the flutters coming from the Signet's finger. The large room was filled with dozens of frames of varying sizes and shapes, each one displaying a piece of the tattooist's art. The tattooist's, and the flayer's and the tanner's . . .

Knowing what Devin had told me about the way they were created, I wanted to vomit. Each piece of beautifully tattooed skin had been inked while still attached to a living human being. Only after the artwork had healed completely was it separated from the awake and aware victim and preserved for display. Devin had told me that this Son of Heaven used the technique to punish those of his servants who had especially displeased him; that the flayers were very skilled and that with the aid of magical healing many of their subjects continued to serve the Son after losing the skin of an arm or shoulder. The craftsmanship was exquisite and horrifying.

Devin himself had an incredibly detailed and gorgeous depiction of the god Shan on his left forearm—a warning. The Son had it inscribed and explained to Devin that it was a down payment of sorts. If Devin ever significantly failed him again, the Son would have the piece expanded to cover every inch of Devin's skin before removing it for display in this gallery.

I couldn't help but look around then to see if any of the half-dozen full-body pieces included the Shan I had seen on Devin's arm, but none did. Hopefully that meant he was still breathing and attached to his skin, and not that it was off being prepared for display or in another gallery somewhere. I despised Devin, but not that much, and I pitied him, too.

"Aral?" It was Faran. "Are you all right? You just stopped. . . ."

"Not really. This is . . ."

"An abomination," hissed Kelos, who had returned from

the far end of the gallery. "One that we will hopefully end today. But we really don't have time to be properly horrified. We need to keep moving. Now, come on!"

As we started after Kelos, I leaned in close to Faran's ear. "This is the Son's failure gallery and I was looking for Devin's hide. I don't see it."

"You knew about this place?" she asked.

I shrugged, though she couldn't see it through my shroud. "Sort of, maybe. Devin told me about it, but I don't think I ever really believed him until today."

As we passed out of the gallery with its brightly burning morning light, and into a shady north-facing hall, I breathed a sigh of real relief, and slowed the flow of nima to my shroud to a trickle. The arrangement here was somewhat different from the formal galleries. A wide hallway ran for perhaps eighty feet with windows facing the garden on one side and open or window-fronted rooms on the other.

I was just reaching up to draw the shadows across my eyes again, when I bumped into Faran. Literally, this time. She was standing in front of the second room off the hall, a small, narrow, almost closet-like space that had been con-verted into a cell by the expedient of installing iron bars a foot or so in from where the windows had once been.

I peered into the cell. "Fuck." We had found Devin, though he was barely recognizable.

"Is he alive?" asked Faran.

It was a good question, and one I couldn't answer at a glance. He lay upon a padded table built in the shape of a spread-eagled human figure. It was tilted up at about a thirty-degree angle, with Devin's head higher than his feet, which were only a yard from the bars. He had been shaved top to toe, and with the exception of a hand-sized patch on his face, every inch of exposed skin was covered in intricate tattoos. If he *was* breathing, it was so slowly and shallowly that it barely moved his chest.

"Devin?" I said, aloud. "Devin, are you in there?" His eyes snapped open and looked my way, but that was the only indication that he was alive or aware in any way. "Devin?"

"He *is* alive," said Faran. "No one deserves this. We need to open this door and get him loose!"

"There's no point," said Kelos, "and no time." Then, when Faran's shadow reached over to cover the lock, he snapped, "Don't! He's not tied down. Not physically, anyway, and for now he's much safer in there with locks and bars between him and the risen than he would be without that protection."

As we spoke, Devin's eyes tracked from one shroud to the next, but again, that was his only motion or sign of life.

"I don't understand," I said. "What's holding him?"

"Word of command," said Kelos. "It's part of the geas we in the Shadow took upon ourselves when we swore allegiance to the Son of Heaven. Devin is alive and aware. He can feel everything that is done to him, but he can neither move nor speak. Not unless the Son wishes it."

"Can't we break the binding?" asked Faran.

"No. Not with the resources we have here and not without many days of ritual and spell work. The only way to free him short of that is to kill the Son of Heaven. So the sooner we do that, the sooner we can do something for Devin. Now come on, we *really* don't have time for any of this."

But I was reluctant to move on and leave someone I had once thought of as my brother in such a state, no matter what had happened between us since. "That's horrible." Then another thought occurred to me. "But you're . . ."

"I should be fine," replied Kelos. "It's the first thing I moved to break when I started chipping away at the geas. But we *really* can't do anything for him here. We need to get down to the far end of the hall and up the stairs beyond." He took three steps and then paused in front of the next cell. "My, my, what have we here?"

I moved forward and looked into the cell. "Well, if it isn't Lieutenant Chomarr." The Hand was strapped down tight with a leather gag to prevent him using verbal magic and his Storm familiar confined in a large blue glass bottle on a table behind him. He had a battle scene in lurid colors about half inked in on his chest. "How do you suppose he ended up here?"

"The Son of Heaven is a capricious master," said Kelos. "I imagine the fact that the invasion of Dalridia failed to result in a single Blade death told heavily against him, and the Son just—Shit! Risen!"

A half score or so of the restless dead came shambling in from the far end of the long windowed hallway. They had their heads raised and seemed to be sniffing the air. Without thinking, I closed the shroud in front of my face, cutting off my human vision in favor of darksight and added concealment.

"They smell the blood of the living," said Kelos. "Dammit! Into Devin's cell, quickly." I heard the lock pop, and a dark blot of shadows slipped inside, dropping down behind Devin. Faran and I followed a moment later, closing the gate behind us with a sharp click. "Quiet now. They can't see well under the best of circumstances and, hopefully, Devin and Zass's presence will mask ours where it comes to whatever other senses they have. He might as well be of some use to somebody for once."

Within a matter of minutes the dead were outside the cell. About half the pack dropped to hands and knees in front of the door and began sniffing along the floor. Most of those quickly moved off into the galleries beyond, heading for the side away from the sun. After several very long seconds, one of those that remained rose and looked in at us. Its rotting hands went to the bars of the gate and shook it gently. But the gate had locked behind us, and it didn't open. The risen pressed its face to one of the gaps and sniffed deeply. Then, shaking its head, it began to turn away . . . only to freeze an instant later.

I don't know how to describe what happened next. One beat, the risen at the gate seemed much of a kind with its brethren, all mindless malice and inhuman horror. The next, it became something more. Inhabited, if you will, filled with presence and purpose. Its milky eyes took on a sort of unholy glow that was clearly visible in darksight when it pressed its face once again to the bars. I could sense the Son of Heaven looking for us through them. . . .

23

———◆———

The Son of Heaven spoke with the voice of the dead. It was a horrible, rasping, impossible sound—words forced up a rotten windpipe by the bellows action of a pair of dry and blackened lungs, the whole modulated with vocal cords and tongue the consistency of jerky left too long in the sun.

"Is there someone in there with you, Devin? I think there might be. Perhaps some of your little Blade friends. I can't see anyone, but I smell more life than I should, both human and . . . that other. Come on, out with it, lad. . . . Oh, wait, you're tongue-tied, aren't you?"

The risen laughed then, a sound like nothing I had ever heard or hope to again—a jackal coughing up its own heart, perhaps. "Should I loosen that knot, do you think? Or should I make you choke on it? It's funny watching a man choke to death on his own tongue. Truly."

Chomarr's voice sounded from the next cell then, but heavily muffled and completely senseless as the gag kept the Hand from conveying anything useful. The risen glanced that way, but stayed where it was and turned back to our cell.

Drawing a rasping breath, it nodded at Devin. "Well, come on then, speak. I command you by the—"

The thing's head came apart like a rotten melon then as a rope of thick black night struck it full in the face. The attack came from the shadows on Devin's farther side where Kelos stood—a burst of congealed magic, like liquid smoke or lightning turned inside out, with a weird, dark, purplish spell-light accompanying it. The five remaining risen all whipped around as one, facing the cell. Kelos killed two more in the next instant with that same dark magic.

I was surprised by his mode of attack, because I had never seen anyone but Siri use the technique, and the first time I'd asked her to teach it to me, she'd flat refused, implying it was too dangerous for me. Later, when I tried again, she refused me again, citing the unstable marriage of elemental powers and the possibility of draining your soul away if you used it too much. That didn't keep me from wishing I could manage the trick. It was more effective than even the most powerful magelightning and it produced none of the Shade-poisoning light that came with that more common magic. Perhaps if Kelos and I both lived through the next few hours . . .

But that would all have to wait for after . . . if there was an after. I moved toward the gate in the wake of his blast, but it was already opening. Black steel licked out of a cloud of darkness as Faran slipped through and took the next one's head. I followed on her heels, stabbing another through the heart as Kelos killed the last with his dark fire.

The time of sneaking was over. At this point, only striking fast and hard had any chance of success. I turned and raced for the far end of the hall, trusting the others to do their jobs without need of any words from me. Someone— Kelos, probably—slammed Devin's cell shut behind us, a small mercy that verified my trust.

Knowing what I might have prepared in the same circumstances, I threw myself down on my belly a few feet short of the door, sliding along the slick jade tiles to pass through the door at ankle height. The vision of the Shades operates equally in every direction, and I was able to focus my attention up and back as I went, watching as a pair of risen leaped forward from either side of the door, only to crash into each other when the life they smelled wasn't where they expected it to be.

They died together, chopped in half by a goddess-forged sword, though whether it was Faran or Kelos who wielded it, I couldn't say. As the impetus of my dive slowed, I tucked into a ball and converted the last of my forward motion into a roll that put me back on my feet. The stairs were just ahead, with four more risen standing side by side on the third step up, forming a gate of rotting flesh.

There were more risen in the room around me, sensed more from movements at the edge of my attention than by truly seeing them. Though darksight may operate in every direction, the human mind—no matter how well trained and highly experienced—simply isn't equipped to fully deal with all the information that comes in that way.

I knew they were there, and I knew that none of them were close enough to prevent me from reaching the stairs, but their exact number and positioning was a thing beyond my ability to know in that moment. Neither did I care. The biggest danger from the risen came when they could use numbers against you. As long as I kept moving, I could ignore those behind me. Of course, if I slowed down, they would swarm me under.

When I reached a point eight feet or so from the stairs, I brought my swords up and back so that the blades pointed over my shoulders, and my elbows were in front of my chin. Then, as I took two more running steps, I snapped them forward and out as hard as I could. Edges met undead flesh at knee height. The risen are hard and tough, filled with a darkling curse that strengthens them against mortal steel. The swords of my lost goddess cut through eight legs like a scythe through wheat. The dead fell around and on top of me as my steel struck the jade-covered walls of the stairs, shattering tiles with a ringing crash.

Behind me, the remaining dead turned in toward the stairs

and their fallen brethren, putting their backs to the gallery . . .
and to my companions, who hit them like a gale of darkness and steel. But I was only vaguely aware of the carnage
behind me as I kept my attention focused up and forward.
The stairs entered the room above in its center, coming up
through a low-walled and open-topped well rather than a door.

With perhaps ten steps left to go I registered a half-dozen
figures moving to cut me off. If they were risen, they were
of the hidden variety, sustained in the counterfeit appear-
ance of life by the blood of the innocent. They wore the garb
of high officials of the church—Sword and Voice both.

Four more steps, and reverse my grip on my swords . . .
five . . . six and a leap up and to the side. As I hit the top of
my jump I jammed my swords down over the lip of the wall
around the stairs, using them like a vaulter's pole to lever
myself up and over the barrier.

I landed in a squat, and flicked the shadows away from
my eyes to get a fix on the room around me. It was a big
open space, with a wide-swung pair of double doors on the
side opposite the top of the stairs. Beyond lay a room I knew
from my last visit—the withdrawing room just outside the
Son of Heaven's bedchamber. I recognized it by the circle
of black swords stapled to a cross section of some enormous
tree's trunk on the wall—swords of Namara, obscene tro-
phies taken from my fallen comrades.

Rage burned through me, but unlike the last time I had
been here, it failed to consume my reason. With gritted teeth
and a gut-churning effort of will, I held my concentration
and finished my survey of the room around me. It was perhaps twice the size of the withdrawing room, and empty
save for a few sculptures, a half-dozen benches, and the dead
clogging the stairhead. Behind them another pair of doors
opened into a grand audience chamber where the Son of
Heaven sat on a white jade throne at the far end—a mirror
of the Emperor of Heaven's own black jade model.

He was tall and pale, almost white, as the men of Dan
Eyre sometimes are, and somehow frail looking. Even from
so far away I could see the wide, fixed gaze of the fanatic

or the madman—the only expression on an otherwise too still face. His robes were white threaded with gold, except for two bright spots of red above his collarbones where the blood that ran from the never-healing cuts I'd left on his cheeks dripped. His hair was thick and black and long, bound up in a braid that trailed down over his shoulder into his lap. In one hand he held the ivory rod of his office. In the other, a human thigh bone with a great green gem on the end, like some obscene mace.

There were perhaps a score of men and women in the room as well, all wearing the trapping of various orders within the church. Most of them looked as alive as I did, but a few had telltale signs of rot cropping up in the shape of pupils gone milky or dark cracks in the flesh around the eyes and mouth or across the backs of their knuckles—the places where the skin needed to bend and twist.

I could never hope to fight them all, but I might be able to get past them to reach the Son of Heaven if I moved fast enough. So, of course, I froze. Here was the moment. Would I end the reign of the Son of Heaven and begin a war that would engulf the eleven kingdoms? Or would I . . . what? Walk away somehow? Crash through the nearest window and hope to escape into the night? I had no exit strategy, no alternate plan, no way to go but forward.

I had come all this way hoping against hope that I would find my way when I needed it most. Perhaps believing somewhere down in the depths of my heart, below thought or rationality, that when I reached this place, my goddess would give me a sign—that, one last time, she would choose my path for me. But there was no whisper in my heart save the flutter of a Signet's dying finger, and no ghost of a benediction to give me solace. There was only the Son of Heaven on one hand and the spectre of war on the other.

Black fire erupted out of the stairhead, blowing apart the dead that waited there—how was Kelos doing that? Raw blasts of magical force burned nima like nothing else could. Was the well of his soul bottomless? Shadow flowed up the stairs and split in two.

"Hold the stairs," Kelos called, as one of the shadows rolled toward the audience chamber and the waiting Son of Heaven.

Finally, I moved—falling in behind Kelos as he headed for the throne, drawn as much by my former master's utter conviction as by my own sense that I must act even if I didn't know what to do. A woman wearing the robes of an arch-priestess of Balor lunged at me, extending long-nailed fingers like claws.

Without any thought or intention I killed her. Reflex flicked my right-hand sword across her throat, half severing her head and spilling her undead life away, though no blood flowed. Another of the hidden risen came at me and I gutted him with an equally reflexive drawing cut. That disconnection felt wrong and surreal, nightmarish. Where normally in a battle I become hyper-engaged, totally in and of the moment, I was sleepwalking my way through this fight, killing this woman and dodging that man without truly seeing any of them, as I tried to make sense of what I should do.

Twice, I might have died if it were not for Kelos and his dark fire, but I simply couldn't make myself care. Kelos should have reached the Son of Heaven long before I did, but he chose not to, moving in parallel with me instead. Before I really knew what was happening, I stood at the foot of the throne's dais, vaguely aware of Kelos standing in a second's place behind and to my right.

"Today is the day you die, Corik." Kelos dropped his shroud as he spoke. He stood sideways to the throne, pointing one sword up at the Son of Heaven's throat and the other out toward the remaining risen—an obvious distraction to allow me to do the deed.

I *wanted* to, but still I dreaded the result—on my hands the blood of kingdoms. I moved forward and to the side still sleepwalking, taking the first step on the dais to the throne.

The Son's eyes passed across my shroud as though I weren't there. "Ah, Kelos," said the Son of Heaven, "I knew that you would return someday. That your arrogance would not allow you to acknowledge your final defeat. You have lost. You know that, right?"

"I don't think so." Dark light rolled down the length of Kelos's lower sword, striking the nearest of the dead in the chest, blowing its heart and lungs apart in a messy spray. "Keep them back."

"Or what?" asked the Son of Heaven. "You'll kill me? I don't think so. I think that if you *could* kill me, I would already be dead. But you can't, can you? The geas still holds that far, even if it no longer protects my followers."

Was that true? If so, any hopes that Kelos might solve my dilemma for me were in vain. This was my decision and my show, as I had always known it must be. So why couldn't I choose? I forced myself up another step. One more and I would be close enough to strike. One more and I would *have* to make the choice. Surely, when I got there, I would know the right answer.

"It does," continued the Son of Heaven. "The geas still binds your hands where it comes to me. If that's true, you're going to die here, Kelos. I have thousands more where these come from." He nodded toward the dozen or so dead closing in on the throne. "Though I don't think I'll need them. If these all rush you at once, you will not be able to stop them, will you? Especially not if: Sithnish Kasht Keenim!"

The unknown words came out as a command, and Kelos went rigid—every muscle in his body straining as if against some invisible barrier. Then his hands opened and his swords fell ringing to the floor in the same moment that the remaining risen rushed the dais. This, then, was my true moment.

And, when it finally came, the choice *was* easy, though not for the reasons I had expected. I turned and dropped my shroud, releasing Triss as I drove my swords straight through the Son of Heaven's heart and throat, pinning him to his throne.

I stared into his eyes as he died, expecting I don't know what. A mighty explosion perhaps? Years to fall on him like a great weight, aging him away to nothing? A black fog that would take him straight to hell? What I got instead was death as it might have taken any man—a slumping and relaxing of muscles that had lost their driving will, as the

Son of Heaven's soul departed for a long overdue appointment with the lords of judgment.

I had just started to relax when I heard a chorus of shrieks and the sound of ripping flesh from behind me. In that same instant Triss cried into my mind, *Ware, Aral! Your swords!*

I ripped them free of the Son of Heaven's corpse, spinning just in time to take the head off a madly flailing knight of the Sword. The next few seconds passed in chaos as I fought off the mindless attack of a half dozen of the risen who—impossibly—had not died with their bond-partner and master.

For some time I was too busy staying alive to think, though I came more and more to suspect that something was horribly wrong with the risen as we fought. When the maelstrom slowed I realized what it was. The wild attacks of the dead fell on each other as much as they did me. There was no longer any cohesion or focus to their behavior, nothing but a blood-seeking madness that tore at anything and everything in its path.

Then, almost as suddenly as the mad battle had begun, it ended. I stood alone. It was only then, as the last of them fell away that I realized I had fought them by myself. Knowing what I would see and dreading it, I looked to the last place I had seen Kelos. He was there still, though lying on the floor now instead of standing. He was covered in blood and had too many wounds to count. But against all reason, he was still breathing—if not for very much longer.

Malthiss had spread himself thin, packing as many of the wounds as he could manage with the stuff of shadow, but still they leaked. I had no illusions about Kelos surviving more than a quarter hour more, if that. As I knelt beside him, I saw Faran coming in through the far door. She was limping, but otherwise seemed sound and unbloodied.

I touched Kelos's cheek and his eyes opened. "Ah," he said, "we won. That's good. I was beginning to—uhng—think you didn't have it in you." He took a ragged breath and forced it out. Then another—a pain-lessening discipline he had taught to me. "What took you so long?"

"I didn't want to start the war that is about to consume the East," I answered.

Oh, my friend . . .

But I didn't respond to Triss. He would still be there in a few minutes, and so would the coming war. The same could not be said for Kelos. Faran came up beside me then, though she didn't say a word and remained standing.

"You always were too soft to make the hard choices," said Kelos.

"I made this one."

"A bit late for me, that." He let out a little hiss. "But don't let it worry you. Whatever you intended, this was always part of *my* plan. I can finally go to face the judgment I so richly deserve."

"I . . ."

"Really, it's all right, Aral. I'd have died soon enough anyway. The black fire I set on the dead burns away my soul, too."

"I wish that—"

But Kelos held up a warning finger and I stopped. "One final lesson, my best student." And now there was blood on his lips. "You made the right choice. Now tell me you did it for the right reason. Why kill the Son of Heaven?"

"Hope."

"Hope?" Kelos sounded surprised.

"Yes. When I saw that you were about to be swarmed under, I realized I didn't want you to die. Not now. Not like this."

"Don't you dare forgive me, Aral," he growled with a tiny bit of his old strength. "I could bear almost anything but that."

"I won't. I promise."

"Thank you. Now, hope?"

"I don't forgive you. I can't. But when I saw that you were about to die, I realized that I hoped that someday I might. That someday, you might *earn* the forgiveness that I could give no other way. Does that make any sense?"

There was no answer, and when I looked into Kelos's empty eyes, I knew that there never would be. Faran put her hand on my shoulder and squeezed.

Though he was dead and gone, I decided that I still needed him to hear my explanation. "It was hope, you see. Hope that was the answer all along. When I realized that I still hoped for us to come to some peace, I knew that hope was the answer to my dilemma about the Son of Heaven, too. Hope is the antidote to fear."

"Aral," said Faran. "He's gone."

"I know. But I owe him this because it was the last lesson he'll ever teach me." I looked down into Kelos's dead eyes, and continued. "I didn't want the responsibility for the coming war. I still don't. But what if you were right? What if this is the one great chance we have to rewrite the way of the world and reach for a deeper justice? I don't know what will rise after the fall of the kings, but I can hope that you were right, and that it will be something glorious. I thank you for that, Master Kelos. And I honor you for it, even if I can never forgive you for Namara."

Aral?

Yes?

I was right to believe in you.

Thank you, Triss.

I stood, then swayed and almost fell as the fluttering in my heart turned into something with claws and teeth.

Faran caught me. "Are you all right?"

"I will be, I think. I just need to sit for a moment."

"Here, lean on your sword for a beat." I had dropped them when I knelt beside Kelos. Now she handed me one. Then, when she was sure I wouldn't fall immediately, she leaped up and yanked the Son of Heaven's corpse from his throne before helping me into it. "There."

I forced myself not to clutch at my chest, or otherwise betray what was wrong. There were still things to do. Which reminded me. . . . "Do you have any idea what happened with the risen?"

"They died or went mad when you killed the Son of Heaven. The rotted ones went down immediately. The hidden type stayed upright—sustained by soaking in the blood of the living maybe—but they completely lost their wits, and I suspect all of them will ultimately fail as well, if they haven't already."

"Ahh, that makes a certain amount of sense. Thank you."

"Are you *sure* you're all right?"

"Again, I think I will be. I need . . . rest. Could you do me a favor?"

"Maybe. What is it?"

"Go grab Devin before he recovers enough to make a run for it. I want him under my thumb."

She looked concerned. "I don't want to leave you like this."

"If we don't catch him now, we won't catch him at all. Please."

"You're hiding something," she said, but then she sighed. "All right, but don't you move off that throne."

"I won't, I promise."

"All right," she said. "Triss?"

My shadow reshaped itself into the familiar dragon outline. "Yes?"

"Don't you dare let anything happen to him while I'm gone."

"I will do my best," said Triss.

She shook a finger. "You'd better."

"I will." He held up one paw as though he were taking an oath.

"Can I at least kill Chomarr on my way to collecting Devin?"

I nodded. "I don't see why not."

As soon as she was out of hearing Triss put his front paws in my lap and peered up into my face. "The finger?"

I nodded and pulled it out into the open, setting it on the arm of the throne. The line of rot had passed the bottom edge of the ring and there were only a few hairs' breadths between it and the ivory plug. The tearing sensation in my heart had increased to the point where I didn't think I would be able to stand if I tried.

"What are we going to do about it?" he asked.

"Hope," I said, and then I swung my sword down on the

finger with all the strength I could muster, aiming for that tiny slice of still living flesh.

Lightning flashed across my vision and then darkness swallowed me up.

When it passed, I found myself in the Gryphon's Head surrounded by my dead. Across the table sat Namara.

"Am I dead?" I asked.

She smiled and shook her head.

"I killed the Son of Heaven, you know."

"I do."

"Did I get that right?"

"That is no longer for me to say. Your way is your own, for now and forever. You have transcended your need of me, and for that I am so very, very proud of you."

"I won't see you again, will I?"

She shook her head and was gone, taking the bar with her, and leaving behind a sense of peace and well-being like nothing I had felt since the fall of the temple. I had made my goddess proud. When I opened my eyes again, I was sitting on the throne of the Son of Heaven, and the previous occupant lay on the floor at my feet.

"Is this justice?" I asked, but he gave no answer.

I had my own opinions. For him certainly, for the thousands or tens of thousands who would now die in the upheavals to come . . . for that I had only my hope.

I speak to the dead. This time there was no answer.

I think it's better that way.

I rose from the throne and stepped over the body of the Son of Heaven. There were things to do and the path of justice to follow. As for the future?

I would live in hope.

Epilogue

We burned Kelos's body high on a bluff above Heaven's Reach. Then we collected his ashes and put them in an urn and hid it within his fallback. That was three years ago. Three years of blood and death and war. Years in which the mantle of First Blade hung on my shoulders like a cape of lead. Where I wanted nothing more than to hang up my swords and walk away from all of it.

I had come very close to doing just that, to returning to the Gryphon's Head and going back to being Aral the jack. I had even begun to drink again for a time. But circumstances and Triss's love had led me away from that place and my own destruction, had put me back on the road I had begun when I accepted the title of First Blade, had brought me here, to a hill above the ruined Temple of Namara.

Across the water, on the island of the goddess, workers were raising a new chapter house for those who now called themselves the Blades of Justice and who looked to me to lead them into the future. It was a fortress and far more defensible than the old temple had ever been. It had to be, for we no longer had the goddess to protect us.

The ruined temple we would leave as a memorial to the fallen, though we'd cleaned up the graveyard and begun to bury our dead there once again. That was what had brought me here today. To bury one of our dead. Rebury, really. We had brought Kelos home. Though we would not place him in the graveyard. Siri and I had agreed that he neither deserved the honor nor would have accepted it.

No, we would bury him in an unmarked grave here on the hillside overlooking the ruin he had wrought. The ruin . . . and the promise.

I turned to Siri then and handed up my shovel. "Do you think he was right?"

She shook her head. "Say rather that he wasn't wrong, and you will strike closer to the truth. The Evindine Free State would have made him smile, as would the Republic of Varya, but what happened in Zhan and, even worse, Heaven's Reach . . ." She shivered a little as she handed me the urn. "Chomarr's brief reign as the new Son of Heaven was ugly."

"But Faran did get him in the end," said Triss.

I placed the urn gently in the bottom of the hole. "That was . . . messy."

"Poetic," replied Siri.

I shook my head as I climbed out of the grave. "Not a touch excessive?"

"Richly deserved," said Triss.

I couldn't argue with that. Instead, I took the shovel back and started to fill in the grave.

I was just finishing up when Faran came over the crest of the hill. "News from Zhan! Harad sends word that Kaelin Fei has been elected to head the new government in Tien, and that she wants to see you."

"That'll be about the warlords on the Chenjou Peninsula, I imagine."

"Probably," said Faran. "Do you want me to go instead?"

"Not instead. As well. I could use someone to watch my back, and it's time you checked in with Harad and Shang again."

She nodded. "I'll go get us ready."

I sighed then and looked down at the grave and shook my head. "Dead three years and still playing us all. I don't think he was any more right about the way things would play out than the Kitsune would have been, not without us doing everything we could to make the future better than the past."

Siri squeezed my shoulder. "Funny, isn't it? He betrayed us all and yet here we are working our hearts out trying to make his mad vision into a bright reality." Then she followed after Faran.

When she was gone, I stood for a few silent minutes more beside the grave, with Triss wrapped around my shoulders in a shadow's embrace, then I, too, turned away. I had a world to build and no more words for the dead.

Terms and Characters

Agutes—A breed of large domesticated mountain goat, sometimes used for carrying packs.

Alinthide Poisonhand—A master Blade, the third to die making an attempt on Ashvik VI.

Alley-Knocker—An illegal bar or cafe.

Altia—A onetime apprentice Blade, once one of Faran's closest
friends.

Aral Kingslayer—Ex-Blade turned jack of the shadow trades.

Ashvik VI, or Ashvik Dan Pridu—Late King of Zhan, executed
by Aral. Also known as the Butcher of Kadesh.

Athera Trinity—The three-faced goddess of fate.

Balor Lifending—God of the dead and the next Emperor of
Heaven.

Blade—Temple assassin of the goddess Namara.

Blinds—Charms of confusion and befuddlement, mostly used
by thieves in the Magelands.

Buried Gods—Undead sorcerer gods of the Others, bound into
the earth by the forces of Heaven after the godwar.

Calren the Taleteller—God of beginnings and first Emperor
of Heaven.

Chimney Forest—The city above, rooftops, etc.

Chimney Road—A path across the rooftops of a city. "Running
the chimney road."

Chomarr—An officer of the Hand of Heaven.

Corik Nofather—The Son of Heaven's birth name.

Corvin—A Master Blade of a much earlier era. Slayer of the Necromancer and destroyer of the Necrotariat.

Dalridia—Kingdom in the southern Hurnic Mountains.

Darkburst—A lightning-like attack based in the element of shadow, magelightning's dark twin.

Darksight—One of the terms used by the Blade to describe the sense that they borrow from their Shade companions.

Death—A goddess.

Demon's Brew—A small river that feeds into the Evindine. It runs hot and smells strongly of sulfur because of its origins in the hot springs of the valley of Demon's Mouth.

Demon's Mouth—A valley full of hot springs and choking fumaroles in the mountains above Varya.

Devin (Nightblade) Urslan—A former Blade.

Dracodon—A large magical beast, renowned for the ivory in its tusks.

Durkoth—Others that live under the Hurnic Mountains. Allied with earth.

Dyad—A binary entity made up of a human sorcerer and their familiar fused into a single consciousness.

Eavesman—A spy or eavesdropper.

Eian Elarson—King of Dalridia and brother to Jax.

Eight Major Elements, the—Light, shadow, earth, air, water, fire, death, and life. Only the first seven are known to have corresponding elementals.

Elite, the—Zhani mages. They fulfill the roles of secret police and spy corps among other functions.

Eva—With Eyn the dual goddess worshiped by the Dyads.

Everdark, the—The home dimension of the Shades.

Evindine—A river, the main source of Evenduin, the sacred lake that holds the island of Namara.

Eyespy—A type of eavesdropping spell.

Eyn—With Eva the dual goddess worshiped by the Dyads.

Falissil—A Shade, companion to Voros.

Fallback—A safe house.

Fallows, the—The strip of land that runs on either side of the Wall of the Sylvain. God-magic prevents any construction from happening there.

Familiar Gift—The ability to soul-bond with another being, providing the focus half of the power/focus dichotomy necessary to become a mage.

Faran Ghostwind—A onetime Blade trainee, now Aral's apprentice.

Fire and Sun!—A Shade curse.

First—The word the Others use to describe themselves.

Garis—A Dalridian messenger.

Garret—A onetime apprentice Blade, once one of Faran's closest friends.

Ghost, Ghosting—To kill.

Godwar—The war between Heaven and those among the Others who sought to rival them.

Gojuru—Mages smiths of Kanjuri. They have the mage gift but not the familiar gift and they use it to ensoul the living swords used by the Hairi.

Govana—Goddess of the herds.

Grays—The traditional garb of the Blade. Usually consists of low boots, flowing pants, a loose shirt, and a yoke and cowl, all dyed in an abstract pattern of dark grays. In colder weather a poncho is added.

Great Khan—Titular head of all the clans of the Kvanas. In modern times, the great khan has primarily served as a figurehead to be raided or traded along with their court by the high khans in their internal battles.

Greatspell—A major permanent work of magic, usually tied to a physical item.

Gryphon's Head—A tavern in Tien, the capital city of Zhan. Informal office for Aral.

Gryss—A shade, familiar to Kumi. Takes the form of huge winged rat.

Gulthiss—A Shade, familiar to Xin. Takes the form of a humpbacked camelopard.

Hairi—The ruling class of Kanjuri, they have the familiar gift but not the mage gift, and use it to bond with living swords created by the Gojuru mage smiths.

Hand of Heaven—The Son of Heaven's office of the inquisition, and one of five branches of the church hierarchy.

Harad—Head librarian at the Ismere Library.

Heaven—The land of the gods, ruled by the Emperor of Heaven.

Heaven's Reach—The temple kingdom ruled over by the Son of Heaven.

Heaven's Shadow—The name the Son of Heaven has given to his organization of Blade traitors. Their grays are slightly red tinted.

High Khan—One of the rulers of the four clans of the Kvanas, nominally answering to the great khan, but in effect absolute rulers of their individual domains.

Holy Guard of Heaven—The security apparatus of the Son of Heaven and one of five branches of the church hierarchy.

Illiana—A master Blade, killed in a suicide attack at the fall of the temple, one that ended the life of the then Signet.

Inaya—A onetime journeyman Blade.

Ismere Library—A private lending library in Tien, founded by a wealthy merchant from Kadesh.

Jack—A slang term for an unofficial or extragovernmental problem solver; see also, shadow jack, black jack, sunside jack.

Jaeris—A onetime apprentice Blade, once one of Faran's closest friends.

Jafsica—A member of the Dalridian royal house, cousin to Jax.

Javan—A onetime apprentice Blade.

Jax Seldansbane—A former Blade and onetime fiancée of Aral's.

Jealousy, Spirit of—A demi-deity or greater spirit, part of the pantheon of the eleven kingdoms.

Jerik—The bartender/owner of the Gryphon's Head tavern.

Kaelin Fei, Captain—Watch officer in charge of Tien's Silent Branch, also known as the Mufflers.

Kayarin Melkar—A master Blade who joined the Son of Heaven after the fall of the temple.

Kelos Deathwalker—A master Blade who taught Aral.

Key of Sylvaras—A mythical item associated with the god Sylvaras.

Kila—The spirit dagger of the Blade, symbolizing his bond to Namara.

Kodamia—City-state to the west of Tien, controlling the only good pass through the Hurnic Mountains.

Kreyn—The oldest branch of the Others. They live in forest enclaves within the Sylvani Empire. Allied with shadow.

Kuan-Lun—A water elemental, one of the great dragons.

Kumi—A onetime journeyman Blade.

Kvanas, the Four—Group of interrelated kingdoms just north of Varya. Sometimes referred to as the Khanates.

Kyle's—An expensive Aveni whiskey.

Kyrissa—A Shade, familiar to Siri. Takes the form of a winged serpent.

Loris—A former Blade.

Mageblind—Mage term for those without magesight.

Mage Gift—The ability to perform magic, providing the power half of the power/focus dichotomy necessary to become a mage.

Magelands—A loose confederation of city-states governed by the faculty of the mage colleges that center them.

Magelights—Relatively expensive permanent light sources made with magic.

Magesight—The ability to see magic, part of the mage gift.

Mage Wastes—Huge area of magically created wasteland on the western edge of the civilized lands.

Magus—The formal title of the chief mage of the Order of Blade, a member of the shadow council.

Malok—A onetime apprentice Blade.

Malthiss—A Shade, familiar to Kelos Deathwalker. Takes the form of a basilisk.

Maryam—A onetime journeyman Blade.

Maylien Dan Marchon Tal Pridu—A former client of Aral's.

Namara—The now-deceased goddess of justice and the down-trodden, patroness of the Blades. Her symbol is an unblinking eye.

Nea Sjensdor—Lady Signet, preceptor of the Hand of Heaven.

Nightghast—One of the restless dead, known to eat humans.

Night Runners—Small sampan like smuggling boats, painted dark colors and optimized for speed.

Nima—Mana, the stuff of magic.

Nipperkins—Magical vermin.

Noble Dragons—Elemental beings that usually take the form of giant lizardlike creatures.

Nuriko Shadowfox—Also known as the Kitsune, a master Blade.

Olthiss—A Shade, familiar to Altia. Takes the form of a Kvani-style manticore.

Omira—A onetime apprentice Blade, once one of Faran's closest friends.

Orisa—God of sailors.

Oris Plant—A common weed that can be used to produce a cheap gray dye or an expensive black one.

Others—The various nonhuman races.

Parsi—One of the Blades who went over to the Son of Heaven.

Pol—A master Blade, long since dead.

Qamasiin—A spirit of air.

Rabbit Run—An emergency escape route.

Rapportomancer—A person with the familiar gift but no mage gift.

Resshath—Shade term of respect meaning, roughly, teacher or sensei.

Resshath-ra—Shade term of respect, roughly sensei of sensei, the Shade equivalent of First Blade.

Restless Dead—Catchall term for the undead.

Risen, the—A type of restless dead, similar to a zombie.

Roric—A onetime journeyman Blade, Avarsi by birth.

Seldan, Dukes of—Varyan nobles, two of whom were executed by Jax.

Serass—A Shade, familiar to Alinthide.

Shade—Familiar to the Blades, a living shadow.

Shadow Council—The ruling organization of the order of the Blade.

Shadow Jack—A jack who earns his living as a problem solver in the shadow trades.

Shadow of Heaven—The Blades that went over to the Son of Heaven, and one of five branches of the church hierarchy.

Shadowside—The underworld or demimonde.

Shadow-Slipping—The collective name for the various stealth techniques of Namara's Blades.

Shadow World—The demimonde or underworld.

Shanglun—A river dragon.

Shan Starshoulders—The god who holds up the sky, current Emperor of Heaven, lord of stability.

Shrouding—When a Shade encloses his Blade in shadow.

Siri Mythkiller—A former Blade.

Slink—Magical vermin.

Snug—A resting place or residence.

Son or Daughter of Heaven—The title of the chief priest or priestess who leads the combined religions of the eleven kingdoms.

Ssassisshatha—A Shade word denoting identity or soul signature.

Ssayath—A Shade, familiar to Inaya. Takes the form of a tuft-eared lynx.

Sshayar—A Shade, familiar to Jax. Takes the form of a tiger.

Ssissathshta—A Shade curse.

Ssithra—A Shade, familiar to Faran. Takes the form of a phoenix.

Ssolvey—A Shade, familiar to Roric. Takes the form of an enormous six-legged badger.

Ssuma—A Shade, familiar to Illiana.

Ssura—A Shade of an earlier era, before the Blades joined the service of Namara. Familiar to Corvin.

Stone Dog—A living statue, roughly the size of a small horse. The familiar to the Elite.

Storm Eels—Huge, sentient, telepathic, freshwater eels.

Sumey Dan Marchon Tal Pridu—Baroness Marchon and sister of Maylien.

Sunrunning—Blade slang for maintaining a shroud in bright daylight.

Sunside—The shadowside term for more legitimate operations.

Sword of Heaven—The military arm of the Son of Heaven and one of five branches of the church hierarchy. Also called the Templars.

Sword Rig—An arrangement of leather straps and blackened steel D-rings that allows a Blade to attach their swords and other tools in a variety of configurations.

Sylvani—The Others who populate the Sylvani Empire south of the eleven kingdoms. Allied with the element of light.

Sylvani Empire—Sometimes called the Sylvain, a huge empire covering much of the southern half of the continent. Ruled by a nonhuman race, it is ancient and hostile to the human lands of the north.

Sylvaras—First emperor of the Sylvain and greatest of the gods who rose from the First. Allied himself with Heaven in the godwar.

Sylvas—Capitol of the Sylvani Empire.

Tamar—A river in the Magelands with its headwaters near Uln.

Tangara—God of glyphs and runes and other magical writing.

Tavan—One of the five great university cities of the Magelands.

Templars of Heaven—The military arm of the Son of Heaven and one of five branches of the church hierarchy. Also called the Sword of Heaven.

Thauvik IV, or Thauvik Tal Pridu, the Bastard King—King of Zhan and bastard half brother of the late Ashvik.

Thiess—A Shade, familiar to Javan. Takes the shape of a huge horned owl.

Thieveslamp/Thieveslight—A dim red magelight in a tiny bull's-eye lantern.

Thiussus—A Shade, familiar to Nuriko. Takes the shape of a nine-tailed fox.

Thornbrindle—A thick shrub with many long thorns.

Tien—A coastal city, the thousand-year-old capital of Zhan.

Tolar—A branch of the Others living within the Sylvani Empire, mostly in the wastes. Allied with fire.

Toragana—Lady Signet of Heaven, preceptor of the Hand of Heaven.

Triss—Aral's familiar. A Shade that inhabits Aral's shadow. Takes the form of a small dragon.

Twins, the—Eyn and Eva, the patron goddess or goddesses of the Dyads. Sometimes represented as one goddess with two faces, sometimes as a pair of twins, either identical or conjoined.

Uthudor—A Durkoth scholar of the earth.

Vesh'An—Shapechanging Others. Originally a part of the same breed that split into the Sylvani and Durkoth, the Vesh'An have adopted a nomadic life in the sea. Allied with water.

Voice of Heaven—The priesthood devoted to the Emperor of Heaven, answering directly to the Son of Heaven, and one of five branches of the church hierarchy.

Voros—A Master Blade, long dead.

Vrass—A Shade, familiar to Maryam. Takes the form of a hydra.

Wall of the Sylvain—Or simply the wall. A giant magical warding in the shape of a five-thousand-mile wall made by the forces of Heaven to bind the buried gods and the magic-using Others into the lands of the Sylvani Empire.

Xin—A onetime journeyman Blade.

Yellow Springs—A valley of hot springs in the mountains above Varya, considered to be a place of healing by the locals.

Yellowtide—A small river that feeds into the Evindine. It runs hot and smells faintly of sulfur because of its origins in the hot springs of the valley of Yellow Springs.

Yinthiss. A Shade, familiar to Malok.

Zara—A Master Blade who died at the fall of the temple.

Zass—A Shade, familiar to Devin. Takes the form of a tayra, essentially, a giant weasel.

Zhan—One of the eleven human kingdoms of the East. Home to the city of Tien.

Zhen-Ki—The Binder of Demons, one of the many gods of the eleven kingdoms.

Zissatha—A Shade, familiar to Parsi. Takes the form of a giant rat.

A complete glossary for all the Fallen Blade novels can be found at: kellymccullough.com/the-fallen-blade-story /fallen-blade-master-glossary-spoilers.

Currency

———◆———

Bronze Sixth Kip (sixer)
Bronze Kip
Bronze Shen
Silver Half Riel
Silver Riel
Gold Half Riel
Gold Riel
Gold Oriel

Value in Bronze Kips

~0.15 = Bronze Sixth Kip
1 = Bronze Kip
10 = Bronze Shen
60 = Silver Half Riel
120 = Silver Riel

Value in Silver Riels

0.5 = Silver Half Riel
1 = Silver Riel
5 = Gold Half Riel
10 = Gold Riel
50 = Gold Oriel

Calendar

———•◆•———

(370 days in 11 months of 32 days each, plus two extra 9-day holiday weeks: Summer-Round in the middle of Midsummer, and Winter-Round between Darktide and Coldfast)

Winter-Round extra nine-day week of holidays
1. *Coldfast*
2. *Meltentide*
3. *Greening*
4. *Seedsdown*
5. *Opening*
6. *Midsummer, which has an extra (festival) week in the middle*
7. *Sunshammer*
8. *Firstgrain*
9. *Harvestide*
10. *Talewynd*
11. *Darktide*

Days of the Week

————◆————

1 *Calrensday*—In the beginning.
2 *Atherasday*—Hearth and home.
3 *Durkothsday*—Holdover from the prehuman tale of days.
4 *Shansday*—The middle time.
5 *Namarsday*—Traditional day for nobles to sit in judgment.
6 *Sylvasday*—Holdover from the prehuman tale of days.
7 *Balorsday*—Day of the dead.
8 *Madensday*—The day of madness when no work is done.